Incendium

R.S. O'Neal

The Quest for the Aura series: Book Five

Books in the Quest for the Aura series:

- The Lightworker Trials

- Terra

- Aqua

- Caelus

- Incendium

To Amanda and Holly
My writing group: Karin, Gabrielle, Jan, Angie and Sarah
Thanks always for the encouragement and support

Linda, my long-time friend—thanks for your belief and your awesome
bookshop
Robert, for your generous expertise
And Mary, for your Venator eyes

"Sox Na'Eatrum," – Quon, Armatura greeting
(May your timing be fortuitous)

"Winter of the soul
Can be lonely and hopeless
Remember the spring"
– Esor, renowned Mimir poet

"Stand up. Walk forward. The rest will come to you," – The Rainbow
Eucalyptus

"The scourge, the plague, the ruination and the destruction," – Madame
Overmantle

Therapeutic Pools
Workshop
Meditation Hall
Ferito Training Shed
Zepp Hangar
Sports Grounds
Lecture Theatres
Pool
Refectory
Fourth Years
Third Years
Common Room
Second Years
Central Admin
First Years
Ponds of Doombee
2 km
Dormitories
Library
Fishpond
Entrance to the Unlit Campus
Receiving Stone
Equestrian Arena
1 km
Bane Rock
Mimir's Domain
Beggarman's Bluff
3 km
S
E
W
N

CHAPTER ONE

EYRE DRAGGED HER POSSESSIONS up the steps of her cabin at Highlight. After they'd arrived, courtesy of Madame Overmantle, Eyre, Beatrice and Abby had left for their own cabins very quickly. No one wanted to talk, and no plans were discussed about the next few weeks. It seemed they all just wanted to go and hide from the world for a while. The trials of the TACI journey to Caelus had left their hearts in tatters.

Eyre did see Nick arrive in a flash of light with Whittaker Ray across the campsite, and she'd given them a small wave before she went inside. But she didn't linger; more than anything, she just wanted to lie down and recover from the events of the past week.

She dumped her bags, a box of books and stationery from her desk, her guitar and her staff on her bed, and then raced down the spiral stairs to the basement with the Book of Bane. Beatrice had given it to her to safeguard in the underground room, which had a powerful ward preventing anyone or anything from entering. Eyre placed the precious record of their secrets carefully in her oak chest, next to her Lightkeeper, where it would be safe from any malign force or prying eyes.

It was tempting to stay there, but she really needed to pause and rest, so she left the basement and trudged upstairs to the attic, searching for the peace it provided, like a moth drawn irresistibly to the light. The late-afternoon sun was sending rays through the beautiful diamond-shaped stained-glass window, and she lay on the couch as the rainbow colours danced across the floor. For over an hour she watched the moving pictures, finding a peace in the artistry of the mystical scenes. She felt that Jolin the Second, the genius who had created these images, would be happy to know how much comfort his brilliant artwork had brought people over the years.

It was the last month of summer, so the sun hung lazily in the sky for long, sultry hours, but eventually it began to lower, and the golden light dimmed as darkness approached. Eyre roused herself and put her feet on the floor regretfully. She had better go and unpack and make her bed. A cup of tea would go down well too. She also wanted to check on Beatrice.

So she quickly got her possessions sorted—there weren't many, really—and made her bed up. She shoved her box of school stuff in her cupboard, and put her staff in beside it. Then she switched on the stained-glass lamp beside the bed and immediately felt better as the glow from the coloured light warmed the room. The light skipped across the glossy polish of her guitar and the magical hues of its rainbow eucalyptus neck, and Eyre placed it in her lap and picked out a few notes, a mournful melody that reflected how she felt. Everything had finished in such a rush; she hadn't even had time to say goodbye properly to anyone. It seemed like they all came back from Caelus and then just disappeared. As she stroked the exquisitely-carved neck of the guitar she thought of Jax, and wondered where he was. Most of all, she wished she'd been able to see him before she left.

After a moment she put the beautiful instrument down. It was no use sitting here feeling sorry for herself, so she ran down the front steps of her cabin and over to the Edmunsun's cabin. A light was on inside and she knocked. Abby answered the door, and smiled.

"Come in, we thought you'd be over. I'll make a cup of tea."

Beatrice was sitting in the lounge room on the Edmunsun's comfortable two-seater. She smiled wanly when Eyre walked in. "The end of the year seems to be forming a pattern for us; drama and more drama." But her voice fell away and tears brimmed.

"Are your parents coming back?" Eyre sat down beside her, her sapphire eyes dark with sympathy.

"Yes, they'll be here tomorrow," Beatrice said. "They are so sad about Blondie. No one in our family has ever lost a Lighthorse before."

Eyre felt so sorry for Beatrice. "Well, let's get Nick over here," she said, changing the subject. "He never showed me his Lightkeeper—have you seen it yet?"

Abby looked amazed. "No, I haven't! I just forgot all about it in the chaos at the Lightness Cup, and then when we got back the subject never came up."

Beatrice shook her head. "I haven't either—how could I have forgotten to ask? I'd love to see it!"

"Call him, Abby," Eyre said. "Tell him to come and have a cuppa and to bring his Lightkeeper with him!"

Abby sent Nick a telepathic message as Beatrice put the jug on to boil and got the mugs out. Her mugs were the 'Lightworker Collection', a limited edition set of eight mugs made of crystal, which she'd got from the Sappir Exhibition at the Sector Fair last year. The mugs had been cut by Sappir alumni who had gone on to become Master Faceters. The money from sales had gone to the Academy's fundraising pool, and Sappir had done very well from their display. Eyre had been with the Clementis in August, when the Fair was held, so she'd missed it completely. It was such a shame, because everyone said the Exhibition had been amazing.

Each of the faceted mugs was one of the seven Sector colours, with one rainbow-coloured one called 'The Aura'. Without thinking, Beatrice placed 'Sappir', 'Hese', 'Tyros' and 'Flava' on the bench. Light caught the crystal facades of the mugs and cast a rainbow reflection on the bench which Beatrice traced absently with her finger.

"It was about this time last year that we took our Lighthorses up to the ridge," Beatrice said, her voice catching. Tears began to drip down her face. In a second, Abby and Eyre rushed over to embrace their friend. Nick walked in the front door and without a word, walked over and hugged them all. Nothing needed to be said; they all grieved for the valiant Lighthorse that had died saving her Lightworker's life.

Eventually Beatrice gave a small laugh and wiped her eyes with the back of her hand.

"Well, the tea's not going to make itself, so I'd better pour the water."

"And then we'll look at your Lightkeeper, Nick," Abby said.

They brought their mugs to the lounge room and Nick and Abby sat together on one of the couches, Abby with her legs across Nick's knees.

"Happy to be a footstool," he joked, pretending to struggle as he leaned over to put his Lightkeeper on the table. Everyone laughed, but Eyre registered the expression on his face. Abby and Nick had become so close over the years and his love for her showed even in small moments like this.

Eyre studied Nick's Lightkeeper curiously; it was the first time she'd had a proper look at it. The little box glowed with shades of purple, blue and red, and the Inguz on the lid was inlaid with black opal. The opal stone was extremely vibrant, with vivid flashes of red, purple and blue running through the dark background.

"The Lightkeeper is made from amethyst, sapphire and ruby," Nick said. "The ruby and sapphire are apparently symbolic of my combination of spiritual and physical strengths, and of course the amethyst is for Tyros. Apparently, the black opal can bring Light to the Aura, so maybe it's a good omen?"

Everyone laughed and then took turns picking up the lustrous crystal box. But Eyre was horrified by a sudden memory. The black opal! Jax had given Eyre a black opal during the hash house harrier run last year, but Eyre had been so angry with him at the time that she had thrown it into her drawer and forgotten all about it. Then she had been burnt in the fire, and by the time she was back on campus the memory of the glowing gem had long faded from her mind. It was probably caught up in the contents of the drawer, which Eyre had unceremoniously dumped into a box when she was moving out. Her heart clenched at the thought that she had treated such a beautiful gift with such disdain, and she vowed to search for it as soon as she could.

Beatrice passed Nick's Lightkeeper to Eyre and she gazed in awe at the flashing crystals. Each Lightkeeper was so unique, Eyre thought, as she studied the exquisite workmanship of the small object. She was glad for Nick; he'd looked so happy and proud as he explained about the crystals. Just a couple of years ago he hadn't even realised he *was* a Lightworker, and now he finally had access to all the history of his family. He had grown up with a violent, brutal father, but now he could find out about family members he could be proud of.

Light sparkled through Eyre's golden quartz mug as she took it back to the kitchen to rinse. She looked over at Beatrice, who was studying the inside of her transparent citrine mug as if reading tea leaves. She looked so sad that tears came to Eyre's eyes; she felt Beatrice's pain as if it were her own. As Eyre upended the clean cup to dry on the sink, she thought hard about a way she could help. The heartbreak behind them and the uncertainty ahead was taking its toll on all of them. They'd all had sadness, and disaster and challenges over the past few years, and not a lot of Lightness, and it was draining the joy and optimism from their lives. *Fun* was what they needed, she decided, and she sat down with her friends again.

"Hey, I've got a great idea. Who wants to organise a New Year's Eve party with me? We could invite everyone and have music; anyone who wants to can stay in our cabins or they can bring a tent and camp."

Abby's eyes sparkled. "Great idea Eyre! I'll be in charge of the invitations and decorations!"

Nick smiled too. "Well, I'll organise the campsite."

After a second, Beatrice's face lightened. "That leaves you and me on food, I guess, Eyre. It is a good idea. Let's make some lists of what we need to do."

"Great! But hang on a minute and I'll be straight back," Eyre said. "I just need to sort something out at my cabin first."

While her friends started to work away compiling lists, Eyre raced back to her cabin as if a Strigis was after her. She burst into her bedroom and grabbed the box from her cupboard, then upended it on her bed. Pens and pencils, paper, books and other stationery spread across her bedspread as she searched frantically through the pile of school stuff. Finally, a flash of fire caught her eye, hidden underneath her 'Tenets of Management' textbook. She seized the glowing object and with a huge sigh of relief, realised she'd found the magical stone that Jax had given her. About the size of a ten-cent piece, it was flattish, and rough, but it glowed with a magical fire—blues, reds and greens radiated in all directions. The stone itself was roughly diamond-shaped, which in itself was quite a rare thing, she knew from her lessons in faceting with the Unlit. Carefully she placed the stone in her bedside drawer, determined not to misplace it again. Then she packed away the school things and headed back to Beatrice's cabin.

They worked away in Beatrice's lounge room for about an hour while Eyre took notes as everyone talked. Nick was going to organise the music, and Abby was going to locate some noiseless Viq fireworks. Beatrice called the guest list; with her razor-sharp memory she was very unlikely to forget anyone. The mood lightened and even Beatrice started to look a bit happier as the plans unfolded.

A grumpy voice from outside interrupted Eyre's scribbling, a voice she knew no one else would hear.

"Dimmog! Dusty, lonely place. Take me back to the stables!"

Eyre dropped her pencil and rushed on to the veranda. Ischyros was standing outside the front door of Eyre's cabin, with the Kikkuli Master by his side. Ischyros still wore his coat, despite the warm temperature, and he was swinging his head around so his good eye—the one with the black spot —could fully see the appalling place he had been brought to.

"Dreadful," he complained. "I can't be expected to stay here for any length of time, surely? The last trip was enough for me!"

Eyre raced over to him as the Kikkuli Master made noncommittal sounds.

"Ischyros!" she hugged him gently. "Are you alright?"

Ischyros harrumphed and the Kikkuli Master indicated some bags stacked by Eyre's front door.

"That's his food and grooming kit. If you need any more food, or anything else, just let me know. You must remember to put the burn cream on every day, to help with the healing. And there's some daily vitamins to put in his feed. I'll leave him with you, as I have to get back. Have a good break, Eyre."

Eyre waved as he left in a flash of light and then softly stroked Ischyros's head. "I'm so glad you're here," she whispered as her friends walked over to join them.

Everyone made a big fuss of Ischyros and he began to look quite pleased. "These people know how to treat a Lighthorse," he commented slyly as Abby braided his patchy grey mane into a single plait. Beatrice was brushing his ratty tail and Nick patted his scarred face and whispered soft words in his ear. It was obvious they were all very moved by the sight of the terribly wounded horse.

"Where will he stay?" Abby asked.

Eyre looked uncertain. "I'm not sure," she said. "I might talk to Jengles."

But Nick spoke up. "We'll build him a stall," he said. "I'm sure the Mimir can help. It will fit quite well at the back of your cabin, Eyre. That way he'll be nearby."

Eyre thought that was an excellent idea. "Let's get started then. We'll want it done before any weird weather comes in."

"Don't forget my feed bucket," was all Ischyros could say.

CHAPTER TWO

THE NEXT FEW WEEKS passed quickly. Between building the stable and organising the party, there was enough to keep them all busy and Beatrice's mind off Blondie. The Mimir came and cut sturdy beams and ironbark logs to build the stable's infrastructure, and they brought smooth river rock up from Coxs River to create the stable floor. The stall doors were made from bloodwood, and Nick carved an Inguz in the centre of them, and Mimir knots, the symbol for courage, along the top and bottom frames. He oiled the doors to a vibrant, glossy red, and attached them with strong brass hinges. Eyre and Beatrice made several trips to campus to bring back straw and feed to stock the grain room, and Abby sewed furiously, creating a colourful patchwork blanket to replace the commercial sheet Ischyros had been wearing. The shapes in the patchwork were made from fabric in rainbow colours, alternating with fabric diamonds cut from the silks Eyre had worn in the Lightness Cup, some of which were purple, and some purple with a small silver Inguz pattern. Then Abby attached Ischyros's silver racing collar, number 11, to the back wall.

Eyre massaged the burn cream into Ischyros's tender skin every day and made sure he got his daily vitamins. And she gently brushed what was left of his coat. Despite his complaints when he had arrived, Eyre could tell that he was glad to be here. He was still obviously in a lot of pain, and he seemed to enjoy the attention and bustle as everyone focused on building him a home.

Finally, the day came when the stable was finished! Eyre led the old horse past a parade of Mimir, lined up on each side of the pathway with Beatrice, Abby and Nick beside them. They all cheered as he walked into the stable to inspect his new abode. Ischyros hadn't been inside since the work started and Eyre was amused to see that he was speechless as he surveyed the beautiful structure they'd built for him. Then she noticed a tear slide from his one good eye and she hugged him.

"We love you Ischyros. Welcome home."

Everyone piled into the stable behind her and clapped as she gave him his first meal in a shiny new feed bucket. Then Abby put the new blanket on him, and Beatrice brought him some liquorice.

"Lunchtime for us too!" Beatrice announced, and Eyre grinned. It seemed that Beatrice was getting back to her old self. As her friends turned to go, Eyre gave Ischyros one last hug. "The Kikkuli Master told me once that no one has ever been worthy of you," she whispered in the old horse's ear. "And now I know why. You are the bravest animal ever. I will try to prove myself worthy of you, old friend."

Ischyros's loud harrumph followed her out of the new stable as she hurried to catch up with her friends.

"My turn to make lunch today," Nick said. "I'll whip us up a feast."

"Toasted sandwiches?" Abby asked innocently, and they all cracked up. Toasted sandwiches were the only thing that Nick ever made for lunch.

Eyre had been to Nick's cabin many times over the past few years, and she loved sitting in his huge lounge suite, which had replaced the original old leather one. Nick had crafted the suite from Blue Gum, a hardwood with a lovely grain, and it had taken him months to make, working on it when he could. Then he had upholstered the cushions in a heavy tapestry, which was embroidered with black cockatoos sitting in a eucalyptus tree. It was an extremely comfortable suite and they sprawled in it as they ate their toasted sandwiches. Eyre noted that the windows, and any other damage in the cabin, had been repaired in the months since Nick had run amok after he was possessed by the demon. That seemed so long ago now, she thought in amazement, as she threw her legs over the side of the massive armchair she sat in. She gazed again at the photograph of Nick's beautiful mother that always sat on the mantlepiece. She had been a powerful and pure Lightworker, and Eyre realised that Nick had taken great comfort in this, most probably because his father was a reviled Ex. Life had taken a foul turn that day and now they all had to deal with the aftermath. Eyre's soul yearned for something that now could never be; a happier outcome to the story. If only that day had never happened, life might have been so different. But then she sighed.

Fairy tales, she thought. Life wasn't like that.

"So how many people have RSVP'd?" Beatrice asked Abby with her mouth full, interrupting Eyre's sombre thoughts.

Abby thought for a moment. "We've got about thirty people coming so far. Ten can't make it and I'm still waiting to hear from twelve. It should be fun."

"I've told Mum and Dad to stay away," Beatrice said. "They're going to Sydney with Lachie for New Year's."

"Whittaker Ray will be with the Echelon over the Christmas break, so he won't be here either." Nick took another bite. "They're trying to find out how much damage Jemima Periwinkle did, not to mention trying to track her down."

"The poor Sergeant," Eyre said. "She would be mortified by this."

"No wonder they didn't get along!" Abby said ferociously. "That horrible woman has the morals of a Tuus Scorpion."

"It was such a strange year," Beatrice mused softly, and then her face fell. "I think I might go and read my book. It's quite nice to have nothing to do for a change."

Eyre agreed. Although it had been fun, they'd worked hard the past couple of weeks to build Ischyros's stable, and it had come straight after the expedition to Caelus. She was still bothered by tiredness after her months of rehabilitation with the Clementis, so she was quite happy to go back to her cabin for a rest, intending, like Beatrice, to lie on her couch and read.

But when she walked inside, she changed her mind and headed for the basement. It had been a while since she'd looked at her Wisdom, and she had a sudden yearning to see her parents. Her grief had lessened over the years and she had become more used to the fact they weren't here anymore, but she still liked to look through the pages and hear their voices. It made her feel like they weren't completely gone.

She passed through the frigid ward and headed down the winding stairs, bathed in the blue light from the walls. She sat down and opened her oak chest and pulled her Lightkeeper out, then used the Tone Blow on her neck chain to summon her Wisdom from the beautiful crystal box. The heavy leather book looked as magical as ever, the cover inlaid with runes and crystals. She would never get used to the wonder of this incredible object. Finally, she took the key from her neck chain and turned the lock on the old book so she could open the pages.

As usual, whichever page she turned to emitted a hologram of her parents talking to her. The first one ever, her mother speaking... *"If you're seeing me here, then I guess I am dead..."* Then the information about the complicated Tyson-Lightward family tree and the message about the Leonid meteor shower. It was all so comforting, it made her feel part of a greater journey and gave her an understanding of her importance in that journey.

The last message Eyre had received was more than a year ago, in second-year, when the Wisdom's Code had been revealed to her. The Code had helped Eyre and her friends to locate the ancient Sea Crone, who had given them further clues about the reinstatement of the Aura. But it had been so long since a new message had come from the Wisdom and Eyre really wasn't expecting any more information.

But the Wisdom seemed to have a life of its own this afternoon. Before she could turn another page, it flipped over itself and immediately the familiar green rays started shooting out from the smooth paper. A hologram of Eyre's mother and father appeared, sitting on the couch that was in the lounge room upstairs, and they twirled slowly around in front of her.

"Hello my darling," her mother said. "The holograms we left in your Wisdom know that it's time to release this message. Congratulations my love —the first three Isars have been located!"

Well, they may have been *located*, but she wasn't able to *keep* them all, Eyre thought dismally. The second Isar was buried somewhere deep in the Underworld.

Her father spoke next. "In order to mislead the Gothak," he said, "the fourth Isar was sent to Incendium..."

Well, we already *knew* that, Eyre thought a bit crossly.

"... and before you get tetchy," her father added softly, "let me add something else. Remember this guide from the Sea Crone:

The fourth Isar can only be seen by the Aether during the Eta Aquariids."

Eyre looked a bit shamefaced, and then gave a wry, lopsided smile that was tinged with pain. This was critical—and *new*—information, but she knew what the underlying message was; she needed to work on her patience! A pang stabbed through her, as the absence of her parents suddenly pierced her. But then they spoke again.

"Don't be sad, Eyre," her mother said, as if she could see Eyre.

"Have faith and you will find your strength," her father added.

"Live with courage and Light!" they said together, and then faded away, still slowly spinning.

As always, Eyre felt a yearning as they disappeared—if only she could be with them again. She ached with their absence. But then she thought about their message. The *Eta Aquariids*. Something to do with meteors, no doubt, she pondered, and resolved to talk about it with her friends later.

Eyre wandered upstairs, feeling strangely glum. After all the stress and pressure of the past few months she was exhausted from being perpetually on alert, and the last thing she wanted was more mysteries and danger. If only life would settle down.

She sat on the brightly coloured couch and picked up her guitar, running her hands along the neck of the beautiful old instrument. Jax had carved a new neck from a branch of the Rainbow Eucalyptus after Ben Perrill had broken the original neck in her first year at the Academy. The wood shone with all the colours of a kaleidoscope, and it seemed to hum with a special energy of its own.

Certainly, it gave the guitar a beautiful tone, Eyre thought, as she picked the strings into a haunting melody, playing an ancient Druid song. She softly sang the lyrics her mother had taught her years ago:

Where are we going
And where have we been
Where is the knowing
Of all we have seen
Will ye come with me
Though dancing with death
Solving the mystery
'Til our very last breath

The old song of courage calmed her painful heart and a sudden tiredness overwhelmed her. She rested her guitar against the couch and in minutes was fast asleep.

CHAPTER THREE

EYRE WOKE THE NEXT morning, astounded to find she had slept all afternoon and right through the night. At some point she had taken herself off to bed, but she'd missed dinner completely. She sat up in her comfortable bed and rubbed her eyes and yawned. The morning sun shone through the stained-glass windows and Eyre realised that she felt so much better today. The peace of Highlight was working on her spirit and she'd finally slept without troubled dreams of Gothak, and Strigis and Blondie.

She poured cereal into an emerald-green pottery bowl and padded to the veranda to sit on the step. It was still quite early and the morning was cool; a deceptive start to what Eyre knew would be a scorching day. The mornings in the mountains often started this way, until the sun took hold of the sky and blasted its summer heat downwards. Kookaburras and currawongs called in the fresh air and Eyre was overwhelmed with a sense of tranquillity. She loved it here, she thought as she took a mouthful.

When she'd finished, she wandered into the stables.

"Good morning, handsome," she called and received a loud grumble in reply.

"Where's my breakfast?"

"Coming right up, my friend." Eyre opened the oiled stable door and cleaned out the old straw with a rake. Then she put fresh straw in, and fresh water, and threw an armful of fragrant lucerne into a feed bucket in the corner. Ischyros tore at the hay with his old teeth and chewed blissfully. Nothing wrong with his appetite! Finally, Eyre poured some grain into a feeder on the wall, and tossed some liquorice in too. The old horse was going to have an abundance of treats for the rest of his life.

As Ischyros ate, Eyre massaged his burnt old body with the special cream. Although he never said anything, over the past weeks Eyre had realised that the therapy hurt him, even when she was gentle. So she'd been giving him his breakfast while she rubbed the ointment in, to take his mind off it.

When she was finished, she gave him a kiss on his head (to a loud harrumph!) and left, leaving the doors open. Ischyros could come and go as he wished; he didn't need to stay all day in the stable.

As she walked out of the stable, she saw Nick stretching on his veranda and she waved. "Be over shortly!" she called.

By the time Eyre had showered and dressed, Beatrice and Abby were up too, and were sitting with Nick on sandstone blocks around the Mantle Basin. Beatrice was holding something in her hand and Eyre tried to see what it was as she approached. She felt a pang when she saw that it was a part of Blondie's mane, braided into a gleaming plait. Beatrice was holding it like a precious treasure and stroking the hair as if she were caressing Blondie herself.

"Whittaker Ray is joining us this morning," Nick said as he ate his vegemite toast. "He wants to check up on us."

As if the man himself had heard, there was a flash and Whittaker Ray emerged from the bright light into the clearing. He beamed as he walked over to them and sat down on a sandstone block. With a snap of his fingers he summoned a cup of coffee and took a sip.

"Ah, I needed that," he said. "It's been a long couple of weeks."

"Have they found Ms Periwinkle?" Abby asked darkly.

Whittaker Ray shook his head. "No," he said regretfully. "Unfortunately, she has completely disappeared." Then he turned to Beatrice and his blue eyes softened. "How are you Beatrice? I'm so sorry about Blondie."

Beatrice's hands tightened on the braid, but she just nodded. "I'm okay."

An awkward silence was about to ensue, so Eyre quickly changed the subject. "Well, I'm glad you're here, sir, because I have more information. I looked at my Wisdom yesterday afternoon and it gave me another message."

Everyone looked at her, suddenly very intent. A message from Eyre's Wisdom was of huge importance.

"My father said that the Isar in Incendium can only be seen during the Eta Aquariids," Eyre said. "I presume that's another meteor shower?"

Whittaker Ray looked shocked. "The Eta Aquariids? Well, that's a surprise. And clever. No doubt it was anticipated that the secret of the Leonids might be 'out' by the fourth Isar. But what a change it makes to our plans for the year." His face was troubled.

"When do the Eta Aquariids occur?" Beatrice asked.

"May," Whittaker Ray answered, deep in thought. "That means we have to get you ready for Incendium by May. No easy task. By far the most dangerous and difficult of the Alterworlds. *This* is going to put a spin on things."

Great, Eyre thought. Something harder. Just what we need. But, "Well, maybe the sooner we get to it, the better," was all she commented.

Whittaker Ray gave a small smile. "Can't keep a good team down, can we?" The four friends shrugged ruefully and Whittaker Ray continued. "Well, I'm very sorry, but I can see that you are all doing well enough here, and I now have to leave at once. I must take this information back to the Echelon—we will have to make plans in the greatest secrecy. This is an advantage that we have over the Gothak, and we must make the most of it. You will have to excuse my short stay; this is of the highest importance."

He stood up and they bid him farewell. "Keep in touch," he said. "Let me know if you need help." And then he disappeared.

"Short and sweet," Nick commented, and a grin appeared. "*What?*"

Beatrice looked serious. "Well, we need to put that message in the Book of Bane," she said. "It's really important."

"And I have something else," Abby added. "I'd forgotten in the furore at the end of the semester."

At their enquiring looks, she continued. "I asked Madame Overmantle about the Lorian message, the one Jax was talking about."

"Well, hang on," Beatrice said. "I'll get a pen."

"And I'll grab the Book," Eyre said, leaving at a run.

Eventually they were all sitting back down, Beatrice with a pen and the Book on her lap, writing the Sea Crone's information from the Wisdom down carefully.

The Third Revelation of the Wisdom

"The Isar can be seen in Incendium during the Eta Aquariids."
Eyre nodded.
"Well, here's Madame Overmantle's puzzle," Abby said. Beatrice wrote in the journal as Abby dictated the message slowly.

The Orbuculum's Enigma
Seek and find the heavy fruit
That holds the juices blue
A means to elude the black pursuit
No other drupe will do

"That's the Lorian fruit, for sure," Beatrice said, thinking hard. "I wonder how it's meant to help?"

Eyre shook her head. "Jax said they'd been trying all sorts of ways, with no success. They've had to give up for now because too many people were dying, trying to get to the Underworld."

A gloom settled over them, and then Eyre interrupted.

"You know, I've had another thought, after my piloting lessons last semester. It's not really anything to put in the Book, but it's something I think we should do."

As everyone looked at her, she continued. "I had a couple of embarrassing moments with Madame Overmantle, when she read my thoughts about her piloting skills."

Her friends chuckled. All of them had experienced the roller coaster ride that was a flight with Madame Overmantle.

"Anyway, I thought that we should really learn to communicate telepathically using the Wisdom's Code, so that anyone who intercepts it can't understand our message."

Abby groaned. "You're joking, surely? *That* mess of hieroglyphics? I'll be graduated before I learn the first row!"

Nick looked thoughtful. "I think Eyre has a point actually. It might be hard, but we can practise over the summer break. Even if we just learn to spell out our message, it's got to be a good thing. We won't know who's listening on campus, or even who the good guys are. It's getting harder and harder to tell."

Beatrice was delighted—any mental challenge was great fun to her. She passed the Book to Eyre. "Here, see if you can get my message," she said, concentrating hard.

Eyre focused on receiving Beatrice's telepathic thoughts and referred to the Code as she scribbled the message on a piece of paper.

"I've got it!" she announced dramatically, and Beatrice beamed.

Eyre held up the paper: "Help, fiend!"

Nick and Abby cracked up and Beatrice looked cross and took the paper. "Well, I guess I need to practise a bit," she said, frowning. "It was supposed to say 'hello, friend'!"

At that they all laughed harder and Eyre closed the Book. "We all need to practise, I daresay! I'll take this back to the basement. And then—what do you think we should do today?"

Nick stood up. "Well, I've got an idea."

As they looked at him expectantly, he continued. "I thought perhaps Bea, you could mount Blondie's braid in your staff? It will give you great luck, I reckon. And we could all put our Inguz Talismans in our staffs too, the ones the Echelon gave us. I've got something else for you too."

Beatrice looked down at the braid in her hand and nodded. Pain coloured her face.

"That's a really good idea, Nick," she said. "I'd like to do that. Mum and Dad and Lachie will be back this afternoon and it would be nice to do it before I get busy with household chores." She laughed, but it was a painful sound and Abby hugged her.

"I'll go put the Book back," Eyre said to cover the awkward moment, and headed off to her cabin with the precious journal.

She was soon back with her staff and Inguz Talisman. She turned the polished rainbow wood of her staff in her hands, loving the way the pink diamond glowed as the light hit it. Beatrice, Abby and Nick had already summoned their staffs and all four of them sat on sandstone blocks around the Mantle Basin.

"The best way for you to attach the braid is up here, using Bingi sap," Nick began, taking Beatrice's redwood staff and indicating where he meant. "But you'll have to carve it out a little to make room. I've brought my carving gouges and sandpaper. I'll help you."

Then he brought some metallic objects from his pocket. "I collected these at Caelus. We can put these in our staffs too, as well as the Inguz Talismans."

'These' turned out to be small Electrum fulgurites. There were four of them, and they shone dully in the light. The power of the lightning that produced them had melted them into jagged shapes and Nick threw them in the air. They scattered in front of the four friends. "I dug them up from the pathway. Pick up the one nearest you."

"Were you allowed to take them?" Beatrice asked as she took the one closest to her and examined it closely.

Nick shrugged. "Approved by Lord Clarembout himself."

Eyre stroked the cool metal. Her fulgurite was shaped like a lightning bolt and it gleamed with a life of its own. Indeed, she knew it was immersed with huge power, as the Electrum fulgurites were used to power the Zepps. It would be an auspicious addition to her staff, she decided. And she was glad to put the Inguz Talisman in her staff too. It was a memory of a huge battle and the success of acquiring another Isar.

For the next hour they worked carefully to carve a bed in their staffs for each of the treasures. Beatrice worked especially hard, and Eyre watched as she carefully measured and scraped her precious staff to fit the gem-topped gift that Madame Overmantle had given her.

All of them already had a ruby set in the wood, which they'd taken from the Pyre of Va in Terra. The ruby was a reminder to them of the courage of their guide, Shuvai, who had died fighting the Gothak. Now they would have other amulets to strengthen their resolve, and as a permanent reminder of this ever-challenging journey.

They'd decided to place the two talismans just above the area they held their staff, and, after measuring the distance, they began to carve away the wood. The cavity to inlay their Electrum fulgurites took quite a while, as each piece was unique and irregular. The Inguz was also a complex shape that required care. They had to take their time so they didn't cut too much wood away, and silence reigned as they concentrated on the task. Eventually they all finished shaping the cavities, and sanded them smooth.

When Beatrice had carved and sanded the space for the neon blue stone that held Blondie's mane, and also the channels for her fulgurite and Inguz, Nick brought out some Bingi sap and Beatrice used it to set Blondie's talisman at the top of her staff.

Beatrice ran her finger over the gemstone that sparkled the colour of the Mediterranean Sea. "I looked this stone up in the Crystals and Minerals textbook this morning," she said. "It's a Paraiba Tourmaline, and it's one of the rarest gemstones on Entis. Madame Overmantle has given me a priceless treasure." They all moved closer to study the gleaming stone. The gem had an otherworldly gleam to it, and yet it seemed to merge with the wood of Beatrice's staff as if it belonged there.

"I know Madame Overmantle has a huge collection of crystals, they're all lined up on shelves around her room, and she has a huge glass cabinet full of minerals and strange rocks," Abby said. "I saw them when I went to ask her about the message in the orbuculum. She said that between her and the Ranger, they have the greatest mineral collection in Entis."

"Well, it's a fitting tribute to Blondie," Eyre said. "Madame Overmantle knew how much you loved her, Beatrice, and she is honouring Blondie's courage."

After Beatrice attached the beautiful gift from Madame Overmantle, they all worked on fixing the other talismans into their staffs.

Eyre studied her staff. Her fulgurite looked like a lightning bolt in the rainbow wood, a golden-silver gleam of power, a mystical offering from Caelus. And the Inguz was a badge of honour, bestowed by the Echelon for their courage. It was something to be proud of.

"Thanks for helping us with this, Nick," she said. "It's so special."

Abby sighed in contentment. Her fulgurite was shaped like an arrowhead and it gleamed amongst the speckled pattern of her leopard tree staff. Beatrice had a spear-shaped fulgurite and Nick's was like the barb on a fishhook. The four fulgurites looked like ancient, mystical Nordic runes.

And the silver Inguz gleamed in their staffs as a permanent reminder of their achievement in Caelus.

"How could you even *think* to collect the fulgurites in all that furore?" Abby exclaimed. "Thank you!" She threw her arms around Nick and hugged him, causing him to turn an interesting berry colour.

"Blondie's braid looks wonderful," Eyre said hesitantly.

Beatrice didn't say anything, but her eyes lingered on the plaited mane that decorated her staff. She seemed happier, Eyre thought. Keeping a piece of Blondie close was obviously a comfort to her.

"Well, I've got to work on the campsite," Nick said, standing up. "New Year is only a couple of weeks away and I have to get it all ready!"

"Good idea," Eyre responded. "Bea and Abby, come to my place, and let's finish off the plans for the party. There's still a bit to do."

"Yes, we have to resolve the guest list!" Abby said solemnly. "Professor Vela still hasn't responded to my invitation!"

Even Beatrice laughed out loud.

CHAPTER FOUR

MR AND MRS EDMUNSUN and Lachie arrived later that afternoon and it was good for Beatrice to have her family back. She disappeared for a few days as she spent time with them and recuperated from the awful shock she'd had. But Lachie was a wonderful presence—he was eleven now and due to start high school next year. He'd grown taller and leaner, but his hair was still sandy like his father's, whereas Beatrice's hair was dark like her mother's. Lachie had lost none of his energy; he ran around the campsite getting into everything and interfering with Nick as he tried to prepare for the New Year's Eve party. Nick, who'd not had much of a family life before coming to the Academy, seemed to enjoy it greatly and Lachie became like his shadow. A rather inept assistant, but one Nick was happy to have around.

Christmas came and went, a quiet day with lots of food. Mrs Edmunsun had cooked up a huge feast with copious amounts of salad, ham, turkey and seafood. They all exchanged small gifts and then the four friends and Lachie went for a hike to the Buyabarra Billabong, spending all afternoon in the cool, healing waters. Nick had stood on the edge of the jump for quite some time before he eventually leapt in. Not from fear, Eyre thought; he just seemed lost in memories. Last year had been very difficult for Nick, and he'd almost died from the mali that had infected his soul. None of them were unscathed from the past few years, and they all had wounds. Nick had plenty of physical scars, but these latest ones were the internal kind; experiences that couldn't be forgotten or erased. Lachie helped, with his irrepressible energy and the way he lifted all their spirits with his antics. When he belly-flopped into the water from the edge of the billabong everyone fell apart with laughter.

As ever, the Buyabarra worked its eternal magic, and the five of them ran home feeling energized and at peace. Every day Eyre, Beatrice, Abby and

Nick worked on their telepathy, staff skills and Ferito, and general fitness. Even Abby didn't complain. None of them underestimated the magnitude of the journey ahead of them.

It had been fascinating to realise that the Electrum in their staffs had given them extra power, and it took them a while to get used to the force that blasted from the crystal at the top of each sturdy branch. They had a hilarious first afternoon where their staffs physically blew out of their hands, or dragged them around the campsite, and generally sent energy in all directions. But eventually, after plenty of practise, they managed to control it.

"Ben Perrill, looking forward to seeing you next year," Eyre muttered under her breath.

Abby, perhaps by telepathy, heard her. "And *I*, personally, will be very happy to introduce our esteemed lecturer, Ms Periwinkle, to my Electrum staff should I ever come across her!"

They grimaced at each other, then let a torrent of fire smash into a rock across the clearing.

"Again, *but better!*" Beatrice cried. Ever since Eyre had told them how Christopher and Tina had cracked the Wisdom's Code, she'd had a great respect for the Unlit.

Ischyros was improving slowly, but he would always have sensitive, red-raw skin from his ordeal by fire. He wandered freely around the campsite during the day, usually commenting disparagingly on this thing or that, before heading back to his stable at night. Eyre was glad he was nearby, as she knew she would have worried terribly about him if he'd been back at the Academy.

Eyre also worked on a special project during those weeks. She'd examined the black opal Jax had given her and decided how to shape the stone to make the best of its exquisite colour, which was a medley of vibrant greens, purples and blues, but it also had an explosion of orange through it as well. Once she had fashioned it into a perfect diamond shape, she polished it with sandpaper and cerium oxide until the colours glowed like the twinkling lights of the Aurora Australis. Then she hammered a wide silver bangle and welded an Inguz made out of gold to it. Finally, she set the diamond-shaped opal into the centre of the Inguz. The result was breathtaking, magical, and all the more special because Jax had given her the stone. Eyre put the silver cuff on and knew she would treasure it forever.

There was enough to fill the hours, and the days flew by in the heat and blue skies of summer until eventually, New Year's Eve dawned. The first thing Eyre heard when she opened her eyes, barely after dawn that morning, was Abby's voice issuing commands. Eyre blearily peered out of her window and saw Abby ordering a dozen harried-looking Mimir around.

"Yes, great, tables over there, thank you lads, and then we want all the seating in groups around the Mantle Basin."

Eyre walked outside, yawning widely, and saw towers of stackable chairs and collapsible tables leaning up against the side of Abby's cabin. What time had they started? she wondered. They weren't there yesterday.

Beatrice was sitting by the Mantle Basin with a cup of coffee, so Eyre made a cup of tea and went and joined her. Beatrice rolled her eyes and shook her head as Eyre sat down.

"It's going to be a looong day, my friend," she said sadly. "Abby's in management mode."

Eyre laughed and they both snickered as Nick sidled around the far side of the cabin to join them.

"Am I safe?" he whispered. "I thought I heard a Saevus out here somewhere."

"Laugh away!" Abby's voice boomed in their heads. "This party is going to be a success if I have anything to do with it! And there is a lot to do today. People are arriving at 5pm sharp and it all has to be done by then! Get with the program, guys!"

And then she whisked by, dragging a roll of white fabric. "Sergeant Ametrine! Could you give me a hand here?"

Beatrice, Eyre and Nick roared with laughter.

"Well, I can't leave Abby to do all the work," Nick chortled. "I'll go see what I can help with."

Within the hour they were all hard at work. Abby's theme for the party was 'The Roaring 20s: Rhapsody in the Blue Mountains,' and she'd organised Art Deco and Great Gatsby-style decorations for the campsite. As they toiled away, Eyre realised what a truly great gift Abby had. The whole clearing was slowly being transformed, back a century to the time following the Great War. A time of wild parties, extravagance and hope for the future. It was a great theme for these times too, as everyone really did need to have some fun after the dire events of late. Any theme that was based on hope for the future was okay by Eyre.

She was helping Beatrice string fairy lights through the eucalypts at the perimeter of the clearing when Mrs Edmunsun walked over to them. Mrs Edmunsun was immaculately dressed as usual, wearing a flowing burnt-orange dress that highlighted the Sector colour of the Inguz on her upper arm—Arant, a vibrant orange. As Eyre studied the striking woman she felt a pang, as she thought about her own indistinct Inguz. The outline of hers was a faint black, rather than silver, with a dull grey centre. She had reconciled herself to this some time ago, but occasionally she felt regretful about it. She would really love to have an Inguz of any colour—as long as it was normal!

But her thoughts were interrupted by Mrs Edmunsun, who stepped over to her and gave her a huge hug. "Your Inguz is absolutely fine, Eyre," she said. "You are perfect as you are."

Eyre was slightly embarrassed that her thoughts had been telepathically picked up, but she hugged Mrs Edmunsun back, hard. Beatrice's mother had become like a surrogate mother to her and she had enjoyed the past couple of weeks being part of a family unit again.

"Thank you, Mrs Edmunsun. I hope you have a good trip."

"Well, I hope you have a great party! And I think you can call me Robyn now. At your age, Eyre. I feel ancient being called Mrs Edmunsun," Beatrice's mother replied, her eyes crinkling. She hugged Eyre and then Beatrice moved in too and Robyn embraced her tightly. "Look after yourself my darlings and call me if you need me. Have fun, and we'll see you before you head back to school."

Lachie ran around saying goodbye to everyone, and Mr Edmunsun also bid them farewell in his quiet way. Then, with a flash, they were gone. It was amazing how the energy of people was a physical thing, Eyre mused. Already the feeling in Highlight was changed; there was a hollowness where their presence had been.

But Abby quickly dragged Eyre back from her thoughts.

"Hurry up you two! We still need to get all the lanterns hung and the food prepared. Then we have to get dressed. There's no time to waste!"

Abby in logistics mode was not to be trifled with, so Eyre and Beatrice redoubled their efforts and within an hour had all the fairy lights and lanterns hung. As Eyre surveyed the lights swaying gently in the breeze, she thought that it was going to look magical tonight. Worth the back-breaking effort.

"Okay, then," Beatrice announced with relief. "That's done. Let's head to the kitchen!"

For the next few hours they worked hard, getting salads made in large bowls, platters of tropical fruits, sausages lined up in trays, towers of bread sliced, and potatoes peeled and prepared for the ovens. Beatrice was looking well-pleased by the time they had everything ready; with her in charge of food, no one was going to go hungry, least of all herself!

Mid-afternoon they had just finished the food when a dishevelled Abby opened the front door with her foot, her arms piled full of mysterious bags that towered above her head. She tottered in and dumped them on Beatrice's couch.

"I am glad to get rid of those!" she huffed. "Awkward to carry! Come and have a look."

Eyre and Beatrice dried their hands on a tea towel and headed into the sitting room.

"These," Abby said grandly, "are for you Bea." She handed over an armful of assorted sized bags. "And these are yours, Eyre!" Eyre received an equal number of bags, and both girls looked questioningly at Abby.

"It's your attire for the evening!" Abby said, delighted by their puzzlement. "I can't have an amazing-looking venue without the hosts being appropriately dressed!"

Beatrice grinned and began to unzip the suit bag. Eyre did the same, curious to see what was inside. She'd been so busy getting the party details organised, she hadn't really thought about what to wear, other than to just grab something out of her cupboard.

"Wow!" Beatrice exclaimed, as she brought out a shimmering yellow dress, the colour of her Sector. The fabric was made of yellow crystal beads that flashed in the light. She held it up against herself, and Abby applauded. The colour suited Beatrice's dark hair and hazel eyes perfectly. Eyre pulled a shining bronze coloured dress made of sequins out of her bag.

"Thank you, Abby," she said as she held the stunning gown up. She was touched by the kindness of her friend. "This is so beautiful."

The rest of their bags contained shoes to match and long ropes of shining pearls, looped with strands of citrines in Beatrice's case, and golden quartz in Eyre's. The final bag had feathered headbands in the same colour as their dresses. Beatrice's yellow beaded headband had a yellow feather at the side, and a circular citrine that sat in the centre of her forehead. Eyre's feather was copper-coloured, and her bronze sequined headband held a square-cut golden quartz.

"Oh, what fun!" Beatrice said as she twirled around, the dress swirling around her legs. Then she ran over and hugged Abby. "Thank you so much!"

Abby beamed. "Well, I didn't want to turn you away because of the dress code! I've got a tux for Nick." She looked a bit shy. "It's got a blue tie to match my dress." Then she looked out the window. "Well, it's time to get dressed, girls. Everything's ready except for us! See you at half past four?"

Beatrice and Eyre nodded, and Eyre packed everything back in the bags. Then she and Abby left for their respective cabins to get ready for the night.

CHAPTER FIVE

GUESTS STARTED ARRIVING AT about ten to five. Zanda, always late to everything on campus, was obviously not one to miss a party, because he was one of the first to zap in, emerging from the light with a stylish woman.

"Thanks Mum," he said hurriedly. "I'll be right now." Getting the hint, his mother waved with a rueful smile and disappeared a second later.

Zanda rolled his eyes. "I'll be glad when I can teleport! Being dropped off by Mummy is not really my style." Everyone laughed. Teleporting was a subject for this year and they were all looking forward to learning how to travel alone.

"Well you do look awesome, Zanda. Your tux!" Beatrice said. Rather than a black tux, he was wearing a rainbow-coloured suit with a purple bow tie and a purple top hat, and he'd brought his staff, which was made of Diospyros Humilis, or Queensland Ebony, with an amethyst crystal at the top. An unusual outfit, but Eyre thought he looked very cool in it—if anyone could pull it off, Zanda could. Nick, more traditionally dressed in his black tux with the sapphire coloured bow tie, slapped Zanda on the back.

"Let's go and get the music organised. Scott's here already, he's been looking for you." They walked off across the clearing to where Nick's lux glowed as it floated in the air. He had tethered it with Viq to stay in place, and tuned the music into it. So when he touched the glowing orb, music began to fill the campsite.

Abby glowed herself as she watched Nick. She looked spectacular in a gleaming blue lamé dress, made from the same fabric as Nick's tie. She had a blue headband with a cobalt feather at the side, and a sapphire in the middle of it, and she'd coloured the tips of her hair in shining blue and silver. She looked so beautiful, Eyre thought, and no doubt happiness had something to do with that.

Flashes of light started to appear around the clearing as more people arrived in their Roaring 20s dress. Carly, Rigmar, Luke and Anders turned up at the same time, and then so many people started to appear it was hard to keep track of them all.

Rigmar walked up to talk to them. He looked very dashing in his tux with a red bow tie, Eyre thought.

"You look awesome, Rig," Abby said and Rigmar bowed.

"As do you lovely ladies. Thank you for inviting me!"

Just then someone spoke from beside Eyre's elbow.

"Would anyone care for a drink?"

Eyre turned and was surprised to see Private Ammonite standing there with a tray of drinks and a twinkle in his eye. He held out the silver platter which held bubbling green drinks in old-fashioned champagne coupé glasses.

Abby grinned. "Jengles agreed that the Mimir would help us out, so they've come to serve. Thank you so much Private Ammonite," she added as she took a glass. "It's a cocktail made from Bibifruit from Terra and pineapple juice. It's the latest thing, and delicious! Try some."

Private Ammonite seemed to be getting a lot of enjoyment from his role as waiter, and he bowed deeply as each person took a glass, no mean feat with a tray full of glasses. "At your service, m'lady," he declared as Eyre took a green cocktail. She laughed. He seemed to treat everything as a huge joke.

"Thank you, kind sir," she answered, and he saluted importantly, then strode off towards another group of people. "So many people, so little time!" he exclaimed in a false-harassed voice as he left.

"A sign of the times," Beatrice said with a sigh, her eyes on Corporal Asscher, who was serving across the clearing. Eyre understood. She knew that the Mimir weren't here to be servants. They were here to keep an eye on things. With all the distraction of a party, and people coming and going, Jengles obviously needed to feel confident someone was on duty when the Gothak had been so active lately. No doubt Jengles was somewhere in the background too, Eyre thought.

Pheria arrived in a flash of light, wearing a silver dress that set off her tanned skin and short dark hair. She hesitated for a moment and then walked over to join them. She had a silver headband with a black feather, and long silver earrings that swayed as she walked. Eyre was still a little unsure about Pheria, but she had to admit that she looked stunning. Over the last few months of the year Eyre had formed an uneasy truce with Pheria, and a reluctant admiration for her athleticism and her focus. She had become a permanent part of their group at the end of last year, and immediately people started welcoming her as she joined them. Eyre noticed that Rigmar stood up a little straighter and Eyre smiled inwardly. Aha! Pheria had won someone's heart, it seemed. And when Eyre noticed the frost thaw a little as Pheria looked at Rigmar, Eyre wondered whether the feeling might be returned somewhat. On the surface they seemed an unlikely match, but perhaps Rigmar was the exact person to crack through Pheria's aloof façade.

Beatrice scattered Eyre's thoughts as she exclaimed "Yes!" with great satisfaction. Beatrice was looking intently across the clearing at a handful of Mimir who were bustling around trestle tables draped in silver and black fabric. "They're bringing the food out!"

A few minutes later the smell of the barbeque began to waft through the clearing as Private Ammonite tossed the loops of sausages on the hot grill. He was obviously relishing his role as head chef and clacked the tongs he held in each hand with all the aplomb of a lead percussionist, his red beard dripping with sweat as he moved the sausages on and off the grill before they burned. Many faces were turned towards him, laughing at his antics.

But then Eyre was distracted as someone walked up to her.

"Eyre," Colton said, so handsome in a tux and light blue bow tie that set off his ice-blue eyes. Eyre had to crane her neck to look up at him—he must be at least six foot three now. His gaze swept across her gown and then focused on her face. "Nice to see you. You look beautiful!"

Then he added. "Are you doing okay?"

Colton was referring to the end of the TACI expedition, which had been shambolic and distressing, with a huge loss of Lightworker and Alterworld lives. And, of course Blondie, which no one would ever get over. None of the TACI expeditions had ended smoothly, Eyre thought dismally, thinking that the Incendium trip was coming even sooner than expected, no doubt with its share of danger and disaster. But her thoughts could not remain gloomy for long under the gaze of the tall, broad boy. She smiled up at Colton.

"The past few weeks have helped," she said simply. "We have to move on."

Colton nodded. Then he took one of her hands in his massive hand. "Would you like to dance?"

Eyre looked out at the dancefloor, which was constructed of large squares of glossy obsidian, the crystal that contained properties to ward against evil, checked with squares of Thassos pure white marble, with its qualities to ground and calm the soul. Abby had constructed a general black and white colour scheme to go with the Roaring 20s theme, and the shining obsidian and marble squares looked amazing under the flickering fairy lights. Already people were dancing on the floor and Eyre followed Colton out, feeling suddenly shy. She reprimanded herself sternly. She'd known Colton for three years now, and she needed to get over herself! But looking at the tall, striking figure in his black tux, she found it hard to reconcile the boy who'd started at the Academy with her, with this grown man.

Colton swept her into his arms, and twirled around the dance floor in a style of ballroom dancing. But his ice blue eyes were twinkling and she eventually exploded with laughter.

"I feel so strange, dressed up like this," she confessed. But Colton's gaze suddenly became more intent and he pulled her a little closer.

"You don't look strange at all," he said softly, twirling her around the dance floor again. But as Eyre looked up at him, and despite his amazing presence, with a feeling of things falling into place, she suddenly realised that although she was in awe of him, she felt nothing more. He was a Lightworker of immense power, a good and beautiful soul. But she knew now that her heart was elsewhere.

The moment was interrupted by an ironic voice by Eyre's shoulder.

"Mind if I cut in?" Eyre turned, already in a fluster, because she instantly recognised the voice. Jax looked down at her with a glint in his bright green eyes, and a crooked smile on his face, like he was unable to quite get it to work properly.

But Colton, cool, and as always, a gentleman, bowed to Eyre. "Of course," he replied. "Thank you for the dance, Eyre."

Eyre's cheeks were flaming, a detail not missed by Jax, who grinned.

"I like Colton's taste in women," he laughed, "but he'd better not do anything that might cause me to use Occido!" He grinned, but there was a glint in his eye that made Eyre's heart race as they began to dance. Jax pulled her close until her face was next to his.

"You look spectacular," he breathed as he kissed her lightly.

Eyre felt a flush of heat travel up her body. "Thank you," she replied when she could finally speak. "You look nice too." *Nice* was somewhat of an understatement. Jax looked like he'd just walked off the set of a Bond movie —the essence of brooding sensuality. His black hair gleamed and those green eyes studied her closely from under straight black brows. And he moved like a jungle cat, with a complete economy of movement, lithe and athletic. Eyre shivered. Jax Jackson only grew more handsome and magnetic each year.

The uncomfortable moment passed, and Jax leaned in to talk to her. "How have you been doing? Is Beatrice alright?"

Eyre nodded. The music was getting louder, and she had to talk close in Jax's ear for him to hear her. "We're all okay. It was a dismal end to the semester really. How was your Christmas?"

"I spent it in Terra," Jax replied. Eyre nodded. That would account for his tanned skin and general look of intense fitness. He'd obviously been working hard in the Alterworld. And she felt a surge of joy that finally he was being honest with her—both of them knew that he would have been secretly searching for information about the Lorian fruit that might help them solve the mystery of the puzzle provided by the beryl orbuculum. If the Lightworkers were to recover the Isar stolen by the Gothak, they needed to solve the problem of how the Lorian fruit could allow them to travel to the Underworld undetected. Jax was obviously still using his skills to work undercover on the enigma.

As Jax twirled Eyre around she noticed Robeson arrive, wearing a sparkling yellow bow tie. Obviously, Abby had sent him a memo, Eyre thought. Robeson walked over to Beatrice, who hugged him and then put her long arms around his neck as they began to dance. Those two probably had half the Academy's IQ between them, Eyre thought as she grinned a hello at Robeson.

Just then a loud gong cut through the music.

"Dinner is served!" Private Ammonite announced. "Step right up, ladies and gentlemen!"

They ate dinner at silver-covered tables, with candles and decorations of pearls and flowers, which Abby had brought in from a function company in the nearby town of Wentworth Falls. Highlight was a riot of colour, of swaying feathers and gleaming dresses, swinging looped necklaces and long ornate earrings, all set in counterpoint to the dashing black tuxedos the boys wore. Above the chatter of voices and the clatter of food being served, the music rose, hauntingly evocative of a bygone era. It was a moment in time, a memory to savour on this last day of the year, Eyre thought as she looked around the scene with a mixture of nostalgia and fear for the future. She was overcome by a feeling that they all needed to make the most of the night. Because who knew what the next year would bring?

The Mimir had just cleared away the dishes, and people were drifting back onto the dance floor, when there was an explosion of light in the clearing that stretched from one side to the other in a blinding glare. The size of the blast disrupted the music from the lux, causing an awful screech of feedback to crash upon them all for a few moments. Everyone covered their ears at the horrible sound, and several students had automatically summoned their staffs, aiming them at the mysterious light.

When they saw who emerged from the light the staffs were lowered, but not by much.

"Keep calm," Eyre muttered to herself as Ben Perrill and a bunch of his cronies stepped into the clearing. The last thing Eyre wanted to do was dissolve into a rage of madness and undo all Abby's hard work. But looking at Perrill's smug face was enough to start her blood boiling.

"It's not you I'm actually worried about," Abby said. Eyre looked over and saw Beatrice marching towards Ben with a look of murder on her face, her Antaraks summoned and gleaming as she raised them high. They looked most out of place with her flapper gown, but no one was laughing, and Eyre realised that if someone didn't stop Beatrice, murder was indeed going to take place. With a burst of speed, Eyre levitated across the clearing and landed at Beatrice's side.

"Stop, Bea," Eyre urged, holding on to the taller girl's arm. But Beatrice shook her hand away, seemingly lost in a world of her own. Several students stepped up to stride forward side-by-side, until eventually there was a circle of students facing each other, some with weapons drawn. The general mood was not helped by Ben's sneering face. He was obviously overjoyed with disrupting the evening.

"Why don't you just turn around and leave, Perrill," Jax said in a low voice. It was not a question.

"My friends and I have come to celebrate the New Year," Ben taunted with a mean smile. "My family does, after all, own one of these cabins."

"I'm going to kill you, Perrill," Beatrice snarled, and hurled one of the Antaraks at his head. But he'd obviously been well trained by Rufa staff, because he raised a hand and shielded, so that the Antarak hit it and dropped harmlessly onto the dirt. Within a second the second Antarak cartwheeled towards him, but seeming to enjoy the situation, Ben stopped that weapon too.

Tears of frustration and rage were running down Beatrice's face as she raised her hands. "You mongrel, Ben." Lightning bolts blasted from her palms. Evidently, she had been practising her fulminology skills, because if Ben hadn't ducked, his head would have been blown off. His smirk faltered a little and colour came to his cheeks.

"Come on then, Edmunsun, try again," he snarled, and raised his own hands. The Curtis twins stepped forward, alongside Tec Langford and Wyatt Rankins. The boys had all grown very big over the past year and their training at Rufa had filled them out. They were vastly outnumbered, but Eyre was starting to feel anxious; someone was going to be seriously hurt if the escalating tension wasn't halted.

Jax moved forward and raised his hand. His ironbark staff appeared and the deep blue sapphire reflected orange flashes from the candlelight as he aimed it at Ben Perrill.

"Someone should have done this a long time ago, Perrill."

He blasted a beam of blue fire towards the hulking boy, but another flash of light filled the clearing and the lethal torrent was deflected to blast into rock at the far side of the campsite.

Jax looked up in surprise, then lowered his staff as Sergeant Tottingham appeared from the light. She strode forward with a furious look on her face, lifted her hands and sent a *whump* of energy radiating around the clearing that knocked every student on to their rear end.

"WHAT are you doing?" she bellowed. "Are you all mad? Stop this at once!"

But Beatrice for once was uncowed by the fearsome Sergeant. She scrambled to her feet and pointed her redwood staff at Ben Perrill, her hand quivering in rage. The emerald at the top blazed as ripples of visible energy travelled up and down the glossy wood. The rest of the students picked themselves up and watched Beatrice, who seemed to glow with an incandescent fury.

"This *mongrel* is responsible for the death of my Lighthorse," Beatrice spat. "The only way he's leaving here is as a pile of ashes."

And, defying the Sergeant, Beatrice moved quicker than Eyre had ever seen her move. Before the Sergeant could react, a stream of scorching fire from her Electrum-enhanced staff smashed into Ben Perrill and hurled him across the clearing. If it wasn't for the shield he had erected at the last minute, he would indeed have been reduced to a pile of ashes.

The Sergeant's face suffused with anger, and again she raised her hands. A zap of crackling energy raced around the whole clearing to encircle the students, instantly immobilising them all. With barely concealed rage, the Sergeant stalked towards the group of furious students and stopped in front of Ben Perrill.

"You and your friends will leave *now*," she said in a low voice. "I will deal with you back at the Academy next semester, but until then you are banned from returning to this campsite." She turned towards the rest of the group.

"Any interaction between you and that group of boys is strictly forbidden, and anyone disobeying this," the Sergeant's eyes lingered on Beatrice, who tilted her chin, her eyes hot, "will be expelled from the Academy. Mark my words." She studied the belligerent group, who seemed disinclined to move.

"GO!" she thundered, and finally the boys left in a flash of light. Everyone else shuffled around uncertainly as the Sergeant addressed them.

"Enjoy the rest of the night," Sergeant Tottingham said. "And try to bring in the New Year in a more seemly fashion."

Then she too was gone in a flash of light.

CHAPTER SIX

EYRE FOLLOWED HER FRIENDS out of the Zepp, carrying an assortment of overstuffed bags and heading for the eastern wings of the dormitory building where the fourth-year residences were situated. Since the dismal finish to the New Year's Eve party, the days had flown quickly until Peter Edmunsun arrived to take them to the Academy.

Eyre thought back to the final days at the cabins as she trudged along behind her friends. The rest of the party had finished happily enough once the Sergeant had left, but it was overshadowed by the violent interaction between Ben Perrill and his cronies and Beatrice. There was a sense of unfinished business, and although the students had welcomed the new year with gusto, an uneasiness pervaded the celebrations. Just the way to start the new year, Eyre thought gloomily. After midnight had rung out, people had dispersed fairly quickly, communicating by telepathy for someone to come and teleport them home.

Indeed, that mood had coloured the rest of the time at the cabins, Eyre thought, so much so that the four of them were well and truly ready to head back to the Academy by the time the day arrived. There was a sense of needing to get on with things, and to face whatever this year was going to bring without further procrastination.

Their room was located down the end of the hallway, and they piled in, dumping their bags and possessions onto the beds. Abby flopped onto her back on her bed.

"I'm exhausted!" she complained. "Travelling is so tiring!"

They all laughed, but there was an edge to it. Life was no longer light-hearted, and Eyre had none of the naivety that had protected her during her past years at the Academy. At least then she had been oblivious to what was waiting out there for them. Now she was all too aware of the dangers, and the magnitude of what they had to achieve. And this year they didn't have the buffer of a whole year before the TACI test. With the Eta Aquariids due in May, they were going to have to study harder than ever so that they would be prepared to face the treacherous environment of Incendium and locate the final Isar.

Beatrice leaned against the wall and used her fingertips to flick through an assortment of colours. She had just changed the wall to blue, then purple and then a vibrant aqua colour, when Abby leaned up on her elbow.

"Go back to that blue colour!" she said, waving her hands in excitement.

Beatrice shot Abby a look, but touched her fingers to the wall to change it back to dark blue, the environmental colours of Caelus.

"Oh, brilliant!" Eyre exclaimed. Etched in silver on the wall was a dramatic picture of a volcano exploding in bright orange flames, in stark contrast with the inky colour of lethal Zeguardagens attacking from the dark-blue sky, while battalions from all the Alterworlds fought desperately on the pumice-filled ground below.

"Caelus," Abby said softly, and they all looked at each other as realisation dawned.

"The Ranger is back!" they said in unison.

"Hooray!" Eyre shouted, and they levitated in the air to give each other a high five.

The Ranger had been 'suspended' halfway through last year, due to concerns raised by some of the parents about his less-than-standard teaching methods. But Eyre understood now that perhaps it was just a political move. The upheaval had been led by a group of parents who'd had problems with the Academy in general and who were looking for any excuse to unseat the current administration. In particular, this disgruntled group cited the Ranger's wild teaching methods with students who were learning to pilot the Zepps, a method that Eyre had found to be one of the best things about the lessons. But this was just petty politics. Eyre had been told that the Ranger was involved in things of much greater significance, and she suspected that there must be deeper reasons for why he had left. Once again, she had to have faith.

"Well, put the Book of Bane in the wall, then Bea," Abby said. "The Ranger obviously wanted us to protect it."

"All very well," Beatrice replied drily. "But where do we put it?"

They all walked over to scrutinise the wall, and Eyre realised that Beatrice had a point. Last year the picture on the wall had been an amusing sketch of a mop and bucket, and the Inguz in the artwork that pointed the way to the secret cache in the wall hadn't been too hard to find. But this elaborate etching had so much detail, it was very difficult to see where the Inguz might be. After several tries at poking the wall in unsuccessful places, Abby suddenly pushed her arm through right up to the shoulder. She quickly pulled it back out again.

"Ugh!" she exclaimed. "It's so cold! I'll never get used to that. The Inguz is on the bottom of Gegenees' chariot, in the design along the base."

Sure enough, Eyre could see the Inguz that Abby indicated. It formed part of a pattern of Xs, but the actual Inguz was slightly different, and located in the centre of the design.

Beatrice pulled the Book of Bane out of her bag and quickly put it into the magical cache. Then she touched the wall until it turned violet, hiding the image.

"Done," she said with satisfaction. "And so it begins, my friends. Subterfuge, mysteries and foul creatures chasing us around. Just another typical year."

"I'll show you a typical year!" Eyre said seriously, and then hurled a pillow at Beatrice, catching her smack in the face.

"Child," Abby intoned, and then whacked her pillow into the back of Eyre's legs, knocking her bouncing on to her bed.

It took another half hour of flying missiles before things calmed down enough for everyone to start unpacking.

When clothes were finally folded and put away, staffs secured in their staff holders, and bags tucked under the bed, Beatrice put her hands on her hips.

"All that work, my friends. It must be lunchtime!"

The Refectory was bustling with activity when they entered. Lines of students stretched across the room, and the Jotnar rushed around refilling food canteens and cleaning tables as students vacated their seats. The Jotnars' demeanour had not improved, Eyre noted, as she took a plate and stood in line; their dark faces were still creased and unsmiling. Catering was clearly serious work.

They were good cooks though, and Eyre's stomach started to rumble at the delicious smells wafting through the room.

"I am so glad to be back!" a familiar voice said in a relieved tone. Eyre turned around and exclaimed as she saw Zanda standing beside Beatrice with a smile on his face. "One more week of my mother's cooking would have done me in I think."

Eyre hugged him and laughed. "I've missed you! How was the rest of your holiday?"

"Hot!" Zanda replied. "I'm glad to get back to the mountains. Sydney is sweltering!"

"Ah, those beaches though," someone else said and Eyre moved over so that Phillip Outray could join them. Phillip lived on a banana plantation in the Atherton Tablelands, so he didn't get much opportunity to spend time on the beach.

Before she could continue the conversation, a telepathic message from Beatrice in the Wisdom's Code flashed into her head. Determined to work it out rather than turn around and ask her, she shut her eyes and thought hard until she finally worked it out. *Strigis alert!*

Alarmed, she swung around, and then understood what Beatrice meant. Walking into the Refectory with Slade Curtis was Ben Perrill. But she barely had time to register this before Beatrice sent a blazing spear of Viq hurtling towards Ben, and he jumped just in time to avoid it. The searing energy blasted a hole in the ground with a huge explosion that sent twirls of black smoke curling up to the ceiling. Several students leapt up in fright, sending their chairs clattering to the ground behind them, and staffs had materialised in the hands of some of the older students. Silence echoed inside the building and no one moved a muscle. Ben's face, which had initially been shocked, suddenly turned a violent red and he raised his hands. A bolt of lightning sliced through the Refectory, just past Beatrice's shoulder, and slammed into the wall. Students began ducking for cover and diving under tables, sending furniture flying.

Eyre felt a fury begin to rise within her, a sudden explosion of rage that she hadn't felt for some time. It was like an eruption from within, and her mind was suddenly blank of anything other than a ferocious, pulsating wrath. Strigis indeed; she faced Ben Perrill as she would the most savage creature from the Underworld.

Slowly Eyre elevated above the floor and an eerie crackling filled the air as her hair stood on end and her eyes took on a golden hue. Then she raised her hands and clapped them together. A deafening boom rent the air and a shockwave of energy radiated outwards, knocking everyone flat.

"Time to die, Ben," Eyre said in a spine-chilling monotone, and she raised one languid hand, aiming it at the prostrate boy. His face registered a deep fear; he knew she was deadly serious.

But there was a blinding series of flashes and in the space of a few seconds, five senior staff members arrived, standing in a ring before Ben and shielding him from certain death.

"EYRE!" Sergeant Tottingham bellowed. "STOP!"

But Eyre was beyond thought or control, and she sent a barrage of jagged lightning hurtling towards Ben. Instantly, the staff members combined to raise a shield and the lightning bolts skittered off it in all directions. Eyre let out a blood-curdling shriek and hurled a spinning corona of blazing fire at the group. Sparks shot off the spinning light and fell to the ground, burning a tattoo of holes into the marble. The corona slammed into the shield with an ear-splitting *whump* and the ground shook. But the shield held.

Suddenly, a form materialised in the air in front of Eyre, who now appeared to be completely engulfed in flames, so red and intense was the energy around her.

The Ranger put up his hands in front of her.

"All is well," he said softly, as if calming a wild animal. "Let it go, Eyre. Let it go."

He continued to talk softly to her until, gradually, the violent energy that shimmered around her began to diminish. Eyre's hair dropped to her shoulders and her eyes slowly changed back to their normal sapphire-blue, and finally she lowered back down to the floor. She felt overcome by a terrible fatigue as she looked around her with growing awareness, and increasing shock.

"You're okay, Eyre," the Ranger said as he dropped to the floor beside her. "Breathe. Come; sit here on the chair."

"You're an absolute nutcase, Lightward," Ben Perrill screamed from across the room. "Loony tunes! My father will hear of this! You'll be out of here next week!"

But Eyre didn't hear any more, as Whittaker Ray ushered the screeching boy quickly from the room.

Eyre tried to breathe, like the Ranger was saying, but spots began to appear in front of her eyes and she was falling, falling...

CHAPTER SEVEN

EYRE OPENED HER EYES and concentrated until she could focus. Her initial confusion was replaced by a dawning realisation as she recognised the ceiling above her. The familiar chequerboard pattern of dark and light squares of amethyst, the crystal of healing, arched above her and she sighed. Once again, she was in the Infirmary. One day they'd erect a plaque for her in here, she thought in resignation, as her head pounded in time with her heartbeat. She seemed to faint more often than a damsel in distress. So annoying.

Sister Murphy came bustling in and beamed when she saw that Eyre was awake.

"Ah! There you are, finally!" she exclaimed. "We were wondering when you'd come back to join us. How are you feeling?"

Eyre shrugged and winced, as even that small gesture caused waves of sickening pain to rocket through her head. Sister's practised eyes noticed, and she reached into the pocket of her tunic.

"Here, take these. They will help with the pain. You've put yourself through an awful ordeal." She put two pills and a glass of water on the bedside table and helped Eyre to sit up. "Your friends will be glad that you're awake. They've been pestering me for two days!"

"Two days?" Eyre exclaimed and immediately regretted it as pain careered again through her brain. "Have I been out that long?" Her immediate thought was Ischyros. She'd been planning to visit the old horse on her first day back and now it was halfway through the week.

"Yes indeed," Sister Murphy said. "It's your own fault you know. You're going to have to learn to control that temper of yours. You use so much Viq at once that your body can't handle it."

Eyre grimaced and was about to reply when three students barrelled in through the door.

"Eyre! Thank goodness!" Abby cried, and flung her arms around Eyre's neck.

"Can you still levitate?" Beatrice asked in a worried voice. "Can't have you going back to that *other* campus again!" Her voice had a slightly-horrified tone when she said 'other', but Eyre knew it was in jest. Beatrice had a particular soft spot for the Unlit, now that she knew how clever and skilled they were.

"You certainly were a human fireball the other day," Nick added. "Your powers must be growing—the staff members only just managed to hold you off."

"Yeah," Beatrice sniffed. "Shame about that. Would have done the world a favour if you'd got rid of that maggot."

Eyre smiled, but her eyes were clouded. "I was totally out of control," she said. "I'm not going to be any use to anyone if I can't use my skills without trying to blow the world up."

"Nah, don't worry," Nick said. "You'll always have us to sort you out and keep you in line. And besides, it was hilarious watching the first-years try to cram themselves under the tables and chairs. They must have thought you were a demon from hell! And I reckon Ben Perrill might agree. How are you feeling?"

"I'm okay," Eyre said. "But my head feels like I've consumed a gallon of Lorian Juice. Hopefully the pounding will stop soon."

"Well, you missed the 'refreshed and rejoicing' and 'gold table' speech this year, so that's no bad thing," Beatrice said, rolling her eyes. "Dean Fraser was in fine form. But I think he needs a new scriptwriter. That speech is definitely getting old."

Eyre laughed, then regretted it as her head thumped. "I was wondering if you know how Ischyros is going?"

"Jengles brought him back to the stables yesterday," Abby said. "But he wasn't er—very co-operative about going back in his old stall." Her voice started to quaver and then Eyre's three friends all began to laugh hysterically.

"Oh Eyre, you should have seen it!" Beatrice exclaimed. "It was so, so funny. The Kikkuli Master told us that Ischyros, in a very reasonable voice, was explaining why his old quarters were no longer suitable, now that he was used to five-star housing!"

"So you needn't worry about him," Abby added. "He's in fine form!"

Eyre lay back against her pillow, relieved to hear that the old horse was doing okay.

"Eyre will be ready to come back to the dormitory this afternoon," Sister Murphy said. "You can talk to her more then. Off you go!"

Her friends left and the efficient nurse disappeared too, off to do her rounds. Eyre stared out the window, watching the late-summer clouds drift by. It was strange to think that it was already a new year. Everything had gone so fast in the past few months.

She heard footsteps down the hall and then someone entered the room, and she turned on her elbow to see who it was.

Her heart almost stopped when she saw the grinning form of a Gothak staring down at her. Eyre's jaw dropped, and a frisson of cold raised the hairs on her arms. Scrambling, she swung her feet over the edge of her bed.

"Hello, Lightward," Mudamir hissed at her. "We meet again."

Eyre summoned her staff without thinking, but she couldn't move fast enough to use it. With a sudden movement, Mudamir had wrapped her hands tightly together with thick black wire, with a black stone at its centre. A similar wire held her feet completely immobile. Eyre wrestled violently against the tight constraint, and opened her mouth to scream. But Mudamir held a powerful, pallid hand across her mouth. His sharp black nails pierced the side of Eyre's face and a trickle of blood ran down her cheek.

"Don't struggle," he said softly. "It only gets tighter. And if you scream, I will kill the first person that comes through the door. Co-operate and no one gets hurt."

Mudamir took Eyre's staff from between her hands and tossed it on the ground. It clattered and rolled against the wall and Eyre's eyes burned furiously. But she couldn't do anything; she was too worried about someone coming through the door.

"I've been sent to get you," Mudamir whispered. "The powers-that-be thought you might be less than co-operative."

He hit Eyre hard across her cheek and her head snapped around.

"If it were up to me, I'd dispatch you now, and be very happy doing it," Mudamir added. "But apparently we require you alive. However, there will come a time when you are no longer needed, and it will be my privilege to dispose of you as painfully as I am able."

Once again, he smacked his hand against Eyre's cheek, and stars appeared in front of her eyes. Mudamir hauled on the wire and dragged her to her feet.

"Must be off," he said in a sharp, falsely jovial tone.

Mudamir moved his hands through the air and a black, smoking line appeared in the room; hanging vertically like a Seam, but dark and ominous.

Eyre pulled back as Mudamir dragged her towards the billowing edges of the rift in the air. She tried to summon enough Viq to fight back, but she was still exhausted after the episode in the Refectory. All she could do was slow Mudamir down as he dragged her inexorably towards the smoking Seam.

Desperately she sent a telepathic message screaming through the atmosphere. If anyone would pick it up, Abby would. "HELP!" she cried in the Wisdom's Code. "Gothak here!" If by some chance her friends received the message, they would be prepared when they came through the door of the Infirmary.

With a huge effort, Eyre focused her mind and mustered enough Viq to prevent Mudamir from pulling her closer to the gaping Seam. He bared his teeth in frustration when he realised that he was unable to drag her any further. He lurched forward and grabbed Eyre in a crushing embrace, lifting her off the floor. His foul breath was fetid on her face as he carried her towards the black opening.

"Keep still or I will knock you out," he snarled under his breath.

But Eyre just struggled harder and he tightened his grip so that she was unable to breathe.

With an almighty crash, the door burst open, and Eyre, barely conscious, looked over Mudamir's shoulder.

Colton came sprinting through the door, his ruby-topped staff aimed at Mudamir, who dropped Eyre to the ground. Her head hit the floor hard and she lay gasping for air as Colton faced the fearsome Gothak.

"And who are you?" Mudamir asked in an arch tone. "I feel I've met most of Lightward's posse, but you're a new one."

He seemed totally unconcerned that he'd been discovered, and a terrible fear blossomed in Eyre's chest. Mudamir was one of the most powerful Gothak, and he was toying with Colton.

"Run!" she urged in a faint voice. "Get out of here Colton!"

But Colton appeared not to hear her as he faced the loathsome being. His eyes did not leave Mudamir as he moved around to stand between the massive Gothak and Eyre.

"Leave," said Colton in a low and steady voice. "You have about three seconds."

Mudamir sneered. "Oh, I—" But whatever he was about to say was interrupted by a beam of vivid crimson light from the ruby on Colton's staff. The ray was brighter than Eyre had ever seen from a student's staff, and it blasted the smoking Seam into nothingness. All humour left Mudamir's face, replaced by an expression of complete shock.

"I'd hate you to leave before the party was over," Colton said softly, and sent another beam blazing towards Mudamir. The monstrous being ducked awkwardly and the blinding light blasted straight through the wall of the Infirmary. As Eyre looked through the hole, flames scorching the edges, she could see the pounding feet of Mimir outside, charging towards the Infirmary entrance. She could hear more frantic footsteps approaching from down the hall, and a look of fury crossed Mudamir's face. A foul expletive erupted from his grotesque mouth as he snapped out some hand gestures, and within seconds, a new Seam appeared. With a furious final glance at Eyre, he dived into it and was gone. But the look he gave her as he left signalled that this business was definitely not over.

Eyre rested her forehead on the ground as the horrible restraints disappeared from around her. Her head felt like it was about to explode and tears of pain ran down her bloody cheek.

Colton dropped to the ground beside her and gently helped her sit. His ice-blue eyes looked deep into hers and he brushed her hair back from her temple.

"You're okay, Eyre. Help is here."

Eyre looked into his eyes, and despite herself, something fluttered in her stomach. His strong arms, his power and his gentleness made the tears come stronger. Colton's large hands softly wiped her tears away and he stroked her forehead as if soothing a wild horse.

Whittaker Ray and Sergeant Tottingham appeared in flashes of light, just as Beatrice, Abby and Nick raced in the door, staffs in hand. Behind them were Jax and Warrigal, and then it seemed a whole battalion of fierce Mimir, with Jengles at the front, was crowding at the door. Everyone looked at Colton holding Eyre on the floor.

"I was with Sister Murphy," Colton said, indicating a bandage wrapped around his arm. A training mishap, no doubt. "I heard the commotion." He picked Eyre up carefully and placed her on the bed, still looking down at her. "I'm glad you're okay, Eyre."

Then he stepped away and began to talk to Whittaker Ray.

Jax pushed through, a strange look on his face. Eyre was so tired she could hardly keep her eyes open, but she registered the mixture of relief and anger in his expression. Jax took her hand and held it softly. He ran a gentle finger down the ridge of holes in Eyre's cheek, left by Mudamir's misshapen fingernails.

"My poor girl," he whispered. "You don't get a break, do you?"

Just then, Sister Murphy shoved her way through the horde that filled her Infirmary: Mimir with various weapons and ferocious expressions,

Lightworkers with staffs, and a cacophony of concerned voices echoing down the halls. The fire had gone out from the hole that Colton had blasted in the wall, but smoke and soot still blackened the room. But the Sister's eyes took in the scene without much surprise. No doubt she had seen far worse than this in her time, Eyre thought wearily.

"It's time to leave. Thank you everyone, but I'll take it from here," Sister Murphy said crisply.

Beatrice, Abby and Nick sent their staffs back with a flash of Viq and waved briefly at Eyre before they left with Warrigal.

"See you, Eyre," Beatrice said telepathically in code. "We'll talk later."

The Mimir left too, apart from two massive soldiers who remained behind at Jengles' instruction. They stood by the window with impassive expressions, Crescent Blades in their hands.

Sergeant Tottingham looked at Eyre with a concerned twist of her mouth, but she too disappeared in a flash of light, without saying anything. And after a moment, Whittaker Ray and Colton vanished too.

Jax looked at the Mimir standing silently by the window and then gathered Eyre in an embrace. "I was too slow," he said in a hoarse voice. "Abby called me, but I was in Terra and couldn't get here fast enough."

The pent-up fear and exhaustion suddenly overwhelmed Eyre and she began to weep violently. "I'm so sick of all this," she cried into Jax's shoulder. "When will it ever end?"

Jax held her tightly, then lay her back gently on the bed. He kissed her softly.

"You need to rest," he said. "It does seem like too much already, but you'll feel better when you get your energy back." He tilted his head as if listening, and then smiled before clicking his fingers. Something squirming appeared in his arms.

"The Ranger asked me to give you this. He thinks it will help."

And then he placed Lenny in Eyre's arms. The struggling bundle of fluff settled straight down and snuggled into Eyre's shoulder. Then the little creature heaved a happy sigh and fell fast asleep.

Another tear rolled down Eyre's cheek and then her eyes closed too.

She could sense Jax staring down at her, and a moment later she heard his footsteps receding down the hall.

CHAPTER EIGHT

EYRE STAYED AT THE Infirmary for another day so that she could rest after her ordeal with Mudamir. At some point Lenny had disappeared, but her Mimir sentries stayed in her room the whole time, and she was able to relax and sleep. Her head had finally stopped aching, but she was weary to her very bones. She vaguely remembered Sister Murphy rubbing her back and feeling her forehead, but mostly she was completely out of it. Every time she woke she would roll over and go back to sleep again. Finally, late the next afternoon, her eyes opened and she realised that her energy was back. She sat up and swung her legs over the side of the bed as the Mimir jumped to attention. For a moment Eyre's head swirled after lying down for so long, but she took a few deep breaths and the feeling quickly subsided.

It was as if Sister Murphy somehow knew Eyre was awake, because a minute later she hurried in the door.

"I see you're feeling better," she said, and circled Eyre's upper arm with both her hands. After a moment she nodded as if satisfied.

"Well, your blood pressure is normal and your colour is much better, so I think I can discharge you." The Sister looked at the Mimir.

"Corporal Adoquin and Private Kerf will take you to Whittaker Ray. He asked to see you as soon as you were well enough."

The two Mimir stood to attention as Eyre jumped off the bed. Then Corporal Adoquin led the way with Private Kerf bringing up the rear as they headed to the Central Administration building. Several students stopped to watch as she walked by, whispering excitedly to each other. No doubt gossiping about the Refectory incident, Eyre thought with a mental sigh. The crazy student who turned into a human fireball.

She did hear one student though. Tec Langford hooted from the pathway.

"Been detained, Lightward? Off to your padded cell?"

Some people never learn, Eyre thought as she sent him cartwheeling into the fishpond with a flick of her wrist. She felt a smug satisfaction as she saw Tec spluttering for breath as onlookers laughed uproariously, although Eyre's escorts were as deadpan as if they hadn't noticed a thing. Well, at least my Viq is back, Eyre thought as she gritted her teeth.

They reached the Central Administration building and Corporal Adoquin indicated that Eyre should enter alone. As she walked through the huge bronze doors, the two muscular Mimir moved to stand guard on either side of the doorway.

Madame Overmantle was hurrying through the foyer, awkwardly carrying a large turquoise-coloured crystal. Bits of hair had come loose from her bun, but she looked extremely pleased with herself.

"Blue zircon," she explained to Eyre, who had stopped to greet her. "It's for my crystal garden. If I fertilize it with lava from Incendium it will grow into the most incredible formation! Sometimes they get as large as a bus."

She looked closely at Eyre. "Oh, I'm sorry my dear. Of course, you don't want to hear about that right now. Go right up." She indicated the elevators. "He'll be waiting for you."

Madame Overmantle bustled away with her heavy load, humming a tune as she headed towards her office.

Whittaker Ray looked up as Eyre entered his office and indicated that she should take a seat. Eyre sat down with a little trepidation. The Dean of Curriculum did not summon students to his office lightly.

"How are you feeling?" he began and Eyre shrugged. It was a hard question to answer. Physically she was fine now, but she felt deeply tired both mentally and emotionally. The year had barely begun and already Ben Perrill was causing his usual uproar. His continued presence on campus both incensed and confused her—why was he still here? In her opinion he should have been banished years ago.

And she had a deep unease that Mudamir was able to venture onto the campus in such a bold and brazen manner. The Academy was supposed to have strong wards in place to prevent the Gothak from accessing the grounds. But no one had been aware that the powerful being had somehow made his way to the very interior of the school. Her stomach roiled when she remembered the malevolent creature dragging her towards that ominous, smoking fissure of black light.

But she raised resolute sapphire eyes to Whittaker Ray, and they flashed with their usual fire as she spoke. "Always ready to fight the Dark Forces, sir." Then she couldn't help herself, and added. "Including Ben Perrill."

Whittaker Ray gave a rueful smile and nodded. "Yes, I understand." But he didn't elaborate about what he understood, and Eyre yet again felt a violent irritation surge through her. But she tamped it down as he continued.

"It has been decided that for your own safety you will be staying and studying with the Mimir until your trip to Incendium," he said. "The Gothak are clearly aware that you alone can see the Isars, and we can no doubt thank our esteemed friend Ms Periwinkle for passing on that information." He shook his head. "So, to prevent a repeat of what happened yesterday, your studies will be conducted by Sergeant Tottingham within the Mimir's Domain."

Eyre raised her eyebrows. Of all the reasons she'd been called in to see Whittaker Ray, being put into protective custody had never crossed her mind. She honestly thought she was going to be reprimanded for her violence in the Refectory. She leaned back in her chair.

"Are you not able to protect the campus from the Gothak anymore?" she asked, and her anxiety rose. Were her friends safe?

"The Gothak will have no reason to breach if you are not here," he said. "So, by removing you, we will not only be protecting you, but everyone else as well. Because, no, we are not certain we can effectively defend the campus when we no longer know who our friends and who our enemies are. Sadly, Jemima Periwinkle may not be the only Lightworker working for the Dark Forces."

A look of such sadness crossed Whittaker Ray's face that Eyre felt like giving him a hug. He must be under such pressure from all directions, she realised.

"Well, I'll do what's necessary," Eyre said, although she felt very sorry that she wouldn't be part of the student body this year.

"Beatrice, Abby and Nick will be going with you," Whittaker Ray said, as if reading her thoughts, and Eyre's heart lifted. "Your friends have proven valiant Lightworkers and will be worthy study companions for you. You will have a lot to cover before your trip to Incendium. The first thing you must learn is teleportation, so you will never be so vulnerable again. It will be hard work, but I'm sure you'll be up to it."

Eyre sat in silence, processing this news.

"What about Ischyros?" she asked. "Will someone look after him?"

Whittaker Ray nodded. "Lisa will take good care of him, and you'll be permitted to come up under escort and visit him occasionally. He'll be fine. The Mimir will take you to the stables now to say goodbye."

"So, when do I leave, sir?"

"Immediately," Whittaker Ray answered. "Corporal Adoquin and Private Kerf will escort you back to the dormitory to collect your belongings. Your friends are waiting for you and you will all go straight to the Mimir's Domain from there. It's imperative to get you safely away—too much is at risk."

Then to Eyre's surprise, he stood and came around the desk to shake her hand.

"You have been very brave, Eyre Lightward, and the difficult journey is not over yet," the old man said, his normally bright-blue eyes clouded. "But in a way, we have more hope than we have had for decades. For so long there was not even the vague possibility of reinstating the Aura, and now, thanks to you, the world may have a chance at it. It is almost a miracle to those of us who have been fighting the Dark Forces for so long.

"So, go well, valiant girl, and the blessings of many go with you."

Eyre nodded, unable to reply, and quickly left the office.

CHAPTER NINE

BEATRICE AND ABBY WERE packed and waiting for Eyre when she arrived back at the dorm after saying goodbye to Ischyros at the stables. The old horse had complained about his quarters as being *less* than suitable for a Lightness Cup contender, but he did wish her well. Eyre tried to keep her face impassive as the tatty old Lighthorse looked at her with his one blind eye, and all his hair burnt away, and told her quite seriously that she should call him if she needed him. She'd hugged him fiercely and promised to do that, then watched with an aching heart as he staggered over to get the piece of liquorice she'd tossed into his feed bucket. He struggled even to walk now, and she doubted he would be able to come if she did summon him, let alone be of any help. At least he was safe though, and she knew she didn't have to worry about him.

"Nick's on his way over," Abby said, interrupting her thoughts. "You'd better get packing."

There was an awkward silence as they looked at Corporal Adoquin and Private Kerf guarding the door, and then all three of them started talking at once, sending them into fits of giggles.

"Blimey, Eyre," Beatrice finally said. "There's never been a dull moment since you arrived! Studying with the Mimir? Let's hope Jengles isn't our lecturer. He'd spend the whole time calling me an ignorant beanpole!"

"Well I'm glad we're all going to be together," Abby said, smiling. "*All for one, and one for all*, and all that!"

"Earth, Air, Water and Fire," Nick said from the doorway, and the Mimir let him through. Eyre knew what Nick meant. It seemed such a long time ago that they had started at the Academy and were nervously preparing for the TEP trials. Beatrice had been in the Earth cabin, Nick was Air, Eyre was Water and Abby was Fire. Although the cabins had merely been assigned by surname, in a way Nick was right. The four of them made a formidable team, each with their own unique talents that complemented each other and made them stronger as a whole.

Eyre finished stuffing things into her bag and unlocked her arms cupboard by placing her palm on the door. Then she took out her staff and Antaraks and picked up her bag. Last of all she slung her guitar over her shoulder.

"Ready!" she said as the others laughed. Then they laughed even harder when Beatrice picked up her large potted plant.

"Me too!" she said as the huge peace lily bobbed up and down. Without any expression at all, Corporal Adoquin took the plant from her and tucked it under his arm.

"Come," he said, and they all filed out after him, trying not to giggle. Private Kerf shut the door and brought up the rear as they headed to the Mimir's Domain.

When they reached the Receiving Stone, Eyre saw that the bronze doors to the Depot were already flung open, lying flat on the ground near the polished square of moldavite. Rows of Mimir stretched back, guarding the entrance, and Eyre could see the curved brass staircase descending into the stone depths. She shivered. She much preferred being above the earth than within it, but she had complete faith in the fierce red-haired creatures who guarded their precious Domain. She nodded a greeting to the troops who stood at attention in a perfectly straight row, then followed Corporal Adoquin down the stairs. Ever since she'd read about St Ria in the History of Light textbook, and then seen the statue of St Ria in the depths of the Mimir's Domain, she'd understood why the Mimir revered her so much— they evidently saw Eyre as some kind of embodiment of St Ria. She only hoped she could live up to their expectations.

The late afternoon sunlight dimmed quickly as they descended, but their way was lit by the familiar blue lights that were set deep into the stone walls. The hot summer air was replaced by a coolness that seemed to emanate from the walls themselves, and the sweat on Eyre's brow dried within minutes. From far above, Eyre heard the bronze doors close with a heavy clang.

Down, down they went, spiralling dizzyingly down the brass steps, until they emerged in a room that Eyre remembered. The Arms Workshop, with its neat rows of unfinished weapons and hot air from the fiery pit where the iron was heated. Large anvils were placed around the room and Mimir workers hammered at weapons in various stages of completion. Captain Spinel marched around giving orders, but he stopped when he saw the group walk in.

"Welcome." the battle-scarred old Mimir said. "Eyre, it's good to see you again. I will be seeing a fair bit of you all in the next few months, as I believe I will be instructing you in the use of your Mnae." His eyes glinted. "I'm looking forward to it."

The way he said it gave Eyre pause, and she wondered if they were going to enjoy it as much as Captain Spinel. From the look on her friends' faces, she saw that they had also picked up the nuance in the Captain's voice, and she smothered a smile. It seemed they were in for an intense education over the next few months.

A loud clang sounded from one of the anvils as a young Mimir dropped the weapon he was working on. A river of molten iron cascaded over the floor and Captain Spinel took a deep breath and strode over to sort out the problem. As the hammering of iron started up again, Eyre and her friends followed Corporal Adoquin through the busy Arms Workshop, and then to another staircase leading downwards.

"Are we bunking in with the Gothak, then?" Beatrice asked in an attempt at joviality, but it fell on deaf ears. Their guide just led them farther downwards into the gloom as the air became more and more frigid.

Finally they emerged into a larger space, or juncture, that had five tunnels arranged like spokes leading away from it, with different coloured lights running in a horizontal row down the middle of each tunnel. Eyre and her friends were familiar with the arrangement of junctures and passages after they had come down to receive their Arms Endowment last year, so they waited for the Corporal to lead them to the right one. As it turned out, he chose the tunnel lined with green lights, and they made their way down the dim corridor, following the lights until they finally reached a large wooden door. The Corporal took them into a room hewn from the stone, with four beds and a sliding door set into the wall. Green lights ringed the walls at waist height, illuminating the room with an eerie glow.

"This is where you will sleep for the next few months. I will be back in half an hour to take you for dinner," Corporal Adoquin said. "You will learn the way quickly enough, but for the next week I'll help you. Please do not leave the room without me or one of my comrades."

Don't worry, Eyre thought. After their experience of being lost in the moving tunnels of the Mimir's Domain last year there was little chance she'd go wandering around alone down here.

After Corporal Adoquin left, they each flung their gear on to a bed, as there were no cupboards to unpack into. The sliding door revealed a small bathroom, but that was the extent of the furnishings.

"Not exactly a five-star guest room," Abby said sadly, and they all laughed. After their experiences over the past few years, comfort was hardly high on their list of priorities.

Beatrice put her peace lily on the ground by her bed, moving it around until she was satisfied with its position in the bare room. Abby chuckled at her styling efforts. "Décor by Edmunsun. That definitely improves the place."

Beatrice lifted an eyebrow, but grinned as she flung herself on the bed. "Just like home now."

She put her arms behind her head and looked at the ceiling. "Let's practise our code," she suggested, and they all agreed that was a good idea. So they lay on their beds and sent telepathic words to each other.

"Cake!" Beatrice yelled, determined to be first, after Eyre sent a message out to them all.

Eyre laughed loudly and threw her pillow at Beatrice. "*Cave*, you dope! You are always much too focused on food, my friend!"

Abby giggled and sent a word out. All three of them got it at the same time and they rolled on their beds with laughter.

"What does cucumber have to do with anything?" Nick chortled.

"Exactly!" Abby said, "I can't make it too easy for you!"

From there the words got more and more ridiculous, so by the time Private Kerf came back to take them to dinner, all four of them had tears of mirth running down their faces.

"Are you sad?" Private Kerf asked in consternation, which caused them to start laughing again. A confused expression crossed the Mimir's face and he shook his head, obviously deciding they were a very strange lot indeed.

He pulled some small shining objects from a bag he carried and handed one to each of them. Eyre saw that it was a round-cut crystal that had a moving dial around the edge and a brass bracket attached to the back.

"You loop the crystal on to your belt with the brass keeper," he said. "And then you turn the dial to where you need to go. It will light the tunnels to guide you to your destination."

Eyre studied the gadget and saw that there were a number of symbols around the edge of the dial, and presumably each one meant something. She threaded the sparkling crystal on to her belt and made sure it was secure. The last thing she needed to do was lose it! She vaguely remembered Jax talking about this system of navigation when they were here last year.

"So which symbol is the Refectory then?" Beatrice asked with great interest, and Abby snorted and punched her softly on the arm.

"Typical!" she laughed.

"Well, you don't need your dial for the dining hall," Private Kerf answered, "because it is always in the same place. You will need it for everywhere else though. We will learn how to use the crystal locator tomorrow, as it's getting a bit late tonight. But to get to the dining hall, you just push here—" Private Kerf pushed against the wall and a hidden circular aperture opened in the rock. A dark tunnel led away from them and Eyre felt uneasy as she gazed into it. She wasn't too keen on dark tunnels beneath the ground. And this one looked like a rather large funnel-web spider's hole.

But Beatrice was very eager to get going, and even the dour Private smiled reluctantly at her enthusiasm. He put one leg in the hole as he explained, "It's called a Chute—just follow me down." Then his other leg went in and he launched himself into the darkness.

Nick's eyebrows rose. "Er, ladies first..." he joked, extending a gentlemanly hand towards the uninviting blackness in the wall.

But Beatrice was undeterred. "Oh, such cowardice! Of course I'll go first!" And within a second, she had disappeared into the dark hole. Abby slowly moved forward, and then stopped when she heard Beatrice's squeals of fright drifting up from far below them.

"Um—" Abby said, looking rather dubious.

"I'll go," Nick said, clambering into the hole. "Wish me luck!"

He pushed off and whizzed into the blackness without a sound.

"Well, I'm not going last!" Abby exclaimed. "I'd better go before I change my mind!" And she disappeared behind Nick with a look of terror on her face.

Eyre wasn't sure what to expect, but she sure as anything didn't want to stay behind in the gloomy green-lit room, so she perched on the rim of the hole and then launched herself into the blackness.

CHAPTER TEN

DESPITE HERSELF, EYRE COULDN'T help screaming out loud, although she wasn't sure if it was because of fear or exhilaration. It was pitch black as she careered downwards, spiralling at increasing speed through the highly-polished rock tunnel. Just when she thought she would pass out from lack of oxygen, she hurtled horizontally out the end of the tunnel into a brightly-lit room.

With a loud *oof!* she landed on a cart covered in an extremely soft, billowy fabric, and the momentum caused the cart to roll all the way across the room until it rested against the wall. The cart tipped up and dumped Eyre onto a bench seat in front of a table, and then it rolled back over to sit below the exit of the tunnel again. A loud "huzzah!" echoed around the hall, accompanied by the thumping of metal on tables.

Eyre shook her head and looked around. Beatrice, Abby and Nick sat at the table across from her, grinning from ear to ear. The rest of the hall was filled with wooden tables and chairs, and at each table sat a dozen or so red-haired, red-bearded Mimir. Eyre looked back at the tunnel as she heard a loud whistling sound, and watched as a rotund Mimir shot out of the hole and landed on the cart. His weight caused the cart to rocket across the room before dumping him into a chair at one of the tables.

"*Huzzah!*" cried the Mimir, and they slammed their copper tankards on the tabletop. Someone slid a copper tankard brimming with purple cider down the table to the most recent arrival, which he downed in one thirsty swallow.

"Not like you to be late for tucker, Gabbro," Private Ammonite teased the portly fellow. Eyre grinned as she recognised Private Ammonite; he was the good-humoured Mimir she had met in the Kit Room last year, and he'd also helped out at the New Year's Eve party. He winked at her as he slapped his friend on the back.

"Gabbro seems a bit like someone we know," Abby said slyly, giving Beatrice a nudge.

"Well, I want to know where to get one of those tankards!" Nick said, not really serious.

But as if someone had heard, four copper steins materialised down the end of the table and scudded along to them. Silence reigned as the four friends looked in bemusement at the frothy purple beverage. Then they grinned and shrugged at each other, picked up the mugs and downed the ciders as quickly as they could.

"*HUZZAH!*" cried the Mimir and lifted their tankards to the four.

Eyre's eyes were watering—she'd chugged the cold drink down so fast that bubbles had gone up her nose and she had a brain freeze. The purple drink was brewed by the Mimir somewhere in their underground Domain, and it was delicious, but made her feel rather light-headed. One was probably enough for her, she decided, as she watched some of the Mimir pouring themselves more cider from tall pewter jugs. She felt slightly bemused as she watched the powerful warriors laugh and joke amongst themselves as they ate plates of steaming food. This was a side she'd never seen of them; they were normally so reticent and stern. And silent. Or face down on the floor before her. Another cheer rose from the side of the room and Eyre raised an eyebrow at her friends, who just shrugged and shook their heads.

A Jotnar bustled in with a huge tray containing four plates of delicious roast beef, roast potatoes, vegetables and all the trimmings. Eyre's stomach rumbled—it had been a long day and she was starving. The Jotnar placed the plates in front of them and then—Eyre nearly fell off her chair—*smiled* at them, displaying sharp pointed teeth like a shark. Beatrice's mouth fell open, but Abby recovered first and smiled back at him.

"Thank you so much," she said, and held the Jotnar's hand. The Jotnar looked shocked, but bowed before scurrying away.

"Well, all I can say is huzzah!" Beatrice said as she shoved food into her mouth.

"Ditto from me," Eyre agreed, and ate until she could fit no more in.

The Mimir kept their distance during dinner, but Eyre was happy with that. So much had happened that day and she needed time to process it all. Nick, in particular, seemed to be loving it! And as Eyre thought about the scars that covered his body, she decided that perhaps it was a perfect environment for him—he had proven himself a warrior already.

When they had all finished, Private Kerf appeared beside their table.

"I'm to take you back to your room," he said, needing to almost shout in order to be heard above the din of the dining room. "We start early tomorrow."

Eyre for one was quite happy to leave, as she was beginning to feel extremely tired. The drama of the past few days had taken its toll, and she still wasn't completely recovered. The others stood up too and they all followed Private Kerf through the crowded hubbub and out a door on the other side of the room.

They walked into a large, roughly-circular space, carved out of the rock with irregular blows of a very sharp implement. The room didn't seem to go anywhere, and the four of them turned to look at Private Kerf.

"You put your foot on one of these," he said, and lifted one polished boot and placed it down carefully. 'One of these' turned out to be circular metal plates, which were inserted into the rock all over the floor. As Private Kerf touched the plate with his shoe, a beam of light suddenly shot upwards, lifting him from the floor into the darkness above. As Eyre looked up in surprise, she realised that the room had no discernible roof, it was just a vast, echoing space that disappeared into impenetrable darkness.

The beams had short vertical prongs branching off them, and they moved slowly up into the gloom. Private Kerf seemed to enjoy their amazement, all the more so when he leapt on to one of the prongs with one foot, and held on to the beam with his hand.

"It's an Uplight," he explained, as he drifted gradually upwards. After a moment he jumped off and came over to show them. "You can all join me on mine, but when there are lots of people there can be ten Uplights going at once. Hang on with your hand and swing on to a prong. If your feet slip, let go and try again. When you're on properly, twist the beam and it will move faster. To go slower, twist it the other way. Have a practise, but jump off before you go too high. I'll have to lead the way."

They all stepped onto a plate and were lifted gently into the air in a shaft of light. It took them a couple of goes until they had figured out how to work the Uplight properly. When they were ready, Private Kerf jumped on first and Abby got on below him. Beatrice followed, then Eyre and finally Nick, and they began to stream slowly upwards into the dark.

"Is everyone on properly?" Private Kerf called. When they all answered in the affirmative, he added, "Well, hang on tight! We're about to speed up!"

And then the beam started to zip very quickly upwards. The rockface, with various doors and windows cut into it, whizzed past them in a blur. Some of the windows appeared to have strange, rather ominous-looking bars covering dark apertures in the rock. Eventually the Uplight slowed as they approached a circular rock door studded with glowing blue lights.

"This is your room," Private Kerf said, and the door opened inwards. A bright path of light appeared from the doorway and grew slowly outwards to the Uplight.

"Step off on to the path as you get near it," the Private said, and he watched carefully as Abby took a tentative step from the Uplight onto the path.

"You'll get used to it," the Private said. "Just don't look down in the beginning. Walk straight into your room."

Eyre needed no instruction about that; there was no way she was going to look down into the gaping darkness below her. She followed Beatrice and marched into the room as fast as she could. Once Nick had joined the three girls in the room, Private Kerf saluted.

"See you in the morning," he said, and he left on the Uplight, which whizzed upwards at tremendous speed. Then with a zap it snuffed out.

They all looked at each other. "I think we were only in first gear," Nick said, looking out into the blackness.

"Well, shut the door or you'll find sixth gear as you head back down!" Abby said crossly, pulling him backwards.

Beatrice was already lying on her bed. She yawned.

"Well, I don't know what time we're getting up, but I'm ready to call it a night."

Everyone agreed with her, and a short time later they were all sound asleep.

CHAPTER ELEVEN

EYRE WOKE TO A horrendous sound that made her simultaneously leap out of bed, summon her staff and use language that would have made her mother weep. The blaring cacophony was surely a combination of an ear-shattering gong mixed with an air-raid siren, and it went on and on without a pause.

Nick was lying face down on the floor with a pillow over his head, Abby had wisely scrambled under her bed, and Beatrice had levitated up to the ceiling.

"By the Light, what *is* that sound?" Beatrice said crossly as she lowered herself to the ground.

Nick lifted the pillow from his head. "Eyre, use your staff to blow the perpetrator of that abysmal racket to Caelus, would you?"

Eyre leaned her staff against the wall as Abby came out from under the bed.

"My hearing will be permanently ruined," she said plaintively. "Will it never end?"

Just then the noise stopped.

"Praise be to St Illuminado!" Beatrice said. "I was about to send *myself* to Caelus!"

The door to their room opened and Sergeant Tottingham walked in.

"Ah," she said brightly. "I see you're up!"

The four of them looked at each other and Nick threw his pillow back on the bed.

"What *was* that noise?" Eyre asked with a tinge of irritation. "The alarm clock?"

"Luckily for you, no," replied the Sergeant. "Twice a year there is a breach drill, and you've been fortunate to experience the first one this year. If the Gothak make an incursion anywhere in the vicinity of the Mimir's

Domain or the Academy, that is the sound you will hear, so you'll know to be ready."

"I'll try not to sleep through it," Beatrice said drily.

The Sergeant put her hands on her hips. "Well, snap to it. Breakfast first, and then catch the Uplight to the red door. Set the dial on your crystal to the Arms Room—that's the symbol that looks like a sword—and follow the lights in the tunnel once you go through the red door. I'll be waiting in the Arms Room."

She left them in the bedroom and Beatrice rubbed her eyes. "I do so love a peaceful start to the morning," she said.

After breakfast they caught the Uplight and, as instructed, exited when they got to the red door. They had all set the dials on their crystals at the breakfast table, and once they walked over the shining path into the doorway, the crystal on their belt turned red. Along the walls at waist height, small lights suddenly illuminated red as well, stretching around the corners and off into someplace unseen. The four friends walked together carefully along the uneven path until Beatrice gave an oath and summoned her lux. It was faster going after that, as they could see ahead about ten metres, and could more easily avoid the rubble and rough patches in the track.

They had just reached a juncture, and were about to cross into the tunnel lit by the little red lights, when there was a rumbling beneath their feet and the ground began to move.

"Wait a minute!" Eyre said, and they tried to balance as the hub moved slowly around. It was like trying to stand on the deck of a yacht in a stiff breeze, with the ground beneath them moving up and down erratically until it finally stopped. The tunnel with the red lights was now behind them, so they turned and headed into it, still following the guiding lights.

Finally, they reached another open area, but this one had a tall wooden door shaped like an arch set into one of the rock walls. There was a heavy bronze knocker on the door and after a moment Nick stepped up and rapped loudly with the circular handle.

The door opened slowly and the four stepped through cautiously. One never knew what might lurk behind an unknown door.

But as they stepped into the dim interior, burning flames suddenly blazed in the sconces mounted high on the walls. A symphony of horns blew and the rhythmic stomping of hundreds of feet began.

Eyre looked around the huge interior in complete befuddlement. What was going on?

As she and her friends got further inside, they saw perfect rows of Mimir standing to attention as heralds blew their horns. Sergeant Tottingham and Whittaker Ray stood at the front of the troops on an elevated platform, with Jengles and President Zircon, the president of the Mimir, by their side. There were three other people on the podium, and Eyre felt her mouth drop as she recognised one of them; *Balthazar!* The President of the Determinant Dozen was here? By his side was Rigmar's father, Andrew Essendon, the Chairman of the Echelon. And then to her absolute delight, she saw the Ranger on the podium too. *What* was going on?

Eyre's friends were equally nonplussed, and they all stopped walking, unsure of what to do. The trumpeting of the horns stopped, and President Balthazar spoke. The acoustics of the room were such that his voice seemed to boom from wall to wall.

"Welcome, brave friends," he said. "Please come to the front and join us on the stage."

As they walked up to the stage, the Mimir all clapped, until the sound ricocheted off the walls around the room. The four friends climbed the steps to the podium and the applause stopped.

"We are here to celebrate your courage," President Balthazar said. "Not only most recently in Caelus, but also in Aqua and Terra, where you have performed as a Lightworker should, at great cost to yourselves. Normally you would receive your Mnae with the rest of your fourth-year cohort at the Bestowment ceremony after your proficiency trials, and with your families in attendance. However, this year has been a very strange one already, and we have chosen to present your Mnae to you today. You have proven yourselves worthy of your Mnae, and we are pleased to be part of this moment with you. Please come forward and receive this very well-deserved addition to your Arms Endowment. Beatrice Edmunsun."

Beatrice walked forward and shook President Balthazar's hand. He passed her a spectacular Mnae, polished to a perfect sheen, with runes carved along the length of the blade. The Mnae had a shining emerald in the pommel, which matched the one in her staff, and Beatrice took the beautiful weapon with a shy smile. Then she shook Chairman Essendon's hand too, and President Zircon's, the Ranger's, Whittaker Ray's and Sergeant Tottingham's. She stood at the side of the podium, looking quite overwhelmed as Abby and Nick went up to get their Mnaes, to deafening applause. Finally, Eyre stepped forward and President Balthazar waited for the clapping to subside.

"I think we all know the burden that we have put upon this young girl," he said. "She carries the hopes of the Overworld on her shoulders, and it is our duty to support her in the months ahead. Please congratulate Eyre on earning her Mnae."

Once again, applause rang through the air as Eyre shook the dignitaries' hands. She felt incredibly proud to be part of this small group of students, her friends who would die for her, and she for them. What an unexpected and wonderful way to celebrate reaching this milestone! She smiled gratefully at Whittaker Ray. Somehow, she knew he had organised this event; he had known that she and her friends needed something special to happen in their lives after all the fear and disaster of the previous year.

"To the four!" President Balthazar shouted, and the Mimir roared ferociously and stomped their feet as the horns blew loudly.

"Goodbye, and good luck," he said as the noise abated, and then with flashes of light, the VIPs disappeared, except for Sergeant Tottingham, President Zircon and Jengles. The Mimir quickly departed with Jengles, as he peppered out a series of orders. President Zircon bowed and left via a green-lit tunnel and then the room was deserted, except for Sergeant Tottingham and the four friends.

"Don't expect that every morning," the Sergeant said sternly, but her broad smile gave her away.

"Come on then," she added. "Let's teach you how to use those things."

CHAPTER TWELVE

CAPTAIN SPINEL RAISED HIS blade again. "That was pretty good," he said patiently to Abby, "but you need to balance better on your front and back legs. Use that back leg for stability and strength.

"Using a palum is quite different to using the real thing—the weight of the Mnae for a start. Remember to maintain the proper distance from your opponent so that you can employ the optimum force when you strike. The momentum of your body should carry through in the same direction as your thrust." He demonstrated the movement slowly at first, and then faster. The gruff Mimir was light on his feet and made it look easy, but he seemed to register the tiredness in his class of four. Eyre sighed. Their first lesson seemed to cover an awful lot of information in a short time. But Captain Spinel was patient, and not critical at all, as Eyre had feared. He obviously understood it was not easy, Eyre thought, as she traced the faceted pink diamond that decorated the pommel of her blade. A weapon of great beauty and power. Captain Spinel adjusted Beatrice's hand on the grip on her Mnae.

"It's practise, practise, practise to get this right," he said encouragingly as he moved around them, studying their form. "You won't get it in the first day, or the first week even. But you will have ample opportunity to train until you do; you will have lessons in the Clasis for Single-Bladed Weapon every morning, so you can practise. This will be followed by Clasis for Multiple Weapons. I will be taking you for 'Single', and Sergeant Tottingham will be instructing you in 'Multiple'."

Eyre clasped the grip of her Mnae tightly and faced Nick again. She was finding it difficult—no surprises there. She'd never picked things up particularly quickly, unlike Nick, who seemed to have an instant understanding of what was required. Nick was a surfer, so his balance and reflexes were perfectly suited to this. But it was only their first lesson, and she was determined to master her magnificent weapon.

She raised the heavy blade and moved through the movements, first with one hand, then with two, as the Captain had shown them in the session. Her arms were aching from the weight of the blade, but she was determined to focus and prove herself worthy, especially after the moving ceremony when they'd been presented with their Mnaes that morning. Her friends seemed equally resolved, and there was no grumbling or complaint from any of them as they ran through the Clasis over and over again.

There was a flash at the back of the Training room and Sergeant Tottingham appeared out of the light, her own Mnae in one hand, her staff in the other, Kulbeda in her belt and Antaraks in the baldrics at her back.

"How are they going?" she asked Captain Spinel, and he leaned on his Mnae.

"They have done well this morning," he replied. "The first lesson is not easy."

"Well, I guess it's now my turn to put you through your paces," the Sergeant said as she faced the weary students. "We don't have time for you to learn at the normal rate, so you will be extremely tired over the next few months as you learn the new Clasis at an accelerated pace. But we must have you ready in time to travel to Incendium. So take a ten-minute break and then I will introduce you to Clasis for Multiple Weapons."

"Inguz," Captain Spinel said, and bowed, giving them the strange hand gesture with fingers interlocking and thumbs up that meant 'respect' in the Mimir's world. Then he headed towards one of the many doors in the walls of the Training Room and disappeared into the gloom.

When they began again, the Sergeant asked them to summon their full arms endowment, which they lay on the ground in front of them.

"So," the Sergeant said. "Clasis for Multiple Weapons is the most advanced Clasis, and consists of various Levels, from Beginner up to Level 20, which only Master Fighters will ever reach. It takes decades for a warrior to reach Level 20, and only then if they have a supreme gift for it. By the time you leave for Incendium we hope for you to reach Level 5, which means that you will be proficient in summoning your various weapons in an adversarial situation and have the ability to use each one to their best advantage. Being able to respond immediately and appropriately in a critical situation will save your life.

"However, it is a difficult Clasis to learn, because there are so many facets to it. Which weapon to use and when to use it? For how long? How can you conserve your Viq so that you can use multiple weapons? And how do you read the combative situation to make the right decisions about all these factors?

"Incendium is the most perilous of the Alterworlds, and not just because the Gothak will be looking for you most intensely this time. It has some of the most extreme geographical features, as well as native wildlife that is tremendously savage."

"The Armatura, for example," Beatrice said drily, and her friends burst out laughing. However, at the look on the Sergeant's face, they spluttered into silence.

"You might be well advised about laughter, since we're on that subject," the Sergeant instructed. "Don't do it."

Eyre raised her eyebrows and drowned a smile. In a class of four, every gesture and comment could be seen and heard.

"So—the Clasis for Multiple Weapons, or just 'Multiple', as the fourth-year students call it. Our training will consist of three focused sections. The first will be practising with each weapon and becoming adept in its use. So, the Clasis you have already learnt in previous years—Basic, Single and Two—will be practised and employed to this end, and of course Captain Spinel will help you to become skilled as you practise the Clasis for Single-Bladed Weapon when using an actual Mnae. You will also practise with your Kulbeda so that you become proficient in its use.

"The second area of focus will be the summons. You will practise summoning your weapons until it is second nature and you can do it without thought. It is the single most critical part of Multiple, because if your weapon doesn't arrive on time, all the skill in the world at using it will be of no use to you. To strengthen your skill with the summons, you will also learn to summon other objects. We find that this increases your ability to summon your weapons when needed.

"The third area of focus will be what we call 'switching'. Changing weapons in the middle of a fight is a strategic move that can unsteady your opponent and change the balance of power in your favour. So you will need to learn when and how to switch weapons at a fast rate, something that takes intense Viq and is very challenging."

The huge Sergeant shifted on her feet and leaned on her staff. "Your skills of Aditus and Tego will never be more important than in this Clasis. Attack and Defence are the keys to knowing when to switch weapons, and to which one.

"So, let's get started by running through the Clasis that you know already, and then we will do some elementary switching between weapons. Begin!"

And so followed an exhausting hour and a half of constant movement and the use of Viq, combining exacting physical movements with intense mental energy to summon the various weapons. Eyre was struggling to breathe and dripping with sweat, and was having trouble even raising her arms by the time the Sergeant called a halt for lunch. They'd been working with their weapons for more than three hours, and all four of them were shattered.

"Go down the Chute for lunch," the Sergeant said, indicating a recessed circular section of the rock wall. "Then catch the Uplight to the yellow door, behind which is your lecture theatre for the afternoon lectures."

"What's on this afternoon?" Eyre hardly dared to ask.

"You'll be learning to teleport," the Sergeant answered. "And then one of our Armatura comrades will begin to teach you about Incendium."

"By the Light," Abby said brightly. "Exactly what I was hoping for!"

They all cackled as they jumped into the Chute one by one, and headed down for lunch.

CHAPTER THIRTEEN

AFTER LUNCH THEY USED an Uplight to shoot upwards to the yellow door. Eyre was wincing as she held on to the beam of light—over the lunch break her over-taxed muscles had begun to seize up. She was going to be in agony by tomorrow, she realised, and she could tell from the expressions on her friends' faces that they were feeling the same way. At least they were done with the physical exertion for the day, she thought with relief as they stepped into the yellow room.

This room was set up like a small lecture theatre, with three banks of seating; ten seats in each row and a blackboard at the front of the room. Waiting by the blackboard was a familiar face, although Eyre thought she might have preferred an Armatura to be standing there. Or even a Saevus. Dr Botolfe looked at them impassively through bright-green cat-eye glasses and indicated the chairs with one purple-nailed, taloned hand.

"Welcome. Have a seat. I'll be teaching you the art of teleporting over the next few months."

It made sense, Eyre thought, since Dr Botolfe was the Head of the Psionic Department at the Academy. But, she thought gloomily, it was going to make the afternoons less than enjoyable if the humourless professor was their lecturer for a whole hour. Abby looked at Eyre and her mouth drooped. Evidently, she was feeling the same way.

But to Eyre's immense surprise, Dr Botolfe sat down in the first row beside them.

"We had a less than auspicious start to our relationship at the Academy," she said, addressing no one in particular, but really referring to Eyre, they all knew.

"I deeply regret that, and my behaviour, and I hope I can build a new trust between us all. Learning to teleport is essential for you and your safety in the coming trials, and I intend to do my best to get you ready for whatever you may face. So please feel free to ask me anything about any subject."

She stood up and moved to the front of the room. "Essentially, teleporting is very similar to using a prohemium and moving through a Seam. Except there's no hand gestures or beam of light conjured up. Your 'hand gestures' are created in your head, and the equivalent of the Seam is merely a shift in energy that you generate and travel through. Getting the energy to shift in the first place, and ending up at the intended destination, they are the challenges to this skill."

Dr Botolfe summoned a pen which she held up and then placed on the desk in front of her. Holding her hands out, she made the pen first move away from her, then towards her, and then spin around in a circle.

"Telekinesis. You can all already do it. Well, teleporting is telekinesis on a grand scale. You are simply moving yourself from one place to another. Once you understand that, the mechanics of achieving it become easier. So you focus in your mind on *pulling* yourself to the place you want to go. It requires a huge amount of psionic force, which is why it is the last of the skills to learn, and why it will take you a great deal of time to get the hang of it. But that is all we will be doing in this hour, every day, and eventually you will understand how to achieve this essential skill."

Dr Botolfe snapped her fingers and a pen appeared in front of each of the students. "Stand up and start by pulling the pens towards you as I did. Once you can do this without effort it will be easier to translate it to a larger scale."

So for the next hour they pulled the pens, pushed them, spun them, and even sent them tumbling through the air, as they tried to understand the association between telekinesis and teleporting.

As Abby's pen plummeted to the floor yet again, she grumbled, "I feel I may be looking for the Isar in the Simpson Desert with these skills."

Beatrice chuckled as her pen crashed and burned over the side of the desk. "I'll be there right with you, my friend."

But Nick wasn't struggling so hard. He'd always had a knack for the psionic forces, and Bullio, or producing and shaping bubbles, was one of his particular gifts. In no time he had his pen cartwheeling through the air across the room and back again, and then landing gently on his desk. Dr Botolfe looked quite impressed.

"I see you're already quite adept with the psionics," she said. "Now try to work in your mind with yourself as the object this time. Start simply. See if you can move yourself from your desk to the wall. Once you've learnt how to travel a short distance, it just becomes an extension to go further."

Eyre wasn't doing too badly, but she was reflecting that she seemed to do her best work when she was totally incandescent with rage. Her pen was sliding back and forth across the table and lifting off the surface quite well really. But she felt it was going to take some time before she could move herself anywhere. Other than by an Uplight. Or a Desert Cyclone.

Eventually the hour passed with no one doing anything more spectacular than calisthenics with the pen. Dr Botolfe teleported herself from the front of the room to the chair beside Abby, causing her to levitate in fright.

"Your powers are growing," Dr Botolfe said to them all. "This is a necessary step in learning the technique. One day it will happen and you'll never look back. Good session! See you next time."

And then, in a flash of light, she was gone.

Beatrice rolled her eyes. "Easy stuff, hey." With an annoyed expression on her face, she made the pen lift off the desk and travel towards the blackboard. With a click of her fingers, she summoned her staff, and as her gobsmacked friends watched, blasted the pen into flecks of soot. They drifted down in a flurry to land all over the carpet.

"Done," Beatrice said with satisfaction.

"I'd say *too* well done, burnt actually," Abby giggled and then they all burst out laughing.

It was probably poor timing, because as Eyre looked up, she realised someone was standing at the side of the room.

"Ah..." she gulped. "Hey..." She nudged Nick and he turned around with a big smile that immediately faded.

"*Bea, Abby!*" Eyre hissed. Her two friends stopped laughing, with puzzled looks on their faces.

"What...?" Beatrice started, and as the Armatura moved forward to the front of the room, she added, "Oh. Oops!"

He did not look happy and Eyre knew that he was highly offended by the laughter in the room. Not a good way to start the semester. So she stood up and brushed the tears of laughter from her face.

"Please excuse our poor timing," she said. "Thank you for coming to teach us."

The Armatura stood in silence for a second and then nodded.

Eyre sat down and studied the fierce warrior in front of her. It was really the first time she'd been able to look at an Armatura closely. Most of the time she'd been running away from them as fast as she could, or standing side by side with them as they all battled the Gothak. Not much time for scrutiny in either of those situations.

What an incredible creature he was! Over two metres tall, his red skin was embedded with jewels and covered with golden scrolls and symbols. He had a gold bar through his nose and round earrings in his earlobes that stretched them into a huge hole. His massive muscles strained against the leather and metal armour he wore.

"Sox Na'Eatrum," he said. "In my language, l'Ajn, that means greetings. Translated literally it says 'may the volcano lie dormant', but in essence it means *may your timing be fortuitous*. I am happy to teach you about my world, and I hope to prepare you well for your quest to find the shining bar. My name is Quon."

His students sat completely still, and silent. Not one of them was game enough to interrupt the mighty warrior, and so he started his lecture on the world of Incendium. Molten rivers traversing towering rockfaces. Creatures with huge teeth and wings, and poisonous creeping things. It was a world of nightmares and Devil Wolves.

The only way to move around Incendium, if you weren't born there and immune to the intense temperature, was in a Zepp. And if you had to venture outside, it was necessary to use Viq in a unique way to guard against the extreme conditions. All in all, it sounded like a delightful place, Eyre thought gloomily. How fitting to end the heartbreaking and disastrous search for the Isars in a place like that.

However, the Armatura was fiercely proud of his savage home. Which shouldn't be surprising really, Eyre supposed; he was born there. She settled back into her seat, determined to listen and learn, and perhaps find out what there was to like about this strange world.

The time passed quickly and Quon eventually finished his discussion about the types of rocks found in Incendium.

"Tomorrow we will begin working on the prohemium for Incendium," he said. "Please review our discussions today before then."

Walking in perfect formation and saying farewell in very polite tones, with no laughter, the four friends exited as fast as they could.

✕✕

"Whoa," Abby said over dinner, her voice raised to clear the hubbub. "What a frightening creature he is!"

"By the Light," Nick agreed. "I'm glad he's on our side!"

"Well he is, until you laugh at him," Beatrice said dourly.

That made them all laugh.

"Well here's to our education," Eyre said, raising her purple ale. "Let's hope it sinks in!"

"Hear hear," her friends said, clanging their tankards against hers. "To being smart!"

The morning after their first lesson, the four could hardly move, they were so stiff.

"Call the doctor," Abby said feebly from her bed. "I've got tetanus. None of my muscles will move."

"I'm in agony," Beatrice moaned as she rolled on to the floor and lay there. "Kill me now."

Nick slowly sat up and slouched on the end of his bed, shaking his head, and Eyre gave a muttered oath as she tried to sit up and failed.

"I can't get out of bed," she said. "Let alone lift a Mnae."

But after hot showers and breakfast they felt slightly better, although every one of them moved very slowly and cautiously.

"The Clasis will be in slow motion today," Eyre said. "My mind is willing but my body is incapable!"

Various mutters of agreement greeted her statement, and, with the look of inmates heading for the hangman's noose, they each took a stand on the Uplight and headed upwards to begin their torture.

CHAPTER FOURTEEN

THE NEXT MONTH PASSED quickly despite the intense pain and exhaustion of training and the massive amount of information they were supposed to absorb in a short time. The days blurred together and there was an awful feeling that it would never end, but at the same time, each minute registered intensely.

"When is it going to get easier?" Abby complained in despair, with her hand over her eyes. She was lying on her back on her bed, where she had fallen the moment she'd walked in the door, and she'd not moved for an hour as she lamented her fate.

Beatrice yawned. "At this point I'm convinced it's never going to get easier," she said gloomily. "I'm more interested in when it's going to be *over*. Five weeks, four days, and ten hours, to be exact."

"Well at least we're getting a break tomorrow," Nick said as he polished his Mnae. "It will be nice to get above ground."

Eyre agreed. Tomorrow they were having a day off so they could visit and work with their Lighthorses. The trip was being taken in the utmost secrecy, so they wouldn't be able to visit their friends and say hi. Despite the fact that Eyre, Abby and Nick felt terrible for Beatrice, they were all looking forward to it. And Beatrice had assured them that she would be okay with visiting the stables, as she would really enjoy a walk in the fresh air.

Eyre knew Beatrice was just being brave, but she was sure she was also being honest when she said she would enjoy visiting the Academy as much as the others. They'd been hidden away under the ground for so long that Eyre had almost forgotten what the wind and sun felt like. And not having to practise the prohemium, or try to teleport, or wield a Mnae with an adequate amount of balance on the back foot, was going to be *great* for a change, even if it was only for a day.

She folded her uniform on the chair beside her bed and tucked her polished and oiled boots neatly under her bed.

"What do you…" she began, but then heard something that made her stop. After a long moment, Abby raised her eyebrows.

"What do I *what?*" Abby asked, laughing. "Want for Christmas? Like the most as a potential hair colour? Think is the most fascinating constellation? So many absorbing questions begin with those words."

Beatrice and Nick cackled, but Eyre's head was tilted, focused.

"Can you hear that?" Eyre asked, ignoring Abby's humour.

Her three friends stopped chuckling and listened, but Beatrice raised her eyebrows and shook her head.

"Nope, can't hear anything. You sure it's not tinnitus from the clanging of the Mnaes?"

A tear ran down Eyre's cheeks. "Oh, it's so sad." She said. "Such a mournful song."

Nick jumped up quickly. "Uh oh! It's happening again." At the blank looks Beatrice and Abby gave each other, he stumbled over himself to explain. "Last year—when we were here and we all ended up on that goose chase! Through the tunnels. Eyre said she was following some singing—it's the Isars! Quickly Abby, call the Sergeant. Bea, sit on Eyre with me until the Sergeant gets here."

So Beatrice and Nick literally sat on Eyre for half an hour, despite her protests and struggles, until Abby managed to call the Sergeant. The big woman hurried in with an annoyed look on her face, but when she saw what was happening, she immediately understood.

"It's fortunate there are two of them down here now, as the sound is far less intense when they keep each other company. And also, Eyre seems to have more self-control now. But it's good you called me," the Sergeant finished as she snapped her fingers. A vial of bright yellow liquid appeared, which she tipped down Eyre's wide open, complaining throat. Eyre gagged and then fell into an instant sleep.

"By the Light, it was like riding a bucking bronco," Beatrice said peevishly. "Just what my tortured muscles needed!"

"Well, I owe her one," Nick said ruefully, referring to his possession by a mali last year. Eyre had helped drive the mali out of him, and probably saved his life.

"I will instruct the Mimir to build up the walls around the Isars for the remainder of your stay so that Eyre can't hear their singing," the Sergeant said as she left. "Eyre will sleep through the night now, so you can all rest.

I'll be here in the morning to take you back to the Academy, so be ready on time. Sleep well."

"I will now," Beatrice grumbled as she clambered into bed. Five minutes later they were all snoring.

XX

The next morning the Sergeant met them at their room after breakfast.

"Leave your weapons behind," she instructed. "With any luck you won't be needing them. But I trust you are accomplished enough with your summons by now to fetch them if you do need them. I'm sure I don't need to remind you that this is a highly confidential trip and you are to not to use telepathy or communicate by any other means with anyone on campus but yourselves. Staff members excepted. Right! Step up and hang on to each other and here we go."

A second later they were standing in the Equestrian Centre, in the middle of the arena. The Centre was deserted, so Eyre surmised that lessons had been cancelled for the day in honour of their visit. But shortly after they arrived in a flash of light, a familiar diminutive figure strode lithely across the dirt to greet them.

"So good to see you!" the Kikkuli Master said, shaking each of their hands. "It's been a very calm and ordered school since you've been gone!"

"You should see what they've done to the Mimir though," the Sergeant said in a deadpan voice, and the four of them had to look twice to make sure she was joking. The Sergeant undoubtedly *did* have a sense of humour, but sometimes it was very deeply buried.

"I'll leave you to it then, Armando. Thank you."

The Sergeant disappeared, leaving the Kikkuli Master to survey the four students, who were looking at each other with eyebrows raised.

"Yes, I do indeed have a first name," he said, correctly interpreting their expressions. "And a last one too, actually. It's Lopez, in case you were wondering."

"Oh, er, sorry, sir," Nick stuttered, and the Kikkuli Master laughed out loud.

"I forget my own name too some days! Understandable you might think I was born being called the Kikkuli Master."

Then they all laughed. Several Lighthorses neighed from down the corridor and Abby, Nick and Eyre looked over in anticipation.

"You go ahead, guys," Beatrice said, trying to say it lightly, but her voice caught in her throat.

"Oh Bea," Abby cried. "Come and ride Cojo with me!"

But she was interrupted by a cacophony of neighing and stamping of feet, and then the unmistakeable sound of high-speed galloping coming straight towards them. A horse came storming out of the alleyway, pawed the air and then charged at top speed around them, creating such a dust cloud they couldn't see.

"Do you need help to catch him?" Nick offered as the horse thundered past again and the Kikkuli Master shook his head in the swirls of dust.

"No, actually, it's a her, and all is fine."

Eyre shut her mouth tightly to avoid swallowing half the arena, and then jumped as the horse skidded in right next to her. Beatrice, who was standing next to Eyre, called out in shock. But the Kikkuli Master didn't move, and so neither did they, until the clouds of dirt had settled back down on the ground, Eyre's eyes were stinging, but she did a double-take when she recognised that it was Eclipse standing beside her! The mare she had ridden to Caelus last year. And then she noticed that Eclipse had her nose in Beatrice's hand and was nuzzling her arm with her head.

Beatrice looked over at the Kikkuli Master with a hopeful expression on her face that nearly broke Eyre's heart.

"Yes," the Master said softly. "Eclipse has chosen. You are to be her Lightworker."

Eyre was filled with joy for her friend, and she threw her arms around Beatrice, and then the dark-brown mare. Beatrice was shaking her head as if she couldn't believe it.

"You don't mind?" she asked Eyre hesitantly.

"Of course not!" Eyre said softly. "Ischyros is my Lighthorse. Eclipse only agreed to help me in Caelus; she never chose me. I knew that. I'm *so* glad for you."

Eyre stroked Eclipse gently. "And what a good choice you've made, my friend," she whispered in the glossy mare's ear.

Abby clapped her hands in delight and Nick stood to the side, quietly happy for his friend. They all knew the grief and pain that Beatrice had dealt with in the past months. Eyre knew Eclipse would never replace the love Beatrice had for Blondie, but Eyre also knew that Eclipse would forge a unique path of her own in Beatrice's heart.

Abby, Nick and Eyre walked down the corridor, leaving Beatrice with Eclipse and the Kikkuli Master. The Master was going to run them through their paces in the arena, so they could get acquainted.

Nick stopped at Prenzel's stall and the massive brown thoroughbred whickered at him as he unlatched the gate. A few stalls further on was Cojo, hanging his head over the door in excitement. The black and white

Appaloosa tossed his head up and down as Abby approached, and she stopped to scratch his black forelock.

"Yes, it's the paddock today, my beautiful boy," she said happily as she entered his stall.

Eyre walked all the way to the end of the stables, where Ischyros's loose box was. He didn't get on with the rest of the Lighthorses, so he'd been allocated his own area away from the general population. Last year, in an outburst of pain and rage, he had destroyed his stall, and Eyre had meticulously rebuilt it as an act of penance to the old horse. She had worked hard at it, but it certainly wasn't a patch on his luxurious lodgings at the Highlight cabins, and she could hear him complaining as she approached.

"Really," he said loudly. "One would think that an ex-participant of the Lightness Cup might be housed in quarters slightly more fitting! And yet, here I am. Back in the same old place. It's an outrage, really."

Eyre knew that *he* knew she was there. But she played the game anyway.

"Hello Ischyros," she said softly, leaning over the gate.

"What? Oh, it's you! You nearly gave me a heart attack, sneaking up on me like that. Well, you'd better come in, then."

Eyre's heart clenched when the old horse swung around, trying to see her out of his one good eye. She would never get used to seeing him like this. But she casually brought some liquorice out of her pocket and put it in his feed bin where he could see it. She removed the protective sheet from his back and took the burn cream down from a high ledge and started to rub it into his gnarled, red skin. Ischyros's coat hadn't grown back at all, but his skin was feeling more supple. It was clear that someone had been attending to him in her absence, which was such a relief.

"That other girl has much softer hands," Ischyros said slyly. "I like her."

"Lisa? Has she been doing your cream?" Eyre asked.

"Yes, that's the one. Very nice, and patient." Ischyros nodded his head and Eyre turned away so that he couldn't see her smile.

"Well, I must thank her," Eyre said. "She's taken such good care of my Lighthorse."

Ischyros stopped chewing the liquorice. "I thought I saw that flashy mare go by just before. No class, that one."

Eyre kept her face deadpan. "Ah yes, Eclipse. She's chosen Beatrice to be her Lightworker. They're practising in the arena with the Master."

"Oh well, of course." Ischyros said offhandedly. "She wouldn't pick you, obviously."

"How could she?" Eyre said, hugging him around his scarred neck suddenly. "I already have a Lighthorse."

Ischyros cheered up after that, with only a few complaints and caustic comments tossed into the conversation. Eyre told him what she was doing at the Mimir's Domain, and what she and her friends were learning. Despite himself, Ischyros seemed to be listening attentively and forgot to appear disinterested. Eyre gave a pleased mental shrug and kept talking.

There was the clatter of hooves down the corridor as Eyre put the jar back up on the shelf. Abby was leading Cojo, with Nick and Prenzel behind her.

"Come to the paddock, Eyre?"

Ischyros looked worried for a minute, but Eyre jumped in. "Of course!" she replied. "We'll meet you there."

She deliberately waited until Abby and Nick were well on their way to the paddock before she unlatched Ischyros's gate. She didn't want him struggling to keep up, so she took her time and let him lift his head to the cool autumn air, and to rub his neck against a few fenceposts. She was more than happy to take it slowly too—after all the weeks below ground she intended to make the most of a day in the sun and fresh breezes. Definitely no need to rush.

Abby and Nick and their mounts were waiting in the paddock when Eyre and Ischyros arrived. Abby's blue eyes were hesitant.

"We were just going for a ride—?" she began.

"Go! I want to lie in the grass," Eyre said quickly. "I do not want any physical exercise whatsoever after this past month!" And that was partly true—lying in the sun did seem a wonderful idea. But so did flying, and as Abby and Nick took off, Eyre's eyes followed them wistfully for a second.

Then she turned back to Ischyros, glad she had the old horse outside for a walk.

"Let's do the perimeter and then roll in the grass!" she suggested, and Ischyros gave a little leap in the air despite himself.

"That will be quite satisfactory!" he said.

CHAPTER FIFTEEN

EYRE FASTENED THE LAST buckle on Ischyros's sheet and pulled it straight. Abby and Nick had still been out flying when Beatrice finished her tuition with the Kikkuli Master, so Beatrice and Eclipse had flown off to join them. Eyre didn't mind. She'd used the time to polish Ischyros's feet and fill his feed bucket. She had so nearly lost the recalcitrant old beast, she would never feel bad for missing out on the things he couldn't do, ever again. She was quite content to potter around and look after the wounded old hero.

Footsteps sounded from down the corridor and the Kikkuli Master came into view.

"Would you come with me, please, Eyre?" he said in a stern voice, and Eyre stopped her fussing and turned towards him.

"Sure," she said in a surprised tone. She tried to open the gate, but Ischyros was being difficult again. He'd wedged himself against the latch so she couldn't undo it.

"Ischyros!" she said in exasperation, embarrassed at keeping the Master waiting. Ischyros wouldn't budge, so Eyre levitated over the gate and landed next to the Kikkuli Master.

"Sorry, sir," she said awkwardly.

"Right, well follow me then," the diminutive man said, and walked back toward the arena.

"Don't go," Ischyros said plaintively, but Eyre ignored him, and the Kikkuli Master didn't seem to notice.

They were halfway along the corridor when Eyre saw the Sergeant arrive in a flash of light. The Sergeant raised a hand and smiled, but the Kikkuli Master grabbed Eyre's hand tightly and she experienced a violent wave of vertigo as she was teleported away.

When she opened her eyes, Eyre realised that she was standing in the Transit cave, amongst the tall shards of multi-coloured crystal. The cave was lit by a flickering flame, which cast eerie shadows up the walls. The Kikkuli Master was still holding Eyre's hand tightly, and a deep sense of unease started to rise within her.

"Ah, sir...?" She indicated her trapped hand and the Master finally let go. Eyre shook her fingers to return the circulation. "What are we doing here? And where are the others?"

"There was an incursion," the Master said. "We are here for your safety. Please sit and wait until I know all is clear."

There was a noise at the side of one of the tunnels and the Master moved forward quickly. Someone was there! Eyre did as she was told, and remained seated, but her ears strained to catch what the conversation was about, and who the Master was talking to.

"Yes, now," the Master said softly, but his voice echoed faintly in the chamber and Eyre could hear. "She must go to the Reconciled One."

The Reconciled One! From the quatrain? Eyre thought anxiously. What did that mean? She half-stood as the Master returned, when there was a flash of light that lit the interior of the Transit. The light reflected so brightly from the facades of the crystal formations that Eyre was temporarily blinded. The unease she'd been feeling kicked into full gear, and without thinking she flung herself behind an outcrop of garnet.

"Come out, Eyre," the Sergeant called as she stepped through the light.

"Yes," agreed the Master, stepping up to face the Sergeant. "Show yourself!" But then, with a *zap*, each of the Lecturers summoned their staffs and, to Eyre's horror, a violent battle began. She realised with a terrible shock that one of them must not be who they seemed, but which one? Until she knew for sure, she intended to stay exactly where she was. Beams of light shot across the interior, each one of them fully capable of inflicting Occido on anyone it hit. Then, with a zing of energy, the weapons switched to Antaraks, and the flashing crystal blades twirled and spun as the combatants tried to destroy each other. They were perfectly in sync, anticipating each other's thrust and parry, and countered each move with a counter-move, almost as if they could read each other's mind. The sheer energy of the fight was frightening and impressive, and Eyre cowered in fear behind the clump of crystal.

The Kikkuli Master spun around again and suddenly a Mnae was in his hand. He chopped at one of the Sergeant's crystal Antaraks and it cartwheeled out of her hand, digging deep into the sand of the cave where Eyre hid.

After thinking furiously, Eyre made a decision. Leaping forward, she picked up the Antarak and tossed it over the garnet formation towards the Sergeant. "Sergeant!" she called, and the Sergeant grabbed the crystal blade smoothly as it spun towards her. Without a pause, the big warrior continued fighting ferociously.

Eyre kept looking nervously towards the tunnel opening, where earlier, someone had been lurking and conversing with the Master. But they kept themselves hidden. Eyre knew she also had to stay hidden, at all costs, so she sidled around behind the crystals until she was well out of sight. She raised a mask and kept completely still while watching the fearsome battle being fought in the centre of the cave.

With a mighty blow as she crossed her Antaraks, the Sergeant sliced and smashed the Mnae out of the Master's hands. He leapt backwards and used the couple of seconds reprieve to morph into Jemima Periwinkle. The tall woman was more than a match in size for the Sergeant, and as Jemima Periwinkle used her Viq to pull her Mnae back up from the ground and into her hand, the Sergeant summoned her own.

"So, sister," Sergeant Tottingham said in a low voice. "This is how it ends."

"For you, maybe, but not me!" Jemima Periwinkle snarled, as their Mnaes met mid-air with a spark of flame and an ear-splitting clang. Once again, they battled back and forth across the cave floor—silently so as to not waste breath. Eyre had her hands at her mouth, not wanting to interrupt the Sergeant lest she take her attention away. The two massive women stepped in closely to each other, their blades crossed together and straining with the force of formidable muscle and immense Viq, and then a strange look came over Jemima Periwinkle's face. A mixture of confusion and total surprise. She stepped back and looked down to see a Kulbeda embedded in her chest.

"Clasis for Multiple Weapons," Sergeant Tottingham hissed. "I was always better than you!"

Jemima Periwinkle crumpled to the ground and became still, as a pool of blood spread widely around her. Her Mnae rested for a second against an obsidian crystal outcrop, then clattered down beside her.

At that moment dozens of Mimir burst from the tunnel, Jengles at the fore.

He hurried over to the Sergeant, who was bent over, leaning on her Mnae in exhaustion.

"Where is she?" Jengles cried, and the Sergeant pointed at the garnet outcrop. Jengles raced over and pulled Eyre out as the rest of the troops quickly searched the cave and tunnels. The echo of their stomping feet filled the air, but they found nothing.

"Are you alright, Eyre?" the Sergeant asked between heaving breaths. Eyre rushed over and hugged the huge woman.

"Thank you, Sergeant," she said, and the Sergeant patted her on the top of her head.

"How did you know which one of us was false?" the Sergeant asked.

Eyre stepped back and shook her head. "I didn't know for sure. But you both seemed to anticipate each other's moves so well, it seemed like you were very used to fighting together. So I took a guess that Ms Periwinkle was one and you were the other. Which meant really that it had to be the Master who wasn't genuine, if I was right. Besides, Ischyros tried to tell me not to go. He knew something was wrong. I should have listened."

The Sergeant gave a tired smile. "The Unlit would be impressed with your logic and problem solving, Eyre. You are right. Jemima and I grew up honing our skills together, and we knew each other's moves so well. Her failing was that she was overconfident—she always expected to win."

A look of pain and regret crossed the Sergeant's face as she silently regarded her sister lying lifelessly on the ground.

"She has brought our family great dishonour," was all she said. Then she bent over and pulled the Kulbeda out of Jemima's chest and turned her back on the still form.

"I think you're probably ready to go back now?" she asked Eyre.

Eyre couldn't agree fast enough, and in a flash she was transported back to her room, far, *safely* underground.

"So, how did the Sergeant find you then?" Abby asked. "How did she know where you were?" They were all sitting in the dining room having dinner. But it was a far more subdued affair this time, and several of the Mimir were looking surreptitiously over at them. News had travelled fast, and the mood was solemn. Everyone knew that if Eyre disappeared, so did the future of the Overworld.

Eyre laughed shortly. "Apparently, I have a tracker under my skin, here —" she indicated the back of her shoulder under her shirt. "It's made of chalcopyrite, and the Sergeant told me that it has an energy vibration they can trace. Sister Murphy put it in when I was at the Infirmary, after Mudamir tried to grab me. On orders from the Determinant Dozen. And a good thing too, I guess. But I'm not sure how I feel about my every move being known to anyone and everyone. No sneaky midnight feasts for me!"

They all smiled, but without much humour. Such a wonderful day had nearly ended in disaster. And it had brought them back to the stark reality of what they must achieve in the next few weeks, let alone the next few months.

Beatrice shook her head. "The poor Sergeant," she said softly. "Imagine having to kill your sister."

"And she will be feeling devastated that her sister was a traitor," Nick added.

There was a long silence as they all contemplated the awful events of the afternoon.

"Did you enjoy your flight?" Eyre eventually asked, trying to lighten the mood. Despite the sombre atmosphere, her friends couldn't help themselves and all three beamed, Beatrice most of all.

"It was fantastic," she said. "Eclipse is beautiful."

Eyre smiled. She knew how smoothly the exceptional Lighthorse flew, and she was happy for her friend.

"We saw someone out there while we were in the air," Abby said coyly.

Eyre raised an eyebrow in query.

"Jax came to meet us. He was very disappointed you weren't there," Beatrice said. "He said to say hi."

Eyre smiled, although she felt wistful. She wasn't surprised that Jax knew she'd been staying with the Mimir. Last year he had been down here himself, secretly studying with the Mimir, but also trying to find the source of the treachery within the Lightworking world. Well they knew now, Eyre thought sombrely. Quite a few questions had been answered in the past year. Jax had also been sourcing the Lorian fruit, which held the key to penetrating the Underworld. *That* puzzle hadn't been solved yet though, Eyre thought. Not everything was clear.

Eyre felt a great yearning to talk to Jax, with his cool head and his unerring certainty about the way forward, even at the cost of his own reputation. She wondered how he was, and felt an inexplicable feeling, almost like grief, she realised, for the life she might have had without the endless search for the Isars. A life of simplicity and security. And things with Jax would have been different too, she was sure of that. She wished she'd been there with her friends today. But her personal desires didn't seem to be a factor on the path that life was currently taking her down.

Abby chuckled, misinterpreting Eyre's preoccupation. "He's going to try and visit you soon."

Eyre smiled at her kind friend. What she wished for most was a more peaceful world, so they could all live their lives normally.

They were interrupted by the Sergeant, who crossed the dining room to their table. "Eyre, I need you for a moment, if you've finished eating."

"I'll see you back at the room," Eyre said to her friends.

The Sergeant held Eyre's arm and they teleported to a large rock cavern that Eyre knew was the Mimir's hospital. It held many rooms with beds, and bustling Mimir attended to the occupants. There was always some injury or other from weapons or mining or misadventure, and the hospital was never empty.

Sister Murphy waited for them in the entrance area.

"My sister found you by tracking you like I did," the Sergeant said and then paused for a long time. She shook her head and continued. "Jemima killed Sir Rayburn, then posed as him in a meeting of the Echelon, so she knew how to find you. It was discussed in great secrecy, but of course they didn't know she was there. We also don't know who else now knows about the tracker, so we've decided to remove it. Unfortunately, it means that you will have to remain here until we go to Incendium. It is too dangerous for you to leave—the Gothak will be planning some other way to get to you."

The Sergeant sighed heavily. "I am sorry, Eyre. My sister has caused such damage to the Lightworking world."

"Hold still," Sister Murphy said, and turned Eyre around so she could reach her shoulder blade. Then she put a small gadget against her skin and there was a light zap.

"That's it?" Eyre asked as Sister Murphy put the gadget back in her pocket.

"All finished," the Sister said. "Take care, Eyre."

There was a bright flash and she disappeared.

Eyre rubbed her shoulder, but could feel nothing. Untagged, just like that.

"I'll send you back to your room now," the Sergeant said.

But Eyre had remembered something while she had been eating dinner. "When I was at the Transit, Ms Periwinkle was talking to someone in one of the tunnels. They were talking about 'the Reconciled One'. I thought I should mention it. Do you know what it means?"

The Sergeant frowned. "After your trip to Aqua we had a special meeting of the Echelon. Whittaker Ray discussed the fact that the Sea Witch had referenced the Nostradamus quatrain, which mentions the Reconciled One. But we haven't been able to work it out. Although it seems that whoever it is, they are aligned with the Gothak." She sighed. "Riddles and puzzles. Way beyond me. But I'll pass it on. Thank you, Eyre."

A moment later, the Sergeant had sent Eyre back to her room, where her friends waited, full of questions.

"The good news is I'm right for a midnight feast now, my friends," Eyre said.

"Hooray!" cheered Beatrice.

CHAPTER SIXTEEN

THE WEEKS PASSED QUICKLY after that. The four of them were getting fitter, and they were certainly more focused, Eyre realised, after the events at the Academy. Now that they weren't in mortal pain every time they woke up, they were able to focus on improving their skills as well as their fitness. In particular, Eyre had seen how effective the Clasis for Multiple Weapons could be, and she worked hard at improving her proficiency in that discipline. Eyre had 'Vulture Killer', the bow Rachis had given her, as a weapon to bring into combat as well, which added an extra layer of difficulty to the training.

Sergeant Tottingham looked at her approvingly after a particularly hard training bout with Nick. Both Nick and Eyre were exhausted after summoning and switching between weapons for fifteen minutes.

"Well done, Eyre. Nick has been hard to match in this Clasis, but that bout was a draw. Both of you are to be commended—you have shown extremely rapid progress."

Abby had finally managed to teleport, to everyone's delight. It had taken so many hours and so many headaches trying to learn the skill that they'd begun to believe it may never happen. But then, one moment Abby was there, and the next she had disappeared in a flash. Everyone was so surprised that their mouths hung open, as Dr Botolfe beamed delightedly. A second later Abby was back, looking as gobsmacked as her friends were.

"Well done, Abby," Dr Botolfe said. "Now, for the rest of you!"

Beatrice followed suit the next week, and arrived back, after somewhat of a delay, with ice-creams for everyone, including Dr Botolfe.

"I visited the Academy Refectory," Beatrice said, looking hopefully at Dr Botolfe. After a moment, the professor raised her hands in mock defeat.

"You've earned it, I guess."

So they all sat around and demolished the ice-creams before starting their practise with renewed determination.

"If that's what I can do with the skill, then it's given me great motivation," Nick laughed.

Eyre and he managed to teleport a couple of weeks later, Nick one day, and Eyre, finally, the next. It had become somewhat of a rite of passage to bring something back from their teleporting, so Nick came back with a pink camellia for each of them, 'to remind them there is indeed a world up there,' and Eyre, who wasn't allowed above ground, scrounged wooden spoons from the Mimir's dining room.

"My last-place memento," she said as everyone laughed.

"Three weeks to go," Dr Botolfe said. "Hardly a wooden spoon effort from any of you. You are to be commended for your focus. Many student Lightworkers graduate without having learned the skill—it can take years.

And then, to their immense surprise, she summoned purple ales for them to celebrate with.

Quon hadn't warmed to them during the weeks he lectured, but he doggedly pursued the curriculum, teaching them about Incendium and the many perils that awaited them. As always, Eyre thought, Incendium was notable for its various lethal, biting creatures, inhospitable environments, and the chance of death at every turn. She almost yawned. No surprises there. It would be more of a surprise to find they were heading to a peaceful, safe haven with gambolling, friendly inhabitants.

They learned that Devil Wolves could be tamed, and that many Armaturan homes had the vicious creatures as guards and companions. And they also learned that the most powerful volcano in the Overworld, Mt Incendius, was located in Incendium, and they would access the Alterworld through the volcano's inner chamber. Unlike Mt Crepitus in Caelus, which lay dormant most of the time, Mt Incendius was active, and violent, and extremely dangerous.

"Charming," Beatrice muttered, rolling her eyes, and Eyre put her face on the desk to prevent Quon from seeing her grin.

They all had learned the prohemium, which had seemed easier after they'd managed to teleport. It was as if a dimension had opened in their brains, and it was hard to imagine a time when they couldn't teleport. Sort of like riding a bike, Eyre thought. Once you 'got' it, it was with you forever.

They also needed to learn the hardest Incendium skill of all—making a Viq 'helmet' to protect themselves against the extreme temperatures outside during the daytime. They would be issued an Institute suit and gloves to guard against the inhospitable environment, but they needed to generate the protective energy around their heads, like a shield, themselves. Using Viq meant they could see properly in all directions, and once they had learned to create and lock the helmet in, it would stay there until they themselves extinguished it. The skill was not generating the helmet, as that was not particularly difficult, but to maintain it for any length of time. So, after they learned to create their helmets, they would sit through class trying to keep it in place for as long as possible. Over the weeks their ability improved, until it was second-nature to produce and sustain the defensive barrier for as long as needed.

Eyre hadn't mentioned it, but she was quite dejected that as the weeks went by, Jax hadn't contacted her. She wouldn't have expected him to, except that he'd told her friends he would. So her mind worried at it like scratching a mosquito bite. She couldn't leave it alone.

She'd given up hoping he might come, when one day, he did. Just like that. They were having lunch in the dining room when there was a zap and Jax appeared, sitting by Nick on the long bench. Nick immediately grabbed Abby and shielded her with his body.

"Cleared by traffic control," Jax said hesitantly as he took in their startled expressions.

Then Jax waved his hand and suddenly he was sitting by Eyre. He looked her like a man lost in the Simpson about to take his first sip of water.

"At last," he said uncertainly. "I'm so sorry, they wouldn't let me come earlier."

It only took a second, and then Eyre pulled him towards her and kissed him desperately. She didn't care about anything other than that he was here. Because despite everything, 'At last' was just what she felt too, as she stared into the green eyes that she loved. No rhyme or reason, no backing backwards. There'd never been a choice really, ever since she'd first swum in Lake Altrum and bumped into him. *You're mine and I'm yours.* Only forwards from here.

There was a long moment and then Beatrice coughed.

"Hello, Jax, nice to see you."

Jax and Eyre pulled apart and Jax laughed.

"My manners!" he said in a courtly tone, and leapt to his feet and gave a deep bow. "At your service, ma'am!"

Nick rolled his eyes and conjured up a purple ale. "Sit down, my friend," he said. "You're setting a bad example."

"Well, you've been doing it for years, mate," Jax chuckled as he looked at Nick's protective arm around Abby.

"JACKSON!" Gabbro roared, sliding a sloshing pewter jug the full length of the tables to teeter in front of Jax. Red-haired faces looked up at the commotion and then looked elated as they saw the dark-haired student at the table. A rhythmic thumping on the tables began as Private Ammonite jumped up and raced over to clap Jax on the back.

"Dimmog, we've missed you!"

And then one of the Jotnar, smiling unexpectedly with its razor-sharp teeth, emerged from the kitchen to bring Jax a heaped plate of food. Beatrice raised her eyebrows.

Jax Jackson was certainly popular in these parts.

As Jax began to eat, the four friends filled him in on their studies and what they'd been doing, as Jax reassured them that they hadn't been missing much at the Academy.

"Vela's still there," he said, shaking his head. "Maybe best you stay underground for a while."

"I think I'm even missing Vela," Eyre said. "It's so hard being down here."

After a moment, Jax nodded. "It's definitely oppressive down here. But at least you're safe." His eyes lingered on Eyre as he said it, and she felt a warmth skimming over her skin as Abby nudged her with her foot.

"You've all done really well by the sound of it," Jax continued, dragging his eyes away from Eyre's face, "I felt very claustrophobic down here and I struggled too. But I had no choice. I had to stay here to maintain the ruse, and now it's your turn."

He laughed and poured them all a purple ale. "The burden of the true Lightworker, I guess."

Then he continued apologetically, awkward at having a conversation that he would rather be having with Eyre alone, but knowing he needed to speak.

"Eyre, I would have come earlier, but the powers-that-be didn't want me to disrupt anyone's concentration with above-ground tales. I was not permitted."

Abby huffed in sympathy with him, and after a moment, Eyre huffed too.

"Well, anyway, how is everyone up there?" Beatrice asked. Jax's eyes clouded for a moment, and then he spread his hands in a noncommittal gesture.

"Oh, you know, everyone is going well in general. Robeson may be slightly sad at the moment for some reason, not really sure why, although your brilliant mind might work it out Bea?" Beatrice gave him a look that would have caused most students to run for the mountains, fast! Jax just grinned at her. Everyone knew that Beatrice would be glad to hear that Robeson might be missing her.

Jax continued his update about their friends back at the Academy, although as he spoke his voice was a bit bleak. "Some are doing better than others. Warrigal's a bit tired with his studies. Everyone is on edge with the way things have gone, and you're definitely missed, all of you.

"In general," Jax continued, shrugging, "it's been good. People are a lot more serious about studying this year. Perrill's been up to his usual antics, of course, and has caused a lot of trouble. But his father came and talked to him and he's been better since then. So just the usual stuff, really."

He talked more about various students and what they were doing, but Eyre noted that he didn't mention Colton. There was definitely tension between Jax and Colton, at least from Jax's side, and she knew it was because Jax was jealous. She didn't know how he could be so unsure of her feelings for him.

And then he mentioned Pheria, and how she'd been exceptional at Single with the Mnae, better than most of the students, to everyone's surprise. Pheria was an athletic girl but hadn't shown unusual blade talent before. Jax and Pheria were old friends, and he'd shown many times that he wasn't interested in anything but friendship, despite Pheria wishing for more. But as Eyre felt the fire of annoyance rising within her, she had to laugh at herself. She was just as jealous as Jax was.

Just then she caught his eye, and the open smile he gave her and the warmth in his eyes dispelled all the roiling thoughts. She smiled back, just grateful that he was here.

Finally he stood. "I have to go," he said regretfully. "The Sergeant said I could stay for dinner only. But, I've been cleared to let you know that I'm coming to Incendium with you."

"What?" Beatrice exclaimed. "You could have started with that, you dope! That's great news!"

"There's going to be a few of us on this trip," Jax said. "So, I'll actually be seeing you all in a few weeks."

Then he walked around the table and swept Eyre into his arms. Before she could react, he kissed her deeply, his lips warm on hers.

"See you soon, my love," he whispered, and disappeared.

"What an exit!" Beatrice chortled.

Eyre couldn't say anything. She felt so overwhelmed; her heart was filled with joy from seeing him, and loss that he'd been and gone so quickly.

"See you, too, my love," she sent telepathically, and hoped he would hear it.

CHAPTER SEVENTEEN

EYRE WOKE WITH A hard knot in her stomach. She hadn't slept well, tossing and turning all night, despite knowing that she really needed to rest to prepare for the ordeal ahead. She sat up quietly, not wanting to wake her friends, and leaned against the rough rock wall behind her pillow. The last few weeks had passed in a whirlwind of intense training and preparation, until now the day was suddenly upon them.

Incendium. Just the name sent a wave of dread through her. Not only the dangers of the unfriendly Alterworld, but the fact that the Gothak might be there, lurking with deadly intent, ready to kill her beloved friends, or indeed, any Lightworker. And above all, she felt the overwhelming pressure of being the only one with the ability to find the Isar. Now, more than ever, it was crucial that she found the 'shining bar', as Quon called it. She felt exhausted and sick before they'd even begun.

Beatrice stirred and rubbed her eyes. She sat up and smiled at Eyre.

"Here we go," she said, and Eyre just nodded. Beatrice's eyes were sombre. She was under no illusion about the next few days of their lives.

They roused Abby and Nick and they all quickly dressed, then headed down for a hot breakfast in the dining room. Eyre was aware of the eyes of the Mimir upon them. A mixture of hope and tension filled the room. They all knew what was at stake on this journey.

Half an hour later Eyre and her friends stood in the Training Room and waited for the Sergeant. Jengles was already there, and in a rare display of physical affection, he hugged each of them tightly.

"The Light be with you," he said gruffly. Beatrice looked so gobsmacked that on any other day Eyre would have laughed out loud. But her nerves were wound too tightly to do anything other than wait for the rest of the Incendium team, whoever they might be. She knew that Jax and Gegenees would be coming, but she had no idea about the rest of the team.

Her questions were answered soon enough, with a series of bright flashes of light in the room. The Sergeant was first to arrive, standing with her hand on a large cardboard box.

Next to appear was Sir Philius Clarembout, closely followed by Gegenees, who beamed at them all, but at Abby in particular. Abby smiled back and lifted the gold medallion around her neck that Gegenees had given her two years ago, which made his smile broader.

"Lovely day for a jaunt!" he boomed. Jax emerged in another flash, and finally, to Eyre's delight, Ranger Chrysanthe followed, wearing a black tuxedo with a rainbow-hued flashing bow tie and matching shoes. The beetles twirled around his bright green hair and the overall effect was quite astonishing. When everyone burst out laughing, he looked delighted.

"Dress for the occasion, I always say," he said.

"Right, speaking of dressing," the Sergeant said, opening the top of the box. She began to hand out clothing that Eyre knew were the heat-resistant suits for Incendium.

"You know what to do," the Sergeant said, passing silver suits around and Eyre pulled hers on over her clothes. The suit was made of a thick white cotton-like substance from Terra, which was then coated in mica crystals infused with Viq. When she moved, the suit sparkled like diamonds. Everyone but Gegenees and the Ranger put one on. With their inexplicable, mystical powers, they evidently didn't have need of the protective covering.

The Sergeant led the way as they walked a short distance through hubs and tunnels until they reached a docking station, where a small silver Zepp was parked. It was similar to the one she had taken when she'd gone to visit Aowx the dragon a couple of years ago, Eyre thought. The Ranger had driven their Zepp then too—he was such an expert pilot that he had been called in to be part of the team to Incendium. But she hoped they weren't in for the stomach-churning ride they'd had on the way to Aowx's lair.

Everyone climbed aboard the Zepp, except Lord Clarembout and Sergeant Tottingham. As they buckled themselves in, Eyre saw that there was only rock in front of them, and rock to the sides. No tunnel going straight down, she noted with relief.

Then Sir Philius and the Sergeant performed the prohemium to Incendium, perfectly in sync, in front of the Zepp. When they finished, a tall shining Seam, wider than usual, opened in a blinding vertical strip. They both stepped quickly aboard the Zepp, closing the doors firmly behind them. As they sat and buckled up, the Zepp started to roll towards the Seam and was quickly swallowed up in a wave of bright light. There was a huge judder of turbulence, followed by a loud splosh and a sudden jolt, and then Eyre could see through the large windows that a sea of bright orange surrounded them. Except Eyre knew that this sea was made of molten rock, which warmed the sides of the Zepp so quickly they were uncomfortable to touch. The Zepp moved violently along, firing through the magma upside down and then right way up again, taking them on a dizzying and stomach-churning ride, until suddenly the Ranger called, "Hang on, folks!"

The Zepp started to move upwards vertically at incredible speed, like a torpedo in a waterspout, until, with a violent blast that seemed likely to rip the sides off the Zepp, they were blown out the top of Mt Incendius. Then the Zepp flipped, tumbling over and over in a sickening spin until Eyre, almost losing her breakfast, was starting to wish they *had* in fact been heading for Aowx's lair. This was absolutely heart-stopping, and she looked frantically out the window at the ground far below.

BTL! she panicked, her stomach churning as she held desperately with both hands to whatever she could find in the Zepp. *It's like XXXL, that horrific ride at the Ekka, she thought, but by the power of a hundred!* She couldn't even stand up in the gyrating vehicle, but if she could, she would have found the exit as fast as she could. Anything to get out of there.

Reaching the top of its trajectory, the flying vehicle stopped altogether for a second and then started to hurtle back downwards, spinning wildly again. But, with a rev of the Electrum-powered engines, the Ranger cranked some gears ferociously and the Zepp shot sideways at Mach speed, away from the volcano—heading for the blackened plains beyond the magma.

The Ranger finally righted the Zepp in the turbulence as the passengers exchanged glances, slightly green-faced. "People pay a lot of money for that experience back in Entis!" Ranger Chrysanthe cried jovially, shoving into fourth gear with a loud and ominous clank. Unsurprisingly, no one answered him.

Finally, Eyre could breathe a bit easier as the Zepp bounced through the volcanic gas and tephra that had erupted from the volcano. She gulped and took several deep breaths, steadying her stomach. The current flight path was not pleasant, but it was bearable, and the Ranger's extraordinary piloting skills kept the silver ship on course.

"Let's hope the Isar isn't somewhere in Mt Incendius," Beatrice said drily as she looked back at the heaving volcano. Black roiling pyrocumulus clouds hung around the sides of the colossal mountain, and vivid rivers of magma rolled slowly down to the base. Eyre agreed. It was not somewhere she wanted to explore closely.

With a soaring swoop the Ranger banked the Zepp and wheeled steeply downwards to land on the black plains with scarcely a bump.

"Well done, Leo!" Lord Clarembout declared. "Superb navigation, as usual!"

The Zepp idled for a few minutes and then the engine cut out.

"We are waiting for Quon," the Sergeant said. "He will guide us through Incendium. Hopefully, it won't take long to locate the Isar."

Eyre looked out the window, feeling stress rise in her. Not much pressure, just the hopes of the entire Overworld, she thought gloomily. She strained her eyes, but couldn't see the vertical beam of light that would tell her where the Isar lay.

As they waited, Lord Clarembout began to talk. "It was decided by the Determinant Dozen that only a small group should come on this expedition. Any troops, or other Alterworld presence, would have drawn attention to what we're doing. Unfortunately, there are spies in every Alterworld, so we have to be careful. However, the troops are on standby should they be needed."

"Well, I'm going to ask the obvious question," Nick said "Why are we three here?" He indicated himself, Abby and Beatrice, and Beatrice nodded.

"I was wondering that too. I'd like to think we were critical to the mission, but I do feel that perhaps you could actually cope without us."

Everyone laughed, and Eyre thought it was just as well Quon hadn't arrived yet.

Sergeant Tottingham answered. "You are here to help validate the cover story we have put out there. Because the Gothak don't know that the Isar can be seen at this time of the year, we are hoping they won't notice our presence. But if they do, disinformation has been spread amongst the community to let everyone generally 'know' that this is an advance scouting party, to learn the lay of the land. It has been heavily emphasised, *secretly* —" Everyone laughed as the Sergeant made quotation marks in the air, making it obvious that this was something the Determinant Dozen wanted widely broadcast, "—that a successful scouting mission would ensure the rapid recovery of the Isar in November. So, we're hoping the Gothak don't notice what we're doing, but if they do, they will think it in their own interests to leave us alone. The only danger is if they try to kidnap you again, Eyre. But at any sign of trouble, our Mimir and Lightworking troops will be called in. They are on high alert and can be here at short notice, along with the Armaturan forces." The Sergeant looked at Beatrice. "So you three are part of the cover story. You make us look innocuous."

Everyone laughed again at Beatrice's expression.

"And I thought it was my Clasis for Single skills," she said with mock offence.

A loud hammering at the door interrupted the conversation and Eyre could see Quon standing outside. The Ranger slid the protective window between the pilot and the passenger compartment shut, and everyone activated their Viq helmets and put on their gloves. When they were completely protected, the Sergeant heaved the Zepp doors open and Quon clambered in, accompanied by a blast of heat that felt like a physical blow. He took an empty seat beside Eyre and lay his studded club and curved sabre on the floor, as the Sergeant shut the doors behind him.

When the air was stable inside again, the Ranger opened the window.

"Which way, boss?" he asked the huge Armaturan. Quon turned his massive head to the pilot's cabin. The gold bar glinted in his nose as he spoke.

"We head south. Towards the Crevasse of Ji."

And without further discussion he leaned back in his chair.

Great, Eyre thought. He'd decided to start with the kilometre-deep chasm in the earth, created by massive earthquakes aeons ago. The Ranger was going to have to fly across the crevasse, and it was notoriously dangerous. Eyre didn't know why they were starting in that direction, but she supposed they may as well get it over with. She stared out the window in front of her, but occasionally looking out the window behind her too. Perhaps if she spotted the Isar early they could all go home. She had to concentrate. But she also had a question for Jax, who was seated next to her.

"The Sergeant didn't say why *you* were here," Eyre said. "Are you part of the cover story too?"

Jax looked down at her for a long moment. "I asked to be here," he answered, and Eyre's stomach flipped at his tone. She took his hand and he placed his other hand over hers. "Thank you," she whispered. If anyone made her feel safe, it was this tall, bronzed boy. She was very grateful he was by her side.

The Zepp trundled on over the scorched earth. Nothing living was visible; over time the land had been decimated by falling rock and the searing rivers of pyroclastic flows. Occasionally Eyre saw a Plains Eagle hanging in the air currents above. The two-metre, scarlet-feathered bird was looking for carrion, which it ate in addition to hunting small animals. Out here on the plains the occasional animal wandered too far and died on the heated earth, and the raptors soared above, searching for carcasses with their sharp eyes. Eyre thought of Florence and an ache went through her. She missed her three-eyed Venator so much, and she was very keen to get back to campus and see her again.

They travelled for a couple of hours over the flat black earth and Eyre watched intently out the windows, desperately searching for a sign of the Isar. But by the time they reached the rim of the Crevasse of Ji her eyes were red and sore, and she had still seen no trace of it.

The Ranger gunned the engine and charged for the edge of the plunging canyon. Eyre's stomach dipped as they shot into space and dropped ten metres, but then they levelled out and began the ten-kilometre flight across the chasm.

Below were incredible structures that had been formed from volcanic eruptions many centuries ago. Eyre knew from her studies that they were igneous-type rock formations, but because the composition of the magma that formed them was different to Entis, these towering mountains rising from the bottom of the crevasse looked like pyramids of coloured glass; they were made up of thick stacked plates in various reddish hues. The light from the two suns of Incendium shone through the glassy formations, casting red, orange and yellow prisms of light all along the sides of the canyon. It was awe-inspiring, on a scale Eyre had never seen before.

Halfway across the crevasse, Eyre's attention was grabbed by something glinting in the distance, something shining from the ground to the sky. Then another one. Could it be the Isar?

But Quon's dark eyes had also spotted the spikes of light on the horizon and his expression was grim.

"Chrysanthe!" he called, but the Ranger had already noticed the lights. He banked sharply, heading away from the bright lines of light.

"Hold on!" he called, and revved the engines, flying away fast, in what Eyre knew from her lessons was top gear. She craned her neck to look back at the lines in the distance.

"What are they, Quon?" she asked, hoping she hadn't forgotten something from class. She couldn't remember him talking about anything like this.

"Metallo-thermal geysers," Quon replied after a moment, his eyes fixed on the sight behind them. "Rivers of molten metal run continuously underground and they periodically erupt like a geyser, spouting hundreds of metres into the air. But because the temperature in the atmosphere is cooler, the eruptions quickly solidify into metal rods. Very dangerous. We don't want to get caught in that. They could fire straight through us."

Nope, not an Isar, Eyre thought, feeling sick, and she felt her leg trying to pump the gas, as if she could speed the Zepp up. But the geyser storm was gaining on them and suddenly a metal pillar shot up outside Eyre's window with a loud explosion. The Ranger turned sharply away, but then another rod burst upwards beside them. Eyre held Jax's hand tightly. She could hardly breathe.

And then something wondrous happened.

"Here we go, folks!" the Ranger called cheerily, and began to fly the Zepp between the bars as they exploded into the air around them. He tilted sideways, dived straight down, and slowed and sped up again so that none of the lethal shafts came anywhere near them. Zooming upside down, banking and accelerating; it was a magnificent display of a genius pilot at work. It was almost as if the Ranger knew the metal rod was coming before it even arrived, and he whooped and hollered as if he was having the best time of his life.

Eyre regarded her friends' white faces, and knew that they probably weren't having the best time of *their* lives, but it was evident that the Ranger had everything under control. So she held on tight and tried to enjoy the ride, until the eruption eventually stopped and the Zepp levelled out again.

"And *that* is why we bring the Ranger," Sir Philius said. "Well done, sir!"

The Ranger turned around and his purple eyes twinkled. "A bit of fun, hey?"

Abby rolled her eyes and lifted her eyebrows, but said nothing, and Eyre smothered a laugh. With Quon sitting beside her now, it wouldn't be a good idea to laugh, especially with that rather lethal-looking sabre at his feet.

She hadn't even relaxed back in her chair when suddenly a whirlwind exploded from under them. Without warning, a massive sandstorm rose from the bottom of the canyon and slammed into the Zepp, strafing the windows with waves of sand and making it impossible to see.

"Extra-terrestrial cyclone!" Lord Clarembout bellowed. "Hang on!" The massive tornado grabbed the vehicle in its fist and hurled it across the canyon. The Zepp smashed against the ragged face of the towering cliffs and came to rest wedged between two huge rocks. As the Ranger desperately tried to right the listing vehicle in the maelstrom, the doors of the Zepp blew off and the vehicle teetered for a second and then tumbled down into the canyon.

"Viq helmets!" the Sergeant cried as she fell out the doors backwards into the canyon and disappeared. Eyre followed, cartwheeling into the air. She had managed to generate her helmet, but she didn't know how she would survive the plunge into the canyon.

"Eyre!" Abby cried as she tumbled from the sky beside her, and then disappeared back into the vortex. Briefly, Eyre saw everyone else toppling out, before they too were swallowed again by the churning sand. The Zepp was now hurtling straight down towards the ground far below them. Lord Clarembout appeared momentarily from the sheets of stinging sand, and then he was flung sideways in the swirling tornado and out of sight again. He called something out as he was engulfed by the maelstrom, but Eyre couldn't hear him. Gegenees appeared and disappeared and then Eyre was blown out of the iron grip of the turbulent storm and slammed hard against the rugged walls of the crevasse. She grabbed a boulder with desperate fingers, and hung on, her feet dangling into the abyss. Bruised and bloody, she gasped for air as she looked down into the void below.

And then a strong arm grasped her wrist.

"Use your feet, Eyre," Jax shouted above the howling wind. Eyre looked upwards with tears streaming from her eyes, and dug her toes into the cliff face until gradually she pulled herself up with Jax's help. They sheltered in a crevice in the cliff face as the wild storm continued on.

Then, just as suddenly as it had come, the awful tempest stopped. Sand fell from the sky to land in an irregular heap at the bottom of the canyon, and the air became eerily still.

Eyre and Jax stood up cautiously and scanned the ground below them, then the horizon, but there was no movement except for a solitary Plains Eagle that soared above, already looking for carrion.

Jax brushed the sand from his body. "You okay?" he asked.

Eyre nodded. "I hope everyone else made it through." She had a terrible anxiety for the rest of the unit and her stomach felt like it had a rock in it. How could anyone have survived this? She sighed painfully.

"We'd better climb up, I guess," she said, studying the cliffs above them. "We were lucky to be flung in here. At least we're not at the bottom. Will you check my suit?"

Jax looked Eyre up and down carefully and turned her around to make sure there were no rips or tears in the fabric to let the lethal outside atmosphere in. Then Eyre did the same to Jax. When they were confident the suits were sound, they began the slow climb to the top of the canyon.

It was gruelling work, as handholds were few and far between. Eyre's elbows and knees hurt where they'd been injured against the rockface, and although they were safe from the outside temperature, the extreme heat was still very uncomfortable. And her legs strained with the effort of pushing herself upwards without adequate purchase in the rocks. Several times the unstable ledge crumbled underfoot and slammed them against the uneven rockface. Eyre was sweating and hurting from the exertion as they toiled up the side of the cliff.

But finally, they reached the top of the canyon and lay on their backs on the sandy ground. Eyre gasped for breath as her muscles quivered with exhaustion. She didn't want to get up. But after a short break, Jax looked over at her.

"We should go, Eyre. We need to find somewhere safe before it gets dark." He gently pulled her to her feet.

Eyre turned to take a last look at the crevasse and then paused.

"What is that?" she asked in a trembling voice.

Far away, lying on the bottom of the canyon, was a small black heap, burning furiously. Black smoke curled up to the skies.

After a moment, Jax nodded sombrely, his eyes on the wreck. "It's the Zepp, Eyre, but I'm sure everyone will have survived." He shook his head and turned away from the canyon. "For now we just have to keep going— you've got to find the Isar."

With a heavy heart, Eyre also turned away and they started to walk forward, across the dry, flat plain.

CHAPTER EIGHTEEN

THE GROUND UNDERFOOT WAS dry and sandy for quite some time, and then it started to change. The bare earth gave way to waving fields of white grass that smelt like perfume. Busy flying creatures, like a cross between a grasshopper and a lizard, whirred overhead and periodically landed on the sweet-smelling grass, grasping the broad leaves with their ten legs. Eyre knew from her studies that the grass was pulped and spun to make fibre that had a multitude of uses, and that the creature was called a Claes, after the man who had first researched them.

She pushed her way through the close-growing crop and then stopped. What was that? Something large was skittering through the grass towards her, causing the tops of the plants to sway. She stepped back cautiously, and then noticed the grass was moving in all directions. She looked at Jax and realised that he'd noticed it too. Without hesitating, they both summoned their Antaraks and stood back-to-back as the circling creatures approached.

Something heavy and hairy crashed into her leg and then raced off back into the grass. Eyre swivelled her head to try and see it, when *another* of the unseen creatures slammed into her and then disappeared. It was quite big, whatever it was, but too quick for her to see. Eyre could tell from Jax's bemused expression that he'd also encountered the fast-moving creatures.

"Cut a clearing around you," he said, his eyes staying on the grass. They sliced quickly, so that there was a three-metre space around them. Staring into the grass at the edge with her Antaraks drawn, Eyre suddenly let out a surprised gasp. She'd realised that something was staring *back* at her! Before the creature could escape, she reached in and grabbed it.

"I thought so!" she said triumphantly, holding the metre-long, squirming creature tightly while her Antaraks lay discarded on the ground.

Jax looked at her and burst out laughing as he re-sheathed his Antaraks.

"A Desert Hirtus! Oh, well caught, Eyre!"

The timid creature snuffled in fear and looked at them with bulbous eyes that stuck out on stalks. Eyre and Jax had encountered the creatures at the TEP trials, when three Hirtus had escaped into Entis through the Seam. It had been a hilarious experience catching the terrified, skittish creatures, who had tried very hard to escape on their eight legs.

"No need to be so scared of me, little one," Eyre said as she put the rough-haired Hirtus down. It scuttled back into the grass and they could see the stalks bend as it moved off.

"I wonder why they ran into us?" Eyre mused, watching the grass moving. "In Entis they seemed to be trying to get as far away from us as possible."

She picked up her Antaraks and put them back in her baldrics.

"Cute little things."

Then Jax pointed. "Look out," he said. "Here they come again."

Eyre looked where he was indicating and could see the swaying of the plants as something approached the clearing. She levitated two metres.

"Well, I'm ready for them this time. I don't need any more bruises, thanks very much."

Jax did the same, and then something exploded from the grass below them. Eyre did a somersault in fright as a fast-moving, most unfriendly-looking creature struck with huge fangs at her ankles. Fortunately she was too quick for it and it missed, before rearing up on its tail to try again. *A Napiat Serpent!*

But before the creature could move, Jax had drawn his Antaraks and with a smooth move, he sliced the head off the lethal snake. Black blood dripped from the body as the head kept snapping.

"After the Hirtus, I guess," Jax said and landed on the ground. "That's why they were running into us."

"The terrible Napiat Serpent. You saved me from one after all!" Eyre said with a rueful smile, and Jax laughed. She was referring to the time in first-year when the students had swum in the river at Lightning Ridge and Eyre had thought, with her overactive imagination, that there was a Serpent on her. Embarrassing at the time, but Jax had been a gentleman and hadn't laughed at her.

"I didn't know there were Strigis here," Eyre mused, as, after a further moment of carefully looking out over the swaying grass, she too lowered down.

Jax re-sheathed his Antaraks. "Nothing is normal in the Overworld at the moment," he said. "The Gothak are rising and Strigis have been noted in many of the Alterworlds. Terra is permanently on high alert; Gryllus Wetas and Sublabor Pedes have been seen in their forests. The Gothak are sending the Strigis everywhere."

"Well, they didn't cover *that* in our Incendium classes," Eyre grumbled as they pushed their way through the grass.

The suns of Incendium were on their descent, and while the associated drop in temperature was welcome, Eyre and Jax both moved faster. Neither of them wanted to be caught in the dark in Incendium. They pushed through the grass, following the lowering Bottom Sun, which they knew indicated the way to Armaturan settlements. Eyre estimated they had about three hours of light left, so she put her head down and marched hard. Maybe they could make it before Top Sun went down.

They were nearly out of the kilometre-wide crop, when Eyre saw the grass moving again. She stepped back and drew her Antaraks as her eyes scanned the plants. Suddenly, a small, rotund form barrelled out of the grass and came to a stop in front of her, jabbering. After her initial fright, Eyre relaxed and once again re-sheathed her Antaraks, because she knew what this was. *One of the Tumba*, Eyre thought. The Tumba were allies of the Lightworkers, and although it was the first time she'd actually seen a real one, Eyre recognised them from her classwork. Round and squat, with dark-grey, leathery skin like an elephant, they stood about a metre high, which was useful when working on the land or in the mines. They were a communal society that worked together, and like the Jotnar, tendered for various jobs in the Alterworlds. The Tumba had made a submission to the Academy for a three-year catering contract when Eyre was in second-year, but it was unsuccessful and the Jotnar had been signed up again for the job.

However, although she knew the little being was an ally, Eyre definitely could not understand anything it was trying to say. The more bemused she looked, the more it gesticulated wildly until, with a look of exasperation, it grabbed her arm and hauled her off, chattering madly and pointing ahead meaningfully.

Eyre turned and gave Jax a baffled look and he grinned as he obediently followed. She noticed that he kept his weapons out and ready. He'd obviously had one too many surprises today.

They left the grass crops behind and followed the banks of a strange, hissing river. The river was bright red and bubbled and jumped; a lava river, Eyre thought gloomily. Where's a real river when you need one? Because she was becoming seriously hot. The suit she wore protected her from the worst of the Incendium environment, but she could still feel the extreme temperature, and her skin was becoming very painful from the heat. Inside her Viq helmet her face was steaming and she was beginning to feel like a

Christmas turkey on slow bake. She turned to look at Jax and saw that he was suffering as she was, despite the fact there was only one sun in the sky now.

She was just about to ask the Tumba let her go so she could sit and rest when they rounded a corner. To her relief, they began walking under some trees and it was cooler as they headed further into the shade. Rocks with real, crystal-clear water splashed down from ten-metre-high coloured-glass rocks, like the ones in the Crevasse of Ji—all different shades of red, orange and yellow, and transparent from the water running over them. Then Eyre's jaw dropped. Sitting under the trees in a clearing were Beatrice, Abby and Nick, with Eclipse, Cojo and Prenzel grazing on some strange plants beside them. More of the Tumba were sitting amongst her friends.

Eyre gasped in shock, and then ran over and hugged them all. She felt like crying, she was so relieved to see them.

"I can't believe it," she said, her voice hitching, "I thought we might have lost you."

"Oh, By St Illuminado, we thought you were both gone too," Beatrice replied, hugging Eyre back.

"So, you summoned your Lighthorses?" Eyre said as she sat beside them. "I didn't know they could survive here."

"Me either," Abby admitted. "But Lord Clarembout shouted at us to call them. I was just about to faceplant at the bottom of the crevasse when Cojo saved me." She looked fondly over at the black and white Appaloosa. "He flew under me and I landed on his wing."

"Me too," Beatrice said. "So, Eclipse has already saved my life. It was terrifying! I thought I was going to leave bits of me all over the bottom of the Crevasse of Ji."

Nick gave a wry grin. "Well, Prenzel found me hanging on to a tree growing from the side of the canyon. One of those Plains Eagles was about to make a meal of me. Hard to fight 'em off when you're hanging from a tree over a one-kilometre drop!"

They all started to laugh and Eyre stretched out on the strange grass. It was flat and spreading, more like a lichen really than grass. But it was so delightfully cool and she felt the heat draining away from her skin. It was wonderful to have some respite from the searing temperature. Up above her a huge blue flag flapped in the breeze on a mast at the top of a Bingi-sap tree. The flag had a yellow symbol, like a child's drawing of the sun, in the middle of it, and a small purple bird was perching territorially at the top of the mast.

"We were waiting," Beatrice said. "We flew for a couple of hours over the crevasse looking for you and all the staff. But we couldn't find anyone and our Lighthorses brought us up the canyon and over those fields. Goong Goong here," she indicated the little Tumba who was watching them with delight, fascinated by the interlopers, "hailed us and brought us to the clearing. She is my very good friend."

Goong Goong nodded animatedly and took Beatrice's hand, looking at her adoringly. More of the Tumba were sitting down and Eyre noticed that they were stroking her friends' skin and putting their arms around them, holding their hands and playing with their clothing.

"Goong Goong is going to come back with me and give lessons to Jengles on how to treat a person, aren't you Goong Goong?" Beatrice said solemnly.

Goong Goong nodded enthusiastically, although Eyre was sure she didn't understand a word.

"*Goong Goong!*" Goong Goong said, which explained her name.

"We don't know why we're waiting," Nick said. "But every time we go to move, they make us sit down again."

Goong Goong nodded and pointed up at the flag and everyone smiled indulgently. Eyre had no idea what she meant.

"Well, I've been trying to call everyone telepathically—you, the Sergeant, Lord Clarembout—and no one has answered," Abby said, sounding a bit miffed. She wasn't used to her power not working.

"I wonder why," Beatrice mused, sliding into academia at the first opportunity.

Eyre looked at the splashing water, and realised that she was dying for a drink. She was so dehydrated after the exertion and travelling across the scorching earth. But she couldn't remove her helmet yet; until the second sun went down the temperature was deadly. It had been hours since Eyre had eaten or drunk anything, and her mouth felt like cardboard.

But suddenly there was a rumbling in the air and as they looked up, a Zepp soared over the top of them. It swooped down and landed on the side of the molten river, then lumbered over to the clearing where they sat. The doors were heaved open and the Sergeant stuck her head out.

"Well done, students," she called. "Send your Lighthorses back and get on board! We've got to keep going!"

A few minutes later, delayed somewhat by the forlorn farewells from the Tumba, everyone was back on board the new Zepp. The Sergeant was there, and Lord Clarembout, and Gegenees. Even Quon had somehow survived the terrible storm. When the doors were shut, the Ranger slid open his window and beamed at them all.

"Had to go get another rental car! And now, onwards for more adventure!"

Eyre noticed that no one else in the Zepp seemed to be quite as excited about that idea as the Ranger. The Zepp left the ground with a roar and took to the skies as the Tumba waved madly from below.

Eyre sank back in her chair and turned off her Viq helmet. It was a relief to finally drop the energy required to maintain the protective shield. The Sergeant passed around sandwiches and flasks of water and Eyre took huge gulps of water as the Zepp flew away from the grassy fields. She listened as the Sergeant explained that, like Beatrice, Abby and Nick, she and Lord Clarembout had summoned their Lighthorses when the Zepp blew apart in the maelstrom, and Gegenees had called for his chariot and caught Quon as he fell out of the sky. The Ranger had flown to safety on his striped carpet. And Lord Clarembout explained that Lighthorses could indeed travel anywhere in the Overworld; they had been bred to survive in any of the extreme environments. It made sense to Eyre; Lightworkers had to travel all over with their Lighthorses. She hadn't really thought about it before.

The Ranger had found them by spotting the Tumba's flag; apparently the symbol on the flag meant 'Lightworker' in their limited language. And Lord Clarembout told them that the reason for the "downtime" in telepathy was that when the extra-terrestrial cyclone was over it left a residue of microdust in the atmosphere, comprised of quartzlike minerals from the canyon. The red quartz was piezoelectric, so under pressure it generated electricity that interfered with all sorts of wave transmissions for several hours.

Beatrice lapped all this up, but Eyre was only listening with one ear, as her attention was focused out the window. As the Zepp flew on, she searched the sky, looking for any sign of a vertical beam of light. Bottom Sun was long gone, and she could see that Top Sun had about an hour left before it disappeared too.

And then something caught Eyre's eye, and she looked closer. Far away and glinting in the fading light of Top Sun, she realised she could see the spires and rooftops of some sort of settlement. Quon was looking too.

"My city, Fer'It-Ynon," he said. "It means, "City of Fire". In our world, it is a beautiful name."

"Will we go near there?" Eyre asked, studying the glinting city, and then she did a double take. Because shooting up from the *middle* of the rooftops, was the beam of light from the Isar.

"Sergeant Tottingham!" she said, her voice shaking. "I can see the beam!"

Everyone turned to her in astonishment.

"Already?" the Sergeant asked, obviously not expecting this.

"Yes, it's in the middle of—er, the City of Fire," Eyre answered, not taking her eyes off the shining beam, feeling like she might lose sight of it if she did. She felt an overwhelming relief and she realised how much she had feared she might not locate it on their expedition.

"Well," the Ranger called, "I'll find the carpark, and you can all go in and find what you're looking for!"

He headed straight for the city as the darkness rose, until by the time he had parked the Zepp on a paddock outside the city, night time had fallen.

At night they did not need their Viq helmets outside the Zepp, because in contrast to the searing days, the temperature plummeted after the suns went down. They all removed their protective suits and stored them under the seats. It was a world of harsh extremes, Eyre thought, as she disembarked. She shook her hair out with relief, rejoicing in the feel of a light, cool breeze on her skin.

All around them, fairy lights sped industriously through the air, and Eyre knew they were the Incendium firebeetles. The beetles stored sunlight in two little circular packs on their backs during the day, and at night the packs glowed like golden coins. As they flew by it looked strangely like two eyes were moving eerily in the dark.

Quon led the way along a cobblestone path made of orange glass rocks. The path led over a bridge and into the town, which heaved with good-natured activity. Eyre and her group did not look out of place in this collection of people and creatures from all parts of the Overworld; Caelites talked animatedly as they strode along the street with Jotnar, and the Nemoris from Terra sat at tables in deep discussion with Lightworkers that Eyre recognised as Unlit. She even saw a Pinnae from Aqua stride by in his protective suit, speaking Thalassa to a huge Armaturan warrior. Her mouth hung open as she took in the bustle and the smell of food cooking, the music playing somewhere across a courtyard and the wild array of coloured fabrics that hung along the front of the buildings. One place, obviously a bar, was extremely popular, with patrons spilling out the doors and on to the pavements. Somewhere inside a band was playing Armaturan music, which was performed with eight-stringed instruments like cellos, and a wind instrument that sounded a bit like the tortilis from Caelus. It was a rollicking sound, accompanied by foot stomping and voices singing. Eyre's mouth watered at the cooking smells and she looked a little wistfully in the door of the tavern. It would be nice to sit down in the middle of that happy throng.

But then she looked up and located the shining beam of light again. They had no time to stop and relax. Maybe sometime, on the other side of this nightmare journey, if the fairy tale came true and the Aura was reinstated, she could come back here. The jovial vibe and sense of relaxation was the last thing she'd expected from an Armaturan city and it was very alluring. But, as she had come to realise over the years, the only thing one could ever expect as a Lightworker, was the unexpected.

She led her group through the city, following the beckoning light from the Isar. Eventually she stopped, as the beam was blindingly close now. However, there was a problem. Everyone looked at her questioningly.

"Well, as far as I can tell," she said, "the Isar is down there."

She pointed at a stone well that was evidently used for water, as a bucket hung from a rope attached to a winding mechanism.

For the first time ever, Eyre saw Quon look disconcerted.

"Oh," he said.

Great, she thought. What does '*oh*' mean? *That* doesn't sound positive. Especially from a two-metre-tall warrior with a scimitar in his hand. It seemed that this was not going to be easy after all.

They all leaned over the edge of the well.

"The well was built a long time ago," Quon said. "It's deep."

The Sergeant also looked concerned as she peered into the black water, and then over at Eyre.

"The Isar is definitely down there?" she asked, and Eyre just nodded, mentally shaking her head. *Of all places for it to end up! BTL!*

"The walls have a number of rocks jutting out as you go down," Quon said, drawing a picture in the air with his massive red hands. "Eruptions have caused them to crack and shift over time."

"So the Isar could be anywhere on the way down," the Sergeant mused. "Stuck on a ledge. Wonderful. That means only Eyre will be able to find it. How deep is it?"

Quon looked at the Sergeant with his dark eyes. "It's impossible to say, as the quakes can cause the bottom to shift up and down by up to twenty metres. But we think it's on average fifty metres to the bottom."

"Do you think you could make it using circular breathing?" the Sergeant asked Eyre.

Eyre looked into the water, trying to see where the Isar lay, but all she could see was the beam shooting upwards. She couldn't tell how far it lay below the surface. Her stomach flopped queasily at the sight of the narrow opening; she didn't do well in confined spaces. And she might not make it back—fifty metres was a long way down. But although she didn't know if she could survive the dive to search for the Isar, she *did* know that she couldn't live with herself if she didn't try.

"I'm sure I could," she said, with a certainty she did not feel at all.

"And there are toxic, blood-sucking slugs in the water," Quon added. Eyre, already nervous at the thought of going into the black water, felt significantly worse.

The Sergeant paused for a long moment and then shook her head. "It's an impossible task, then," she said in a disappointed tone. "We'll have to come back another time. At least we know where it is now." But her eyes looked around at the crowds thronging the square and Eyre knew what the Sergeant was thinking: *and so do any spies who might have been listening to them talking.*

Lord Clarembout and the Sergeant moved off with Quon to discuss the problem. Eyre could see by their hand gestures that they were trying to work out a way to retrieve the Isar safely. Undoubtedly, formulating a plan so they could come back and get it quickly, before anyone else did. Eyre felt terrible that she couldn't go in and retrieve the Isar.

She turned her head suddenly. She had an overwhelming feeling of being watched, and she scanned the crowd with troubled eyes. Her sixth sense had gone into high alert for some reason.

"Eyre," Abby hissed. "Look over there!" Abby was indicating a flight of stone steps that was filled with beings of all types. And then Eyre's stomach dropped at the sight of a familiar face, illuminated by the hanging lights.

Carrison Hamlen was here? That black-hearted *maggot*—how on Entis did he find them? And now he was spying on them and *must* know the location of the Isar! It was a total disaster; all their planning had not anticipated this outcome. In a moment the place would be swarming with Gothak. A rage began to build in her, a wrath so intense that for a second she couldn't see. Carrison had tried to kill Nick last year at the Lightness Cup, and no doubt he had been influential in orchestrating the Dark Forces that had nearly caused Eyre and Ischyros to die. He was the worst kind of traitor, betraying not only the Lightworkers but the whole Overworld. Carrison's face looked demonic under the downlights and Eyre thought that the lights showed him as he truly was. A monster. But a coward as well. Sneaking around and eavesdropping; too spineless to show himself properly.

She lifted her hand and sent a searing bolt of energy forged from pure fury blasting towards Carrison's head. But the powerful boy snapped into action and deflected it with a quick movement of his hand. There was a deafening explosion as the re-directed energy demolished a rock wall, and Lord Clarembout and the Sergeant looked up in shock. Gegenees, as usual, had been listening to Abby and he was already halfway up the steps, his huge hands reaching out to seize Carrison's shoulder. But, too quick for him, Carrison performed a strange prohemium and a second later he had disappeared into a smoking Seam. To the Underworld, no doubt, Eyre thought, with a feeling inside her like Mt Incendius itself was about to erupt. Carrison *couldn't* be allowed to win!

She hesitated for only a second before she dived into the unfathomable water of the well and followed the shining beam of light inexorably downwards. Fury fuelled her strong strokes as she swirled deeper and deeper into the dark water.

The circular breathing she'd learnt in second-year kicked in and she forced her mind not to panic as the narrow walls of the well closed in on her. The silver beam led straight down and she followed it slowly, allowing her ears to equalise periodically. She didn't look back up and she didn't look beside her. She knew it wouldn't take much to send her screaming in panic for to the surface. She concentrated on her breathing and her stroke and kept going steadily down the shaft of the well.

Where was the Isar? Eyre thought desperately. She'd spent ten minutes looking down at the beam of light and her eyes were quite blinded. From the amount of time that had passed, she knew she must be at the fifty-metre mark by now. But she still hadn't reached the bottom, and she was beginning to get cold; the temperature of the water had dropped considerably and her teeth were chattering.

Finally, after only a few more strokes, she could dimly see the Isar below her! She presumed it was on the bottom of the well, but it was hard to tell as everything was completely black, apart from the guiding beacon. The sight of the elusive bar was enough to make her kick harder. As she neared the brilliantly shining treasure, the light shone on her suit, and she realised that she was covered in black, blood-sucking water slugs. The hideous creatures were crawling all over her, but fortunately hadn't pierced her clothing.

Eyre ignored them and reached for the Isar, which she could see now was sitting on a ledge. She still hadn't reached the bottom, and she could see more of the wall stretching down into the gloom. She shuddered. It was terrifying down here. Time to get back to the surface! Carefully she reached for the Isar and grabbed it—the last thing she needed was for it to tumble down into that fathomless pit.

Instantly, the light snuffed out, and with horror Eyre realised that picking up the Isar had turned the guiding light off! She felt an instant of total panic in the pitch blackness, and thrashed around in the water when she lost her circular breathing and swallowed a mouthful of water. *Stop it!* She shouted in her mind as she choked on the water. *Breathe!*

She held on to the Isar with one hand and the ledge with the other until she was finally able to get her breathing back under control. She was exhausted and freezing cold now, and desperate to go back up.

But all of a sudden, something grabbed her from the darkness below, wrapping around her leg and pulling her down. Eyre couldn't let go of the ledge, but she was terrified of dropping the Isar, and was caught in a terrible tug of war with the unknown creature. And then a huge mouth bit into her other leg with sharp, pointed teeth.

A horrible minute went by, and Eyre resigned herself to death. Her strength failed and she was ripped away from her handhold on the ledge, and quickly the powerful creature dragged her downwards. But just as she was about to pass out from the struggle, a booming voice filled her mind.

"Did I sacrifice a piece of myself for you, only to have you die without using it?" a furious voice shouted. Eyre could barely think, she was dizzy and disorientated, and she vaguely wondered what the Rainbow Eucalyptus was doing in a well in Incendium.

"YOU CAN DO BETTER THAN THIS!" the ancient tree bellowed in her head, and Eyre finally reacted.

She used the last of her Viq to summon her staff, although she could barely hold on to it when it slammed into her frozen hand. Instantly, the pink diamond began to glow, illuminating the rocky walls that lined the narrow well. Eyre looked down at the creature that was dragging her to her death, and screamed. It was a giant Latcher, with a massive single eye. One of its enormous, muscular tentacles was wrapped around her arm, and she was powerless to stop the relentless drag to the bottom.

But at least she could see now, thanks to the pink glow from her staff, and she roused herself enough to point the sturdy weapon at the Latcher. Desperately she sent a beam of light straight into the Latcher's eye and it screeched in agony. With a horrible slither, one tentacle uncoiled from Eyre's leg and the Latcher spat Eyre's other leg out. Somehow, she found the energy to propel herself up, away from the writhing animal.

She floated slowly higher, unable to kick hard enough to move faster than a gentle upwards drift. And then, a godsend! A rope came plunging down from above, lit by the dim light from Eyre's staff. Something was attached to it and Eyre threw her arms over each side. *The bucket!* Whoever was above registered the change in weight on the end, and began hauling her up at great speed. Within a couple of minutes she had reached the surface, and strong arms pulled her out.

As Eyre coughed and spluttered, her back against the wall of the well, she registered that Lord Clarembout had seized the Isar and was gone in a flash of light. Everyone was patting her on the back and congratulating her. Someone threw a blanket around her. And Jax had kneeled down beside her, his eyes grave as he tied a bandage tightly around the deep wounds on her leg.

"Are you alright, Eyre?" he asked for the second time that day.

"I'm okay," Eyre said weakly, "just get these damn things off me!"

And the next few minutes were spent pulling grotesque slugs off the fabric of Eyre's suit and tossing them back into the well.

"The beam disappeared, so we knew you'd found the Isar," Abby said as she squeamishly picked off a slug. "Gegenees sent the bucket down and pulled you up. He used all his arms and turned the handle so fast he looked like a grinder in the America's Cup!"

Eyre smiled gratefully at the huge five-armed man. And she sent a mental message to the entity that had really saved her.

"Thank you for the gift you gave me," she sent telepathically to the Rainbow Tree. "I will try to prove myself worthy of it."

"You'd better," came the succinct reply.

CHAPTER NINETEEN

THE NEXT FEW WEEKS passed rapidly. The Incendium Isar was now safely ensconced deep within the Mimir's Domain, along with the two from Terra and Caelus. Eyre had healed quickly from the bite marks of the Latcher, and her other scrapes and bruises were gone too. The four friends had returned to the Academy and were soon back in Graduate class, studying and training hard again. The November TACI test was going ahead as normal, so Eyre joined in the tuition about Incendium and the Clasis as if she too were going. In actual fact, she wasn't sure what she'd be doing, but she wouldn't mind going back to the inhospitable Alterworld if it meant she could have a meal in the city of Fer'It-Ynon.

Eyre visited Ischyros every morning, and she was surprised to see Florence occasionally sitting on the door of the stall. Evidently, the thawing in Ischyros's mood that had begun at Highlight was continuing back on campus. He didn't seem to mind that Florence came to see him, although he still referred to her as 'that silly flapping creature.' Florence, for her part, seemed to idolise the decrepit old horse, and watched him incessantly with her three golden eyes.

Eyre, Beatrice, Abby and Nick also practised the Wisdom's Code whenever they could, on their Felsics or telepathically. They were getting better at it after all their practise, and were now able to put simple sentences together, and understand any received. They also began to learn to use their Felsics without a stylus. This involved more telepathy—transferring thoughts from their heads on to the obsidian sheet.

"What does XPTzN mean?" Nick asked, after trying to write a word using his mind.

"I'm not sure," Abby said, studying his Felsic, "but I'm sure it's closely related to QyBF." She held her own screen up and everyone burst out laughing.

"Oh, this is going to be a long road," Beatrice bemoaned. She only had lines and scribbles on her Felsic, and Eyre had nothing at all.

But slowly, they made progress, and by the time first semester was drawing to a close they could write words on their screens instead of just hieroglyphics.

Madame Overmantle was elated. "You will get quicker now. Your brain has attuned to the process and soon you won't need a stylus at all!"

Eyre's routine was to run every morning to visit Ischyros and rub the burn cream into his skin. Now that she was back on campus, she didn't miss a day. She loved the early morning half-light, the sound of the birds, and the smell of the cool air, and she would lean against the back wall of the stall and talk to Ischyros as he ate the breakfast she'd given him. He'd listen and occasionally toss in an acerbic comment, but she could tell that he liked her chatting to him.

"Only a couple of weeks now and you'll be back in more suitable quarters," she said, and he tossed his head in long-suffering agreement.

Eyre contemplated the time since their return. After Incendium, it had been assumed that since Carrison had been lurking around there and had seen them, the Dark Forces might realise that the Isar had been recovered by the Lightworkers. The Echelon had decided that there was little risk of Eyre being abducted now, because there were no more Isars to find. So she and her friends had been allowed to resume their studies on campus instead of underground with the Mimir, much to the foursome's relief. They'd made the most of their time back with their friends, and were desperately trying to catch up on the lectures they'd missed.

A sound from the passageway made her look up and she began to smile when she saw Warrigal walking by. But he appeared not to notice her raised hand and she let it drop uncertainly. Worried, she walked to the front of the stall and watched him disappear down the alleyway. He hadn't looked well for quite some time, and over the past few weeks he had become more and more withdrawn from the student body. He ate alone and didn't participate in any of the student activities that he used to. Many people had commented on it and tried to talk to him. But he was unwilling or uninterested in communicating with anyone, and Eyre felt sad that his last year at the Academy was finishing this way.

Someone else walked down the alleyway with their Lighthorse, returning from an early-morning ride and Eyre was ecstatic to see it was Jax and Firestorm. Eyre hung over the stall door, and coaxed Firestorm to her with the offer of liquorice.

"You traitor," Jax said to his Lighthorse, who moved swiftly to take it from Eyre's hand. "So easily led astray!" His eyes were merry as he looked at Eyre.

"Something for me too?" he asked innocently. Eyre flung the door open and raced over to him, kissing him recklessly. Then she looked deep into his dancing green eyes.

"Always," she breathed.

Jax latched Firestorm into his stall and walked with Eyre to breakfast.

"I'm worried about Warrigal," Eyre said as they sat down at their usual table. "He's looking quite unwell."

Beatrice looked over at Warrigal, who, as usual lately, was on his own. "Especially the past few weeks," Eyre continued. "I've tried to talk with him, but he's just not himself these days. The only one he seems to communicate with is Colton."

Jax's eyes flickered at the mention of Colton, but his face didn't react. Eyre suspected he would always be a bit jealous of the other boy, but was too proud to admit it.

"Do you think the staff are aware?" Abby asked, her cornflower eyes troubled as the studied the hunched form at the far end of the cafeteria.

"Surely the Ranger would be?" Beatrice replied.

"Maybe we should go and ask him," Nick said, and everyone looked at him.

"Well, what a genius idea!" Beatrice looked appalled at herself for being so slow.

"Yes, poor Warrigal." Eyre agreed. "Let's skip Ferito and go after breakfast. This is too important."

They were all in agreement, so they cleared their dishes away and marched out of the Refectory.

But they didn't get very far down the path.

"Er," Jax frowned and looked at the Academy's buildings, then raised an eyebrow. "Does anyone know where—?"

"Nope. No idea." Nick replied.

"I don't even know if he *has* an office," Abby finished.

Stumped, they looked at each other.

"After all these years," Eyre said, astonished, "I've never found out where the Ranger's office is."

"Well, I know someone who would know," Beatrice said, and led them to the Library.

Mrs Abnett, the elderly librarian who had been Eyre's babysitter many years ago, smiled at them as they walked in.

"What are we after today, dears?" she asked. "Lightworking History? Details of Strigis? How to Spy on an Echelon meeting?"

Eyre, Beatrice, Abby and Nick looked startled. They didn't realise Mrs Abnett had known about *that*. Jax was amused and carried on as the others struggled to speak.

"We'd just like to know where the Ranger's office is," he said.

Mrs Abnett gave a jolly laugh. "Ah, the Ranger doesn't have an office in one particular area. In fact, he's all over the place. You'll have to track him down using the Rangerometer." She picked up an object and placed it on the counter in front of them.

Eyre looked confused. "Really? It looks like a stapler." She picked it up and turned it around.

Mrs Abnett's eyes twinkled. "It is a stapler. He's right behind you."

They all jumped in surprise and turned around. The Ranger grinned.

"You are seriously spooky sometimes," Beatrice said in an annoyed tone, holding her heart.

"Walk with me," the Ranger answered. "It's a beautiful morning."

As they tried to keep up with his long strides, Abby jumped in. "We wanted to talk to you about Warrigal as he's just not been himself, and we're worried about him, and we wondered if you knew what was going on with him in case there's anything that we need to do for him and—" The sentence was so long, and she was so puffed as she took two strides to each of the Ranger's one, that she ran out of breath before she ran out of words. She inhaled deeply as Beatrice finished the thought.

"—and you've been teaching him for so long, we were hoping you might know why he's changed so much."

The Ranger stopped suddenly and they all nearly cannoned into each other, like balls on a billiard table.

For once his purple eyes had no laughter in them. He regarded the group seriously as the iridescent beetles whirled around his clown-like hair. He seemed about to say something, and then his eyes shadowed.

"You are good friends," he said in a soft voice. "Warrigal is okay. The last year is tough for everyone and he's finding it especially hard. But you have no need to worry about Warrigal!"

He looked at them for a long moment, and then the mischief was back in his eyes. "I must go to perform important duties. Away to water my pot plants!"

They all laughed as he charged away out of sight.

But then Beatrice pursed her mouth. "I can't say that I'm convinced."

Eyre shook her head. "Me either."

Abby shrugged. "But there's nothing more we can do, really. If the Ranger can't help, *no* one can."

After a long moment, they nodded and headed off to their respective classes.

CHAPTER TWENTY

EYRE FINISHED WRITING TELEPATHICALLY on her Felsic. *Perrill's life expectancy is about six months. I'm going to get him!* She was examining the back of Ben's head as if she might somehow psychically slaughter him right then and there.

Rigmar looked down at the lumbering boy and 'wrote' back, *Occido. Awesome. I'll be trying hard too. As long as one of us gets it done!* His eyes smouldered as he shared a mental high-five with Eyre.

All the graduate students had been clumped together and divided into a few small classes. They weren't divided into Sectors as in previous years, and Eyre had the great misfortune to be in this one with Ben. Few of his cronies had come through into the Graduate year, but Wyatt Rankins sat beside him for telepathic writing lessons on the Felsic. The energy of the Felsic helped the process of telepathic writing, or 'clairography', but the aim was to eventually master clairography on any medium, a skill that could take years to develop.

Madame Overmantle waited a moment. "Are there any questions? Well class, please finish—"

But she didn't get to even finish her sentence before a deafening siren blasted. Aghast, the colour drained from Madame's face as she turned towards the window.

"Get to your rooms and stay there!" she cried urgently. As the shocked class looked at her, she disappeared in a flash of light.

Everyone jumped to their feet and looked around at each other. The hair on Eyre's arms rose as a dread settled in the pit of her stomach.

"We know what the siren means," Abby said.

The Graduate students didn't have a dorm supervisor this year, as the Academy Board felt circumstances were so dire in the Overworld that the staff who usually assisted them would be better serving elsewhere. And there was a growing attitude regarding the Graduate students, that in any case, they should be old enough to supervise themselves by this age. But precisely because of that mentality Eyre felt uncomfortable hiding in her room if the Gothak had breached the campus. If they were old enough to supervise themselves, they were old enough to fight.

"Maybe we can help?" she proposed, and everyone nodded. None of them wanted to go to their rooms.

They raced to the front of the lecture theatre and out the door, heading for the Central Admin building. But even though they'd been on campus for a few breaches over the years, what they saw stopped them in their tracks. Several buildings had been completely demolished by explosions of atra. Gothak streamed over the grounds, Zyx flew through the air in grotesque black swarms and, to Eyre's horror, she saw a Sublabor Pede and a Tuus Scorpion crashing through the Equestrian Centre in the far distance. Someone had wisely let the Lighthorses free and they soared above the Centre and out of sight. She desperately hoped they had looked after Ischyros too.

But initially, as willing as they were, the students couldn't work out what they could do to help; they were so overwhelmed by the sight. They stood aimlessly, staffs in hand, as Saevus thundered through the campus. A few Lightworkers battled the hordes valiantly at the front of the Academy and Madame Overmantle was an army of one as she cut swathes through the Gothak with her staff.

It was the sight of the diminutive old woman fighting bravely alone on the battlefront that suddenly galvanised Eyre into action. Do *anything*, not *nothing!* she berated herself, and raised her staff.

"Come on!" Eyre shouted, and felt her fear replaced by rage. She charged with Beatrice, Abby, Nick and Jax into the fray and shot down five Gothak with her staff in one blast. As the Zyx swooped down on her, she sent a searing corona of lightning at them and burned them from the sky. A dark, deep-set joy assailed her as she finally understood—she was bred for this! For the first time she felt comfortable with her Lightworking skills and she switched between weapons, cutting down swathes of the hideous creatures. *Whatever kills the fiends the quickest,* she thought as she chopped them apart with whichever weapon came to hand first. A Rufa Lightworker fell beside her, sightless, and his companion turned towards Madame Overmantle desperately.

"Where are the Mimir?" he cried. She didn't answer and disappeared in a sea of Gothak.

Eyre kept fighting in a frenzy of fury—her only focus was killing as many Gothak as she could before they killed her. If this was *it*, she'd take as many of them with her as she could.

The man who had cried out to Madame Overmantle was himself suddenly felled by a bolt of black lightning, and Eyre turned despairing eyes towards her friends. How long did they have? And where *were* the Mimir?

And then suddenly, vast vertical beams of light appeared, and a ferocious, roaring horde of massive creatures came flooding out of them. The Armatura were here! And from another Seam, the Caelorites, and then the Nemoris from Terra. When a huge wave of frothing water smashed down upon the Gothak, Eyre knew that the Pinnae had arrived too. With the vast numbers of the Overworld forces fighting ferociously beside the Light forces, the tide was turned, and within a short time the Gothak had been pushed back outside the Academy's perimeter. The Sublabor and the Tuus were dead and smouldering on the ground, and the Zyx disappeared into smoking Seams to the Underworld. The clash of weapons stopped and there was an eerie silence as the forces wearily took stock of their losses. Bodies of both Gothak and Overworld forces lay heaped on the ground, but Eyre knew the toll on their side would have been so much worse if the allies hadn't turned up.

Desperately, she looked around and finally relaxed when she saw that Madame Overmantle was unharmed. Professor Vela was nursing an ugly wound in his arm, but he walked around, checking on anyone else who might need help before he went to the Infirmary himself. Dr Botolfe had lost all her usual chic, and her hair stood on end. Black soot covered her face and she was stained with blood. Eyre supposed that she must look like that as well. A heavy despair hung over the campus. *What* had just happened?

And then it got worse. Pandemonium erupted again as hundreds of running figures emerged from an eerily smoking Seam, and Eyre realised with shock that it was the Mimir, escaping from some unseen horror behind them. Then another shadowed Seam appeared, and another. Filthy, exhausted and grievously wounded, the Mimir carried their dead out with them, row after row. Private Ammonite staggered by, all mischief gone from his face, as he helped a burnt and suffering comrade towards the Mimir's Domain. Lightworkers stumbled out too, coughing, covered in blood, and missing limbs; they lay down to die as they left the Seam. It was an apocalyptic scene of sheer horror, as hundreds of troops emerged defeated from the Underworld.

Jengles lurched out of the Seam, carrying a young Mimir in his arms who was unconscious and gushing blood from a wound in his leg.

"Medic!" Jengles bellowed, and another Mimir came running.

Eyre and her friends could only try and do their part to help the wounded, as cries of pain and despair filled the air. Eyre worked silently beside Abby as tears of grief coursed down their faces. They tied bandages, assisted the wounded to the Infirmary and to the Mimir's Domain, and covered over corpses so the Jotnar could carry them away. Eyre wept bitterly as she pulled a sheet over Corporal Cabochon, the young, blushing Mimir who had helped them make their staffs in first-year. He had been terribly wounded in the battle with the Gothak and died as Eyre held his hand. Healing powers or not, she couldn't help him, and her heart broke as his hand slipped from hers. The forces of the Alterworlds called their first aid support and medicine people, and all beings present toiled to try and save as many lives as they could. Finally, many hours later, the wounded and the corpses were gone, and the Alterworld troops went home. The campus was deserted and a frigid wind howled across the blood-stained ground, as if death itself had arrived to scour the land for more trophies.

Eyre and her friends held each other and wept for the brave souls who had fought and died so valiantly. Then they trudged dejectedly to their rooms, exhausted and devastated, and afraid to the very core of their beings.

CHAPTER TWENTY-ONE

A HORRIBLE SILENCE HUNG over the campus. From their window, Eyre could see that Jotnar were quietly sweeping sand over the bloodied earth and picking up debris from the battleground: bandages, armour, weapons and in some cases, body parts. Smoke still coiled from craters where atra had struck, and in the distance the Equestrian Centre smouldered where a wall had been completely knocked down and incinerated. She turned away from the sight and sat on her bed. A weariness weighed her down so heavily that she thought she would never move again, and she knew Beatrice and Abby felt the same. None of them could even muster the energy to talk. The only bright point of the morning was that she knew Ischyros was safe; the Kikkuli Master had sent a telepathic message to reassure her of that.

A quiet knock came at the door, and after a moment Eyre opened it. Madame Overmantle stood there, her face scarred and pitted by atra burns. She had a deep cut across her forehead that disappeared into her hairline and her arm was in a sling. But worst of all was her air of desolation. Eyre had never seen the old woman look *old* before. Today she seemed bent and defeated.

"There is a meeting of the Determinant Dozen in the boardroom at 11am," she said. "No need to hide in the broom cupboard this time. You are invited." She was obviously trying for humour to help the distressed girls, but was unable to muster a smile herself.

"The rest of the Academy, except for the Incendium expedition, will be sent home today until further notice. That is all I can tell you at the moment." Her eyes softened and she patted Eyre's arm, and then she left.

Eyre looked at her friends and a tear slid down her cheek. "What a way to get an invitation," she said.

At a quarter to eleven, Eyre, Beatrice and Abby walked into the boardroom and took a seat at the back on one of the undamaged crystal benches. Sunlight was streaming into the room where a comet of atra had smashed through the ceiling, leaving a gaping hole. The fluorite boardroom table was in pieces, and shards of a massive quartz crystal had tumbled through the hole in the roof and speared into the floorboards. *At least it isn't raining,* Eyre thought. *One small mercy.*

Jax and Nick walked in and came to sit with them, and the staff filtered in and onto the podium. Whittaker Ray and Madame Overmantle were first to take a seat around the chunks of the broken boardroom table. Dean Fraser wasn't there, and Lord Clarembout was missing too. UD1 entered on crutches, with a bandage wound tightly round his head and over one eye. Gegenees and Sergeant Tottingham followed, and sat in the front row of the audience after acknowledging the students. And finally, Ranger Chrysanthe arrived, wearing a black suit and not a smile to be seen. Although he was a permanent Honorary Guest of the Determinant Dozen, he sat silently beside the Sergeant. The mood of the staff told Eyre all she needed to know; there had been a disaster of unprecedented scale.

Through the hole in the roof, Eyre saw the blue Zepp of the Echelon fly over the Central Admin building. Shortly afterwards, the rest of the Determinant Dozen arrived. President Balthazar walked in the door first, wearing purple robes and a gold turban. The handsome black man was sombre as he nodded to the staff and took a seat. Kyori, the Caelite who had guided them through Caelus, was next, followed by a ferocious Armaturan warrior who they knew, from their spying in first-year, was Field Marshall Xenolith. Chaga O Ton, a Nemoris they also recognised from first-year, came next, and finally Princess Nacre, one of the Pinnae Royal Family.

Interestingly, Eyre noticed that unlike last time, there were no members of the Thantos Nex present. The aloof race had evidently declined to be part of the proceedings. *Good!* Eyre thought furiously. She hated the powerful beings for having the means to intervene against the Dark Forces, but had chosen not to. They *should* stay away and not show their cowardly faces.

Academy staff filed in and filled the next two rows of the boardroom, along with various other members of the Alterworlds. Many of them were wounded, and all of them were silent and shell-shocked. Eyre noticed that amongst the group were other members of the Echelon—Carrison Hamlen's father, whose devastated face echoed that of Professor Perrill, who was also in the audience. How could two good men produce sons like Carrison Hamlen and Ben Perrill, Eyre wondered. Their faces were tinged with shame, and showed that they wondered the same thing themselves. Slowly, the auditorium filled up with Lightworkers. Some were parents that Eyre recognised—Peter and Robyn Edmunsun amongst them—but there were many people she didn't know. All of them had the same sombre look on their faces.

As President Balthazar stood up, two late arrivals limped in the door. Professor Vela and Dr Botolfe quietly took seats in the front row beside Gegenees.

"It is with sadness that I open this meeting of the Determinant Dozen, the Light Bearers of the Overworld," President Balthazar began in his soft voice. "As President, I have to say that this is one of the hardest things I have ever had to do. We are missing some members and I report with sadness that Cecil Fraser was killed in action yesterday."

Eyre and the other students looked at each other with horrified eyes. The Dean was dead? Tears filled Eyre's eyes as she thought of the good-natured Head of the Academy and his kindness towards the students.

"Lord Clarembout and Andrew Essendon have been grievously injured and are unable to attend this meeting. However, I have been told that they will recover," President Balthazar continued. "President Zircon and General Gel Lithium Silica send their regrets; they are unable to be here as they are attending to their wounded forces and re-establishing the defence of the Mimir's Domain. However, I have been briefed and I will give a report on their behalf.

"As many of you know, in great secrecy a decision was taken by the Determinant Dozen recently, to send a select army of Mimir and Lightworkers to try and reclaim the lost Isar. Several missions have been attempted over the past year to try and enter the Underworld without being detected—all of which were unsuccessful." Balthazar sighed heavily.

"And so, it was decided that greater force might be the only way the Overworld would ever recover the fourth Isar. Yesterday afternoon that army courageously risked their lives to make the recovery attempt. I regret to report that the attempt was unsuccessful."

This was crushing news for the audience and shoulders slumped as a low buzz rose and then faded. Those who had known about the mission were talking in soft, despairing voices. Eyre was devastated to hear that the sacrifice had all been for nothing. It was such a catastrophic loss of all those lives.

There was a long silence as President Balthazar composed himself. Then he sighed and looked around. "Worse news, if possible, is that our plans were leaked to the Gothak, and they took advantage of the fact that the Mimir forces were significantly reduced in the Mimir's Domain. Regrettably, the three Isars that were secured in the Mimir's Domain have been stolen." He sighed heavily. "And... all the Mimir left behind were slaughtered."

A horrified gasp ran around the room as he spoke and Whittaker Ray shook his head slowly. He'd obviously already known about this, but his strained face showed how hard he was finding it to process. Eyre felt like she'd been hit hard in the stomach with atra.

Stolen? She felt sick, and hopeless. For three years she had endured terrible ordeals and faced death and destruction to acquire the four precious bars, and losing one of them had been hard enough. But now the Gothak had all *four!* This could mean the end of the Overworld. For a moment her head spun with shock, and then Jax took her hand. She looked up at him with her eyes brimming, but couldn't say a word. The Allied forces were perched on the brink of annihilation.

President Balthazar spread his hands. "I don't need to tell you how dire this situation is; you all know what it means. I implore you to reach out to your contacts and engage your most erudite advisors to try and solve this crisis. We must find a way.

"Finally, I think at this time when the Mimir have made such a terrible sacrifice for the Overworld, it is appropriate to remember the words of the ancient Mimir poet, Esor, who was renowned for his wisdom and learning. In his 'Enlightened Anthology' he wrote these words:

'Winter of the soul
Can be lonely and hopeless
Remember the spring'

"We must remember the spring, my friends. Thank you, and the Light be with you."

A low hum rose within the boardroom as the audience began to file out of the room, talking softly to each other. All faces were shocked and apprehensive. This was a complete catastrophe.

Eyre and her friends left too, shattered by the revelations. No wonder Madame Overmantle had left in such a rush from class yesterday, Eyre thought—she knew about the mission, and she knew exactly where the Mimir were when the Gothak attacked. But no one could have foreseen the cataclysmic disaster that would eventuate. And as for the source of the leak, it could only be Ben Perrill, surely. Her heart roiled both with fury and fear as she walked out the door.

Whittaker Ray called to them as they came out into the wintry sunlight. He stood beside a sad tangle of three destroyed Zepps. The Zepps normally docked at the front of Central Admin, but now they looked like they'd been through a car crusher at a demolition yard.

When they reached him, his blue eyes were grave.

"Are you alright?" he asked.

"Did Ben do this?" Eyre asked furiously, rage brewing in every pore.

"He has disappeared," Whittaker Ray said after a pause. "But we are not jumping to conclusions."

Beatrice gave a snort that Ischyros would be proud of.

Whittaker Ray took in their pale faces.

"The Gothak entered by the Transit and used the Isar they had to find the others—the Isar pulled them along the passageways to the rockface where the other three bars were hidden. Then they blasted the rock to get them out, and there was no one to stop them. It will be distressing for you to hear that they killed all the troops that had remained behind. But I wanted to tell you what happened so you could understand the courage of the proud Mimir. They sacrificed everything to try and recover the Isar from the Underworld. And whatever happens," he said, "you have proven yourselves to be Lightworkers of incredible courage and determination. The Overworld could not have asked more of you. And we are not done yet."

"But what can we do when no one can get into the Underworld?" Abby said miserably, and Eyre knew she was thinking of the beryl orbuculum and her inability to see anything in it.

"Madame Overmantle could not see either," Whittaker Ray said softly, also reading Abby correctly. "Do not take that on your shoulders. We will figure something out."

Then he looked across campus. "The Determinant Dozen wanted you to be part of this out of respect for what you have achieved. You are also part of whatever the way forward might be. For now, go to the therapeutic pools and relax. There is nothing to be done at this moment. Then you can pack and I'll send you home. Beatrice, your parents have gone on ahead and they said that they will see you there."

He regarded the dismal students in front of him and smiled. He picked up a piece of metal that had fallen off a Zepp, and looked at it for a moment before throwing it back into the twisted heap.

Whittaker Ray seemed lost in thought and spoke softly. "We must adopt the attitude of the Mimir, and never give up."

"It's a beautiful verse," Abby sighed, her eyes filled with emotion. "I hope Esor is right."

Jax looked at Whittaker Ray with intense green eyes. "Sir, I don't want to go back to the cabins, or to the therapeutic pools. Let me go and help the Mimir. I don't mind what I do, and there must be some way I can contribute."

Eyre replied instantly. "Count me in!"

There was a chorus of agreement and Whittaker Ray paused for a moment and gave them a long look. Then he nodded. "Actually, you all know how to navigate down there, so you probably could be of use. Beatrice, check in with your parents and then I'll escort you down there. I know you can teleport now, but the hubs and passages have changed and you'll need a shield as there's falling rock and other hazards. But I'm sure they'll appreciate your help. Go and pack a bag and then I'll help you get there."

The students left at a run, anxious to do *anything* that might help their beloved friends below.

CHAPTER TWENTY-TWO

IT WAS DECIDED THAT they would stay for a week and help clear the tunnels and attend to the wounded. The sheer numbers of injured had overwhelmed the normal infrastructure, and the hospital had run out of medics and beds to accommodate them all. And because so many of the Mimir were either dead or injured, there were not enough workers to fix the extensive damage to the tunnels and rooms. So they took it in shifts, alternating between working at the hospital and taking turns to clear the rock that blocked the passages, using their Viq to blast the fallen boulders into dust.

By far the worst thing was finding and locating the dead, who had fallen while the troops were away. They had to be stretchered to the mortuary, a foul and heartbreaking job. None of it was easy, and a miasma of despair hung over the whole Domain. Not only because of the devastating losses, but for the belief that the future was doomed. When Eyre came across the lifeless form of Gabbro, the jovial Mimir who loved his tucker, she fell to her knees with her head in her hands. She'd formed such a bond with these courageous creatures, and tears streaked down her face as she surveyed the impossible scene.

Fortunately, other support teams came to help as well: Lightworkers—both Lit and Unlit, the Jotnar and the Armatura clinicians. The Armatura were such a ferocious, warlike race that, from necessity, their medical staff were top-notch and well-versed in treating all sorts of battle injuries.

Eyre rubbed her eyes and surveyed the passageway she'd just blasted. The Mimir engineers were fixing the rotating hubs, but the clearing of the tunnels was straightforward, although exhausting work. She was covered in rock dust and her head was pounding from the constant use of Viq and the noise from the explosions. She had created a Viq helmet to keep the dust out, but the coarse residue from the blasts covered her body and found its way into her pores. Her skin was red-raw from rubbing the grit off, it was as if her skin was constantly being scoured with sandpaper.

The work in the hospital, however, was worse than the tunnels. There were so many Mimir suffering in silence and needing attention. Several Clementis had come from Caelus to help with their treatment, and Eyre found her own healing ability had somehow been turned up to full strength in the face of all this torment. She was able to heal minor injuries fairly quickly, and even the major ones improved under her touch. Now it was her turn to help Private Kerf and Corporal Adoquin, the two Mimir who had stood guard over her at the Infirmary. Both of them had been seriously wounded, with Private Kerf the worst of the two, having been stabbed in the stomach by a Gothak's dagger. But after a couple of days of Eyre's constant touch, the wound had healed over enough to enable him to sit up in bed and eat.

"You're an angel," the Private said gratefully as he spooned soup into his mouth. I didn't think I was going to make it. Thank you."

Eyre smiled, though her head was pounding. If blasting tunnels used an extraordinary amount of Viq, healing people took a ton more. But she was determined to make a difference, and she toiled uncomplaining beside Beatrice and Abby as they hastened from patient to patient.

Jengles turned up on day three. He had been deep down in the bowels of the Mimir's Domain, dragging out the dead and then organising teams of the few troops who weren't injured to frantically clear tunnels and stabilize the infrastructure. However, most of all the impetus was to search and make sure that the foul Gothak were well and truly gone.

"I blame myself for this," he said in a voice filled with pain and shame, when he joined the friends sitting at the dining room table. "I should have known something was up and I have failed my people. T'was far too easy in Incendium for you once that Hamlen mongrel disappeared. The Gothak should have been swarming within minutes, and when I heard about that, I should have realised that something was afoot. They knew even then that they were going to steal the bars once we put the third one in with the others, so they *wanted* you to bring it back. That maggot was just observing to see if you got it." He looked down at the table and shook his head. "I was outmanoeuvred, plain and simple."

Beatrice got up and walked around to Jengles and gave the old soldier a hug, causing his face to turn the colour of his beard.

"You are a brave warrior, Jengles, and no one could have foreseen this. You need to stop dumping on yourself or I'll start singing."

Everyone cracked up, as they all knew how awful Beatrice's singing voice was. It was a real threat. Jengles eyes looked moist, and in a way, it was one of the most shocking things Eyre had seen this week. For the ferocious, grumpy curmudgeon to be so emotional, it was a telling sign of how the whole world had been turned on its head.

Beatrice sat down and took a bite of lasagne. She pointed a bread roll at Jengles. "That's your first warning."

But if Jengles was beating himself up mentally, Abby was far worse. When everyone else had fallen comatose into bed after their gruelling labours every day, she would sit late into the night studying the beryl orbuculum, trying to see something in its misty depths. She had brought the sea-green crystal ball with her, determined to try and figure out the secret to accessing the Underworld. But the answer eluded her, and she would fall into bed just before dawn every day for a few hours sleep before starting again. Eyre studied the circles under Abby's eyes, and her pale face, and her general air of dejection, and wished she could help her. But nothing would stop Abby from her punishing routine; it was as if she were trying to atone for not finding the solution before the terrible attempt to retrieve the Isar had been made.

Finally, one afternoon after a week of back-breaking toil and heart-breaking efforts in the hospital, Whittaker Ray arrived to suggest it was time for them to leave.

"You've made an immeasurable difference," he said, "and the Mimir will be grateful to you forever for this. But they have had enough assistance and they will be able to function down here now. All the weapons and stores are secure and the tunnels are clear again. And you have assisted the injured tremendously. You have helped to achieve a lot in a short time, and you are to be commended for your willingness to work so hard.

"There is still a week left of semester break. You should go back to the cabins and relax before you come back to campus. But perhaps first you might take that trip to the therapeutic pools?"

He looked at their exhausted faces. "I don't need to take you back to campus. You have the skills now to take yourself. Thank you to all of you."

Eyre, Beatrice, Abby, Nick and Jax disappeared in a flash of light and reappeared on the moldavite square. The Central Admin building was swarming with Master Faceters, who were fixing the quartz crystals where the atra had blasted through them. Great shards of quartz were being levitated in the air and placed in position, and there were Jotnar pushing stacked barrows of crystals, and the high-pitched whine of a slab saw as the huge repair job got underway. The late afternoon sun cast a strangely beautiful golden light across the jagged ends of broken crystal on the roof. They looked like broken teeth, Eyre thought. But the roof could be fixed; the lost lives were another thing. Her breath hitched as she left the repairs behind her and headed towards the dormitory buildings.

"See you at the pools," Nick called as he and Jax turned off.

"You *so* will!" Beatrice said. "If it's the end of the world, I want to get one last spa in!"

And it did seem like a good idea, actually, on the cusp of annihilation, so they hurried towards their room—off to find their togs.

CHAPTER TWENTY-THREE

EYRE RELAXED BLISSFULLY AGAINST the crimson crystal wall of the therapeutic pool. The crystal vibrated quickly, and the water was the hottest in the pool complex. A small waterfall cascaded down from the pool above, a turquoise pool that Beatrice, Abby and Nick were sitting in. That pool was cooler, but Eyre needed to burn today. Her muscles were so sore and only heat would soothe her aches. She closed her eyes and lost herself in the wonderful sensation of the vibrating water. By the time they'd got to the pools the sun had gone down, and the cool winter air made the water feel all the more delicious.

Someone entered the water and Eyre smiled when she opened her eyes. Jax was slipping into the hot pool to join her. He went right under, immersing himself completely in the water. Then he emerged, pushing his hair away from his face. Eyre took in the sight. He looked like a statue—defined muscles, chiselled features and hair wet and black, sleek as a seal. And that mouth! She took a deep breath as his green eyes looked her up and down slowly.

"You are a sight for my weary eyes, girl," he said. "What a marvel you are." And he moved in and kissed her deeply, sending sensations down her limbs that were not caused by the vibrating crystal walls. Jax's strong hands moved over her body and she shivered, pulling him close.

"I love you so much," she whispered.

Just then, from the pool above, Abby gasped and leapt up, sending a wave over the edge of their pool and splashing heavily down to where Eyre and Jax were sitting.

"By the Light, you scared the Aura out of me!" Beatrice said in a startled voice.

"You guys should come up here," Nick called calmly, and, mystified, Eyre reluctantly pulled away from Jax and slipped out of the warm red pool.

She and Jax climbed over the ruby crystals up to the turquoise-coloured water of the pool above. Eyre stopped in surprise. Something was fluttering and flying over the pools like moths drawn by lamplight. *What were they?* Super-sized dragonflies? And then one turned around and Eyre was astonished as she recognised it. A Faerie! From the Jenolan Caves—they had visited last year and encountered the fragile little beings at the Pool of Reflections. Not wanting to frighten the delicate, shy creatures, Eyre slipped quietly into the warm water of the aquamarine pool and drifted over to sit by Beatrice. Jax followed carefully, his eyes on the Faerie.

The Faerie started to sing, a song of mournful loss, and they flitted above the surface of the pool in a choreographed, graceful dance. Their iridescent wings caught the colours from the pools and the cool light from the moon skimmed across their shining silver hair.

Anguish pervading
Losses so great
Evil invading
Hopeless our fate, but
Remember the Light
Will Darkness assail
And abolish the night
'Til the virtuous prevail

When the Faerie finished the song, Abby smiled. "Thank you, that was beautiful."

"We wanted to thank you for your efforts," one of the Faerie said in a high, lilting voice. "And to give you a message, Nefelibata."

Nefelibata! Eyre thought. The Cloud Walker. One who was not bound by the norm. The Faerie had called Abby that last year, referring to her special skill with the orbuculum. Hovering in front of them, one of the little beings looked at Abby and spoke.

"The lights of Leeawulenna will help to clear the clouded ball, but only Nefelibata has eyes to see."

The little being flew in a gentle loop to land on Abby's shoulder.

"Do not doubt yourself, Nefelibata. Visit Leeawulenna."

And then the Faerie disappeared in a series of silver sparkles, like miniature fireworks in the dark night.

Everyone looked at each other.

"Great," Beatrice said in an exasperated tone. "More puzzles. Grab your towels people, we need to get to the cabins and work it out."

She stepped out, her long, lean body dripping with water, and put her hands on her hips. "Time to save the Overworld, folks; chop chop!"

No one could argue with that, so they scrambled out and headed off to pack their bags and leave for Highlight.

⋈

At dawn the next morning Eyre slipped out early and headed to the stable. The Kikkuli Master had sent Ischyros there when the Gothak attacked and Eyre wanted to see him and make sure he was okay. When she arrived, she was surprised to see Florence sitting at the back of the stall, alert and vigilant with her three golden eyes. She gave her strange cry when Eyre approached and flew up to sit on the stable door. Eyre stroked the sleek Venator as Ischyros turned around.

"Darn thing won't leave me alone! Always sitting there and annoying me; flapping, bothersome chicken. Don't know why you got it, really."

But Eyre could see that he didn't mean it. Somehow, a bond had formed between her two Lightworking companions, and it made her happy. She opened the door and threw some hay into Ischyros's bucket and grabbed the hose to fill his trough with fresh water.

"How are you Ischyros?" she asked. "Are you okay? It was a terrible day at the Academy."

"Wasn't worried," Ischyros mumbled through a mouthful. "Couldn't burn me any more than I am now. Was going to kick any of those horrible running things back to where they came from."

Eyre laughed. She had no doubt that Ischyros meant every word, and part of her thought that he probably *could* kick them back to the Underworld.

When she'd finished mucking out Ischyros's stable, she made a piece of toast and wandered over to Abby's cabin. Abby was already up, drinking a cup of tea at her breakfast bar, and when Eyre arrived she jumped up and made her one too. Abby had just sat down again when Nick arrived, and she leapt up in mock exasperation.

"I may as well make Beatrice a cup too. I feel like a wallaby hopping up and down!"

Eyre and Nick laughed, and Abby was right, because as soon as she'd brought two more cups of tea to the breakfast bar, Beatrice walked in, holding a book under her arm.

"Mum and Dad had already gone last night," she announced. "They and other delegates have been sent to the Alterworlds to be part of crisis talks. They weren't even here when I got back—all I got was a note. I guess I'll see them sometime—maybe in a couple of years?"

Her friends laughed at Beatrice's chagrin and Abby passed her the cup of tea.

"Never mind, you've always got us," she said.

Beatrice shook her head. "But you guys get me into *so* much trouble!"

"Speaking of trouble," Eyre said, "let's get on with the clue that the Faerie gave Abby. We've got to find out what they meant by the lights of Leeawulenna."

"Well, I've solved that already!" Beatrice said triumphantly, holding the book up.

"WHAT?" Three incredulous faces looked at her.

She grinned, loving it. "I couldn't sleep last night. I kept thinking about what Leeawulenna might mean, and worrying about everything and everyone, when I suddenly realised. *I could go and look it up in the library!*"

After a second, Abby started to giggle uncontrollably. "We finally learn how to teleport, and of all the places you could break into, you choose a *library?*"

Eyre and Nick joined in the laughter while Beatrice rolled her eyes. "You won't be laughing when you hear the title," she said drily. "Destinations for the Hiking Enthusiast."

Abby stopped laughing, her blue eyes aghast. "Oh no," she said. "*Hiking?*"

The others began to laugh at her, and eventually Beatrice recovered herself and wiped her eyes. "Who knew the end of the world could be so amusing? Well, anyway, listen. Leeawulenna, or 'sleeping water' is the Aboriginal name for Lake St Clair in Tasmania."

"So we have to go to Tasmania then." Nick said. "Where are the lights? Is there a town there?"

Beatrice shook her head, looking very pleased with herself. "Nope. That stumped me for a while, but I eventually figured it out. Apparently, people go down there to see the Aurora Australis. You know, they're the *Southern Lights*, those rainbow lights in the sky at night? Winter is the time to see them best, and one of the best places at Lake St Clair is Cradle Mountain."

"Mountain," Abby echoed gloomily.

Beatrice punched her on the arm. "Toughen up, princess," she said. "And in any case, what do you think we have Lighthorses for?"

Abby brightened and Nick laughed and put his arm around her. "I'll look after you."

"Will someone give me a lift? Or do I have to hike?" Eyre asked plaintively, which caused them all to laugh again. A feeling was bubbling up in the room—of *hope*. And as they all looked at each other in excitement, Eyre realised she felt lighter than she had for many months.

"Jax is coming later this afternoon," Beatrice said. "I've already called him via brainwave. He's become an unofficial part of Bane, really. We can't call it BANEJ though, so he doesn't get his name on the acronym."

"How about JBEAN?" Abby said.

"NEJAB?" Nick suggested.

"BNJAE!" Eyre said decisively, and then they all fell about again. It was like the glimmer of hope had filled the room with laughing gas.

But Beatrice poured a bucket of cold water on the frivolity. "Now that the Gothak have the four Isars, they could use them at any time to generate the energy to bring us all down. We have to hurry. All this does is—hopefully—enable Abby to see something else in the beryl orbuculum. Who knows what that might be?"

"Or if I will be able to see anything," Abby said slowly, a crease wrinkling her forehead. The levity was gone as they looked at each other solemnly.

"All we can do is try," Eyre said softly. "We've come this far. We just have to see it through." Her words hid the deep anxiety she felt, and which she knew her friends shared. When they were looking for the Isars, they'd had the advantage each year because Eyre was the only one who could find them. So, although Eyre felt pressure to actually find them, there wasn't the overwhelming time pressure they now faced. Until the four Isars were reunited, the Aura couldn't be regenerated. Now, she felt the whole world could blow apart at any time—there was no telling what was going on in the deep, dark recesses of the Underworld. But it was nothing good, of that she was certain.

"Well, get your winter woollies out, it's going to be cold down there," Nick said, standing up.

"There's no point leaving until late this afternoon," Beatrice said. "It's got to be dark. And I for one am not going to sit on the top of Cradle Mountain in the middle of winter, waiting for nightfall! Let's leave about 4.30."

And so it was agreed they would come back at dusk, and they each went their separate ways to organise themselves before the trip.

CHAPTER TWENTY-FOUR

JAX ARRIVED AT 4PM and knocked on Eyre's door. She answered and threw herself into his arms.

"There's never a dull moment with you, my girl," he whispered, and kissed her softly on the lips.

"So, I've got my coat," he said after a moment, looking down at her upturned face. "Dress warm, Beatrice said. Where are we going—skiing?"

"I wish," Eyre said. "But this will be pretty awesome too. We're heading to Tasmania."

She shut her door and as she and Jax walked over to the Mantle Basin, she filled him in on why they were going there. His eyes were serious as he listened.

"You know that whole thing with the Ranger—the so-called 'Fallen One'—being put on 'leave' last year because the Rankins complained, was just a ruse," he said. "The Determinant Dozen asked him to go, but not because he was teaching you to fly the Zepps upside down. He was away looking for a solution to accessing the Underworld without being detected. So while I was trying to *find* the Lorian Juice when I was in Terra, he was trying to work out what to *do* with it. He went all over the place trying to figure it out. He had no success, obviously, and I'm sure he feels bad about it. You know it was him who sent the Isars to the Alterworlds in the first place, don't you?"

Eyre nodded. "And I heard that the explosion was so huge that he can't remember any of it." She shook her head and said softly, "He has sacrificed so much for the Overworld."

Eyre noticed Jax looking at the silver cuff on her arm, with the black opal that he'd given her set into the Inguz, and she held her wrist up. Silently he pulled the plume agate pendant that she'd made for him out from under his shirt and they both grinned.

"Next I'm going to make you an ashtray out of clay," Eyre said solemnly.

"And I will do a popsicle stick and wool decoration for your kitchen," Jax replied.

Beatrice walked down her cabin steps into the clearing and she beamed when she saw them both standing there.

"I come prepared, and thinking positively," she said, pulling a Felsic out of her backpack. "I'll be the scribe when the pearls of wisdom drop from Abby's lips."

Eyre and Jax laughed, as Abby and Nick walked over to join them. They each had a backpack and both were wearing thick jumpers and coats.

"Made out of merino," Abby said, pulling at her jumper. "It's so warm!"

"Dare I ask if you've got the orbuculum?" Beatrice said, and Nick indicated the backpack.

"Well, let's get going then," Beatrice said. "Ready?"

They all nodded and there was a series of bright flashes as they disappeared.

In a second, four of them reappeared on the cold but beautiful shores of Lake St Clair. Just as they were beginning to worry, Nick arrived too, looking sheepish.

"I went to St Clair in Sydney," he explained. "Need a bit more practise."

They all looked up at the snow-covered, craggy cliffs of Cradle Mountain, north of the lake and set in relief as the sun lowered. Streaks of light slanted across the highest peaks, turning them a vivid orange. But dusk was falling fast, and it wouldn't be long until it was completely dark.

Nick looked up at the white peaks. "Well, I guess it's one thing to get it wrong trying to get to the lake's edge—worst case I'd just land in the lake, I suppose," he said. "I've already visited a supermarket parking lot in the other St Clair. But I'm a bit concerned about the co-ordinates up there; with my skills I might end up head-first down a ravine. Or start an avalanche!"

Beatrice laughed. "Me too, my friend. That's why I'm hoping Eclipse will give me a ride. First time in a new place, it's probably better not to teleport, I'd say."

At that, she summoned her Lighthorse and Eclipse appeared instantly, pawing at the fine sand on the shore with excitement. Everyone thought that was a brilliant idea, and Prenzel, Firestorm and Cojo arrived quickly afterwards. All of them looked around with their ears pricked, loving the unexpected summons and ready for whatever action might come next. Everyone mounted quickly, keen to get on with it. Eyre sat behind Jax, her arms around his waist, and she kept her head down as they thundered along the lakeshore and took off. It was very cold in the winter air, especially as they soared upwards towards the mountain's peak.

As they got higher the sun finally disappeared and the dark night sky became speckled with stars. A meteor flashed across the sky above them and the air grew colder with each downstroke of the Lighthorses' powerful wings. It was a new moon, so there was very little ambient light, and the weather was crisp and clear Fortuitously, the conditions were ideal for seeing the lights.

As they rose higher, Eyre began to see the curtain-like waves of the Southern Lights. Normal beings in Entis could not usually see the colours of the Aurora Australis with the naked eye—to them it just looked like white light and they needed a camera to view the colours. But Lightworkers' eyes were attuned to the lightwaves, and as they flew higher, the view of the lights became more and more spectacular. Finally, they reached the peak of Cradle Mountain and the mighty Lighthorses landed softly on the snow. It was so cold on top of the mountain and Eyre's breath came in frigid puffs. When she jumped down from Firestorm, she went knee-deep into the icy snow. It wouldn't take long to freeze up here, she thought, but she was too transfixed by the sight of the Aurora Australis to even care. The colours along the horizon were glorious: vivid greens and oranges and blues. It was a moving feast of colour that was astonishing, and it took her breath away.

Abby took the beryl orbuculum from the backpack Nick wore. She rested it on a high snow-covered rock, digging out a hollow so the crystal ball wouldn't roll away. They all gathered around as Abby stared into the depths of the glowing orb, which had absorbed the lights and swirled with the brilliant colours of the Aurora.

Abby seemed lost in a trance as she studied the magical crystal ball. She rested her palms in the snow on either side of the orbuculum, and didn't seem to even notice the ice on her hands. Eyre saw Beatrice take her Felsic out, and she clenched her hands. They desperately needed a miracle.

And then, the ball began to sing. Notes came out of the glowing crystal in an eerie, poignant melody. They seemed to swirl around the orbuculum and drift away into the night. Abby didn't move for a long time, and then, as the haunting music stopped, her eyes rolled back in her head and she began to recite out loud. The first stanza was the same as the one that Madame Overmantle had seen in the beryl orbuculum and Eyre felt her heart sink. *They already knew that!* She was so tense with anxiety that her fingernails were digging into her clenched palms. But when the chanting continued, the hairs rose on Eyre's arms as two new verses spilled from Abby's lips.

Seek and find the heavy fruit
That holds the juices blue
A means to elude the black pursuit
No other drupe will do
Crack the pit to find within
The fibres that must be dried
Take them and next closely spin
To silk, then blue-juice dyed
The pins of Plumipes alone can weave
A cloak that is the key
But only the young are able to deceive
Too old, and the Dark ones can see

Eyre didn't know what Plumipes might be, or indeed what the verses might mean. But she noticed Beatrice 'writing' them down with her mind and a huge joy overcame her. The Gothak might have the Isars, but the battle wasn't lost yet! There was still a chance that they might be able to change their fortunes.

Abby finished reciting the verses, then slumped to the ground. Nick jumped to gather her in his arms, his face anxious as he looked at his friends.

"Is she okay, do you think?"

Eyre was panicking, but she took the orbuculum off the snow-covered rock and carefully put it in Nick's backpack.

"Send Prenzel back," she said. "I'll organise Cojo. You need to get Abby home. Go! But do try to end up in the right place!"

Nick smiled, but he was too worried to reply, and in a flash of light he and Abby disappeared. A few minutes later all the Lighthorses had been sent back, and then there were a series of flashes as Eyre, Beatrice and Jax teleported to the cabins, leaving the spectacular lights of Leeawulenna behind.

CHAPTER TWENTY-FIVE

THEY WERE ALL UP again just before dawn the next day. Despite the dire situation the world was facing, Eyre had slept like a log after the night on top of Cradle Mountain, and strangely she awoke feeling refreshed. Maybe hope will do that for you, she thought as she pulled on her clothes. Or maybe the fresh air or the magical lights had. Whatever the reason, she was happy to have some relief from the perpetual anxiety and exhaustion.

She padded lightly down the steps and headed over to Beatrice's cabin, where she could see a light on. Late that night they had sent a telepathic message to Whittaker Ray and Madame Overmantle, telling them the message from the orbuculum. They expected that they were passing the information on and that would be the end of their involvement, but an hour after Eyre had gone to bed there was a soft knock at her front door.

When she opened it, Abby was standing there in her pyjamas. "Sorry, Eyre, but I needed to tell you that Madame Overmantle and Whittaker Ray are coming in a few hours. They want to talk to us, so we're going to meet in Beatrice's cabin before sun-up." And then she'd passed the beryl orbuculum over to Eyre and asked her to safeguard it in her cellar. While she was down there, Eyre had also taken the time to write the message from the beryl orbuculum in the Book of Bane. More than ever she was aware of protecting the priceless information, and the orbuculum, against malevolent forces.

Eyre pulled a jacket over her clothes as she ran to meet her friends. Winter was here with a sharp bite in the air, and snow had been forecast for later in the week. She breathed the chill air in deeply and clapped her hands together as she waited for Beatrice to open the door, wondering what the staff had worked out, for surely that was why they were coming here.

Beatrice had a pink beanie on her head, her striped dressing gown over her clothes, and lime green Ugg boots. Eyre grinned.

"I see the Ranger has been giving you wardrobe tips?" she quipped, as Beatrice passed her a coffee in the golden quartz crystal mug.

"He is my fashion hero," Beatrice said solemnly as she took a sip of her own coffee.

Jax and Nick arrived soon after. Jax had bunked in with Nick the night before and he rubbed his eyes and yawned as he took a mug from Beatrice.

"This Lightworking business is exhausting," he said, laying his head on the bench. "Wake me in about three years."

Abby arrived last and pushed open the cabin door with her foot. She had a piece of toast in her mouth and a carried a mug with *'Clairvoyants see Crystal Clearly'* written on it. Her short blonde hair was tousled and she had a line across her cheek where she'd clearly lain face first on her pillow all night.

Not a very prepossessing lot, Eyre thought, for a team who were supposed to save the world.

Two bursts of light flared through the cabin as Madame Overmantle and Whittaker Ray arrived. Madame Overmantle carried a sheet of paper in her hand which she put on the bench, and Eyre could see the words from the orbuculum on it.

"Good morning!" the old woman said brightly, as if the Gothak weren't about to overrun the Overworld and kill everyone. She sounded like she'd arrived for a picnic.

"Thank you for the message," Whittaker Ray said, and his blue eyes had a gleam that Eyre hadn't seen in a long time. "We are cautiously optimistic that you may have given us a clue on what to do."

"The journey continues," Madame Overmantle said. "My faith in you was justified, my dear," she finished, giving Abby a hug.

Everyone took a spot on Beatrice's roomy lounge suite. Evidence of Lachie's presence was scattered around the room. Over the years Lego had given way to worn-out runners and comic books, interspersed with various items of sporting gear and discarded clothing.

"Ah, brothers," Beatrice said, picking a grubby sock off the couch with a forefinger and thumb and tossing it down the hall. "Anyone need a twelve-year-old boy for their cabin?"

Madame Overmantle placed the paper on the coffee table and they all leaned forward.

"Basically, what the message has revealed is how to make a cape—the cloak it mentions—that will render the wearer undetectable," Madame Overmantle explained. "It's a *recipe* for constructing an invisibility cape. So it will conceal a Lightworker in the same way as masking, but the cape is far more powerful because it won't require the vast amounts of energy that masking does. Masking is a short-term option for Lightworkers; this cape will hide a person indefinitely. But it needs a secret ingredient."

"Youth!" Whittaker Ray exclaimed, and then quoted, running his finger along the line on the page. "*'Too old, and the Dark ones will see'*. It means that when we do make the cloak, it won't work if you're too old."

Eyre sat back as understanding dawned. ""So that's why you're here. You need us to go and look for the Isars." There was a brief pause and she rubbed her forehead as she added, "Again."

Whittaker Ray looked apologetic but just nodded.

Beatrice was reading the message. "And we need to make enough thread to make four capes. But what's Plumipes, and what's a pin?"

"Ah," said Whittaker Ray.

"Um—" said Madame Overmantle. Then she dived right in. "Well, it's actually ah, a spider—" She whispered the last word and then charged ahead, "that lives in Boulia. That's near Mt Isa."

"A what?" Abby shrieked. Her hearing had always been good.

"Yes, well, a spider," Madame Overmantle repeated. "A rather large one. Quite humungous, really, and very, very old. She's a mutation of *Selenotypus Plumipes*, the largest Australian tarantula. Venomous, of course, unlike the normal tarantula. But don't worry, she's big but quite placid. Unless it's feeding time, of course."

"Of course," Abby repeated, looking rather pale.

"And actually, it's been decided that eleven of you—the Eleven—will undertake the mission, eleven being a particularly auspicious number," Whittaker Ray added.

"Which also allows for losses," Nick said, raising his eyebrows.

"Yes... indeed. Unfortunately, that *is* also a consideration," Whittaker Ray agreed after a moment. "So, if you agree—and no one would think any less of you if you didn't, you have already contributed enough these past years—we would like you to leave for Terra today. The rest of the Eleven will meet you there. The entire forces of the Nemoris are already gathering the Lorian fruit, thanks to your excellent investigation to find the hidden caches, Jax.

"The second verse of the message tells us how to process the thread from the pit of the Lorian fruit," Whittaker Ray continued. "They've been doing it for centuries in Terra with plants like Va Flax and Terra Vine Pods, although they haven't used the Lorian seed before. And then, according to the message, the juice should be used to dye the thread blue."

Whittaker Ray spread his hands. "*Minutes* may be crucial at this stage. So you are all to leave with the thread the moment it is processed."

"To the spider," Abby said dismally.

"To the spider," Madame Overmantle repeated, nodding. "The pins of Plumipes are the Ancient One's—uh, *legs*, and she will weave the thread into the eleven cloaks."

"Does she know about this?" Jax asked.

"Ah, not as *yet*," Madame Overmantle said, and then laughed at Abby's stricken face. "You are wonderful with creatures, Abby. You are, after all, of the Sappir Sector! I'm sure you'll get on just fine." She stood up and looked at Whittaker Ray, who also got to his feet. Madame Overmantle destroyed the piece of paper with a flash of light.

"Well, Mr Ray and I must keep going as we have six more students to recruit. We will be back a little later this morning to collect you." Then they both disappeared.

Everyone laughed as Abby mimicked using a can of fly spray. "I'll get on fine, she said. Of all things—a *spider*! I'm not too good with anything that has more than four legs."

"A *humungous* spider," Beatrice intoned.

"Well, I got Aowx, so I only think it's fair that you get a monstrous, blood-sucking arachnid," Eyre said reasonably.

Beatrice thought hard, getting it all straight in her head. "So, we make the fibre, dye it blue, the er—Ancient One—spins it into capes for us, which will get us into the Underworld without being seen. Then what?"

"Find the Isars," the others all said at once. The notion of finding four small silver bars in the massive, unmapped and perilous Underworld was so ridiculous that they all cracked up laughing.

Later that morning Whittaker Ray returned, looking utterly exhausted. "We've been all over the place," he said. "And not one of our first draft turned us down! Seems we breed them tough at the Academy. Madame Overmantle has taken the other six to Terra already, and we will meet for lunch at the mess hall of Ionad."

Beatrice clapped her hands. "Ionad! Awesome! I've always wanted to go there."

Noticing Eyre, Abby and Nick's mystified expressions, Jax filled them in. "It's the expat town on Terra, named by the Irish guy who first went there. Ionad is Irish for 'centre', and yep, it's at the centre of Terra. It's also the centre of fun," he added, looking wickedly at them.

Beatrice rolled her eyes. "I was actually more interested in the geology and botany, to be honest. But I could be coerced into a purple cider."

"Just as long as it's not a Lorian Juice," Abby said, and Whittaker Ray chuckled.

"Maybe not a good idea," he agreed. "Put your bags here and I'll send them through first. Then I'll get you to hold on to each other, and I'll get you to the right place," he said. "We don't want you wandering around the Pyre of Va."

Eyre grabbed Jax and Beatrice's hands. The last thing she wanted was to revisit the scorching red desert they'd crossed in their first year TACI expedition. Once was enough! A second later a Seam opened in the living room, their bags disappeared and then they all stepped through to Terra.

Whittaker Ray had brought them to the outskirts of Ionad, and they walked out onto a huge receiving stone, at least two-hundred-metres square. The first thing Eyre noticed was how much warmer it was in Terra. The climate in the Alterworld was more uniform year-round, and didn't have the change of seasons they experienced in the Blue Mountains. Terra's violet sky arched above them and a dense forest of tall trees sat at the perimeter of the clearing.

"Supplies come in and out here," the old man explained. It's the hub of the agricultural and mining sector."

At the moment though, all that seemed to be arriving were truckloads of Lorian fruit, which was packed in crates and stacked at one end of the moldavite square. Jotnar and Tumba worked side by side, furiously unloading the fruit and sending it on a light-beam conveyor belt around the corner and out of sight. They jabbered and shouted to each other, gesticulating in a strange manual code as large-wheeled vehicles collected up the empty crates and took them away.

"How long do you think it will take to process enough fibre?" Nick asked, as they watched the series of light flashes that signified the arrival of each delivery.

Whittaker Ray's eyes followed the activity of the busy workers.

"We are hoping that with the assistance of other Alterworld citizens, two days, perhaps three. But the reason for what we are doing is being kept a secret. You are here under the guise of a Graduate training seminar. It's imperative that it remains confidential; we don't want to give the Gothak any warning.

"Come and we'll get some lunch while we wait for the other students."

Whittaker Ray led them to a swaying walkway made of wide wooden slats, which was strung over a deep gorge with a churning river at the bottom. He spoke over his shoulder as he began to walk across the expanse.

"Ionad is an arboreal city. It began as a way to study the indigenous creatures up close, but evolved into a large community. It's also, in part, a safety issue, but the expats found that they liked their tree-top living."

Eyre saw a Zhuzhu Flutter soar down the canyon underneath the slat bridge, its iridescent wings shining in the sun. The large eyes rolled up to look at them, and then it flapped its wings and was gone.

At the end of the walkway, rough-barked trees with trunks three metres wide stretched from the bottom of the gorge and up the steep sides of the cliff face. Huts made of woven vines were built in the tree-tops, and they appeared to be quite spacious. They had verandas and more walkways connecting the huts, so that it was possible to walk from one end of the community to the other completely in the treetops. Eyre didn't look down; she wasn't keen on heights and it was definitely a long way to the bottom of the forest. Whittaker Ray left, saying that he was going to find the rest of the group, and suggested they eat while they could. He pointed out the mess hall and headed off down the maze of walkways.

The mess hall was located at the centre of Ionad and it was busy and noisy. Patrons came and went, sometimes with a purple cider in hand, and a delicious aroma arose from somewhere within. Zhuzhu Flutters perched on a tree at the side of the hall, and Eyre was happy to spot a Nemoris sitting outside on a chair and whittling with a very sharp-looking knife. A chat was curled up on the ground beside him, and a curl of smoke undulated from the chimney at the top of the mess hall.

The moment the Nemoris spotted Jax, his eyes lit up and he jumped up to embrace the tall boy.

"Jacko!" he exclaimed in his raspy voice. "I thought you were done in these parts. Didn't expect to see you back!"

"Me too," Jax said, hugging him back. "But we've had a slight change of plans. Bon E Hec, these are my friends from the Academy. Friends, this is Hec. Come and eat with us, Hec!"

"Well, I think they've all gone mad," Hec said confidentially, as they headed into the mess hall. "Some bright spark has decided that Lorian fruit is the thing of the future, and this morning literally tonnes of the stuff have been turning up for processing. I mean, it's just not going to work. We can only get a few threads out of each fruit—how on Entis they think it's going to succeed commercially is beyond me. But you know how it goes, someone gets an idea and the next thing it's full steam ahead without much planning. Remember last year with the bat-poo coasters?" His large eyes blinked in bewilderment and he scratched his head with one taloned hand.

"Still, it's livened things up around here, so I won't complain. Do you like beetle salad?" This last question he shot at Beatrice, who was completely unable to respond.

"Uh, er—"

"She loves it," Jax said, smothering a grin. "Is it on the menu today?"

"Sure, every day. They do great food here."

Beatrice could only smile weakly as they took a seat inside.

Fortunately, there were other dining choices and they helped themselves to a feast of seafood brought in from Mooloolaba in Entis. Jax explained that the Ionad management wanted to keep the expats happy to ensure they would stay in Terra, so wonderful food and year-round entertainment was organised in the 'Village in the Trees'.

As they ate, Eyre could hear the high-pitched whine of machinery in the background, and she turned to see where it came from.

"It's the pitting machine," Hec said. "First, they de-flesh the fruit, so the pitter can split the seeds, then they extract the fibres from inside the seed and run them through a desiccator to dry them out, and then they dye them. After that, apparently—I haven't seen it yet—they've got masses of expert spinners organised in a warehouse to turn it into thread. I'll take you after lunch to have a look; I want to check it out myself." His pointed teeth bit into a spoonful of insect salad and the resulting crunch was slightly disconcerting, especially when one of the beetles escaped and scurried off the table.

Just then, someone called from the entranceway.

"By the Light! They obviously let *anyone* in here!" Rigmar walked over to them with a delighted look on his face.

He joined the table and sat next to Jax, and shortly after that, Carly appeared in the doorway, beaming as she grabbed a plate of food.

"Glad to be on the cattle drive!" Carly chuckled, shoving a forkful of roast lamb into her mouth. "Mum was so proud!"

And then a small figure entered the mess hall, looking around curiously.

"Tina! Over here!" Eyre called, elated to see her old friend arrive.

Madame Overmantle flashed into the mess hall a half hour later, bringing the final members of the team. Warrigal turned up, looking pale and strained, but with his usual calm demeanour. And finally, Colton and Pheria walked in the door. Colton sat down beside Warrigal and cast his eyes around the mess hall, taking it all in. Pheria was the only one who looked uncomfortable, and she stood awkwardly for a moment. But Abby didn't leave her standing for long.

"Come on, Pheria, we've organised a beetle salad for you!"

Pheria grabbed a tray and sat next to Abby. Eyre smiled at Pheria. "I'm not sure if it's an honour or not to be chosen for this mission."

Pheria raised her eyebrows. "Not boring I guess, anyway. Have you seen the rooms yet? They're quite nice. Comfortable."

Hec looked around at them all and smiled, showing his pointed teeth. "So when does E-Yire get here? I've been looking forward to meeting him. Is he your guide?" They all looked mystified and then Beatrice began to cackle. "That would be *you*, my friend," she said, indicating Eyre. Eyre looked confounded, but not as much as Hec, who regarded the russet-haired girl with a blank look on his face.

"You've obviously read the guest list," Beatrice said. "It's not E-Yire, it's E-Y-R-E, '*Air*'. Our red-headed friend here." Hec's puzzled face cleared and he slapped his head.

"Oh, my mistake! I thought a Nemoris was joining you." Everyone else laughed uproariously. The mispronunciations of Eyre's name over the years had been a constant source of amusement to everyone. Eyre rubbed her brow in mock pain, but grinned too.

Over lunch they talked about many things, but mainly about the terrible loss of the Isars. But no one mentioned the orbuculum's message—they all knew not to mention that out loud.

"How about I take you to look at the new Lorian fruit venture this afternoon?" Hec said. "We can see what a *wonderful* idea that is. According to my calculations, we might have a spool of thread in a year or so." He rolled his eyes. "Anyway, after that baffling experience, we can visit the Va Bar tonight. May as well indoctrinate you as soon as possible to the expat way of life."

So after lunch, Hec led the way down the swinging bridges, which eventually emerged out on the forest floor at the pitting factory. A large warehouse had been built in a kilometre-wide clearing, and more of the large-wheeled trucks delivered crates of Lorian fruit in the large open roller doors. A hammering, mechanical noise emanated from the building, and when the group walked inside they could see massive machinery splitting the seeds open. Hec slowed as he entered and looked around in bewilderment.

"Whoa," he said. "They're really serious about this. Why? There's far better plants in Terra to make fibre from." He was really mystified, and looked around the frantically bustling factory with his large, dark eyes. The students followed him as he walked slowly through the huge factory. At the other end of the concrete floor, a doorway led to another factory of a similar size. Huge air blasters were blowing hot air over massive drying racks holding the fibres from inside the Lorian seeds. Hec was struck silent as he walked ahead of the students, studying it all. Eventually he leaned up against a noisy dryer and shook his head.

"I don't get it," he said. He picked up some of the dried fibre and looked at it closely, then passed it around. "Anyone else understand?"

Eyre felt the fibre. "Well, it's very silky," she said.

Nick pulled at it. "And strong!"

"Actually," Carly said, holding the ugly brown fibre up, "it's rather pretty I think."

Hec frowned and had another look, then looked around at the industrious workers who spread the fibres around with long tools that looked like rakes. Shaking his head, Hec put the fibre back on the table and kept going through to the next warehouse. Enormous cauldrons of blue liquid swirled around inside, and a steady stream of fibre was sent into the vats and eventually out the other end onto a conveyor belt, where once again they led to desiccators on tables.

"So, it apparently will take a day for the Lorian blue dye to take, and dry, then the spinners will make thread from the fibres. I guess your Graduate seminar is 'The Fibre Industry in the Alterworlds', although I'm completely bamboozled, I have to say. Seems a waste of Lorian Juice, if you ask me."

He looked back at the interlinked warehouses and then back at the students. "So, how about we meet at the Va Bar after dinner? I'm going to leave you here, and when you've seen enough, you can head back to your rooms. I think Whittaker Ray put your bags in for some of you, and the rest of you have already been to the huts. Your huts are all next to each other—you'll find it."

And Hec headed off, studying the moving machinery as if trying to decipher the reason for the massive scale of operations.

Jax laughed. "Poor Hec. Normal Graduate programs are a fraction of the size. He's really struggling with this."

They walked back to their huts and Eyre was slightly disconcerted to see that the rooms were twin share, and her roommate was Pheria. Abby and Beatrice were sharing, and Eyre would much have preferred to share with Carly or Tina, but she didn't feel she could say so. So she threw her bag on one of the two hammocks without comment. The huts had huge windows that looked out into the trees, with a ceiling made completely of glass, so that the trees seemed to enfold the whole space. Unusual birds flittered around the canopy and Zhuzhu Flutters and long, lustrous serpents hid in the vines and leaves of the massive trees.

The huts were arranged in a pod-like structure, set up around a central common room. So once everyone had organised themselves, they met in the middle and sprawled over the soft lounge suite.

"They're pretty organised in the factory," Nick commented. "I wonder how long it will take."

"Not too long, I hope," Rigmar said. "To be honest, I'm surprised the Isars haven't been used yet. I wonder what the delay is."

"Well, I'm not complaining," Beatrice said. "All we need is a bit of time and we might have a chance."

"I heard that the Gothak have invaded Caelus," Carly said. "UDi is co-ordinating the troops there, and the Armatura have gone to help."

A gloom settled over the room. Eyre stared out the window and felt tired. It seemed impossible that they would get the cloaks organised in time, let alone find the Isars. But Rigmar as always dealt with first things first.

"Come on, where's that bar you were talking about? Surely they can feed us there? Let's go get a cider!"

And they all decided that was a pretty good way to start, so they headed out to find it.

CHAPTER TWENTY-SIX

THE VA BAR WAS hopping when they arrived. Expats and Alterworld citizens alike were crowded on small tables, talking madly as they downed all sorts of coloured drinks. Busy Jotnar served hot food, and a band called 'Terra Firma' played wild music from a stage in the corner. It was a mix of guitars and instruments Eyre hadn't seen before, with a particularly good drummer keeping the beat. This group of patrons seemed totally unworried that war had broken out in the Overworld; they seemed more concerned about where their next drink was coming from. Eyre decided that she couldn't do anything at this point, so relaxed with the rest of them and drank her purple cider. As the night went on, the laughter rose and eventually Rigmar pulled Eyre up onstage.

"Come on, Eyre, sing with me!" he coaxed. The band was an alternative-looking bunch comprised of three Nemoris and two Lightworkers. They had piercings in their ears with a "T" and an Inguz hanging off them, and the Lightworkers had dreadlocks threaded with various rough-hewn crystals that swung wildly as they played. The Nemoris who played the drums had a pointed emerald tooth at the front, and wore oversized sunglasses with sapphire-coloured rims. Each of the band members had a tall glass of Lorian Juice by their side, which didn't affect the Nemoris the way it affected those from Entis.

"Yeah, come on up, give us a tune," the drummer drawled. "What do you want?"

They decided on a rollicking song called 'The End of the World,' which Eyre thought was rather appropriate. So she summoned her rainbow-necked guitar and she and Rigmar belted it out. Rigmar had a strong voice and he loved being on stage, so all Eyre had to do was follow along. The audience wasn't particularly critical and they gave the performers a rousing round of applause at the end of it.

Eyre sent her guitar back and sat down again at the table. Someone slid her another cider. She sipped at it for a short time but didn't finish it. "I might head back," she said eventually, standing up, "I want to get a good sleep, just in case."

She was a bit regretful she'd said that, because it cast a dampener on the evening, and shortly after the students started to leave one by one.

Pheria walked with Eyre back to their room, and once they were inside, Eyre decided to face things head on. She sat on her hammock and looked at Pheria.

"So, I know you and Jax have known each other virtually all your lives," she said. Pheria looked at her for a long moment with her amber eyes.

"Yes, we have," she said.

"Well, you know, I understand that," Eyre said eventually. "And I hope that you'll always stay friends. To be honest, I've found it a bit awkward with you, with Jax, you know. And you always seemed so sure of yourself, and so good at everything, that it's been a bit difficult to talk to you about it."

Pheria lay back in her hammock and put her hands behind her head as she looked through the glass ceiling at the dark canopy of trees. After a moment she replied.

"Well, I guess I've been jealous of you," she admitted. "You know I wanted to be more than friends with Jax. But he wasn't interested and I just have to deal with it. There's other guys around." Her face softened for a moment and Eyre wondered again whether Rigmar might have made an impression on the aloof girl. But she didn't say anything.

After a moment Pheria sighed. "I guess I've been a bit of a cow really, and I've learned a lesson this year."

Eyre tried to keep her face impassive at *Pheria* admitting to that. But she realised that this might be harder for the acerbic, competitive girl to do than for other people, and she just gave an understanding smile.

"We've all got regrets, Pheria," she said softly. "And I know I've certainly learned some lessons over the past few years. I'm really glad you've come on this expedition. The Echelon chose well."

Pheria's eyes warmed a bit, and she turned over in her hammock. "We all make a good team," she said, and they eventually dropped off to sleep.

The next morning they were woken by something tapping on the windows. Eyre opened her eyes quickly, going from sound asleep to instantly awake as she always did these days. She leant up on her elbow and stared into the dense bush, looking for the source of the noise.

"It's the branches hitting the glass," Pheria said, passing Eyre a cup of tea as she sat back down on her hammock. "The wind is rising and it's getting wild out there."

Eyre could see that it was blowing a strong gale outside and the leaves of the trees were being whipped into eerie shapes. Scuds of cloud skittered high above the foliage and flocks of small flying creatures rocketed through the air, partly blown by the wind gusts and partly trying to escape the oncoming weather.

"Lovely morning," Pheria commented.

"Well, I'd still like to go out and see how the production is going," Eyre said. "We did say we'd all meet down there and I'd like to see what's happening. It would be good to see the spinning too. I don't want to sit around, I'll just get antsy waiting and wondering how much longer before they have enough."

"Well, bring your wet weather gear," Pheria said as she got dressed. "It could get hairy out there—I've heard about the rainforest typhoons on Terra."

And that was an understatement. As they left their hut and headed out onto the walkway, sheets of rain blowing sideways swamped them instantly. The rope bridge was swinging wildly from side to side and Eyre couldn't hear a word Pheria said over the scream of the wind. Further down the walkways they could see the small figures of Jotnar heading to the factories, holding tight to the ropes as they stepped gingerly on the slippery planks. Sometimes the bridge swung so high it almost flipped 360 degrees and their startled cries drifted up to Eyre as she grasped the rail with both hands.

Eventually, completely soaked through and shivering from the wind, Eyre and Pheria walked into the noisy first warehouse where the pitting machines were. As the wind howled across the entrance to the huge shed, Eyre wiped the hair back off her face and looked at Pheria, who was in a similarly bedraggled state. Both of them grinned and chuckled. Then, with a wave of Viq, they dried the water instantly from their bodies.

"That's better," Eyre said, shaking herself. "Nasty out there."

They wandered through the into the huge interior of the factory, where a massive stockpile of blue fibre was growing higher against the wall with each passing minute. Giant-wheeled trucks trundled up to the stockpile and were loaded by Jotnar and Tumba workers. The trucks were driven along into the third warehouse and their cargo was dumped. There was so much activity going on that there was frequent shouting and gesticulating, and whistles to stop or start the trucks, depending on what was required. To Eyre, it looked like controlled pandemonium. The operation hadn't been going long enough to sort out any inefficiencies; they were only producing so much fibre quickly because they had so much labour.

Eyre and Pheria caught up with the rest of the students at the entrance to the third warehouse. The clatter of rain on the roof and the howling wind made it impossible to speak, so they communicated by telepathy.

"Whittaker Ray said he'd meet us down here," Nick said. "He stuck his head in at the huts to say hi this morning. He and Madame Overmantle have been housed over in the Management Quarters."

Inside the factory, an uncountable number of huge spinning wheels had been constructed, each mounted on a high seat like a penny-farthing bicycle. At every seat was a spinner, who, with deft hands and expertise obviously earned over many years, was transforming the wads of irregular fibres into silken blue thread. When the fine fibres came out the other end they were wound onto large spools, like fishing reels. The sight was mesmerising; the foot spinning the wheel and the hands carefully guiding the precious fibre, and producing a gleaming sapphire-blue thread at the other end. It was magical to watch.

Someone moved up beside the group and Eyre smiled when she saw it was Whittaker Ray.

"The production is going well," Whittaker Ray sent telepathically. "Faster than we were anticipating. One more day, Operations Management thinks, will be enough."

"As long as it doesn't all get blown away first," Abby sent, looking out at the tempest outside.

"Ah, no, they are well used to Terra Typhoons," Whittaker Ray replied. "But there won't be much going on until it passes. So I'll organise for meals to be delivered in to you, if you can figure out a way fill the time while we wait for it to pass."

"Not crystallography!" Eyre and Abby telepathed simultaneously as Beatrice's eyes brightened.

There were grins flashing around the group at that, and one by one the students teleported back to the common room in the middle of the huts. Eyre, Beatrice and Abby had a discussion and then came to sit down with the rest of the students in the lounge suite.

"We have something for you to learn," Eyre said to the group, passing around pencils and paper. "It's a code, the 'Wisdom's Code', and we think you should know how to use it. It's a secret way of communicating if you don't want your thoughts to be read."

"Why?" Rigmar said innocently. "Are you expecting trouble?"

They all chuckled and Beatrice explained to them how the code worked. And for the next three hours, they practised as if their life might depend on it, and indeed, it might. Tina had translated the code last year, and Nick had already been practising for a while, so the five of them helped the others to learn and practise it. They all picked it up pretty quickly, but Warrigal had to go and lie down in the afternoon to rest. Everyone was watching him as he left, but no one said anything. What could they say? Eyre thought. No one could work out what the problem was.

At sundown that night Whittaker Ray and Madame Overmantle came to see them as they were finishing up some pizza. Colton had just sent a message in code to Rigmar, saying, "I want the last bit," when Rigmar picked up the last piece and ate it. "Sorry, didn't quite understand that message," he said as he stuffed it in his mouth.

"You will need to pack up your bags tonight," Madame Overmantle said as she waited for them to clear the table. "The operation has been a huge success and we've estimated that we have more than enough thread for the capes."

Her eyes dimmed slightly as she added, "We do need you to number off as part of this troop, so in case of difficulty, you will know who is—uh—still there." She looked down for a moment and then continued. "Warrigal, you are 1; Eyre, 2; Beatrice, 3; Abby, 4. Nick—you are 5, Jax, 6; Carly, 7; and Pheria, 8. Rigmar, you are 9; Tina, 10; and Colton, 11. Learn your numbers and practise sounding off, please, in the next day."

Everyone nodded; it made complete sense. In a battle, yelling out names wouldn't work, as they wouldn't know who was missing. But their faces were serious as they memorised their numbers. This was getting serious.

"We will leave just after midnight tonight," Whittaker Ray added, "so please be organised. Does anyone have any questions or concerns?"

"Only that Rig ate my pizza," Colton said, his ice-blue eyes twinkling.

Whittaker Ray laughed and then he and Madame Overmantle disappeared. As the students were packing their bags, there was a knock at the door and Hec walked into the common room, carrying a pizza.

"Whittaker Ray said someone was wanting this?" he said, looking around. Hec gave a mystified look as everyone laughed and he put the box down on the table. "Mr Ray told me you're all going tomorrow—I'm sorry you're not staying longer," he said. "I barely got to have fun with you all! You'll have to come back."

Then he rolled his eyes. "Although not for the Graduate Fibre program —someone has figured out pretty quickly that it's a bad idea, and they're already sending people home! Management, hey. I could have told them that."

"It did seem to be a rather lot of work for not much return," Colton said cautiously.

"Best to use all that equipment for something more worthwhile, I'd say," Carly added.

"Well, I'll see you on your next trip to Terra," Hec grinned. "The Light be with you!"

He shook everyone's hands and Jax looked sombre as he watched the amiable Nemoris walk away.

"And with you, my friend," he said softly.

CHAPTER TWENTY-SEVEN

THE NIGHT WAS DARK when they gathered, sleepy-eyed, in the common room, with their bags at their feet. Eyre yawned as she looked out the shrouded window. Sometime in the night the typhoon had passed and the air was so still, it was as if it had blown so hard it now couldn't move at all. The light from the hut threw distorted shadows up the trunks of the trees to the leaf canopy, and Eyre could see an exhausted and buffeted Garman roosting high up in the branches. Normally a ferocious predator of Zhuzhu Flutters, the huge raptor seemed interested only in sleeping. The storm had been too much for even that savage hunter.

"I will take you to Boulia," Whittaker Ray said when he arrived, "and Madame Overmantle will help us to locate Plumipes. We hope it won't take long, but it's an imprecise method. Once we find our arachnid friend, Madame and I will begin to transport the fibres there from the warehouse."

Whittaker Ray asked them to hold hands and there was the familiar, dizzying sensation as they teleported in a flash of light. Eyre had spots in front of her eyes and her head spun. She wondered if she'd ever get used to the feeling.

From their discussions before they left, Eyre realised that she was standing on the Kennedy Developmental Road, or Highway 62, which intersected a stretching, dusty plain. It was cool before the sun came up, but the road still retained the heat from the day before. It was deathly quiet, and dark without the lights of a settlement to soften the darkness. Above her head the Milky Way scattered its stars across the sky, a cascade of shining pinpricks.

"What we're looking for," Madame Overmantle said, casting her eyes around, "is the Min Min lights. They are moving orbs that will guide us to Plumipes, if we are able to locate them at all. You need to be quiet and focus."

They moved their bags to the side of the highway and sat on them. Shooting stars streaked overhead in the tranquil night, but no one said anything. It was so huge out here; there was a reverential feeling and Eyre knew she wasn't alone in wanting to preserve the silence. An hour went by, then two, and still Eyre didn't see anything, other than a Letter-winged Kite that swooped low over their heads and on to its vast hunting grounds.

And then, Abby exclaimed. "Over there!" They followed her outstretched hand and saw two spectral orbs floating above the highway, dancing towards and away from each other. Occasionally they would shoot straight upwards, then skitter away sideways.

"Get your things," Madame Overmantle said softly. "And follow."

The glowing orbs moved inland and the students followed silently in a ragged line. Over rocks and scrubby plants, they pursued the ethereal lights, trying to keep their eyes locked on them.

And then the lights stopped and hovered, up, then down. Up, then down. Then they zipped off and disappeared, just as the first sliver of the sun edged over the horizon.

"Thank you!" Madame Overmantle called. She gazed at the empty space after the lights had gone, then turned to the students. "Some people in Entis think they are the reflections of car headlights, but we know better. They have given us the gift of Plumipes' location. Put your bags down, students, to remember the spot."

As instructed, they all heaped their possessions up to make an untidy and unlikely marker in the middle of the desert.

Now that the sun was rising, Eyre could see uneven ridges of sandstone rock stretching in all directions across the red sandy dirt. Veins of rough colour ran through the sides of the rockface; streaks of red, orange, black and yellow. All over the desert the ground was covered in dry, spiky spinifex clumps and dotted with pieces of rock that had broken off the geographical spine. Eyre shaded her eyes and looked up as a slow-flying hawk circled above, searching the dry grass for prey.

"So what do we do now, Madame?" she asked. "Do we wait?"

"Yes indeed; we wait for Plumipes to digest her dinner. She is a nocturnal hunter and will not want to be disturbed immediately after eating. But we need to find her burrow. So use your possessions as a central point, go in groups and search—quietly—for the entrance to her lair. You'll know it from the silken web around the opening."

Eyre, Beatrice and Abby took a line to the left down the rockface, and walked slowly along as the rest of the group searched in other directions.

"Great," Abby said, looking around apprehensively. "We've been wandering around in the night with a giant, hungry spider. Who might be grumpy if we disturb her too early."

"I know how she feels," Beatrice said, yawning.

"Well, I'm not sure how easy it will be to spot," Eyre said, examining the rocks closely. "Spiders are good at camouflage, I've heard."

"Fairly easy, I'd say" Beatrice yelped, her mouth clamping shut as she reversed suddenly.

In front of them was a cavernous opening in the rockface, about five metres high and surrounded by whiteish-grey strands of web. The opening was shadowed, but Eyre could see the web was constructed like a tube and led into the dark cave. From inside she could hear the disconcerting sound of crunching and scrabbling.

Abby's eyes were round. "Retreat!" she said. "Time to get Madame Overmantle!" And she spun on one heel and headed back the way they'd come. Eyre was quite happy to follow along, and she noticed that Beatrice's long legs were moving pretty quickly too.

"Great work, students!" Madame Overmantle said, beaming. "Well, everyone settle down and we'll wait an hour to make sure we get the kind of welcome we'd like."

Abby sat on the ground morosely. "I suppose we're actually going *in* there?"

Eyre laughed. "And I always thought Ischyros was the worst creature to be stuck in confined quarters with!"

As the students sat down to drink some water and have a snack, Whittaker Ray and Madame Overmantle disappeared. A second later they reappeared further down the cliff face, outside the spider's lair. Before them was a stack of spools wound with blue thread, and they left and returned twice more until there were thousands of reels of the blue thread neatly stacked outside the obscured opening. Along with the spools, there was a cardboard box with the flaps closed.

The sun was rising now and a heat haze hovered over the red dirt like a mirage. Madame Overmantle waved them over, so they packed up their bags and reluctantly went to join the lecturers.

"Well now, we won't all be able to go in at once. We'll go in four groups I think," Madame Overmantle said brightly. "So, who would like to go first?"

After a resounding silence, Jax put his hand up, looking sheepish. Eyre decided she might as well get it over with and raised her hand too, after which Colton, of course, was quick to volunteer.

"Right then, that's our first group—follow me!" Madame Overmantle picked up the cardboard box and walked into the massive hole as if she were walking into the library.

Eyre took a breath and followed her in. Madame set a lux floating above them and it cast a juddering circle of light that only made the journey more unnerving. Eyre's feet kept getting stuck to the web, and when she pulled them off, the strands reverberated, a tactile calling card for the monstrous spider lurking at the end of the tunnel. All the noises she'd heard earlier had stopped, but that only made her jumpier. The hairs on her arms stood on end as they emerged into a large cavern.

At first, she couldn't see anything. Then her eyes tuned in to a small glint of light and she realised, aghast, that it was an eye. One of eight, staring unblinking at them. Slowly, the gigantic creature crawled forward into the light cast by the lux and Eyre's heart nearly stood still. She knew it was a big spider, but not *this* big! It was the size of an elephant, with great brown hairy legs and hideous fangs that were at least a metre long. Two gigantic moth-like wings were folded up by the side of the spider's bulbous body, and Eyre couldn't figure out why, but the spider's back was moving. Then she realised.

"Dinner!" shrieked a tiny voice.

"Yum yum!" another cried, leaping on to Eyre's head.

Then the whole brood leapt off the back of the tarantula and came swarming over to cover the four of them.

"I should have mentioned that perhaps the first group might have a slightly more intense experience than the rest," Madame Overmantle said with a great display of understatement, as she daintily picked one of the spiderling's legs out of her mouth.

"*Children!*" rasped a desiccated voice. "Return!"

The swarm reluctantly abandoned the group and returned to their mother's back, jumping in excitement as they regarded their potential breakfast.

"Stay still," Madame Overmantle instructed.

Eyre stood still. She was so rooted in horror that she couldn't have moved even if she wanted to. Only her eyes inched sideways, where she could see Jax was looking a little green.

"What brings you to my lair?" the spider whispered in a voice as dry as the desert itself.

"We wish a favour from you, Ancient One," Madame Overmantle replied. "We would ask you to weave eleven cloaks from the magical blue thread we provide. These will allow our Lightworkers to enter the Underworld unseen."

"Magical cloaks?" the spider turned the words over in her mouth. "Very curious. And what will I receive in return?"

"I have something for your brood in this box. And we have manufactured three hundred extra spools of the magical thread, which we will leave you for use in your burrow. The thread is durable; you can reuse it when you move."

"And what is to stop me from killing you and taking everything for myself?" the great spider asked craftily.

"Then regrettably, I fear your possession of the wondrous thread would be short-lived," Madame Overmantle replied. "For, unless the Gothak are stopped, they will surely decimate the Overworld and all beings within it."

The eight eyes of the spider gleamed and one hairy leg scratched her abdomen as she thought about the proposal.

"Agreed," she said suddenly, and then her voice turned avaricious. "What is in the box?"

"Coats for your offspring," Madame Overmantle said and took out a knitted jacket. *Made out of clouds*, Eyre realised. She'd taken a coat just like that to the Ranger last year for Lenny.

The spider took the jacket daintily from Madame's outstretched hand and scrutinized the stitches with her eight beady eyes. "Fine work indeed," she breathed and then pushed the floating jacket back in the box. Then suddenly Plumipes became all business.

"Bring me the thread."

Madame Overmantle placed the box on the ground next to the immense spider and then snapped her fingers. Three hundred spools of thread appeared, stacked neatly against the back wall of the spider's burrow. She snapped her fingers again and another pile lay before her.

"Step up then, you flaxen-haired creature," the spider rasped at Colton. As he stepped forward, trying to appear unconcerned, the huge arachnid ran a spiked leg through his hair. "You, I would like to keep," she purred.

Eyre had never seen Colton look disconcerted before, and she found it very amusing. All it took was a giant arachnid for him to lose his aplomb.

As Colton stood still, the spider, surprisingly delicately, picked up a spool of blue thread and hung the hole in the middle on one of her legs. Then she began to turn it, faster and faster, until she could pull a line of thread out and begin to manipulate it between her other legs. Over and under, backwards and forwards, like seven knitting needles clacking at once, she spun and turned the gleaming thread. Occasionally, she stopped to measure up using her fangs, and Eyre thought that Colton, to his credit, did a good job of remaining calm under pressure.

Finally, the masterpiece was finished. It fell from shoulder to the ground, with a belt around the waist and a hood that would flip over and completely obscure the face. When Colton was wholly covered, all you could see was the sparkling sapphire blue of the stitching.

Plumipes sighed with satisfaction as she studied her handiwork, and turned Colton this way and that so she could have a good look. "I suppose I have to let you go," she said to Colton regretfully. "You're done. Out you go. *Next!*"

Jax gave Eyre a wry smile and moved forward. The ancient weaver was fast, and before long, he too had a custom-made robe and had left to join Colton outside.

As Eyre stepped up, Plumipes paused and studied her. "What is your Sector?" she asked, all eight eyes glinting. "I've not seen such a one before." She scrabbled forwards slightly and turned Eyre so she could see her arm better.

"Eyre is an Aether, and a form of Hese," Madame Overmantle said. "She is in our Management Sector."

The spider's eyes glinted. "Very strange indeed. I have heard of the Aether who found the Isars." Eyre said nothing, and tried not to react as the spider seized her and began weaving furiously. Around and around she turned until she was so dizzy she thought she would fall on her face. And then the spider stopped.

"Yes," Plumipes said. "That is nice."

Eyre looked down and saw that, unlike Colton and Jax, the spider had woven a raised letter into the front of her cloak on one side: "H" and on the other, an Inguz.

"You shall have a special robe for your service," the spider said.

"Thank you, Ancient One," Eyre managed to stammer, and then she was ejected as fast as Jax and Colton. She took her cape off to study it and marvelled at how lightweight it was, and how small it could roll up—it was only the size of a golf ball when tightly packed. A magical fibre indeed! As she flapped it open again, Beatrice came to examine the letter. After a moment she frowned.

"Ah... H?" she said. "What does that mean?"

Eyre snickered softly. "Ahhhh... horrified maybe?" Her eyes darted back to the entrance of the cave, as if she thought the huge tarantula might hear her, and then she continued whispering. "Probably Hese. Although, maybe Plumipes thought Madame Overmantle said my name was Hair, not Eyre!"

Eyre's eyes were mirthful as she examined the spectacular cloak and looked over at her lanky friend. "Probably not a good idea to ask for alterations, you agree?"

Beatrice's eyes glinted behind her glasses and she laughed out loud. She patted Eyre on the back as she returned the robe. "This is why you are part of the Eleven," she agreed. "Outstanding deduction!"

While the others took their turn walking into the dim aperture to be 'fitted', Madame Overmantle showed those waiting outside how to use their Viq to activate the invisibility in the fibres. It involved sending a 'sparkle' of light energy across the fibres, making them disappear. It was important that they could do this quickly, Madame explained, so they could activate or deactivate it in an instant if needed. So the students outside spent the time practising the 'sparkle'. Colton would activate Tina's cape, since she had no Viq, and solemnly they decided that if for some reason Colton couldn't do it, Warrigal would, and then whoever was next by number. It was a sobering thought and underlined the danger they were all facing.

For the rest of the day the spider toiled in her burrow, wrapping up her victims in cloaks instead of web. One by one they walked out in their gleaming capes, Rigmar most notably, because he had stumbled on the way out and gathered a swathe of web on his head before he'd managed to straighten up. He'd also accumulated a spider offspring, that scuttled down his back and scurried back inside as Rigmar emerged with the rest of his group. Beatrice guffawed as he jumped in horror when he felt the eight legs of the little spider rushing down his back. Although, 'little' in the realm of the Plumipes was still the size of a lobster. When he tried to wipe the sticky mess off his head, his hand got completely stuck and he looked like he was caught in a permanent salute. Pheria, normally so aloof, was hiccupping with mirth, but trying valiantly to hide it as she helped to release him, which took an awfully long time. Even when the worst of the web was gone, Rigmar's hair stuck out all over the place, and he looked like a cartoon character who'd put his finger in an electrical socket. Everyone was crying with laughter at his annoyance as he tried to smooth his hair back down, but it just wouldn't co-operate.

"Permanent hair gel, my friend! Looks good on you!" Beatrice choked, trying to keep her face straight as tears rolled down her face. Everyone fell about as Rigmar rolled his eyes and sat down, shaking his head.

"At least I lost baby Plumipes ," he said in annoyed relief, causing more laughter at the thought of the youngster who'd thought Rigmar's head was its nest.

"It could have made us 12," Colton said solemnly, and they all dissolved in laughter again.

Finally, by the time the sun was thinking about disappearing over the edge of the horizon, Carly walked out in her cloak, the final one.

The students stood together in their vivid blue cloaks as vermillion streaks painted the sky. Just before the light went completely, they saw a strange sight. A monstrous winged form, with a squirming mass on her back and clutching a web sac of blue thread and a cardboard box in her legs, flew low overhead and then off into the setting sun.

"She's moving again," Madame Overmantle said, watching the diminishing form until it disappeared. "No one ever knows where Plumipes is."

CHAPTER TWENTY-EIGHT

THE FIRELIGHT SENT UP sparks in the winter air as Jengles piled more branches on the matrix, sending the protective silver light beaming out over Highlight. His fiery red beard was plaited in two large loops and threaded with copper wire and garnets, symbols of war in the Mimir tradition.

He turned towards the students, who sat on sandstone blocks with plates of food on their laps. "Incendium was overrun yesterday and Professor Vela has led a contingent of Lightworkers to assist the Armatura in fighting the Gothak. Troops of Mimir are there also, but we have a force staying behind to protect the Domain and the Armament Stores. Our numbers were decimated by the surprise attack at the Academy."

Jax had been busy on the barbeque and he handed around a tray of well-cooked sausages as Jengles continued. "We do not know what the Underworld strategy is, or when they plan to use the Isars. But they have already wreaked havoc across the Overworld, and in Caelus and Incendium there have been many deaths.

"Whittaker Ray has explained what your plan will be, and we stand ready to send reinforcements should you need them. The way ahead for you is hard, and uncertain. Time is precious, and the Echelon has asked that you leave immediately after your meal."

Jengles, Whittaker Ray and Madame Overmantle looked at each other, and Eyre saw a look of deep sadness pass between them. Whittaker Ray stood up.

"The Echelon, and indeed the Determinant Dozen, have asked that I convey their deepest thanks for your courage, and what you are about to attempt for all beings of the Overworld. May the Light be with you."

There was a flash and the Sergeant appeared by the fire. "And remember also to *walk Lightly and carry a big stick,*" she said fiercely, as she walked around and hugged each student hard. For the first time, Eyre heard the

Sergeant close to tears. "I am so proud of you, my novices who have become the mightiest of warriors. Truly the finest of the Defence Force. Our Viq is with you on this journey."

After dinner the students sorted their possessions in the cabins. They had been back only a day, to rest but also to learn the prohemium to the Underworld, the most forbidden of secrets. Dr Botolfe had arrived yesterday morning and spent the day speed-teaching them the technique to open the smoking gates for their perilous journey.

It didn't take them long to master it; they'd already learned four prohemiums and it got easier each time. Their Viq was strong now, after four years, and their Halos should have been removed at the beginning of the year, as they were no longer necessary. But circumstances had interfered with the normal traditions, and the ceremony would probably be conducted at the end of the year—if they found the Isars, if there was an Academy left, if they were even alive, Eyre thought. So many ifs, it wasn't even worth worrying about. They would either succeed or they wouldn't. There were no half measures with this endeavour.

Eventually, they gathered back at the fire to begin their dark journey. So many hopes rested on their shoulders, Eyre thought, and she felt a frisson of dread travel up her spine. She looked around at her travelling companions, each one dressed in their shining blue cloak, and sent a prayer upwards. The Light be willing, they would all make it back.

When they were ready, each one of them sent a sparkle along the blue fibres of their capes, and the cloaks became invisible, hiding the students beneath them.

"Farewell, and be strong," Madame Overmantle called, as Abby performed the prohemium.

"Remember the shorthand," Abby said as a sinister smoking Seam appeared in the clearing. Jax stepped through first, followed swiftly by the others, hurrying before anything could come *outwards* from the Seam and back into the campsite. A minute later the Seam shut, and they were enveloped in an evil-smelling darkness.

As instructed, on arriving in the Underworld they stood completely still, with their cloaks wrapped tightly around them and their hoods over their heads, giving them time to get their bearings. The first thing Eyre noticed was how cold it was. For a place that was supposed to be elbow to elbow with Hades itself, she found that most surprising.

But she was suddenly overwhelmed by an uncontrollable panic. She found her breath coming in shuddering gasps and realised she was terrified; indeed, if she didn't calm down, she was going to faint from lack of oxygen.

She was just so afraid that the cloaks wouldn't work, and that they would be detected immediately, as the Mimir had been. But she forced herself to take a few deep breaths and eventually got her nerves back under control.

The tunnel they stood in was lit by eerie clumps of phosphorescent mould which grew up and down the dank walls. Acrid-smelling water oozed from the rocks and dripped down to splash on the tunnel floor, creating puddles that occasionally sizzled.

"Sulphurous," Beatrice sent telepathically. "We are indeed at the gates of Hell."

As they all hovered in indecision, Nick spoke softly, his voice dark. He pointed at some irregular purple clumps on the wall beside them. "Violite," he said. "Let's keep moving."

Remembering the evil power of the substance that came from the veins of the Underworld, they finally found their momentum and moved forwards.

Swirls of clammy mist curled around their ankles and drifted down the tunnel into the gloom, and occasionally a small, dark creature skittered away into the blackness. After they'd been walking for ten minutes or so, they reached a fork in the passage and Rigmar 'spoke'.

"All in all, rather charming, wouldn't you say? Which way, then? Left to Hell and damnation, or right to the abyss and torture?" Even Rigmar's telepathic voice had a smile, Eyre decided. He was determined to have a good time even in the bowels of the earth.

"The left one seems to be leading downwards, so I'd say left," Abby suggested. "Seems logical."

No one had any idea at this point, so they deferred to the strongest psychic in their team and chose the left branch, setting off down into the darkness.

A symbol suddenly filled Eyre's mind. Warrigal had been leading the way and he'd sent the Wisdom's Code for 'N'—*Stop!* In Terra, when they'd learned and practised the code, they'd decided on a shorthand method of communicating so that no one but they could understand it. 'A' was right and 'W' was left, 'I' was forward and 'E' was back. 'N' meant stop and 'M' was go. Visually the shorthand made sense, and was a lot quicker to send than convoluted messages.

The Code's Shorthand

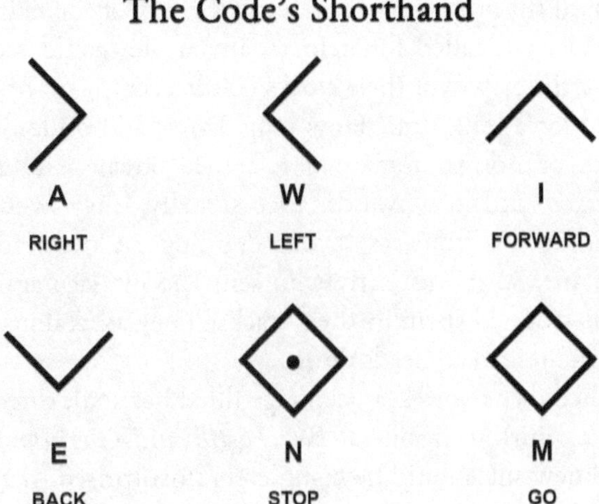

Still, it took Eyre a second to register what Warrigal meant, and she nearly collided with Rigmar, who was directly in front of her. The eleven of them stood deathly still, waiting to find out what Warrigal was warning them about.

Scampering down the tunnel towards them was a huge pack of sightless rats. They had misshapen lumps all over them, patches of fur missing, and their teeth were oversized and stained as they stopped and sniffed the air. Eyre felt nauseous as she looked at their deformed skin and sharp claws. She'd rather have one of Plumipes' offspring on her than one of those hideous creatures.

The rats took a step towards the group, who leaned hard against the tunnel wall. It seemed that they might have been going to investigate further, when a screech of pain came from further down the tunnel. Some creature in mortal agony, Eyre realised, and the rats charged off towards the awful sound.

Eyre let her breath out. She hadn't even realised she'd been holding it. Silently they all started moving again.

As they drew closer, the source of the screams became apparent. A rock had fallen on a Gothak, trapping his leg under it. Unable to move, the rats had taken advantage of easy prey and were feasting on the horrible assortment of his viscera that lay spread over the ground. The Gothak was still alive, but only just, and he wasn't going to last long. Obviously no loyalty between the creatures of the Underworld, Eyre mused.

They sidled by the dying Gothak as the rats gorged themselves, distracted by their banquet from the silent group slipping past. Eyre felt a huge relief when she realised that the Gothak couldn't see any of them; if he had, then surely he would have called for help to anyone he could see. It gave her comfort to have the power of their cloaks confirmed.

They walked for a long time. How long, Eyre had no idea, as there were no visual clues or normal frames of reference down here. She just kept trudging onwards and downwards. Occasionally, they would swap the person walking at the front, as it was draining on the leader to remain constantly vigilant. So it was Carly who sent the message again to stop, so urgently that it stopped them in their tracks. They all crammed against the wall and kept their cloaked heads down.

When Eyre heard the voices, a deep rage filled her soul, threatening to tip her over into a whirling madness. *Ben Perrill and Carrison Hamlen were here?* But she knew she should be completely unsurprised that the two foul boys were mixed up in this.

She gritted her teeth and kept her head tucked in, forcing herself to stay calm lest she give them all away. Carrison and Ben walked past the eleven Lightworkers without even realising they were there.

"He's down this way," Carrison said as he passed, and Ben responded with something unintelligible. "About an hour," Carrison continued. A sneer was in his voice as he added, "the Perseids aren't far now. And then all Hell, or should I say, all *of* Hell, will break loose."

Eyre wasn't sure what they were talking about, but she did believe that the Isars would be in the direction the boys were travelling. Carly obviously had the same thought, because she quickly sent the *forward* symbol to everyone. As Eyre pushed herself away from the wall a small stone tumbled down the rockface, and everyone froze.

"What was that?" Ben said, turning around sharply.

"What?"

"I heard something."

The two lumbering boys listened as their grotesque shadows flickered up the mould-covered walls.

"It's those rats," Carrison said. "They're everywhere."

After a moment, the boys began walking into the gloom again, and this time, unbeknownst to them, they had eleven silent, invisible shadows on their heels.

CHAPTER TWENTY-NINE

"THEY'VE GOT NO IDEA," Ben Perrill was saying as he laboured along the path behind Carrison.

Eyre didn't know what he was talking about, but she was sure he was right. They definitely had no idea about any of it—what was next, what to do or where they were going. All they could do was follow along as they were led deeper into the dank earth. Jax moved past her to take his turn at the lead, and the group silently followed the loathsome traitors in the Stygian darkness, as the path stretched endlessly on.

Finally, the gloom began to lighten slightly and Eyre could see a faint orange glow emanating from somewhere around the corner. The eleven students hung back slightly as Carrison and Ben disappeared ahead of them. Then they inched forward until they could see that the tunnel had opened out into some sort of space. Carrison and Ben were nowhere to be seen, so they hurried forwards in case they lost the two boys.

As they came out of the tunnel, Eyre couldn't help herself, and gasped out loud. They had arrived at an enormous crater; its convex basin tens of kilometres across. An orange glow was coming from pits of bubbling magma, which were interspersed all over the uneven floor of the canyon. Bright-orange molten rock hissed and jumped in the pits, occasionally shooting violently in the air with the force of a geyser, and then plopping back down again. A miasma of sulphurous air hung over the gaping gorge, and chunks of black volcanic glass were scattered over the irregular, steaming ground. The canyon seemingly had no end; it stretched as far as the eye could see. Who knows, Eyre thought dismally as her shocked mind tried to comprehend its size, it might fill the whole of the Underworld.

But the most spine-chilling sight were the Strigis that choked every inch of the terrifying valley. Gryllus Wetas crawled up the sides of the rockface, and Menax Lizards lurked by the sides of the boiling magma, oblivious to the spatters of burning rock that splashed on their thick hides. Eyre watched in horrible fascination as one of the ten-metre-long lizards chewed lazily on some long-dead animal, its feet hanging out the side of the lizard's maw. She heard the crunch as the ribcage was devoured, and then the feet were sucked noisily into the sharp-toothed mouth.

Eyre's horrified eyes saw the thick, scaled body of a Sublabor Pede disappear into a hole in the cliff face, its sharp legs propelling it deep into the mountain. Millions of red-eyed Zyx swirled and cried from above, swooping in to roost in misshapen, hairless blobs and hanging upside down with their powerful claws to cover the ceiling of the huge cavern. Unable to move, Eyre watched in shocked fascination as an old 'friend'—the Saevus—leapt from rock to rock, chasing a two-headed serpent as long as a bus. And a herd of Tuus Scorpions, dozens of them, clattered along the edge of the canyon below, their barbed tails curved over and poised to strike. There were thousands of lamprey-mouthed Characs, and a multitude of other vile creatures, for which Eyre had no name—grotesque and bizarre Strigis she had never seen before.

The immense size of the gorge, and the overwhelming numbers of Strigis, were beyond shocking. They were already uncountable, and yet more creatures were streaming relentlessly into the valley from somewhere beyond Eyre's eyesight. The eleven Lightworkers were struck dumb with shock and dread. How could the Overworld fight *this*?

Finally, Jax sent the code symbol for '*forward*' and Eyre tore her eyes away from the hair-raising sight in front of her. Far around the rim of the valley she could see two small figures walking steadily onwards. Carrison and Ben had followed a narrow track cut into the side of the mountain, and were heading for a dark tunnel further along the side of the basin.

As if the two boys could sense Jax's telepathic message, they both stopped and turned, looking over to where Eyre and her friends stood. They all stood stock still and Eyre scarcely dared to breathe. But after a moment, Carrison started to lead the way again. Thank goodness for the beryl orbuculum, Eyre thought. The secret it had revealed was their secret weapon down here.

They were about halfway to the tunnel when Carrison and Ben disappeared inside the tunnel. The students hurried to catch up, and it was then that disaster struck. Pheria's foot turned on a loose piece of rock and before she could save herself, she had tumbled over the side of the track. The edges of the mountain were sloped but steep, and covered in scree, and as she skidded down the loose rock, her robe flapped open, revealing her head and hands.

Desperately Pheria grasped for a handhold as a landslide of rock tumbled down beside her. The rumble of the rock caused the Strigis nearest the track to look up, and the Zyx screamed in rage when they saw the interloper.

"Pheria!" Eyre shouted. "Use your Viq!"

The panicked girl heard, and finally sent a stream of energy coiling towards the rocks above her instead of grabbing at the rocks with her hands. A lariat made of Viq looped in the air and then held around a boulder, stopping Pheria's frantic slide with a bone-jarring jolt.

But by then the Zyx had located her, and swirling masses of them had broken away from the ceiling and were plummeting towards the dangling girl.

"Cover yourself!" Abby screamed, all telepathy forgotten. Dazed, Pheria pulled her hood over her head and dragged the robe to cover her hands and body.

When she suddenly disappeared, the Zyx screeched in frustration. A couple of them were too late to stop their predatory dive, and smacked into the rocks beside Pheria.

Carly was already halfway down the cliff. Her strong frame and arms handled the gradient with ease, and she slid down carefully until she reached Pheria.

"The rest of you make a chain down the hill," she called. "Hurry!"

Because, by now there were masses of screeching Zyx above them, and the Saevus had turned away from the snake it had caught and was watching the cliff with great interest. It wouldn't be long before half the Strigis in the valley were on them, Eyre thought, as she desperately flung herself over the edge to join Carly.

Forming a human chain roughly by size, they reached Pheria. Carly held tightly around the exhausted girl's waist and then they all pulled her up using their Viq. The whole thing had only taken a few minutes, but it was now obvious that they were in trouble.

The effort of the rescue had caused a couple of their robes to slip, and bits of them were showing. Colton's arm had fallen from his cloak and Tina's hood had slipped off in the effort. Beatrice's long legs appeared through the front opening and Rigmar's face was uncovered from the effort of hauling Pheria up the cliff face. By the time they landed panting on the track, the air above them was dense with Zyx and the Saevus was bounding up the cliff face towards them. Menax Lizards had roused their sleepy bodies and were clambering over the rocks towards the track.

"Time to get going," Jax said tersely as everyone readjusted their cloaks. He sent a message in code saying '*up five metres*' and '*silence!*' then he put his arm around Tina and levitated quickly above the track, moving them both forward and out of range. The others followed as the Zyx landed on the pathway behind them and rooted around, searching for the prey they could smell but not see. The Saevus arrived and scattered the black scavengers, but it couldn't find the students either, who were now out of sight and up in the air. As the group moved forwards and back down onto the ground inside the tunnel, they left the frustrated Strigis behind, still searching for them.

"Are you okay Pheria?" Eyre asked telepathically as they stood in the darkness. After a moment the girl replied, but her 'voice' was wobbly, and Eyre felt for her. They'd all had a fright, but Pheria had almost rolled the whole way to the ground, and was probably hurting as well.

"I'll be fine," Pheria said. "Let's keep going." They headed along the tunnel without communicating, unsure now where Carrison and Ben were. There was only one tunnel though, so at least they didn't have to make any decisions on which way to go. Through the dark, foul-smelling and damp passageway, they walked for quite some time behind Nick, who was taking his turn at the lead. Eyre's anxiety was increasing by the minute. How would they ever get out of here? And what an incredible long-shot they were playing by venturing into the lair of the malevolent Gothak! They must be mad.

Suddenly, Nick stopped without sending them a message, and they all cannoned into each other. Then his telepathy reached them, a soundless shriek of '*STOP!*'

The tunnel had again opened out into another large cavern, and ahead of them was an area the size of a small city. It had a landscape of slippery, mould-covered rocks with dark holes carved into them, and pallid Gothak were coming and going from inside the holes in their strange sideways-forwards movement. Characs, with their scaled skin and wide-set eyes, lurked under the rocks and in the holes, their small, wide-spaced eyes glinting.

Like many-storied buildings, the rocks formed a terrace of tilted caves that stretched through the open space. Several Gothak sat on boulders and ripped at raw flesh with their sharp teeth; dining al fresco, Eyre thought with a shudder. Their dead eyes looked around incessantly, searching for prey no doubt, but they couldn't see the students who hid beneath their protective cloaks.

Eyre turned her head slowly, aghast, as she took in the expanse of black rocks and the erratic cityscape. It resembled nothing so much as a row of rotten, broken teeth. There must be thousands of Gothak in here; lurking, pale vampires skulking in the dark. With a surge of relief, she spotted Carrison and Ben in the far distance as they tramped across the open space. At least they had caught up to them. Then her heart fell. Their cloaks were powerful, there was no doubt of that. But would they get them across *here*? Despite her worries, one thing was certain—they were more vulnerable staying in the passageways, where someone or *something* might bump into them, so they needed to keep moving.

Eyre strode to the front of the line, ahead of Nick. She took a deep breath as she looked at the sight ahead.

"My turn to go first," she sent in code. "No point waiting, let's get going."

CHAPTER THIRTY

EYRE TOOK A STEP into the gloomy cave and held her breath. None of the Gothak looked up or even registered her presence. She sent a careful message in code, '*forward,*' and like an invisible caterpillar, the students stepped quietly into the cave. With their hands on each other's waists, they moved single-file through the dank city. Only the sound of flesh being torn apart by razor-sharp teeth could be heard; the students slipped by the hideous beings without a whisper of a breeze. Occasionally, a Charac swivelled towards them and tilted a large ear, but the Eleven remained undetected. Eyre tried to set the pace so they could all move with extreme care, but at the same time not lose sight of Carrison and Ben. Because one thing was sure, she didn't want to be stuck in this grotesque place any longer than necessary.

After walking for about ten minutes, Carrison and Ben entered a violite-covered rock building. Eyre felt sick as she stopped at the entrance to the hole they had disappeared into. What to do? On the one hand, they might be led to the exact things they were searching for. But on the other, it left them extremely vulnerable to discovery. And the sight of the violite was terrifying. She studied the shadowed entrance and then sighed. There was no choice, of course. All they could do was follow. She stepped forward into the shadows.

The entrance was short and Eyre sent up the '*stop*' symbol after only a few steps, because she could hear Carrison's voice close by. He seemed to be goading someone, and Eyre imagined it was Ben for a moment. But as she cautiously stuck her head around the corner, she could see that Ben was standing behind Carrison. The tunnel had opened out into a shadowed atrium that was lit by burning sconces, and around the walls of the roughly circular space were cavities hacked out of the rock and secured with thick iron bars. A prison! Eyre thought. So who was Carrison talking to?

"Nearly the Perseids, tenant," Carrison sneered. "Tomorrow's the day. No more excuses."

Ben walked over and kicked the bars of the cage. Eyre heard a scuffling, as if someone or something was backing away. Ben leaned forward and held the bars, thrusting his face close to them.

"And then we will open the gates to unimaginable chaos," he said in a menacing tone.

Before Eyre could gather her wits, both boys turned and started to leave —heading straight for the students. '*Up!*' Eyre messaged in code and the ten who could levitate headed instantly to the rock ceiling while Tina sidled along the wall out of the way.

Carrison and Ben passed underneath the students hanging in the air, oblivious. It was just as well they didn't look up or they would have seen twenty legs dangling above their heads. After making sure the coast was clear, they lowered down slowly to the wall where Tina waited.

Eyre hesitated, staring at the door where Carrison and Ben had exited. Should they follow? Then she looked in at the prison, her mind churning. But it was no decision really. They *couldn't* leave anyone locked up here. Get them out and send them home, and then follow the boys.

Moving quickly, she crept into the room. All the other cages were empty, and she couldn't see anything other than shadows in the one Carrison had been talking to.

"Who's there?" a croaky voice called.

Eyre was bemused. How could the person know they were there? She moved closer and peered in.

Her immediate response was overwhelming sorrow. An emaciated old man sat at the back of the cage, his white, scraggly beard hanging to the ground and curled in a snarled heap in the dirt. His eyes were milky and blind, and his gnarled, filthy hands reached out in front of him, feeling for the intruder he sensed was there.

"Quiet, old man," Eyre whispered, pulling her hood off. "Tina, can you help?"

"Who are you?" the decrepit creature cried, as Tina dropped her own hood and dashed over beside Eyre. "What are you doing here?"

"I am going to get you out and send you home," Eyre said in a low voice, as she put her hands on the heavy brass lock. "But you have to be silent. We only have a few moments."

Tina produced her lock picks from inside her boot, and then, concentrating hard, both Eyre and Tina began working on the lock of the cage. Tina probed inside the lock while Eyre sent a thin beam of Viq to assist in holding up the pin stacks as they were aligned.

"Standard Gothak issue?" Rigmar said with a laugh in his voice as he dropped his cowl to study them. The other Lightworkers followed suit and there was an expectant silence as Tina's hook picks clicked softly in the lock.

"Not sure why they bother really," Eyre replied, and she and Tina grinned at each other as the lock snapped open.

"Twenty seconds," Carly said. "Awesome work girls!"

The old man was bewildered and stood up unsteadily. "Who are you?" he asked again as he took a shuffling step forward. His rheumy eyes swung around sightlessly in a futile attempt to see them.

Eyre didn't answer him, not wanting to waste time with explanations, or to draw any attention from outside. So she quickly performed the Underworld prohemium. But the Seam didn't appear. She tried again with no success. What was wrong?

Suddenly, Abby exclaimed as her telepathic senses kicked into high alert. She turned to the old man and put a warning hand out to Eyre.

"Eyre, he's—"

But it was too late. There was a flash of light and an explosion, and all the Lightworkers fell to the ground. Running feet came from outside into the entranceway.

"Hide your cloaks!" Eyre sent urgently to her friends, and she pulled her cloak off, revealing herself, then rolled it up into a tight, invisible ball, and shoved it down her boot. The others understood. They had been discovered, but they wanted to keep the existence of the cloaks a secret. So by the time the Gothak burst through the door, all eleven students had shaken off their cloaks and were visible, standing in front of the old man. A tall, thin Gothak with a cruel face moved forward from the entrance.

"And who do we have here?" he whispered. "Lightworkers? *You're* a little off track, my dears."

"We've come for a Management Meeting," Nick said, and received a hard backhander for his trouble.

"I can see why you have so many scars," the Gothak said softly.

Then he turned to the old man. "Thank you for the alert. You may get back in your cage."

The old man obediently felt his way through the gate and back into the darkness at the corner of the cage. He sat down in silence as the Gothak slammed and locked the gate.

"Our tenant sent us a message to let us know we had guests. Good of him to give us a heads-up. So I will be off to let our—uh, what did you call it?—*Management* Meeting know. But first, let me arrange your accommodation."

The Gothak was enjoying this, and took his time opening up all the cells in the room. Then other Gothak shoved each student into a cell and locked the gates.

"They will not be so easy to get out of," he rasped. "Your prohemium will not work in here. It's much too far underground. We've had far tougher clients than you come and stay with us. The old man has tried innumerable times to escape, and we always catch him." The Gothak's eyes were cruel as he added. "He paid for his indiscretions, and he's learned the foolishness of attempting an escape. He has now wisely become one of us." Eyre's eyes flickered to the old man cowering at the back of the cage. He had so many scars on him that it was almost impossible to see any clear skin. Despite her rage at his betrayal, she felt a stab of pity.

There was a ruckus outside and the sound of crashing and snarling. A massive Gothak entered with a Saevus straining violently on a heavy chain. He tied the Saevus to an iron ring in the wall and then left. The Saevus snarled and gnashed its teeth and lunged at the cages, which greatly amused the Gothak in charge.

"I think he likes you," he said. "But I suggest you don't try and play with him. See you in a little while, my dears."

And then he left, obviously unconcerned about the captives mounting an escape.

Eyre turned wounded eyes to the old man. The treachery of his actions had rendered her speechless. She felt so stupid for endangering the mission, and of course their lives, like this.

"They know I will not leave," the old man said, speaking to the room in general. "No need for a lock at all, really." Then he turned his face towards Tina, who was already busily trying to undo her lock. "You won't be able to do that one. It's sealed with dark energy. If you unlock it, it will blow you up." How he knew what Tina was doing was beyond Eyre, but he seemed to have a sixth sense in the overpowering darkness.

The shrunken old fellow fell silent, and Eyre stood up and walked over to speak to him through the bars, asking him virtually the same questions that he'd asked her a few minutes ago.

"Who are you? And what are you doing here?"

But the old man seemed to be asleep. He didn't answer her and Eyre sat back down, trying to figure out a plan.

CHAPTER THIRTY-ONE

IT WAS A LONG night. The old man had been correct—there was no way to unlock the mechanisms that secured the cages. And try as she did, Eyre could not raise a Seam, and neither could anyone else. It just didn't work in here.

So they sat on the floor and talked telepathically all night, trying to come up with a plan.

But there was no way out of the current situation. They were locked in, and even if they did get out, the Saevus was waiting. And if they got past the Saevus, there was a whole city of Gothak out there.

"At least they don't know about our capes," Jax said in code. "We've *got* to keep that a secret. Leave them in your boots; let's hope we find a way to use them."

"And maybe it's good we're seeing 'Management'," Abby said encouragingly. "It might give us a clue of where we have to go next."

So they settled down and waited for 'morning'. It was impossible to tell the time of day, of course, but they had an innate sense of how much time had passed. None of them slept much. The snarling of the Saevus and the scamper of the horrid blind rats kept them awake most of the time. But strangely, now that they were in dire peril, Eyre felt calmer. Once they reached the point of no return the fear had disappeared.

"Bring it on," she whispered, as she huddled in the corner.

Many hours later, the gate to the building clicked open. A contingent of Gothak walked in, armed with Luxoccisors, the tall spears with the strange curved blade at the top. A contingent of subservient Characs followed behind, their greasy scales reflecting dully in the dim light. Creatures of the night who belonged in this abyss, Eyre thought.

The same Gothak who had spoken to them previously was at the front of the party and today he was all business, with none of the sneering joviality he'd displayed the night before.

He motioned for the huge Gothak they'd seen yesterday to unchain the Saevus, and it was dragged away down the tunnel. A short Gothak with a mohawk approached the cage doors, holding a flickering flame in a hammered brass lamp. He held the flame close to the brass padlock and an oily black smoke emerged from the keyhole and a foul stench filled the air. Then the black smoke was sucked violently into the lamp's flame in an explosion of green sparks. The short Gothak held out a grotesque key shaped like a malformed snake, and as it neared the keyhole the snake began to snarl and writhe, its leathery, lumpy skin moving as if something was creeping along beneath it. The Gothak shoved the head of the snake in the lock and it slithered inside. After a moment the shank sprang open and the misshapen head of the snake appeared as it slid back out of the keyhole. It wound its way through the bars to each lock until all of the brass contraptions were open, and the gates swung wide.

"Out," the one in charge ordered. The students walked forward and waited in the central area. The leader walked over and undid the old man's cage.

"The Perseids begin today," he snarled. "Time's up."

The scrawny, sightless man stumbled forward to join the Lightworkers. His beard was so long it trailed behind him in the stinking water, and if possible, he seemed even more frail than he had the night before. Despite his perfidy, Eyre couldn't help feeling terribly sorry for him. He was such a pathetic figure.

Three Gothak fell to the back of the room and three more stood at the front, flanking the students and the decrepit old man. The ones at the front led the way out of the building and the ones at the rear prodded the Lightworkers with their sharp blades, and they all stumbled out into the stinking city. Behind them trailed the Characs, mouths open and hoping for someone to fall so they could tear them to pieces.

For a long hour the Eleven walked through the stench of the mud and the carcasses of dead creatures. Over slippery rocks and through stinking mould until they were covered in filth that turned their shirts black. If anyone slowed they were prodded along with the curved blades and Eyre could feel a trickle of blood run down her back where one of the weapons had broken the skin.

But by far the worst-off was the weak old man, who struggled so much, it was apparent that he hadn't walked for a very long time. When he fell to the ground he was beaten with the spears and kicked until he got up again. Eventually he fell and lay face down in the putrid ooze and didn't move, despite the blows that rained down on him.

"Stop!" Jax shouted at one of the Gothak and knocked him into the mud, then stood in front of the old man's prostrate body. One of the Gothak smashed the end of his staff into Jax's cheek and he fell into the filth too. He quickly got to his knees, but a rage unlike anything Eyre had ever seen in him glowed violently from his eyes.

"It's not over yet, vermin," he said in a low voice as he stood unsteadily, wiping the grime from his face. He lunged forward again, but three enormous Gothak held him tightly, and he struggled violently as he tried to break free.

While they concentrated on Jax, Eyre ran forward and helped the feeble man to turn over. Then she sat him up. A tear ran down his cheek, tracking through the rancid mess on his face, and Eyre's heart clenched as she wiped the mud from his creased cheeks. In that moment, he reminded her of no one so much as Ischyros; old, weak and beaten.

"Don't give them the satisfaction," she said under her breath, and helped him to stagger back to his feet.

"If you want him to get there, you will have to slow down," she shouted, with fire flashing from her eyes as she swung from one Gothak to the other. "If you beat him again he will never get up."

The leader turned and looked at Eyre as if he wanted to beat her too. But he waved the Gothak back to the rear. "I am glad you are going to be watching the show," he said softly. "We will soon see how feisty you are."

Jax and Colton took an arm each and helped the old man to walk with them. But it seemed the Gothak had listened to Eyre, because the pace was slower and they managed to continue along the uneven track.

Then the path started to wind upwards and out of the vile, fetid city, much to Eyre's relief. The stench of the rotting carcasses and the sulphurous fumes had made her feel sick to her stomach, and there wasn't an inch of her that wasn't covered in the disgusting muck. She turned her weary eyes upwards and saw that they were heading to an edifice that looked completely out of place in this wretched place.

A massive gothic castle loomed from the jagged rocks; a demonic cathedral, constructed from severe planes of obsidian, with sharp spires and small black windows. It stood proudly with a cruel beauty, constructed from razor angles and harsh lines. The building looked like it was alive; the black, evil heart at the centre of the Underworld. Distant shrieks of agony echoed down the mountain towards them, and Eyre had no doubt that whoever was housed behind those small windows was suffering unspeakable horrors. She gritted her teeth and flashed a coded thought to her friends.

'Strength'.

As they neared the towering fortress, Eyre heard a soft, familiar sound. A haunting singing drifted down the bleak sides of the mountain and she struggled to place it. Then she remembered. It was the melancholy notes she'd heard last year in the Mimir's Domain, when one of the Isars was singing to the other. A song of such loneliness and desperation that Eyre took a deep, painful breath. The sound seemed so appropriate in this seemingly hopeless situation.

The lead Gothak stepped up his pace and led the group to the huge iron doors at the entrance to the castle. They were wrought with the faces of creatures in agony; snarling Strigis, and Lightworkers being decimated by ugly weapons. The Darkness celebrating its unholy successes.

As they approached the entrance, there was a clanking from within and the doors slowly opened. Inside, Eyre could see a huge crowd of Gothak standing and watching them silently, waiting for them to enter. A multitude of Characs were jammed in amongst the audience too, their oily scales gleaming and their black eyes glinting in the red light. Eyre knew they were hoping for roadkill; for someone to fall so they could feast.

As the Eleven were led through the doors, the Gothak drew weapons and beat them as they passed, and the silence was broken with a low-pitched, ominous chanting. "Eredicco, *Eredicco!* EREDICCO!" Eyre didn't know the language, but the meaning was clear. Kill, *Kill,* KILL! Over and over the words filled the huge chamber like a demonic roundelay. Long clubs covered with studs were bashed against the Lightworkers' arms and legs, and sharp spears poked bloody holes in their backs as they moved further up the hill. And then, one of the Gothak slashed the old man across his leg with a curved sabre. He staggered and fell to one knee as blood spurted from the wound. Warrigal turned with a look of searing rage. Before Eyre or anyone else could caution him, he had burned the Gothak to a screaming crisp, using a burst of powerful Viq that left Eyre dumbfounded.

Immediately, the horde fell upon Warrigal, beating him with their clubs and shrieking like a pack of snarling jackals. Eyre's heart almost failed her; she thought they would kill him, but the lead Gothak intervened.

"Stop!" he roared, swinging his club violently and smashing the Gothak away from Warrigal. "We need him alive."

Warrigal staggered to his feet, his arms and legs cut and bruised. One of his eyes was black and swollen, and he had a deep cut across his forehead that dripped blood down his face. He spat blood from his mouth and his eyes were wild. Eyre had never seen him this way; despite his injuries he looked ready for another round.

"Don't," she whispered desperately. "Be calm Warrigal."

Rigmar patted Warrigal on the shoulder and the Gothak gave a nasty, amused smile.

"Next time I'll let them continue," he said, as he turned and walked before them into the atrium. Carly, her eyes flaming, helped the old man up and they followed Warrigal as the Gothak prodded the students through a great stone door and into the castle.

Inside, at the end of a long passageway between tiered seating, was a large amphitheatre with a raised stage in the centre. Crowds of Gothak jammed the seating racks and spilled down to cram in front of the stage; a rabid pack of pale faces and manic, evil eyes, alight with black anticipation. An eerie red light lit the area, beaming down from glowing tubs of magma set high on the walls, and streams of molten rock oozed down the sides of the cathedral, creating weird channels in the poisonous mould that covered the whole interior.

A Gothak was speaking to the crowd gathered around the stage, and behind him, a stone throne was occupied by a hideous being. The creature emanated evil and power like a foul stench. Eyre recognised him—he was the grotesque creature she'd encountered in Terra almost three years ago. *Rhabdor.* The monstrosity who ruled the Underworld.

The Gothak pushed the Lightworkers roughly through the crowd, their passage accompanied by hoots and jeers, until they reached the front and were shoved onto the stage. Despite herself, Eyre's stomach clenched in fear because she recognised the Gothak who was speaking to the crowd. It was Mudamir, who had harboured a deep hatred of Eyre ever since she killed his brother Kaar when she was in first-year. Mudamir had already tried to abduct her from the Academy, and it looked like he was now going to get the opportunity to exact his revenge.

Eyre was disgusted at the sight of the malevolent, brooding being who sat behind Mudamir and grinned as the prisoners approached. Nothing good could come of this meeting, she was sure. But she raised her chin and walked with a straight back up onto the stage. *No way* were any of them going to see her fear.

The old man stumbled and Eyre caught his arm. His eyes turned towards her, almost as if he could see. "Thank you," he whispered. "I have been waiting a long time to meet The Eyre." Eyre was so surprised she didn't answer. How did he know her name? And when had he heard of her?

But Beatrice wasn't lost for words. "Well, *The Eyre* would be in a lot better position if it weren't for you, as would every one of us, including *you!*" she snapped, fearless even in these circumstances.

Eyre waved her to silence. She knew that trauma and isolation could do strange things to the mind, and she had already forgiven the old man. Who knew how long he had suffered on his own in that cage. And it was done now; what she needed to focus on was how to get the Isars and get out of here.

"And now, for the main event," Mudamir was saying. "Our entertainment for the evening!"

The Gothak pushed the Lightworkers to the edge of the stage and a roar arose from the audience. The old man was shoved so hard that he fell flat on his face before the throne. The jeers grew louder as he got to his hands and knees. For a moment it looked as if he might stay there, but then he managed to struggle to his feet. His face held such a desperate look of resignation, and a weariness so profound, that Eyre felt like weeping.

And then a strange silver glow started to shine from the cathedral door, and it tracked its way in, cutting a bright path through the red light. As it neared the stage, Eyre saw with dread that the light emanated from four Gothak, each holding a shining Isar above their head, and moving slowly through the crowded auditorium. It was an obscenity to see their filthy hands touching the sacred bars. As they passed through the horde, the vile creatures shouted in guttural grunts, and punched their weapons to the sky. It was spine-chilling, and Eyre felt an anguish permeate her soul. All was lost.

And it was her fault.

CHAPTER THIRTY-TWO

"BEHOLD! THE ISARS!" MUDAMIR roared to the crowd. "We have waited many years for this day; to reunite the four and claim the power for the Underworld!" The crowd roared its approval, their hoots and cheers filling the air.

The foul creature stalked around the Lightworker students with an evil glee.

"And we have an audience to witness the bestowing of power. Our thanks to these eleven illustrious students who have travelled so far to be part of the spectacle." More jeers arose from the audience as the Gothak laughed at the students who stood exhausted, bleeding and filthy on the edge of the stage. And then a deafening sound like thunder began, as the audience stomped their feet, over and over. As the noise increased, the grotesque creature sitting on the throne waved a languid hand for silence, and he stood up. The gross masses fell silent.

"Indeed, we have waited a long time," the misshapen thing said in a voice so low it could hardly be heard. He was nearly two and a half metres high and was huge of girth, covered in sores and pustules and suppurating wounds. His head was completely hairless and he grinned a horrible smile, showing rotten, malformed fangs. Eyre trembled, despite herself. The evil that emanated from him was a physical force.

"Behold, the Protector, the Betrayer!" Rhabdor pronounced, indicating the shrunken old man in the middle of the stage. "Bound as we were until the Perseids began, the Isars have waited until the stars were aligned. And now this man, who has waited decades for this moment, will regenerate the energy that once surrounded the earth, down below with us. With this power, we will conquer the Overworld!"

Aghast, Eyre realised that the innocuous, weak old man standing broken before her, was the Lightworker who had betrayed the Overworld and caused the 'Proditio', the Betrayal. He was the traitor who had tried to deliver the power of the Aura to the Gothak, which ultimately led to the Ranger breaking up the Aura. He had been here ever since, waiting to reunite the Isars once they were found.

"Kill him," Jax sent urgently in code. "He *can't* get hold of the Isars!" And before anyone could react, Jax's incredible reflexes had summoned his staff and shot a beam of pure energy at the bent old man. But surprisingly quickly, the ancient ex-Lightworker deflected the beam and it shot upwards, blowing a chunk of obsidian off the ceiling. The huge shard hurtled down into the audience and shattered, and Eyre could hear the screams of the Gothak that were impaled by the lethal fragments. And then, with a flash of blinding light, the old man disappeared.

Her initial shock gone, Eyre summoned her staff, blasting burning spears of light around the room. Nick now had his Antaraks in his hands, and all the other Lightworking students had weapons drawn, standing back-to-back as they faced the seething crowd, searching for the old man who had betrayed the whole Overworld.

"He's gone," Abby said between her teeth. "That old fraud."

"I'm sorry," Eyre said bleakly. "I have ruined everything."

"We'll take a few of 'em with us," Warrigal said, his battered face grim in the red light.

But there was a sudden flash and a dome of light covered them over, trapping them on the stage. No matter how they blasted with their Viq, or cut with their weapons, they couldn't shift the energy to get out and fight, let alone escape. Even Colton's mighty Mnae glanced ineffectually off the barrier of the shield. Panting, exhausted, they eventually stopped, realising it was hopeless. Nothing would budge the power of the light.

Eyre dropped her head and a desolation filled her soul as she saw the grimy old man reappear on the stage. The Gothak were jeering and laughing, vastly amused at the impotence of the students, and entertained greatly by their despair.

And then the worst cut of all. Led by Gothak guards, striding through the crowd were Carrison Hamlen and Ben Perrill. They swaggered along with their arms above their heads, carrying a black, rough-hewn metal box, half the size of a coffin, between them. The sides of the box were decorated with pewter images of snarling beasts and the faces of Lightworkers contorted in mortal agony. Like conquering heroes, and playing to the loathsome crowd, Carrison and Ben strutted, energised by their gross importance. The guards mounted the stage and put the Isars in front of the Betrayer. Carrison and Ben, struggling with the weight of the hideous box despite their bravado, walked up the short steps too, almost stumbling as they placed it at Rhabdor's feet. A horrible premonition travelled down Eyre's spine as she watched Carrison slide the lid off the box. Then he and Ben reached in and pulled out a huge, pulsating black object, and placed it beside the box. Eyre shivered as she looked at the repulsive thing that resembled a diseased brain more than a rock. *The Egeo Blackstone!* The Blackstone throbbed on the stage like a living creature, dark and malevolent. All the students could do was watch with desolate eyes as Carrison and Ben walked across the stage and stood at the side, grinning maniacally as they waited for the show to begin.

Eyre looked at Carrison and, despite her own despair, was gobsmacked to see how he had changed physically. At some point since she last clapped eyes on him, he had morphed into a bloated, boil-covered, red-eyed demon, uglier even than the Gothak. Maybe not so surprising, she thought dismally, as the last of her resolve flickered and died. This was, after all, the well-known fate for a Lightworker who rejected Lightness—to become a malevolent chimera of dark heart and evil energy. How could they have a chance against this overwhelming force? With a dread feeling that time itself was about to end, she saw Ben gibbering in glee as he watched the bent old man, the *Betrayer*, approach the Isars. So, the Betrayer's heart had not provided the Egeo Blackstone, despite the fact that his soul was black enough to do so. It was hard to think that there could be any creature more foul, more traitorous than this one. So where did it come from?

Rhabdor sat back down on his throne, ready for the spectacle, a gloating smile on his deformed face. The grimy, decrepit old man walked up to the Isars in front of Rhabdor and gave an obsequious bow to the leering creature. Then the Betrayer—not the *Protector*—Eyre thought furiously, seemed to make an effort and stood up straighter. Looking out at the hundreds of creatures before him, he spoke in a raspy voice, no longer the feeble wreck that Eyre had helped out of the stench on their way to the castle.

"The Perseids had to begin in order to reconstruct the energy of the Aura," he proclaimed, lifting one of his thin, wrinkled arms in a victory fist. "Today is the first day of the Perseids, so we can *finally* begin! Only the Protector is able to regenerate the Aura. The secret I have guarded, the means to reform this singular energy force, is to create the rune of the Inguz by using the Isars. Thus, the inert Isar, the rune of stagnation and blockage, will be transformed into the Inguz, the rune of harmony and fertility—of the ultimate power!"

Silence had fallen over the auditorium as the Gothak hung on the old man's words. His filthy beard dragged on the ground as he picked up one Isar and crossed it over the second.

"The Isars were hidden in four Alterworlds by one of the Thantos Nex, the most notorious, and indeed, awfully *terrible*, 'Fallen One'," the Betrayer said, laughing, as he placed a third Isar on top of the others.

"Yes indeed, he did fall a very long way!" Referring of course to the Ranger tumbling from the sky after the Aura exploded. The whole crowd of Gothak guffawed at the Betrayer's words and Eyre's fury rose. The sound of that skinny, disgusting man making fun of the most courageous soul Eyre had ever met made her want to blast them all to pieces. But she was trapped inside the dome and all she could do was clench her hands ineffectually as the Gothak sneered. Playing to the audience, the Betrayer sniggered too. "Oh what a traitor! Appalling, really, how some people behave."

The whole crowd hooted and grunted and cheered, and the misshapen being on the throne lifted one lip, revealing horribly discoloured fangs, as if he approved of this japing. Playing to his audience, the skinny old man grinned as he considered the first three bars on the stage before him.

"Until this auspicious day, these powerful forces were unable to be reunited."

It was then that Eyre heard a sound; a soft wail of terror. She was confused, but then she realised—it was coming from *the Isars*. They knew they were in mortal danger and were sending out panicked cries for help.

The Betrayer picked up the fourth Isar and held it aloft. "Finally, the Isars are together as they were intended! All energy to the Underworld!" His voice rang out through the red-lit room and echoed from the obsidian walls. He looked directly at the students under the restrictive dome and spoke to them by telepathy. "Say hello to Doron Helios for me."

"NO!!!" cried Eyre in despair as the Betrayer lowered the final silver bar, and the Isars shrieked in fear. Rhabdor stood up in anticipation and the Gothak in the audience hooted deafeningly.

And the Betrayer placed the fourth Isar on top of the other three to form the Inguz.

For a second the auditorium was filled with an incredible golden glow. Then, with a violent eruption, the whole place exploded with a power that rivalled Mt Incendius itself. The stage caved in and a violent, fiery blast roared outwards through the building. Under the dome of energy, the Eleven were protected, but the rest of the room did not fare so well.

Carrison Hamlen was engulfed in a tornado of fire and disappeared with an expression of abject terror on his deformed face. Mudamir had dived sideways at the first sign of the explosion, but lay inert, face down at the edge of the room where he had been blown by the shockwave. Hundreds of Gothak lay dying on the ground, surrounded by the carnage of missing limbs and spurting black blood. There was no sign of the Egeo Blackstone on the fractured stage. And the Betrayer was gone, blasted into pieces by the detonation.

The students had been thrown painfully to the floor by the force of the blast, and when it was over, the energy shield was gone from above them. Eyre's ears were ringing so badly she couldn't hear a thing.

"What just happened?" she called telepathically to her friends. "Where is Rhabdor?"

They staggered around, trying to get their bearings. The force of the explosion had caused Eyre's thoughts to spin like a vortex, and she fell to her knees.

And then, with startled, intense fury, she caught sight of a familiar lumbering figure, stumbling amongst the ruins and debris, and climbing over the mangled corpses of the Gothak.

How did Ben Perrill survive? She was horrified and incensed that he was still alive; it just didn't seem right! She watched him rooting around and digging in the rubble like an opportunistic looter, and violent rage filled her mind. It was so unbelievable; he *absolutely* shouldn't be alive—he, *so* unworthy, and yet still with luck on his side. When so many brilliant

Lightworkers had sacrificed their lives for the good of the Overworld, it seemed the ultimate travesty.

Exhausted, she slowly put a hand on the burning ground, despite the pain, and lifted one leg up in the ashen ruins, steadying her foot to stand. It was a gargantuan effort, and she hung her head to breathe before she finally lifted her glowing, golden eyes and sent a pulse of Viq through the destroyed chamber. *Come!*

Eyre's staff flew from across the smoking black rocks and into her hand as she staggered to her feet and turned towards Ben Perrill.

What was he doing? she thought, as she turned the gleaming pink crystal atop the rainbow branch towards her hated foe. Her head was spinning and her eyes couldn't focus, but she stumbled through the ruins towards him. Groggily, she sent a stream of energy blasting towards Ben, and he looked up in horror as the energy beam smashed into the wall beside him. She shook her head to clear her vision, determined that her next shot would hit its mark.

But fortunately for him, a flood of Gothak began to pour through the doors. Ben Perrill held a shining Isar aloft as the first Gothak reached Eyre.

"Bad luck, Lightward," Ben sneered, as he collected the fourth Isar. "That's the last one!"

And he shoved it into a backpack with the others, and charged out the doors as Gothak and Characs swarmed over the Lightworkers.

CHAPTER THIRTY-THREE

"FIGHT!" JAX SHOUTED, AND summoned his staff. Galvanised by hope, the others moved fast too.

Eyre's rage at Ben Perrill was bad luck for the particular Gothak who had grabbed her shoulders. Without even a spark of fire, he dissolved straight into dust at her feet. Not even looking at that, and with her Mnae raised, she turned her gaze to Ben Perrill, desperately trying to keep track of him. But he disappeared out of one of the many broken walls, and as the hordes of Gothak and Characs swarmed in, she could only raise her staff and prepare for Multiple Clasis.

"We can get out the window up there!" Rigmar cried frantically, pointing way up the wall as he blasted a dozen Gothak with his staff.

Together, the Eleven fought ferociously, cutting down the vile Underworld creatures as they drew close. Gouts of fire blasted from their staffs, and any that got within range were sliced in two by the formidable Mnaes.

"Vile. Foul. Mongrels." Beatrice shouted, cutting a Gothak down with each swipe. Eyre had summoned Vulture Killer, and had passed the precious bow to Tina, who was dropping Gothak and Characs with every shot. The rest of them were using Multiple Clasis to wreak havoc on any Gothak who approached: using staff, Mnae, Antaraks and Kulbeda.

The reek of sulphur, and the particularly foul stench of Gothak and Charac blood, filled the air and corpses were heaping up in front of them, but it seemed to be a hopeless battle—there were just too many of the vile Underworld creatures. Only the smoke billowing from the burning stage saved them from being completely overwhelmed—the Gothak couldn't see them properly in the haze and fumes.

Then a message came blasting through in code from Abby, the most powerful telepath of them all.

Eyre's wild mind struggled for a moment as she tried to focus while swinging her staff around, scorching several Gothak into tumbling embers, as the symbols from the Code shone painfully in her mind. And then suddenly she worked it out. Of course! *Capes!* Thinking swiftly enough so that no one else would understand—Ben Perrill most of all—Abby had sent the message in code so that the Gothak would not realise that the Eleven possessed such a powerful weapon.

Eyre pulled her cape out of her boot and sent a wild blast of Viq from her staff arcing in front of her, providing a distraction while she swung the supple garment up and over herself. Several Characs were charred into a heap in front of her as the cool blue drape floated around her shoulders, and she crouched down, sending a sparkle across the fibres, and hoping that what she'd done hadn't been noticed. Her disappearance didn't seem to have been noted by anyone—Lightworkers or other—the battle inside the demonic cathedral was total chaos. Eyre raced to the side of the smouldering building and heard a voice in her head again. This time there was no need for code.

"*Blast* 'em!" an invisible Abby bellowed from beside Eyre's shoulder, and Eyre needed no further encouragement. Together the cloaked friends raised their staffs and sent deadly streams of Viq from the glowing crystals at the top of the sturdy branches. Any Gothak that entered the ruined castle doors were incinerated the moment they arrived. The obsequious Characs proved their cowardice;, once the conflagration began, those inside tried to scuttle to safety, and no more attempted to enter.

This respite gave time for the Lightworkers to dispatch the Gothak inside the interior, and then they swiftly covered themselves in their cloaks. Seconds counted, and as smoke spun upwards from the glowing embers of the conflagration, the students gathered at the wall as fast as they could.

"Wait, are we all here?" Colton asked, and they counted off.

"1," Warrigal sent into the ether. Telepathic voices followed quickly. "2,3,4,5,6,7, 8..." There was a horrified pause as everyone waited, and then a feeble voice cried, "9!" as Rigmar pulled himself from beneath a smouldering beam of ebony.

"10, 11!" Tina and Colton finished off, and Eyre felt a wild exhilaration flood through her. They were all still here! By the Light, they still had a chance! And then a seething rage filled her whole being as her hot eyes searched the area around her friends with a burning certainty. These foul, underground creatures did not walk Lightly, and she was determined to introduce them to the *big stick* the Sergeant had made them experts in, as soon as possible. She twirled her mighty staff around and it felt *good*!

Sending a beam of light from her pink diamond like a laser, she pointed upwards to the arched windows in the walls high above them.

"Quickly, before more of those mongrels arrive—let's get up there!"

Eyre levitated up to the window frame and she used her staff to blast a hole through the glass. Then she leaned back into the building and beckoned to the others below.

"Come on!" she screamed telepathically. "Quickly!"

One after the other, the others flung themselves through the air to reach the window, as Eyre sent burning missiles downwards to create more smoke and confusion. Tina did a perfect tumble in the air, using the momentum to launch herself up the wall of the cathedral. Cracks in the obsidian, and the sconces embedded in the rock provided purchase as she clambered upwards. Soon, they were all perched precariously outside on the roof as the horde of Gothak surged underneath, piling into the building.

Zyx were starting to fly above and there were signs of other Strigis being summoned to the fortress—the Eleven could hear the hair-raising screams and roars of heavy creatures thundering up the mountain. And the revolting Characs were beginning to regroup at the bottom of the slope.

"Time to move," Nick muttered unnecessarily.

Jax walked gingerly over the steeply-pitched roof to the back of the building, and after a moment he sent a telepathic message for them to follow.

"We can get down over here," he said. "They haven't come around this side yet."

"We've got to find Perrill," Eyre said, frantically scanning the pathways for the lumbering boy. "He's got the Isars."

Jax was already descending, sliding down the roof and then using levitation to slow his fall to the ground. "We'll find him. But first we have to get out of here."

Eyre slid down after Jax and the rest followed, landing heavily on the ground. Nick cut his arm on one of the obsidian corners, which were as sharp as a knife, and he was bleeding heavily as he landed on the ground beside them. Abby wrapped her belt around the wound as they waited for everyone else to descend.

"Another scar," Nick said wryly as he tightened the belt. "Good. I don't have nearly enough." Abby's bright blue eyes glowed, and she kissed him softly on the lips as the others gathered together.

Everything had happened in such a panic and in such a short time that Eyre's head was ringing and she was still trying to collect her thoughts. The old man had saved them, that was clear, but they were no better off, as they now had to find Ben Perrill somewhere in the abyss of the Underworld. It was such a huge, impossible task that it seemed pointless to try.

But she had made a decision. "There is no need for us all to die. You go back and get help. I'll search for Perrill. It's probably going to be futile anyway. He could be anywhere, and I don't want you to die because of my mistake."

The other ten students were silent and then Rigmar laughed. "If you think I'm going to miss out on all the fun, think again! You're stuck with me."

"As if," Beatrice said hotly, and Abby linked arms with her and Nick. Warrigal just grinned out of his poor, smashed face, and Tina and Carly high-fived.

Pheria smiled wryly. "I wouldn't be much of a friend if I deserted you," she said.

Colton looked intently at Eyre with his ice-blue eyes. "None of this is your fault," he said softly, and wiped a smear of mud from Eyre's cheek. Eyre knew he was only offering support, but Jax's knitted eyebrows moved slightly downwards.

However, Jax just nodded. "We all signed up for this. Let's get going, and find that mongrel Perrill."

They sidled around the building, hiding amongst the boulders and the foundations of the fortress as the Gothak searched furiously for them below. In the chaos and confusion, none of the Gothak seemed to realise that the group had exited out the window.

"That way," Jax whispered, indicating the ridge line that ran around the valley where the castle stood. In the distance a black hole signalled the beginning of one of many tunnels that dotted the walls of the basin. "They're focusing the search down below, and if we can avoid the Zyx we might make it to the tunnel up there. We have a head start, but we're going to have to *motor!*"

"Wait a minute," Colton said. He stood stock still and concentrated hard. After a moment, from across the valley there was a loud rumble and a jolt of seismic energy that shook the ground. The walls of the cliff face began to tumble in a violent landslide. The rest of the Eleven stared at Colton, astonished. The power to create such Viq was something they'd rarely encountered. Eyre began to wonder if practising with his Lighthorse was the only thing Colton had been training for in secret over the past years.

"My man," Rigmar said in an awed tone. "You're on my Gympie gold-prospecting team next year!"

As the cliffs continued to split apart the Gothak roared and stampeded down the mountain, shaking their weapons in the air and thundering back into the stinking city. Hordes of Characs scurried behind them, teeth bared in their cavernous mouths, hoping for a feast. Then the Strigis were sent out, and their savage screeches made Eyre's blood run cold.

"Come on!" Jax urged, and bending low, he started to run up the side of the mountain. "Keep your cloak tight and your eyes peeled for Ben; he can't have gone too far."

The group raced desperately up the side of the mountain, moving as silently as they could over the rocky terrain. It was hard work; they were clambering almost vertically in their efforts to reach the track. Eyre's chest was heaving and she continually scanned the terrain to see if they'd been detected. They finally reached the rough-hewn path and started for the tunnel. But Eyre knew they were in incredible danger; they would be completely exposed now to anyone to see who might look upwards and see a foot or arm escaping from a cloak.

They made it three quarters of the way when there was a scream of fury that reverberated around the whole valley. Carly's hood had slipped off for only a second before she pulled it back up, but it was enough.

"Come back you cretins!" Mudamir shrieked as he staggered from the side of the castle. The unruly army of Gothak, Characs and Strigis stopped dead in its tracks, halfway across the city.

Eyre looked back at the foreboding castle. Mudamir was leaning against the broken front door, black blood cascading down his face. A look of intense madness consumed his face, contorting his features so it seemed that something was crawling under his skin. He focused intently on the track where he had seen the glimpse of Carly's head. With a flick of his wrist, Mudamir hurled a comet of atra at them, and it blasted into the side of the mountain with a scorching *boom*.

"RUN!" Jax shouted, and he frantically ushered Tina up the track. Tina didn't need encouraging, she raced along the uneven ground at incredible speed. Eyre put her head down and sprinted as fast as she ever had, as a swarm of Zyx swooped down towards them, locked on to their scent. Jax brought up the rear and fired his staff at the horrible creatures as they plunged, their venomous claws extended.

Jax was last into the tunnel and barely made it through when the Zyx reached the opening. Some of the foul beasts tried to follow, but he incinerated them with a blast of Viq, and they died in a screeching heap.

"We need to find somewhere to hide and regroup," Eyre called desperately.

"Should we split up maybe?" Beatrice suggested as she dashed along the path.

"No," Warrigal said emphatically. "We need to stay together."

Amid the mayhem, Colton was the calm voice of reason.

"We've been discovered," he sent telepathically. "And we have no idea where Ben is in this endless, monstrous world. We have lost our advantage. We need to get out of here. Nothing is served by our deaths. There is nothing noble about sacrificing ourselves without reason. We must go, and live to fight another day. That is the basic tenet of Tego, of Defence, which we've all learned is a strategy in itself. We have our capes, and we can come back. The Sergeant would not be proud of us for being stupid."

There was a silence in which Eyre once again felt the weight of the situation she had caused. If only she had remained hidden from the old man. They could have stayed undetected and followed Carrison and Ben, possibly to the Isars. Her single disastrous decision had brought them to this.

Rigmar, the ultimate tactician, was the first to agree with Colton.

"Colton's right. There's no point dying senselessly. We've got to get out and report back to the Echelon. Which means we have to find the tunnels that go the fastest way upwards to reach a point where we can generate a Seam. Stop a minute and look."

Heaving with exhaustion, they stopped their mad run along the passageway while Rigmar generated a lux. It bobbed along the tunnel, sending eerie shadows around them. Hundreds of the filthy, blind rats scampered along the ground and many of them sat and waited, their noses quivering. Waiting for something to die, Eyre realised with disgust.

Eventually they located a hole in the roof, a rough tunnel that headed straight upwards.

"Go!" Jax urged, and Nick levitated into the hole, checking ahead of him for any threats. Then he put one foot on either side of the narrow tunnel and began to climb furiously. Carly followed, dragging Tina behind her, and then the rest of them flung themselves upwards. Rigmar pulled his lux into the fetid hole with him and Eyre could see that the passage did indeed go straight up, too far to see. She launched herself into the tunnel behind Warrigal and then Jax followed. Colton, being the largest, was the last one in, and he pulled a rock upwards from the tunnel below and wedged it tight with Viq to block access.

Then there was a mad hour of climbing vertically, using the sides of the passage to lever themselves upwards. It was gruelling and slow—rushing did not work on the slippery, mould-covered surfaces. All of them were burnt and bruised and bleeding from the fight in the cathedral. They were wounded and exhausted, and Eyre could feel her Viq failing. It was an arduous ascent through the bowels of the earth.

They had to take their time to make sure their feet didn't slip and send them crashing onto the others below them. And all the while, as she struggled upwards, Eyre had a terrible feeling that Mudamir was going to come blasting in and kill them all. The thought gave her enough impetus to force her shrieking muscles into further action, to keep putting hand over fist beyond the limits of her quivering body.

Finally, when she thought she couldn't climb another inch, the tunnel curved around horizontally. When they finally clambered out, all completely covered in slimy, stinking mud, the Eleven lay for a few minutes on the tunnel floor, completely spent. The heat from the lava below, and from their exertions, was almost unbearable, and they flipped their hoods off to try and cool down as they lay flat on their backs and gasped for air.

Eventually, groaning with the effort, Rigmar leaned against a rock and got to one knee then tiredly waved his hands in the prohemium for Entis. A smoking Seam appeared. Everyone gasped and sat up slowly.

"Thank the Light," Beatrice breathed, wiping her sweaty hair from her brow as she staggered to her feet. "We're high enough. Let's get out of here!"

But then the Seam was snuffed out.

"Oh, I don't think you want to thank the Light," a rasping, repellent voice drawled. "Not any Light down here, my dears." The Gothak leader from the prison moved forward, followed by Mudamir, who grinned at them without a trace of humour.

"Don't worry about hiding now. I know you're here, and I am going to enjoy this," Mudamir whispered, and moved forward, as an army of Gothak crowded the tunnel behind him. Eyre turned and looked behind Colton, and saw an equal number of Gothak flooding up the vertical shaft and into the tunnel where the students stood. They were trapped! After long moments of willing her mind to find a way out, Eyre resigned herself and summoned her staff. It snapped into her hand and the pink diamond glowed. She prepared to die fighting to protect her friends.

"I'm going to enjoy it too, you sickening creature," she said in a steely voice, and blasted a stream of raging pink fire from her staff. Mudamir ducked and his features contorted in rage as he sent a blast of atra down the tunnel towards them. Carly deflected the burning fire with a snap of Viq, and it rebounded past Mudamir and scorched through the pack of Gothak behind him. Shrieks of agony and the acrid stench of burning flesh filled the air.

"Attack! DESTROY THEM!" Mudamir screamed, and the deathly figures at both ends of the tunnel ran towards the students.

"For the Light!" Jax shouted, and they all echoed as one. "FOR THE LIGHT!"

But before they could move, the ground began to shake. The path broke apart and rock from the ceiling exploded and rained down into the tunnel. *'Shield!'* Colton yelled telepathically, and on hearing the panic in his normally controlled voice, Eyre performed a shield faster than she ever had in her life.

And just in time. A Sublabor Pede smashed through the ranks of Gothak at the rear of the tunnel and crashed its way towards the students. It opened its massive mouth and swallowed Colton and Jax. Eyre fell heavily to the ground and tried to blast the creature, but the ground was moving so erratically and she was tossed around as the horrible beast scrabbled rapidly towards her. Her staff was wrenched from her hand by a fall of rock and then darkness engulfed her as the Sublabor swallowed her too.

Eyre had a strange feeling of falling, of being tossed around and smashed flat. An awful burning liquid surrounded her. Was this how she was going to die?

But Rigmar's voice filled her head. "Make a Bullio shield around you! Blow the acid out of the bubble! I'll get Tina." Blind, and with acid burning and blistering her skin, Eyre simply obeyed, unable to do anything but follow Rigmar's instructions. She floated in the empty Bullio, now protected from the stomach contents, but her skin was still covered in the searing liquid.

"Who's in here?" Abby sent desperately, between her screams of pain.

"All of us," Carly said, groaning. "We need to blast out of here!"

"Hang on, I'll do it," Jax said, coughing weakly. "We don't want to hit each other."

Eyre was overwhelmed by mind-numbing agony, and she tumbled over and over, her protective Bullio rolling her around in the juices of the Sublabor's stomach. "Hurry up," she thought. "I don't think I can survive this."

Through the searing pain, another voice slowly entered their minds. "Be strong," Madame Overmantle called to them. "Stay there for a few more minutes. Be still."

And the Sublabor smashed its way upwards, through the Gothak and the rock while the students shrieked in agony in its stomach.

CHAPTER THIRTY-FOUR

EYRE HAD NEARLY PASSED out from pain and the exhaustion of maintaining the protective Bullio, and the voices of her friends had died away one by one. She felt herself spinning through the Sublabor's stomach, enveloped in endless torture. She knew she had to listen to Madame Overmantle, but she wanted an end to this horrible torment. Each second that passed was beyond excruciating.

Just when she felt she could bear it no longer, the monstrous creature heaved itself, and Eyre could hear the smashing of rock as it broke through a huge impediment. It was still for a moment, and then its stomach started to contract and Eyre heard Pheria let out a piercing cry. Soon she too was mashed by the contraction of the stomach, and she was expelled explosively onto the ground. Her Bullio evaporated and she lay, unable to move, as the other students were deposited on the ground beside her. Every part of her body was screaming in agony and she felt she was close to death. Her frantic eyes roved over the bodies that lay nearby, and she could see that all their hair was burnt off and their skin had peeled back in irregular scraps, like old fabric patches. But worse, she realised that only ten of them were there. Someone was missing. She studied the still forms on the ground, more like corpses really, and realised that it was Warrigal. He'd been at the rear of the group and she didn't even know if the Sublabor had actually eaten him. He might still be back there, caught by the Gothak or trapped beneath tonnes of rock. Her heart contracted and a tear ran down her face.

The Sublabor reared on its many legs and let out a primeval roar that filled the air. Eyre wanted to blast the horrible creature into a thousand pieces, but she couldn't move, let alone summon any Viq. The massive centipede crashed off into the eucalypt forest and an uneasy silence filled the clearing.

There was a flash of light and Madame Overmantle appeared.

"By the Light," she said softly. "You have been so brave."

Whittaker Ray arrived a second later, his blue eyes deeply concerned, and then the Ranger appeared in another flash of light.

"Where did it go?" the Ranger asked, but didn't wait for an answer when he saw the wide trail of destruction through the bush. He set off at a run into the gaping chasm.

"Hold on, students," Eyre heard Madame Overmantle say soothingly. "Just hang on for a couple more minutes."

She saw the flash of vertical white light as a Seam opened, and then they were all pushed through. Vaguely, as she descended into unconsciousness, she realised that she recognised this place.

A Clementis put a gentle hand on her brow and everything went black.

Countless hours passed before Eyre finally woke, encased once more in a Bullio bubble. But instead of being in blinding agony, this Bullio contained the soothing syrup from Medela Island in Caelus, and she floated weightlessly in it, blissfully aware of the absence of pain. She could hear a tortilis playing softly, and saw the irregular shape of a tall, thin form moving around the room.

A few minutes later, the golden orb was pushed over and immersed in a bubbling spa. The Bullio melted and released Eyre into the warm water. It felt wonderful on her skin and she lay with her head resting on the side.

What had happened? The last memories she had were so filled with torment she couldn't remember properly. The Sublabor had swallowed them, but somehow, they had escaped. A weariness came over her. Her mind wasn't ready to process it yet.

Someone moved into the room, moving gracefully on long limbs. Large dark eyes regarded Eyre calmly.

"You are the first to recover," it said. "As before, you have healed very quickly. But your friends will be out soon."

"Is Warrigal here?" Eyre asked. The Clementis looked at her for a long moment and then shook its head.

"I'm sorry."

A tear ran down Eyre's cheek and the peace was gone. A crushing guilt weighed her down. *All for nothing.* The Isars gone and Warrigal dead. She turned away from the Clementis and shut her eyes.

By the end of the day the rest of the students had been released into the spa and given fresh uniforms. Thanks to the mystical healing powers of the Clementis, their hair and skin had already grown back. Physically, apart from an overwhelming tiredness, they were back to normal. But Eyre could see a terrible pain in everyone's eyes. It had been a horrific experience and they had lost one of their friends. And the dread of what might be coming hung darkly over them as they silently dressed.

"Whittaker Ray has asked to see you," the Clementis said when they were ready. The graceful creature generated a Seam and sent the students back through one by one.

Eyre walked out of the Seam and realised she was in the Dean's office. Whittaker Ray sat in the Dean's chair, and his eyes held a sadness as he walked around to join her.

"I've been promoted," he said heavily. "After poor Cecil's death, the Echelon held a special meeting, and for practicality it was decided that I should step in. I am missing my old friend." Eyre could only nod. Dean Fraser had been a good man.

The Dean's office had a similar arrangement to Whittaker Ray's old office, with a leather lounge suite and coffee table. Someone had organised extra chairs in the room and as each person arrived they took a seat. Eyre sat on a chair near the door, feeling keenly the absence of their good-natured Dean. There was a long silence as Whittaker Ray poured cups of coffee and handed them around.

"I trust you are feeling better," he began. "You have had a terrible experience, physically and emotionally. We are just fortunate that so many of you made it out."

Just then, there was a knock at the door and Eyre stood up and opened it. Her mind went completely blank when she saw Ben Perrill standing there, before an explosive rage overtook her and she moved without thinking. She punched Ben hard on the nose, and he grunted in surprise, holding a hand out towards her as blood spurted down his shirt. Eyre summoned her staff and blasted a stream of fire at him, but he had already teleported behind Whittaker Ray's desk.

Immediately, the other nine students had their staffs in hand, pointed at Ben's head.

"Who will do the honour?" Beatrice said softly, her eyes aflame.

But Whittaker Ray jumped in front of Ben.

"Stop!" he shouted.

Ten bewildered faces looked at him. But slowly, after a long moment, they lowered their staffs.

"Ben is on our side," Whittaker Ray said urgently. "He has been since last year, and has been working under cover, spying on the Gothak."

Eyre had to sit down. A wave of shock ran over her so completely that she thought she might pass out. She could not fathom what she was hearing.

Ben cautiously walked around the front of Whittaker Ray's desk and leaned against it. He held a tissue on his nose that was quickly turning bright red.

"I think you owed me that," he mumbled to Eyre as he held the bridge of his nose tightly.

"Sit down," Whittaker Ray said to the confused students. "Let me explain. First of all, so that you don't slaughter Ben here, let me assure you that all four Isars are with the Mimir, secure in the Mimir's Domain."

Eyre's jaw dropped and she looked at Beatrice and Abby. *What?*

"He took them straight there from the Underworld," Whittaker Ray continued.

Ben took the tissue off his swollen nose and spoke softly to Eyre. "Something changed in me when you saved me last year from the fire," he said slowly, in a muffled tone. "Like a miracle, the blackness that I had fought for so long was suddenly gone. I've been told that your self-sacrifice drove the mali out, *finally*, after feeling like I was drowning for years. It was like I'd woken from a long nightmare, and it was such a relief. I am so sorry for what I have done to you over the past few years, Eyre. I wanted to stop myself, but I couldn't." Seeing the huge boy so abjectly apologetic was a very odd sight, and Eyre glanced in astonishment at her friends.

Whittaker Ray finally sat down, satisfied that no one was about to blast Ben to smithereens. "Ben came to see me while you were with the Clementis last year, Eyre, and asked to go undercover to spy on the Gothak. Carrison Hamlen did not know about him, and together they were supposedly working for the Dark Forces."

Eyre looked down, thinking. No way was she okay with this. But out of respect for Whittaker Ray, she tried. "So you were just pretending in the Underworld? Just for show?"

Ben nodded. "I didn't want the Gothak to pursue me with the Isars. They were so focused on catching you so I slipped out without them realising. And I was pretending at the end of last year too. I didn't want Carrison to realise there was anything different about me. I'm sorry. I wouldn't really have hurt any of you."

Beatrice sat back in her chair and exhaled loudly. "Ben Perrill, working for the Light? I'm *so* confused."

"The old man," Abby said, trying to catch up. "I heard him summon the Gothak when Eyre tried to rescue him. Rhabdor called him the Protector *and* the Betrayer. Was he a good guy or a bad guy?"

Whittaker Ray was sombre. "As it turns out, he was a good guy, and a very brave Lightworker. He was the Protector of the Aura, a Lightworker with the ultimate power to protect the Overworld, and supposed to defend the Aura at any cost. He had been locked up in that cell since the Aura split apart in 1908; everyone thought he had died when it blew up. And they also believed that he had indeed betrayed the Lightworkers by forsaking his Light-given duty and trying to help the Gothak steal the Aura." He looked down and let out a sigh of regret. "I thought he had betrayed us too, and for all this time the Protector's name has been reviled. None of us knew he was still alive. Ben found him in the prison and talked with him—he found out the truth."

Eyre thought back to their time in the demonic cathedral, and the last moments before the explosion.

"The Protector," she began, feeling so sorrowful that this man had been labelled 'The Betrayer' throughout Lightworker history, "said to say hello to Doron Helios. I don't know who that is."

Whittaker Ray thought for a moment, and frowned slightly. "Well, it's a name that sounds like one of the Thantos Nex. So I guess because the Ranger and he were friends, and the guardians of our world as it turns out, maybe he meant the Ranger." He looked upwards as he thought. "Ranger Chrysanthe's first name is Leo—so that would sort of make sense. L-i-o rather than L-e-o. Maybe the Protector just wanted to say farewell, not hello." But then the esteemed lecturer's voice hitched, and in a rare moment of vulnerability, his eyes glistened as he shook his head slowly in disbelief.

"I have to confess, I'm still struggling with the injustice of what we have done to one of our own, leaving him trapped below for so many years. *The one we should have fought for with all our might.* We have done him a great disservice, in so many ways. But unfortunately, we must maintain the charade for a bit longer. We can't give the Dark ones any hint of the truth. We have to keep them guessing. Hopefully the day will come when we can carve the real story into an obelisk." Whittaker Ray looked as sad as Eyre had ever seen him, and she desperately wanted to give him a hug.

She rubbed her forehead as she tried to make sense of her chaotic thoughts. "So who did betray the Lightworkers so the Gothak could try to steal the Aura, if not him?"

Again Whittaker Ray looked regretful. "Carrison Hamlen's great grandfather, Adolf Hamlen. He and the Protector were in the Determinant Dozen, and Adolf helped the Gothak to pursue and kidnap the Protector, hoping to take the power of the Aura and the Protector down to the Underworld. If the Ranger hadn't intervened and blown the Aura to the

Alterworlds, the Gothak would have inherited all the power, and the Overworld would have been decimated. Unfortunately, the Ranger lost his memory in the blast, and since then it has been widely believed that the Protector had joined the Dark Forces. In reality, he waited patiently, trapped, trying to fool the Gothak and waiting for the moment when he was able to help. The Gothak knew he had the secret to reinstating the Aura's power. So he made many excuses to delay doing anything. Once the Gothak had the Isars, the Protector said anything to make them think they had to wait to use them: he told them it was dependent on the time of the day, on temperature fluctuations, on the magma explosions in the Underworld, and even the number of Gothak in the city. His excuses became bizarre and quite hilarious. Ben told me that one day Mudamir sent three quarters of the city's population off to the Strigis Canyon because the Protector told him that might help. Apparently, they all spent the day running away from creatures that were ready to eat them! It seems that Strigis are not completely controlled by the Gothak."

He smiled, although without much humour. "I think, although the Protector couldn't see it, that it must have given him great satisfaction to deceive his captors. Anyway, he fed them all manner of misleading information to prevent the reconstruction of the Aura's power. He bided his time, waiting under excruciating conditions. He was so brilliant and courageous—manoeuvring circumstances so the Isars could be returned to the Overworld. I'm not sure why he couldn't use them to escape, but he sacrificed his life for the whole Overworld. He deliberately summoned the Gothak so that they would take you to where the Isars were, and then when you were all safe, he crossed the bars—something we now know you must not do—to cause the explosion. He sacrificed his life so that the Isars would be returned to the Overworld."

Beatrice looked thoughtful. "*The Reconciled One.*"

"Yes," Whittaker Ray said. "Nostradamus's quatrain referred to him, losing all his time. Reconciled to his fate. And the quatrain told of the injustice of the Lightworker's belief about the Protector in its words: 'will not be without debates'."

The students sat in silence and Eyre's heart broke for the lonely, courageous old man who had sat in filth for decades, knowing his name was reviled. Faith and honour had sustained him until he was able to make the ultimate sacrifice for the Lightworkers and the Overworld. He had indeed been the true Protector.

Ben spoke hesitantly. "I knew that something momentous was down there, but not what it was, and I didn't know where we were going when

Carrison took me into the prison. He wanted to impress me by showing me the Protector. I didn't have long, but I was able to speak briefly to the old man. He warned me that he was going to cause the explosion, and told me to hide beneath a shield when he put the last Isar in place. Afterwards, in the confusion I found the Isars in the rubble. I'm sorry I left you all, but I had to get them out." He shrugged apologetically. "And if I stuck around, one of you was going to fry me."

Eyre blinked hard. *This* was taking a bit of getting used to. Ben Perrill a *good guy*? But it was true. There was something different about him. Now the mali had left him, his demeanour had deflated radically. He seemed strangely ordinary as he leaned against the desk. All the same, she felt uncomfortable being near the hulking boy. It would take her a long time to believe he had really changed.

"We couldn't generate a Seam down in that foul city," Eyre said to Ben. "Didn't you know that?"

Ben shook his head. "I only went to the city once before, just to look at it, and I didn't try to make a Seam. Carrison and I walked through the tunnels to get there and back. I guess *he* knew, but he didn't tell me."

"So, we know now," Whittaker Ray said, "that a Seam generated by an Overworld citizen won't work below a certain level. It requires too much energy. No wonder so many of our brave Lightworkers never made it back."

They all looked sombre. They didn't want to think about what they had experienced.

"So how *do* we reinstate the Aura with the Isars then, if not by crossing them?" Pheria asked.

"We are working on that," Whittaker Ray replied. "Regrettably, we still don't know."

But then he revealed the most amazing news of all.

"Warrigal is alive," he said. There was a mass gasp and the students exchanged looks of delight.

"But how?" Rigmar asked. "Where is he?"

"He is locked up, deep in the Mimir's Domain," Whittaker Ray said, then continued after a long pause. "Warrigal was the Sublabor who ate you. He saved you all by getting you out of there, but at great cost to himself."

Whittaker Ray rubbed his brow and sighed. "The Ranger had been training Warrigal in therianthropy because Warrigal had shown an exceptional gift for it. Together they were attempting something never done before—to transform into a Strigis, and for months they had worked on achieving the impossible, at great physical cost to Warrigal. The plan had been to send him down to spy, if he'd been able to transform. He had come close but never achieved it until your journey to the Underworld. But unfortunately, Warrigal has been unable to change back; it seems he is stuck as the Sublabor. So now The Ranger is working with Warrigal, trying everything conceivable to get him back. It may take some time, if indeed it is even possible."

Abby's face fell and she looked like she might cry. "Warrigal might stay as a Sublabor?"

"We hope not," Whittaker Ray replied in a soft voice. "He was very brave to attempt it. And he showed the most extraordinary control of his Lightness, by regurgitating you all at the surface. A feat of superhuman mental strength. We have to hope he will prevail."

A silence fell over the room as the students finished their coffee. Eyre rested her head on her hands, feeling conflicted. The news about the Isars was incredible, and she was still trying to absorb that all was not lost after all! But her elation was tempered by Warrigal's situation. She couldn't bear to think that they may never see the clever, wise boy again.

"I wanted to thank you all for your courage, and for what you have achieved," Whittaker Ray said. "The Academy remains closed, so I have let your families know you are coming home to rest. We ask that you keep this mission completely secret, apart from your immediate family. At this point the Gothak think you all are dead, eaten by a Sublabor. And they do not know that we have the Isars, as Ben believes none of the Gothak who saw him take them have survived, thanks to you. You killed them all with your staffs when you were escaping. So this secret is an advantage that we want to keep. They could spend months looking for the Isars in the rubble from the explosion. So, go Lightly, and enjoy your well-deserved rest. And of course, I'll see some of you back at Highlight in a few days."

Ben had always known when to make an exit, and he left quickly. The rest of the students all embraced each other.

When Jax reached Eyre he looked down at her, his green eyes serious, and his lips brushed hers in the tenderest of touches. "See you soon, Eyre with the red hair," he said.

CHAPTER THIRTY-FIVE

EYRE, BEATRICE, ABBY AND Nick were sitting around the Mantle Basin at Highlight, discussing the events they'd experienced in the Underworld. The rest of the group had returned to their homes for a few days to spend time with their families, but ultimately, they would all meet again when they went to the Front to join the Allied forces.

It was taking a while to work through what had happened and understand the dimensions of it all. Chief among the topics for discussion was the strange turnaround of Ben Perrill. Abby looked uneasily over her shoulder at the cabin at the far end.

"Is he still in there?"

Eyre nodded. "I don't think he's left since we came back. It's sort of creepy knowing he's down there."

Beatrice's eyes were hot as she turned to study the cabin. Eyre knew that her friend realised that Ben wasn't the cause of Blondie's death, but she could tell it was hard for Beatrice to let go of the hatred that had built up. Eyre felt exactly the same. She knew that they all accepted that Ben might have changed. But she also knew it would take a long while for them to forgive and forget.

"So, the Protector was actually a hero," Abby said softly.

Everyone shook their heads, and a long pause ensued as they all stared into the light of the Mantle Basin.

"I'll personally make sure the truth is in the history books," Beatrice replied fiercely, after a long silence. Eyre realised Beatrice would forever regret her last harsh words to the old man. It had been such a terrible situation, and they'd all misinterpreted it—although largely, because that was what the Protector had wanted. But what he'd sacrificed for the Overworld was beyond comprehension—for decades, locked away, suffering, but still working for the Light. Beatrice said she would set the record straight, and Eyre was absolutely sure her friend would do that. Mrs Abnett would have a few more tomes for her library in due course.

But Eyre herself also burned from guilt, because she would always feel she might have saved the Protector somehow, if she'd just been a bit more savvy. Somehow she felt she should have seen through the Protector's ruse, and helped the old man. But it was too late now.

Nick spoke after a long moment, contemplative as he looked into the flames of the silver matrix. "Whittaker Ray was so—well, the word isn't really *happy*, but it's the closest I can think of, last night. He didn't say much, but I could tell it's been a burden on the Echelon, and all the Lightworking community for decades, believing that something so unbelievably shameful could have been perpetuated by the most powerful Lightworker of the time. Mr Ray was beside himself—and I couldn't think why. But then I suddenly realised why he was so joyful. It was *hope*. Hope that somehow we might get out of this mire".

Eyre nodded. That made so much sense, and it echoed what she had been feeling today, despite the dire situation the Overworld was in. A lightness that fluttered within her, despite the terrible events she'd been through. And Nick was right—it was *hope* that fuelled the light.

Eyre stared into the shining matrix, contemplating the recent events. Whittaker Ray had arrived last night at the cabins, and he and Nick had clearly had their own debriefing session. Whittaker Ray had become like a father to Nick, and Eyre knew that Nick probably knew more than he would ever let on. Eyre would never press him for information; she was just happy that *he* was happy.

But at least for the moment, the Isars were safe. They just needed to work out what to do with them.

Whittaker Ray walked out of the cabin with a mug of coffee and sat on a sandstone block opposite Eyre.

"How are you doing?" he asked them all. He got various noncommittal responses and smiled wryly.

"Yes," he said. "I know how you feel. It's a bit like we're in a holding pattern. Stuck in a wide circle, going nowhere."

At that moment he was swooped by a blur of feathers, as Florence dived past him to land on a sandstone block beside him. Her three eyes seemed delighted she'd made him jump. Eyre laughed. Her Venator had arrived shortly after they'd returned to Highlight, and Florence had stuck close by Eyre ever since. It was as if she sensed that she'd nearly lost her Lightworker partner. Eyre had brought Ischyros to the cabins too, and had spent many hours with him. Being so close to death definitely helped you get your priorities in order, she'd realised.

Robyn and Peter Edmunsun came out of their cabin and Beatrice shuffled over on the sandstone block so they could sit and join her. And then, as if a telegraphic message had been sent, Ben Perrill's cabin door also opened. Despite herself, Eyre felt a stab of dread go through her as the heavy boy headed down the steps towards them, followed by his father, Dr Perrill. It was going to take a long time before she could relax around Ben, if ever. Whittaker Ray broke the awkward silence that had fallen over the group.

"The Edmunsuns, Dr Perrill and I need to go," he said heavily. "War has broken out in Terra and the Echelons of Entis and the Determinant Dozen are meeting this morning to discuss strategy. The Gothak are rising, in such great numbers it is feared we cannot hold them off for long." His clear blue eyes were troubled and he shook his head. "Lord Clarembout is leading the fight in Terra, but he has reported huge losses." Whittaker Ray stared vacantly across the clearing, his thoughts in another world. "We are losing."

"What do we do?" Nick said.

"You wait," Peter Edmunsun replied softly. "The time is coming when all must fight. For now, you rest."

A deep silence fell over the group at that and Eyre felt a wrench of foreboding. Despite all their efforts over the past years, the Overworld was still in great peril. And she felt like a speeding train was headed their way, out of control and unstoppable. She shivered.

A few moments later the members of the Echelon left and the rest of them sat and looked at each other. A great unease hung over them all.

"I think I'll go back to my cabin," Eyre eventually said. She stood up to go.

"Wait." Ben stood up too. "I'll walk over with you."

Eyre was completely nonplussed. It was such an improbable notion, it was as if he'd offered to do a pirouette around the campsite in a pink tutu. The only time she could imagine Ben Perrill wanting to walk with her alone would be to dispatch her permanently to the ether. But she knew that Ben had risked his life, and endured months of abuse from those who thought he was working for the Dark Forces, so she bit her tongue and nodded stiffly. She walked apart from him, but together, towards her cabin.

"I want to apologise again," Ben said softly. "And I understand if you want nothing to do with me. But for what it's worth, I'm deeply sorry. I will try to earn your tolerance, even if we can never be friends. My father is very disappointed in me and I am so ashamed."

The large boy sighed and looked away with such an anguished look on his face that Eyre actually felt a little sorry for him. But she still couldn't handle the thought of chatting socially with him, so she turned to walk up her steps. But Ben put his hand on her arm to stop her.

"Wait." He didn't hold her hard, but she flinched, and a shot of fear ran through her veins. Ben realised what he'd done and he stepped back.

"I'm sorry," he said. "I didn't mean to scare you. But I have something for you."

He pulled something white out of his pocket and handed it to her.

"It's from the Protector," he said. "He said to give it only to you."

Eyre looked confused. "Are you sure?" she asked, as she took the envelope and turned it over to look at both sides. It was blank.

"I'm sure," Ben replied. "He said to give it to the red-haired one. That must be you." He grinned suddenly and his whole face was transformed. He looked like a different person when he smiled. Against her instincts, Eyre smiled back ruefully. Yep, red hair certainly couldn't refer to anyone else.

"I put it in an envelope to protect it," Ben said. "I think it's a Peragro."

Eyre was intrigued. A Peragro from the Protector? She stood awkwardly for a moment. Although Ben was officially on the Lightworkers' side now, she still couldn't handle the thought of chatting socially with him, and she certainly wouldn't open this with him present, even though it wouldn't activate with him here. It was too personal, and it would take her a long time to trust him.

"Well, thanks," she said, and she went into her cabin.

She sat on her lounge suite and opened the envelope to take out the blank piece of paper inside. Sure enough, it was Light Paper—a Peragro indeed! The paper was burning in her hand and as she watched, words appeared across it.

Take the Isars to The Wurm to produce a torch—P

Then the Light Paper burst into flame and burnt quickly to ashes. Eyre sat back, desperately memorising the words. Beatrice was good at remembering things quickly; it wasn't Eyre's forté. So, reciting the words over and over in her mind, she raced down and grabbed the Book of Bane from the basement and then sped out her front door.

Everyone had left the Mantle Basin, so she ran up Beatrice's stairs, sending a telepathic message to Abby and Nick: *come!* She still wasn't ready to entrust Ben Perrill with anything, let alone something potentially so crucial, and she didn't want anyone intercepting the message, so she sent the message in code.

Beatrice gave a startled look as Eyre barged in.

"A pen, Bea!" Eyre exclaimed and flung herself onto the couch. She opened the Book of Bane to the next blank page and Beatrice sat down beside her.

"Write this in," Eyre said, reciting. "Take the Isars to the worm—that's 'the' with a capital and 'wurm' with a capital and spelt w-u-r-m—wait, where's your pen?"

"I don't need it," Beatrice said with satisfaction and Eyre watched in amazement as the words she'd said appeared on the page when Beatrice looked at it.

"What comes next?" Beatrice said smugly, and Eyre fed her the second half.

"Impressive," Eyre said. "Clairography—I still struggle with my Felsic."

Just then Abby burst through the door, followed closely by Nick. They were alarmed, searching for the threat, but sat down with relieved expressions when Eyre lifted an apologetic hand.

"I've had a message, well actually, it was a *Peragro* given to me by—would you believe—Ben Perrill? The Protector gave it to him to give to me," Eyre explained. From their faces, Eyre could tell that her friends were as astounded as she was.

Nick read the message. "What does a worm have to do with a torch?"

Eyre looked mystified. "I'm not sure. And I don't know what The Wurm —with a 'U'—is. Or where to find it."

Beatrice was thinking. "I do," she said. "Remember the old Sea Crone in Aqua? She was talking to you about 'besting the Wurm' and didn't she mean Aowx? Wurm is an ancient term for dragon."

Eyre's eyes cleared. "You're right," she said. It had been two years ago, but the ancient woman had indeed referred to Aowx as the Wurm, as well as the 'old lizard', which Eyre was sure Aowx would not be impressed by. "Yes, so take the Isars to Aowx. I'm sure he meant all of them."

"And 'torch'," Nick mused. "Perhaps he has to create a fire for some reason."

Eyre shrugged, unsure. "Aowx might know what it means." Then she rolled her eyes. "I guess we have to go and see him. Problem is, he's not exactly a fan of mine."

Abby studied the message and her mouth turned down. "We really misread the Protector," she said softly. "I feel so bad about that."

Eyre nodded slowly. "Such a brave man. He waited so long for the chance to best the Gothak. It is remarkable how powerful he was. He looked so feeble and crushed."

"Not powerful enough to get away, though," Beatrice said. "Every time he tried, they found him. Our capes saved us. And Warrigal."

They all were silent for a moment, remembering the incredible sacrifice of the Protector, and the courage of their friend.

"Well, the message doesn't say why exactly," Eyre finally said, feeling a rising hope and excitement. "But thanks to the Protector, it's clear what we need to do next. Abby, can you contact Whittaker Ray and let him know about this? I'm just going to put the Book of Bane away—meet you at the Mantle Basin."

Eyre was back in a few minutes and re-joined her friends at the fire pit. But Abby had a strained look on her face and Beatrice looked worried.

"I can't get hold of Whittaker Ray," Abby said.

"Or Mum and Dad," Beatrice added.

"I've tried all the staff," Abby said miserably, "and no one is responding."

"The war is escalating," Nick said softly. "Everything is falling apart."

A foreboding rose within Eyre. To be unable to contact *anyone* was unheard of.

"Did you try the Sergeant?" she asked.

"I'm only getting chaos and blackness," Abby said in a small voice. "I have a bad feeling about this."

As if to punctuate the disquietude they were feeling, a comet of atra shot across the sky above them and disappeared out of view. A few seconds later there was a huge explosion in the bush somewhere towards the Buyabarra Billabong. And then black streams of Zyx swarmed across the sky, above the protective Mantle.

Nick watched them flap over, his eyes serious as they followed the inky swarms. "In the daylight," he commented. "That is not a good sign."

Flames reached to the sky as a eucalyptus tree caught fire from the atra and formed a flaming torch. A billowing cloud of dense grey smoke grew ominously and cockatoos took off in fright, screeching raucously as more searing blasts of atra rent the sky. In the distance Eyre could hear screams and the roars of the Mimir, and the sound of a huge battle being fought out of sight. She sent up a prayer for their safety.

Dust swirls twisted across the dry earth in the overwhelming silence. Distant fires had turned the sky an ominous orange. A group of Lighthorses flew overhead and disappeared over the horizon and Eyre felt suddenly hopeless. For a moment everything felt totally futile.

As if Abby sensed her mood, she jumped up and spun her staff around like a baton-twirler in a marching band.

"Come on!" she exclaimed. "Let's go take the Isars to that dragon of yours, Eyre."

She struck a pose. "I have my drupe cape in one boot and I'll put an Isar in my other! And I'll march it all the way to The Wurm!"

Eyre laughed and her dark mood lifted. "Well then, let's teleport to the Mimir's Domain and get those Isars!"

CHAPTER THIRTY-SIX

EYRE STOOD ON THE moldavite square and looked at the brass doors to the Mimir's Domain. They were shut tight and she contemplated the problem as a lone leaf skittered across their surface.

"Hmmm. What do you reckon? Bang on them with a staff maybe?"

But then the doors slowly creaked open. Those hinges need oiling, Eyre thought, which was unheard of in the Mimir's Domain, where everything was normally maintained in pristine working order. A true sign of the times.

Private Ammonite stuck his head out and looked at the four of them.

"Quick," he said. "The campus won't be deserted for long—the Gothak aren't far away. Get inside."

Eyre moved quickly across the moldavite square and started down the curving brass stairs past Private Ammonite. Nick was last to enter and when he came down the stairs the heavy doors swung shut with a clang. Private Ammonite looked at them.

"Why are you here? I thought you were back at Highlight. No one is on campus; this is not a good place for you. We heard movement up here and I was sent to investigate. Just as well. In another hour you would be target practise for the Gothak."

Abby leaned against the brass railing and her face was sad. "I can't get hold of anyone and I have a terrible feeling that things are not good. What's happening?"

The normally jovial Private was sombre. He looked down and shook his head. "The last twenty-four hours have been grim, I can't lie. It seems the Gothak are making their stand in the Overworld, Isars or no Isars. And they have unleashed their terrible force in all of the Alterworlds."

Eyre felt desolate. "So Jengles is not here? Or President Zircon?"

Private Ammonite shook his head. "They have been gone for days. Our forces were decimated by the attempted raid at the Underworld earlier this year, so we have only a skeleton crew here at present."

He looked at Abby's distraught face and his gaze softened. "I'm sorry, little bird," he said. "But the reason you can't get anyone is because they are not *able* to be contacted. The staff are all leading troops across the Overworld, trying to hold back the attack of the Dark Forces. The last I heard, all Academy students were being enlisted in the fight too."

"Things are that dire?" Nick asked softly.

"Things are that dire," Private Ammonite echoed.

Beatrice's eyes flashed. "Well, there's no point hanging around the staircase. If they've enlisted the Curtis twins, then things are *really* desperate! Take us to the Isars!"

Private Ammonite looked startled, then let out a deep belly laugh. "Straight to the point, I see. *If* we were to have the Isars, and I'm not admitting anything, then I would *imagine* they were supposed to be concealed in the most secret of places, and *supposed* to stay there."

Eyre had a sudden loss of patience with beating around the bush. "We need your help," she said. "There's no one to talk to and we have information that might help to reinstate the Aura. And by the sounds of it, the Light Forces could use it right now. But we need to get the Isars."

The Private looked shocked. "What do you mean you 'need' them. You mean, you want to take the Isars away from the Domain?"

Eyre nodded, her eyes locked onto his.

Private Ammonite looked at each of them, his sense of duty warring with his instincts. He was never one to obey rules that didn't seem sensible, and Eyre could see that he wanted to help. But the Isars had been hidden in the utmost secrecy, to be safeguarded by the Mimir and no one was supposed to know they were there.

In the end, Private Ammonite's nature won out. His sharp mind and his sense of adventure overrode his sense of duty and he seemed to make a snap decision. He smiled suddenly, big white teeth appearing in his bushy red beard.

"Well, if you've got information that might help get the Aura back, then I will take you to the Isars," he pronounced, "even though it may be the end of my illustrious career as a Private. But *I* will be their appointed guardian. Wherever they go, I go. That's the deal."

"Fine by us!" Eyre exclaimed. "Come on, let's go."

Private Ammonite, once he made a decision, was not slow to act. He raced down the stairs and the students hurried after him, their feet making the bronze steps ring like cathedral bells, the mellow tones echoing down the tunnel in layered waves.

They branched off and travelled down until the stairs ended at a hub. The Private activated a crystal on his belt, and instantly a row of lights lit up one of the tunnels, guiding the way. Without hesitating, the Private thundered into it, charging ahead as fast as he could run.

Abby staggered along, trying to keep up with her faster companions. Eyre and Nick were super fit, and Beatrice's long legs meant it wasn't hard for her to keep up with the speedy Mimir. But Abby was red-faced and puffing by the time Private Ammonite stopped at the end of the tunnel. She put up a hand in a mute request for a rest, but the athletic Mimir didn't take any notice.

"Follow me!" he said dramatically, and jumped into a chute. Abby groaned and sighed as she leaned up against the wall. But not wanting to lose him, Eyre leapt in the dark hole and slid down the shaft after him, with Beatrice and Nick following quickly after.

"Come on Abby," Beatrice called as her voice receded down the slide, "Fortitude!"

Abby took a deep breath and jumped.

They landed in yet another tunnel, and again it lit up with a line of guiding lights. Eyre cocked her head. She could hear something. And then she smiled. The Isars were singing!

Private Ammonite led the way as they hurried along the dark passage. Not once did they encounter another Mimir and it made Eyre very uneasy. It was a sign of how bleak things were if the Mimir had moved most of their troops away. It was only because the Gothak did not know where the Isars were that the magical bars were safe, despite the lack of protection. The Dark Forces would not be looking for the Isars here because they thought they were still buried somewhere in the Underworld.

As they travelled further down the tunnel, Eyre could hear the singing more clearly and she knew they were close. They rounded a corner and suddenly, she saw the four Isars.

They were embedded in the rock wall about a metre apart from each other, and they glowed a brilliant silver. As they sang, the wall seemed to pulse in time with the haunting melody, and the rock was luminous from their reflected light. Eyre stood in awe before the beautiful, powerful entities.

Private Ammonite seemed to share her sentiment, because he spoke in a soft, reverential voice. "If you can get them out, you can take them with you. But I come too."

As if in a trance, Eyre moved slowly towards the rock wall. It was like the silver bars had hypnotised her, and she walked like a robot towards the glimmering rock wall. Without thinking, she reached out to the rock and plunged her hand inside it, grasping the Isar. The silver bar was ice cold to the touch, despite its glowing light, and she pulled it smoothly out of the wall.

"I guess I'm going with you then," Private Ammonite said softly. "I didn't think you'd be able to do that."

Eyre wasn't listening. She took the Isar and slid it into her boot. It was a tight fit, but that was a good thing really, as it was unlikely to fall out. The Private suddenly turned and left, but Eyre was too focused on her irresistible desire to get the Isars out of the rock to wonder where he'd gone. She left her staff on the ground and went to the second Isar. When she pulled this one out, she took it to Beatrice. "Put it in tightly," Eyre said, and headed back to the wall. In a short time, all four Isars were out and concealed within each of their boots. Private Ammonite returned at that moment with squares of soft black leather.

"Got them from the Kit Room," he said. "Put them over the top of the Isars so the light doesn't shine out." He passed them each a swatch and they tucked it over the Isar so that it didn't show at all.

"So... now what?" Private Ammonite asked with a grin. He was actually enjoying this. Eyre had to give him credit. From being a reluctant participant at the start, he was now embracing the mission whole-heartedly. His enthusiasm made her smile. It might be the end of the world, but the fearless Mimir was going to risk everything for one last chance at a road trip. And to save the world, of course.

"I wonder if you know how we can get to Aowx?" Eyre asked, and judging by his reaction, he did.

"I'll just dictate my obituary then," Private Ammonite said, and laughed really loudly.

CHAPTER THIRTY-SEVEN

HE LED THEM TO an Uplight, but this time they were going down. A long way down, Eyre remembered. The 66th floor, she recalled from her last trip to visit Aowx. Private Ammonite stepped out over the vertical chute onto a prong and twisted the beam so the light whizzed downwards at incredible speed.

Eyre held her staff tightly with one hand and grasped the beam with her other as she found a foothold on a short strut. Then she twisted the beam and she too descended quickly. Their time with the Mimir earlier in the year had made them adept at the use of the Uplights, and before long she was standing at the bottom beside Private Ammonite. When the other three arrived, the Private led them down a tunnel to a small set of bronze doors that he pulled open. Beyond them was a loading bay where a compact silver Zepp was docked. And incredible heat. Eyre had forgotten how oppressively hot it was down here.

"I do have a slight problem," the Private confessed, looking with longing eyes at the Zepp. "I can't drive one of these. Only trained Mimir are permitted near them, and I'm not exactly known for my—ah—*prudence*, so I was never considered suitable for lessons. So, it means one of you is going to have to do it."

Beatrice, Abby and Nick looked immediately at Eyre. She was the logical choice, after her piloting lessons with the Ranger. But her friends didn't know what they were in for. When she'd visited Aowx the last time, the Ranger had piloted the Zepp, and it was a stomach-churning, difficult trip to handle even for an expert aviator. Eyre wasn't sure if she could even keep the vehicle on the track, let alone get to the destination. But she smiled confidently. "Sure, no problem. Climb aboard, folks!"

Just then, there was an earth-shattering crash from somewhere behind the thick granite wall; the ground shook and the Zepp rattled. Pieces of rock cracked from the roof of the tunnel and fell on to the ground. They all froze. A wild shrieking started and the thudding of something very heavy smashing into the rough-hewn walls. Eyre knew only too well what it was. Once you'd heard the Strigis, you never forgot it.

Private Ammonite raised a hand at their panicked looks. "It's okay," he said. "Come and see."

He led the group down the tunnel to a massive hammered bronze door. It had a cast bronze circular handle with crossbars, like a bank vault, and whatever was making the terrible noise was locked behind the door. Eyre thought perhaps it might be better to stay on this side, but Private Ammonite turned the huge handle and swung the heavy door open.

Inside was an amphitheatre-like stadium, with tiered seating positioned around a sunken circular arena the size of a football ground. In the middle of the arena a prodigious battle was taking place. A Sublabor screeched and writhed and reared up on its back end as the Ranger flicked a long golden whip at it. Gently, not touching the animal, just using the sound to encourage it to move around. Eyre couldn't hear what the Ranger was saying, but every movement was measured and calm, and she could hear the tone of his voice was soft amongst the tortured screams of the colossal centipede. The Ranger was very thin and looked exhausted, but his focus was completely on the tormented beast in front of him, and he didn't look up as they entered.

"Warrigal," Nick said softly.

Private Ammonite nodded. "The Ranger has been working with him constantly since you came back from the Underworld." He paused and then added in a pained voice, "without much success, unfortunately."

They watched for a few more moments and then Private Ammonite turned to lead them back out. But before they left, Eyre called out to Warrigal. "Be strong, Warrigal. Come back to us." The Ranger looked up briefly and smiled at them, then carried on flicking the whip in the air. As the hefty door closed behind them, there was a deafening squeal and the thunder of many running feet. The Ranger has a way to go yet, Eyre thought bleakly.

They reached the Zepp and Eyre jumped in the pilot seat. Sweat was running down her face, and it wasn't just because of the heat down here. She hoped they were going to make it.

"Buckle up, babies," Eyre said, quoting the Ranger. "Here we go!"

She put the Zepp in gear and it trundled forwards, then launched off the edge into the tunnel. Like a roller coaster in top gear, the Zepp roared up in the air and then plummeted downwards, executing sheer turns right and left and once, even a loop-the-loop that the Ranger would have given her top marks for. It was a wild ride, with Eyre struggling desperately to keep the magical vehicle under control. On the positive side, it completely drove the sadness of Warrigal's plight from her mind. She scraped around the corners and pulled wildly on the steering wheel; trying to slow it down, clunking the seven gears and stamping on the two clutches like she was trying to put out a fire. Indeed, the vehicle was sending off so many sparks as it scraped along the rock that it was a miracle it didn't catch fire. Finally, the Zepp stopped with a shuddering *whoosh* at the entrance to Aowx's cave. Eyre took a deep breath and unbuckled her harness with shaking hands.

"You have arrived at—Middleworld" she intoned in a voice like a train conductor. "Please disembark."

Private Ammonite, Beatrice and Abby exited, followed by Nick, who laughed as he shut the door behind him.

"Top piloting skills, Eyre, impressive!" he grinned, but Eyre noticed he had a green tinge to his face.

All four of them were looking around curiously, and Eyre supposed that like Beatrice, Abby and Nick, Private Ammonite hadn't been here before either. Unfortunately, Eyre knew what was coming. She wiped her brow— the heat was incredible and sweat was already pouring off her. And no doubt partly due to nerves, she was sure.

She led the way through the sparkling curtain of diamonds into Aowx's chamber. It was incredibly hot and the bronze sconces high on the walls were aflame with burning flares, which only increased the temperature. Uneven piles of gold and jewels were heaped up in every corner, tossed aside like toys in a spoiled toddler's toybox.

Even though she'd been before, Eyre was still overwhelmed at the size of the dragon's lair, and the massive pile of priceless treasures. Beatrice, Abby and Nick's mouths hung open as they slowly turned and took in the enormity and extravagance of the hoard. The glow of golden artifacts illuminated the rock walls, and gemstone necklaces lay coiled like colourful crystal snakes throughout the mounds of coins, artifacts and uncountable riches. Priceless art hung higgledy-piggledy on the rock walls, with no particular order or care. It was an unbelievable display of greed and avarice, and absolute pointlessness. All this beauty and genius craftmanship, Eyre thought, hidden kilometres beneath the ground for no one to see.

Eyre spotted a small spiked triangle moving through the golden dunes and she smiled inwardly, recognising the tip of Aowx's tail. The others watched curiously as it approached like the fin of a shark, and with a blood-curdling roar, Aowx heaved his massive bronze body out from beneath the riches. Golden *objets d'art* and chests of gold coins tumbled around him as he rose from the sea of gold. His wings were extended to their full span of twenty metres, and fire blasted from his nostrils as he pointed an accusing webbed toe at Eyre.

"You dare to come back?" he bellowed, and slammed his front feet down in the shimmering pile, sending a goblet spinning in the air. He bent down and sent a stream of burning fire at them. But it flipped up and over the shield Eyre had whisked into place a second before the flames reached them.

"Where's. My. Orbuculum!" the dragon tantrummed, as he melted a pile of dinner plates into a golden puddle.

Eyre was starting to think this was a very bad idea. Aowx was having such a fit he couldn't hear a word she was saying, and she thought she could well end up eaten or fried before she could be heard.

But then something magical happened. A shining bubble a metre tall appeared and drifted up in the air near the dragon's ear. Aowx swiped at it in a fit of temper but missed, and it gently bobbed up and down for a moment, then wafted to sit above his back.

The irate dragon flicked around and whacked at it with his powerful tail. But the bubble was elusive and remained just out of reach, even when Aowx lunged for it with both arms. He missed completely and fell on his face with a disbelieving roar of rage. That did it! He fired golden treasures at the quietly rising bubble, trying to burst the maddening object, and he screamed in annoyance when every single one missed. The bubble gently reached the roof of the cave and started to bounce along, away from them all. And did Eyre hear a snigger of laughter coming from it?

With an oath, Aowx flapped his powerful wings and rose into the air. He spun around and gave one mighty down beat. The air came rushing down, sending gold coins tumbling and spinning. Then Aowx *chased* the bubble, following the elusive orb around the roof of the cave, up and down the sides of the rock walls. Sometimes he flew, other times he clambered across the rock, but he never managed to catch it. Eyre was trying not to laugh, but he looked like an extremely frustrated and annoyed tabby cat chasing a feather on a stick.

Somewhere in the middle of the whole performance, they heard a strange sound. Rusty, dry, and deafening, almost like the squeak of a seldom-used hinge that badly needed oiling. Eyre looked up at the scrambling dragon in astonishment. Aowx was *laughing!* Chasing the orb across the mounds of gold and leaping to grab for it and hooting with glee! And then Eyre noticed Nick, who was watching the whole performance with great delight. No, not *watching.* She suddenly realised that Nick was *orchestrating* the whole thing. He had created the Bullio bubble and was teasing the great dragon with the floating orb, sending it in whirls and eddies like it was alive. He was having a wonderful time, Eyre realised, just as much as Aowx was.

Finally, after flying the length of the cave and back twice, guffawing loudly as he sped along at breakneck speed, Aowx grabbed the bubble and it squeaked, then exploded in his face. The wicked old dragon sat on the treasures in the middle of his cave and laughed until tears ran down his leathery cheeks.

"I don't believe I've laughed since the 14th century," he hiccupped. "I'd forgotten it could be so much fun, much more fun than chasing and eating people. You..." he pointed his claw at Nick, "must come back again!"

"Oh yes, that can be arranged," Eyre said swiftly, seizing the moment, "but we would just need a favour first."

The dragon's eyes narrowed and he frowned. "You are too tricky by far," he said to Eyre petulantly. "And you take the fun out of everything. I don't like you. What are you scheming?"

"The Overworld is at war with the Underworld," Eyre said. "We have been instructed to bring you these—" she pulled the Isar out of her boot and laid it down on a golden tray.

"We have been directed to ask you to produce a torch," Eyre pronounced confidently, not knowing what it meant, but trying not to show it.

The old dragon looked crafty. "That will be four favours then," he said. "I told you last time that I don't care about the Overworld or Underworld and their boring struggles. But I am well-pleased today with the entertainment. So I will grant you the torches, but this one—" he indicated Nick. "Will promise to come back again and play." The dragon's eyes chilled suddenly and the hairs on Eyre's arms rose.

"You must give me your word you will return. Don't make me come and get you.

Nick raised his hand and gave a sweeping bow. "It would be my honour, Great One."

The mighty dragon was most pleased by this and his good humour returned. He picked up the Isar and threw it in the air so that it twirled like a baton. When it was halfway back down to the ground, Aowx blasted it with a stream of fire. Then he caught it nimbly and bent it with his powerful feet. The combination of the force and the heat of the fire created a bar that was bent in half with a sharp-edged corner, like the angle of a mathematical set-square.

Eyre was horrified. "What are you doing?" she cried. "That's not a torch."

The dragon turned unfriendly eyes towards her. "Yes it is. Pass me the others. Or don't, I really don't care."

Abby moved fast and removed the Isar from her boot. Then she threw it high in the air above the wily old dragon so that it spun wildly like the first Isar. Aowx cackled in delight and blasted it with flames as it whirled towards him. Then he bent it in half as he'd done with the first.

The next two bars were treated the same way until all four Isars lay cooling on the top of a treasure chest.

Beatrice was intrigued by the puzzle, as usual.

"You say it's a torch, but how can that be when they are not on fire?" she asked.

The dragon looked as if he might ignore her, but then his desire to brag and show that he understood the riddle won out. Eyre thought her own presence probably helped in this situation; the vain dragon was still smarting from her besting him when she was last here, and he wanted to show how clever he was.

"This *is* a torch," he declared, picking up the still-hot Isar. "I have created a Kenaz from the Isar. The Kenaz is a rune meaning 'torch' and it is a symbol of fire, of awakening knowledge and finding the path."

"But what do we do with them?" Eyre asked desperately.

"Ah, but that would be another favour," the dragon answered with a cunning look in his orange eyes. "Will I grant it?" He was performing, pretending to think it over, and Beatrice jumped in to push his buttons.

"He will have to work it out another day, Eyre," she said sadly. "Unfortunately, he doesn't know the answer to that puzzle."

Aowx frowned and looked at Beatrice for a long moment, as if she might be a suitable appetiser on his midday menu. But his ego made him take the bait.

"Anyone with half a brain could see that the Kenaz can be placed to form the Inguz," he snapped, arranging them roughly on the top of the treasure chest.

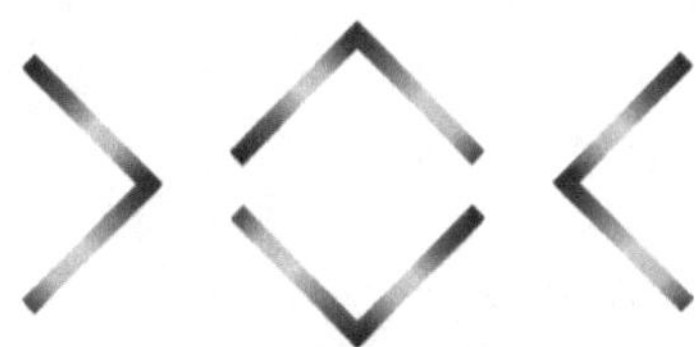

"Of course, they have to be pushed together," he finished.

Eyre didn't wait. She raced forward and shoved the four Kenaz together to make the Inguz.

Then she looked around, waiting for something to happen.

Aowx looked startled, then guffawed, relishing the opportunity to take his annoying adversary down a peg.

"Not *you*, you ridiculous creature. The Protector has to do it. You must take the Kenaz back to him."

Eyre felt like she'd been punched in the stomach. "But the Protector is dead," she whispered.

"Ah well, you're stuffed then," Aowx yawned. "You can't do it." A crafty gleam appeared in his eye. "They're no use to you at all. I'll keep hold of them if you like?"

Eyre sat down heavily. After all this? *Impossible*? For a second, she wanted to lie on the ground and have a tantrum worthy of Aowx.

They all looked at each other. Now what?

CHAPTER THIRTY-EIGHT

AOWX GAVE A CASUAL yawn. "However, for a favour, I could make a suggestion..." he said with a glint in his eye that belied his nonchalance.

Eyre rubbed her brow, thinking hard. But before she could reply, there was a movement beneath the treasure pile at the back of the cave; some subterranean shift that caused a tidal wave of golden objects to start sliding down towards them. A rolling crest of treasure. Aowx turned his head in surprise. As they watched, a strange creature rose from beneath the dragon's hoard. At least thirty metres in height, it had three snake-like heads and multiple red eyes in each of them. The heads writhed and snapped with razor-sharp teeth, and the creature screamed so loudly the cavern reverberated with the sound. Abby covered her ears, her cornflower eyes looking at the monster in disbelief.

"What. Is. That?" she breathed.

The great snake rose out of the golden mire and focused on the group below. Then it charged towards them, hissing and lunging with fearsome speed. Eyre was so petrified that for a moment she couldn't move.

"*Elapidus Viper*," Beatrice whispered in dread as she took a step backwards. "The apex Strigis."

Aowx turned, his orange eyes furious, and he lifted off the ground with a huge sweep of his wings. He flew like a bullet up the hill, with an unearthly shriek and fire blasting from his nostrils.

The two massive creatures met in a screaming tangle in the middle of the cavern. The impact of their crash caused an enormous shockwave that extinguished the burning flares, before they flickered and re-lit. Eyre summoned her staff, but what good it would do in this titanic battle, she had no idea. Huge teeth tore at each other and Eyre's hair stood on end at the vicious shrieks and roars as the two behemoths fought to the death.

Aowx got in early and bit one of the heads of the viper off with his formidable jaws. Black blood exploded in a spurting gush and ran down the dangling neck. The other two heads of the Elapidus hissed and screamed and one of them lunged and sunk its teeth into Aowx's neck. While he was struggling to free himself, the other head darted round and bit Aowx's tail completely off. The monstrous snake held the wriggling tail in its mouth like a bird with a worm as Aowx bellowed in agony. Without his tail as a stabilizer, he was unable to lift himself in the air and the snake smashed him down onto the pile of treasure. With blood streaming, Aowx staggered to his feet but was unable to repel the Elapidus, and the vast dragon dropped to his knees.

Eyre charged up the golden heap. Aowx was a conceited old creature but she didn't want him to suffer. She sent a stream of fire at the massive snake and burnt a hole in its skin. It screeched in agony and let go of Aowx's neck. Then Eyre sent another blazing beam from her staff to cauterize the stump where Aowx's tail had been. But the old dragon had lost too much blood, and he fell back weakly on his pile of treasures, his blazing orange eyes fading as he roared in defiance at the Strigis.

Beatrice, Abby and Nick started up the heap with their staffs too, and Private Ammonite ran beside them until they stood beside Eyre. Together they formed a barrier in front of Aowx and fired scorching beams of light at the Elapidus to stop it plunging down to finish its defeat of Aowx. But it was a desperate effort, Eyre knew, and they were only delaying the inevitable. The Strigis was too powerful, and it was only a matter of time before the monstrous creature wore them down and killed them all.

But just then, the pile beneath their feet shifted as another seismic jolt hit, and Eyre stumbled and dropped her staff. Beatrice, Abby and Nick fell over, struggling to keep their balance on the shifting infrastructure, and Private Ammonite fell completely and rolled down the slope.

Eyre was on her hands and knees as the hoard of treasures buckled and shook. As she looked up in horror, a Sublabor broke from beneath the surface. Golden artifacts fell from its skin as it pushed upwards into the chamber. A gaping hole appeared in the field of treasure, a shining crevasse that disappeared into a bottomless pit. Aghast, Eyre watched as Aowx slipped sideways into the cavernous void, roaring in rage as he cartwheeled over and over until he disappeared from sight. The chasm widened as a jagged crack split the surface, and Eyre shouted in horror as it overtook Private Ammonite and sucked him down into the rift. The ground shifted again and the crevasse closed, leaving no sign that either of them had been there.

Eyre looked upwards with fierce eyes and staggered to her feet. An Elapidus and a Sublabor?

"BRING IT ON!" she screamed in fury, facing the two leviathans without an ounce of fear. Beatrice, Abby and Nick managed to struggle to their feet, and stood beside her, their staffs raised.

But a curious thing happened. The Sublabor didn't attack them; instead, it launched itself at the Elapidus! With an almighty roar, it snapped its massive pincers and chopped a second head off the Elapidus. The snake screamed and struck back at the Sublabor, wrapping its tail around the thick body of the huge centipede. The two crashed to the ground and rolled together, writhing in a mighty, violent struggle. Golden objects flew in the air and the walls reverberated with the thud of their bodies as they smashed against the rock, but eventually the thrashing ceased and an ominous silence filled the air.

Then the Sublabor raised itself on its back legs and roared a deafening screech of triumph. The Elapidus slumped to the ground, its black blood spilling over the shining golden objects and pooling like oil.

The Sublabor smashed back to the surface and turned towards the group who stood with staffs raised. Eyre took aim.

"Stop," the Ranger said from behind them. Eyre jumped in fright. Beatrice, Abby and Nick turned to look at him and then back at the Sublabor. Horrified understanding dawned and they rapidly lowered their staffs.

"Come on, friend," the Ranger whispered. "You can do it."

"Warrigal, come back," Abby pleaded, tears running down her face.

And then the Sublabor began to writhe and scream in agony. It twisted and turned, seemingly trying to fight itself, until gradually it began to reduce in size. It coiled into improbable shapes and bent over backwards, morphing gradually, inexorably into the crouching figure of a Lightworker. *Warrigal.* He looked up at them with a tortured expression and then fell face forward into the golden heap.

Nick and the Ranger raced forward and sat Warrigal up. After a moment he began to stir and his eyelids fluttered. Then his eyes opened and he jumped up, struggling to get away from their supporting hands. He was totally disorientated, Eyre realised. He didn't know where he was, and she stood anxiously as the Ranger spoke in a low voice, trying to calm the panicking boy. Was he alright? Eyre wondered. He'd been through so much, and she desperately wanted confirmation that their friend was unchanged.

Finally Warrigal's eyes cleared and he stopped fighting. He drew a deep, shuddering breath and rubbed his forehead.

"I'm sorry," he whispered. "I'm so confused."

At that, his friends rushed up to hug him. "Thank you, Warrigal," Eyre said softly. "That's the second time you've saved our lives. You are so brave."

They all stood silently for a moment, then together they turned and looked at the mountain of treasure, ploughed with furrows from the violence of the battle. The corpse of the Elapidus was sinking slowly into the pile like a trapped animal in quicksand; it wouldn't be long before it was completely swallowed by the golden quagmire.

A tear ran down Eyre's cheek as she searched the slope. There was no sign of Aowx or Private Ammonite, and no chance of finding them beneath the tonnes of treasure. A deep sadness filled Eyre's soul. More casualties of this vile war. Sighing, she straightened her staff and turned away.

"We should get going," she said heavily. There is nothing for us here."

The Ranger put Warrigal's arm around his shoulder and helped him down the unstable hill. Eyre picked up the four Kenaz and gave one to each of her friends.

"Keep them safe," she said. As they walked towards the diamond curtain, the Ranger filled them in.

"Abby called me for help," he said. "And I left Warrigal behind. But he followed through the underground tunnels. It seems that his desire to save you overcame his instincts as a Strigis, and conquering those impulses was the catalyst that ultimately enabled him to transform back to himself."

"I'm not doing it again, though," Warrigal joked weakly. "You don't taste very good."

As they reached the Zepp, the ground beneath them rocked with a powerful explosion. Dust blasted out of the tunnel and far away a siren howled. The lights in the tunnel flickered and died, and with the flick of a wrist, the Ranger sent up a lux. His face was shadowed as he looked at the ceiling in the wavering light.

"The Gothak have invaded the Domain," he said softly. "And this time, they won't be leaving. Hop aboard the Zepp. I'll take you to Highlight."

Cracks appeared in the walls and rocks rained down on them as they jumped aboard the silver vehicle. The Ranger gunned the engine while everyone buckled up, and in a flash of light, the silver ship disappeared.

CHAPTER THIRTY-NINE

EYRE HELD HER FAVOURITE green mug as she sat on her front step. The campsite looked odd with the Zepp parked like a family wagon at the side, but Eyre decided she rather liked it. She'd always wanted one of the magical vehicles, and for now, they had one. Not that she was going anywhere in it; they had found out that war had overtaken all the Alterworlds and all countries in Entis. Lightworking troops were battling the Gothak in every dimension, and, sadly, losing. Lightworking soldiers had been decimated across the board; the force of the Gothak was too great, and despite the unity of the Allies, they were being forced back relentlessly. The Lightworkers had known for years that the Gothak were rising, and now the Dark Forces were breaking free of the Underworld with a horrifying momentum. And Rhabdor had been seen in Incendium. Somehow, he had survived the explosion in the Underworld and was leading the evil forces in their increasingly successful raids.

A deep gloom settled on Eyre's shoulders. The Kenaz were hidden in her basement, and protected by the ward, but also protected by the fact that no one, save the group here, knew where they were. But they couldn't do anything with the Kenaz anyway, so in effect they were worthless. Without the Protector, the Kenaz had no power. And if the Aura couldn't be reinstated, it looked very much like the Gothak would triumph.

Over the past few days life had been weirdly uneventful, in contrast to what was happening in the Overworld. Warrigal had bunked in with Nick, and was improving but still needed to rest. The Ranger had stayed to help him begin his recovery from the therianthropy overload, but had left to confer with the Echelon once Warrigal was showing signs of getting better.

Eyre hadn't seen much of Warrigal; or any of the others—everyone was feeling exhausted and depressed about the failure of their mission, and had been keeping to themselves. On the positive side, Ben Perrill had disappeared. Gone to join the fight, the Ranger told them, but Eyre wasn't really interested. As long as he wasn't *here*, that was all that mattered.

She sighed. Was this how their journey of the past few years would finish? Fizzled out in a dead end? She stared into her mug and came to a decision. They'd had enough time to recover, and she wanted to be a part of the defence. Tomorrow, she would go and join the fight, wherever she was needed. This inertia was not accomplishing anything.

The thought made her feel better and she took her mug back to the kitchen. She leaned against the sink and wished for the millionth time that her parents were here. It had been quite a while since she'd cried about their deaths, but now, the loneliness and fear overwhelmed her and tears streamed down her face. She felt like a complete failure, and she'd give anything to be able to talk to them.

Right at that moment, Beatrice walked in the front door and Eyre rubbed the tears quickly from her face. But Beatrice knew, and she gave Eyre a sympathetic hug.

"I wish Mum and Dad were here," Eyre said.

Beatrice's mouth turned down. "I'm so sorry, Eyre," she said. "You must miss them so much, especially right now. I'm so sad and depressed too—I don't know where Mum and Dad are, or if they're even okay, and it feels like everything is *lost* right now. But your Mum and Dad would be so proud of what you did achieve, my courageous friend."

Abby and Nick arrived and Beatrice patted Eyre on the shoulder. "Come on, Eyre, take us to your basement. I want to look at all the messages in the Book of Bane."

Eyre took them down the hall and helped them through the ward. They tramped down the steps to the basement and sat around her old sea chest with the Book of Bane on the floor in front of them.

"Speak to me, Banes," Beatrice said, and everyone winced at the pun.

"Awful, Bea," Abby groaned.

They flipped the Book opened and scanned through the information they'd acquired over the years, trying to figure out what their next step should be. Nothing seemed obvious.

Abby eventually pointed at the Sea Crone's prophesy—"*when all seems forsaken...find the Golden Beryl,*'" she said, and sighed loudly. "Well, it seems we're in a fairly hopeless position now, so perhaps it's time to look for the meaning of that prophesy? Do you think it might have something to do with the Transit? There are so many crystals there."

Eyre sat back. "Maybe. I guess it's as good a place to start as any." But she felt deep down that they'd reached the end of the road with their quest, and she doubted they'd find anything in the Transit. And if that was a dead end, then there was no way to know where the Golden Beryl was.

Eyre closed the Book of Bane with a finality that had been four years coming. "We can go look. But if we don't have any luck today, I'm going to the front tomorrow," she said. "I feel like I've been sitting around too long while others are risking their lives."

There was a silence and then her three friends nodded. "We're coming too," Beatrice said. "You're right."

Eyre packed the Book of Bane back in the sea chest, and then got her Wisdom out. "I'll meet you at the Mantle Basin," she said. "I just want a last look."

When her friends had gone, Eyre opened the ancient book. She wanted to see her parents again before she left; she knew there was no guarantee she'd ever be back. She leafed through the pages, soaking up the vision and the voices that she loved so much. She reached the final page with the Revelation about the Eta Aquariids, and then, out of habit, turned the page over.

To her great surprise, as she watched, words appeared across the middle of the blank page.

When Sir Daljeet fights the mighty Djinn
One of the two triangles can pass to learn
The path to the Aura, which lies within
But the traveller who enters will not return

Eyre took a deep breath and stared at the page. Just when she thought there was nowhere to go, another clue. What did *this* mean?

She wrote the rhyme in the Book of Bane: *The Fourth Revelation of the Wisdom.* Then she carried the Book up to her lounge room and telepathed her friends. A few minutes later, Beatrice, Abby and Nick returned, looking very curious when they saw the Book of Bane on the table.

Eyre turned to the new entry and tapped the words. "This was in my Wisdom," she said, and sighed. "Really? More puzzles. One of the two triangles. *Which* triangles?"

Beatrice dragged the Book over and read the Revelation aloud. She looked upwards for a minute, thinking and then nodded. "Remember at the meeting of the Determinant Dozen we watched in first year, Madame Overmantle mentioned 'One of the two Triangles'. She meant 'one' as in a person, an *Aether*. It refers to the symbol on the genealogical chart, it's just the way she phrased it that's a bit confusing. So it means an Aether—you,

Eyre—can go somewhere to uh, *find out*, I guess, how to reinstate the Aura." She drummed her fingers on the coffee table. "But where? Somewhere Sir Daljeet is. Who is he? And what do they mean by *when* he fights the Djinn? We can't really go back in time, sadly. Wouldn't that be a great Lightworking power!" Everyone laughed, a bit ruefully, and again Eyre's thoughts turned to her parents, and she felt the familiar pain of their loss. Indeed, wouldn't that be wonderful. To be able to change the past.

"There are many Lightworking powers I wish I had," Abby said softly, and Eyre understood. She was no doubt thinking of her own father. "But some things are not possible."

"What about the Library?" Nick suggested after a moment. "Maybe we're supposed to look in a book for information. The old methods!" Everyone laughed. All the students at the Academy loved the Library—mostly because of the wonderful Mrs Abnett, who made learning, and books, exciting. Even the most precious of works was available and accessible to students, provided they treated them with the respect they were due. If not, Mrs Abnett would send them to the Academy cafeteria for a week, where the Jotnar would teach them a few life skills.

"The Central Admin building has several sculptures and there are a few Saints and Lords amongst them," Beatrice mused, and then she shrugged wryly. "Not that I know who they are." Everyone laughed half-heartedly. They didn't know who the old sculptures were of either. Eyre felt a sudden shame. Now that the Overworld, and the Lightworkers themselves might be in such peril, she wished she'd taken more notice.

"Or could it be a museum somewhere?" Nick said. "Sydney has a Lightworking Museum in the Rocks."

They sat in contemplation for a long while. Abby sighed. "Well, the campus is not safe at the moment, if the Gothak have taken over the Domain. But perhaps we could get in and get out of the Library quickly? Surely, they're unlikely to be in there?"

Eyre nodded slowly. "It's worth a try. We really don't have any idea what that Revelation might mean at the moment, and the Library might hold the clue."

Nick grinned. "Let's teleport to the Genealogy section. We know no one's been in there for several decades! Even the Gothak would fall asleep in there."

Everyone laughed. Jemima Periwinkle had ensured that Genealogy would remain the most unpopular subject on the Academy's curriculum.

Beatrice's eyes glinted. "Excellent! At least we'll be doing something, instead of sitting around here with a question mark-shaped lux above our heads. And we can look for information about the Golden Beryl too. Let's go!"

Eyre stood up. She was happy to go and look, and if they were careful, their presence would be undetected. Teleporting was so quick, they could disappear in a second if the Gothak noticed them on campus.

They stood in a circle and then, one by one, they disappeared in a flash of light.

CHAPTER FORTY

EYRE BREATHED HARD AS the Library shimmered into sight around her and she held on to the counter for stability. Vertigo always seemed to accompany her when she teleported, and it took a second for her to recover. Her friends appeared beside her and they immediately looked around them for any signs of the Gothak. They walked cautiously along the walls and crouched behind the reception desk.

When it was obvious there was no movement outside, Eyre motioned to her friends that she was going to check out the front of the building. She moved forward slowly and peered out the window.

What Eyre saw broke her heart. The college grounds were completely decimated. The Central Admin building was scarred with atra burns and several large shards of the infrastructure were broken into irregular chunks, which lay scattered in the lot where the Zepps normally parked. The dormitories and lecture buildings had been attacked and bombed, and walls were missing in many of them. Trees were toppled and hedges and gardens uprooted. Several of the beautiful sculptures and carvings had been smashed. It was sad, and eerie. The grounds had a curiously deserted air, and yet Eyre still felt like she was being watched. Her skin crawled. The sooner they got back to Highlight the better.

"I'm going to look for information about the Golden Beryl," Beatrice said, her face grim. Eyre thought that made sense—Beatrice's favourite game was Crystallography, so perhaps she could work out the puzzle of the Golden Beryl. It seemed to be the key to everything, so her smart brain was undoubtedly the one to try and work it out.

"I'm going to search for anything about the Djinn, and Sir Daljeet," Eyre said. The Fourth Revelation was obviously an important part of solving the enigma of the Aura, and because her parents had sent the message to her, it was a personal thing for her to try and solve the riddle.

"Well, I guess I'll look for any history on the Tunguska Event," Abby said after a moment. "Maybe there's something that will help us there."

"And I'll stand guard," Nick said emphatically. "We don't want you all sliced to pieces with a book in your hand if the Gothak sneak up on us."

They all smiled at each other. A plan! Finally, after dithering for days on what to do next, it seemed like they might be able to move forward. Quickly, they separated, heading for the relevant sections of the library, and Nick stood guard at the front of the building. His senses were on high alert; he wouldn't miss a movement out on campus if any malign being came in sight.

Beatrice was already plunging into the section on crystals, and Abby headed down the aisle to find the history books that might reference the Tunguska Event. Eyre decided after a moment that the best place to start might be in the 'Lightworkers of Note' section, which included cabinets containing ancient weapons and memorabilia of those people who had been so important in Lightworker history. As she studied the old artifacts, Eyre saw that Beatrice and Abby were already sitting on the floor, surrounded by dusty old tomes, and they were turning the pages furiously.

Eyre eventually found a book about famous Lightworkers and looked for a reference to Sir Daljeet. She found it quickly enough, and as she read, she realised he was revered in India for his courageous effort in defeating the terrible Djinn of Jodhpur. The Djinn had destroyed many towns and killed thousands of people. Crops had been burnt and homes razed to the ground, and the people had lost all hope until Sir Daljeet came. He battled the Djinn for hours until finally he destroyed the Djinn's lamp with his powerful Mnae. He had saved the people, and they had erected a bronze statue of him in his honour. As she looked at the picture of the statue, something was familiar about it. And then she realised—he was depicted in one of the images in her attic window. In the window he was standing strongly with his Mnae as a huge wind blew around him. She had never known his name—no doubt her parents would have told her if they were alive. She'd always just seen him as a symbol of the strength of Lightworkers, rather than a real person.

But that didn't help much. Perhaps she needed to study the image in the window at Highlight more closely—that might give a clue. Or maybe they needed to travel to the statue? She closed the book and looked for more references. She found quite a few, and spent an hour studying the information within. It supported what she'd already read in the first book, but she could find nothing else that might solve the clue that the Fourth Revelation had given them. She put the books back, feeling exasperated.

Why didn't the Revelation just *tell* them what to do? It would make things so much easier. But she already knew the answer to that—it had to be hard, so that the power of the Aura could not fall into the wrong hands. When her Wisdom was constructed, unfortunately her desperate parents didn't know who to trust. And riddles helped to keep the secret safe.

A telepathic whisper reached her from the front of the library and she looked over. Nick had disappeared under his drupe cape.

"*Gothak*," Nick cautioned. "Time to go."

Beatrice and Abby jumped up and quickly started putting the books back —despite the mess of the campus they would never leave them out. Mrs Abnett would follow them to the ends of Entis!

In a flash Eyre swung her cape over her and sent a sparkle down it so that she disappeared from sight. Her stomach churned as she saw the number of Gothak sauntering around the campus as if they owned it. And then she despaired because she realised, at that moment, that they really *did* own it. What she actually wanted to do was blast them all with searing Light energy, but it wouldn't help anything to reveal their presence, so she gritted her teeth. Suddenly. from around the corner, a huge Saevus charged across the grounds towards the Library, teeth bared and green drool slavering from them. The Gothak didn't know Eyre and her friends were there, but the Strigis had scented them.

Beatrice shoved the last book on the shelf and then in a blaze of light they all teleported back to Eyre's cabin.

No one said anything as Eyre made them coffee. No need for a kettle any longer—she boiled the water with a blast of Viq. Abby summoned a plate of lemon slice from her cabin.

"I made it yesterday," she said. "I reckon we've earned it."

They all sat on Eyre's comfortable couch and after a moment she sighed.

"Well, who wants to go first? I'm not sure I have anything helpful, to be honest."

Beatrice jumped in. "Well, I found out where several Golden Beryl fields are. I guess we could visit them. And one of them is in Russia—where the Proditio occurred. That might make sense. Except there was also a reference to the Transit having all crystals of the world. I feel like the Golden Beryl must be close by, so perhaps we should start there."

Abby took a sip of her coffee. "My books told me that there was a powerful clairvoyant in Russia called the Tomsk Prorok. So maybe we could go there and see if anyone remembers anything she said. Apart from that, all the books I read only told me information that we already know about the Proditio."

Eyre sighed again. "That was pretty much the same as me. The books I read all had the same information about Sir Daljeet, but at least I know who he is now. He killed an evil Djinn who had slaughtered thousands of people in Jodhpur in the 17th century. There's a statue of him there, so perhaps we should go there and look. But you know, one of the moving pictures in my window is of him, so it might hold a clue. I think we should look at that first."

Nick shrugged and laughed. "It's close by. I reckon we should start with that."

So they trooped up the narrow staircase to the attic and sat on the floor. The window was moving in the mid-morning sun and the colours were as vibrant as ever, and they stared at the beautiful images until the one of Sir Daljeet came up. He stood proudly in the howling wind with his Mnae in front of him. It was an image Eyre was familiar with, as she'd looked at the window so many times over the years. She stared at it, trying to find something that she might not have noticed before, but when the image moved on to the next, she still hadn't come up with anything.

"Anyone see anything?" she asked in frustration. Everyone shrugged, and the window kept rotating through the scenes. After the third, infuriating time through the whole series, Eyre decided there was nothing to find and started to stand up. But then she noticed Beatrice had a very intent look on her face and she knew it meant she'd had a thought. After a long moment of consideration, Beatrice looked at them.

"What if," she said slowly, "I mean, it's a bit of a stretch—but what if, 'one of the two triangles', which means an Aether, like we said before—i.e. *you*, Eyre, can enter the window when the image of Sir Daljeet appears?"

There was a long silence as everyone thought about it.

"I've never touched the window," Eyre said, frowning. "It's such a masterpiece I wasn't game. So I don't know."

"It certainly is magical," Abby said softly.

Eyre was unsure. *Could* the miraculous window be some sort of a transit —she wasn't clear where to—but to solving the Aura's mystery? Eyre had never touched the glass because it had seemed too precious to do anything other than look at it. Jengles organised one of the Mimir to wash it carefully whenever it needed doing. All those hours she'd spent staring at the beautiful windows, not imagining there might be a huge secret hidden in it. Possibly the solution to the problem that had plagued the Overworld for more than a hundred years. But the idea of being able to go in there seemed so surreal—the stuff of fantasy. She shook her head dubiously.

"The words say the traveller won't return," Nick said, and silence crashed down on them all. No one said anything and then Eyre managed a laugh.

"Well, I'm not entirely convinced you're right, Bea. It seems a bit far-fetched." She looked apologetically at Beatrice. "But we're all going to die sometime," she said. "And a lot more of us, and a lot more *quickly* if the Aura isn't reformed. I'm the only Aether old enough, so if this is indeed the meaning of the Revelation, I have to go."

She looked at her friends' sombre faces and stood up. "Come on, we can't waste time. I'll try it. I might just smash through the window and out into the garden. But if not, and I don't come back, I'm happy, actually—the Revelation has taken us one step further in our quest, after all these roadblocks and all the hardship over the years. If I can help to work the mystery out, that's brilliant. An hour ago, I thought all was lost, so this is actually fantastic." Even to her own ears she sounded like she was trying to convince herself. She walked towards the window, trying to seem confident. But in reality, she was terrified. Was she going to her death? Would she ever see her friends again? It sounded like—if she did get into the window—she might never come back. A paralysing dread filled her and she had to force herself to keep going. She felt she understood how someone might feel when they were heading to the gallows.

The scene currently showed a million butterflies wafting through a glade filled with weeping willows, and traversed by a tumbling river. It was intricate and peaceful, and it depicted a couple in a canoe reclining as they drifted down the current and out of view. But Eyre's stomach flipped in fear, because she knew that St Daljeet was only a couple of panes away. She froze in place when the celebrated knight appeared with his gleaming Mnae. And before she could crank her brain into gear, the scene changed again.

Eyre looked down. "Sorry," she whispered. "I wasn't quite ready."

Her friends ran over and embraced her, and all of them were crying. "We love you, Eyre," Abby said as tears dripped down her cheeks. "What will we do without you if you don't come back?"

They sat silently in front of the moving window, close to the glass, and watched the breathtaking art change for a whole rotation. After half an hour, nearly all twenty scenes had moved past their eyes. Eyre was watching a glorious winter waterfall scene in the Snowy River, but her stomach was knotted, despite the tranquillity. Next up was St Daljeet.

But this time when the old warrior appeared, she didn't stop to think. Without looking at her friends, she shut her eyes and launched herself towards the window.

CHAPTER FORTY-ONE

EYRE HAD A DISORIENTING feeling of vertigo, and rainbow colours shimmered in front of her eyes as she passed through the glass. Then she was falling, falling. Down she went, unable to stop herself until she landed awkwardly in spiky branches at the top of a tree. Breathing rapidly, she held tightly to one of the limbs and peered cautiously down through the leaves. Somehow, she'd landed in the middle of a baobab tree, a strange and ancient tree from Africa. It was just as well she had landed in the canopy, because it was a long drop to the plateau below, where Sir Daljeet battled the malevolent Djinn.

Sir Daljeet swung his Mnae with great force. "Come on then, you blighter!" he bellowed at the three-metre-high red spirit. It spun in the air before him, its top half incredibly muscled and the bottom half gradually fading to red smoke that emanated from an ornate lamp. The creature wore a golden turban and its sharp features were distorted in rage. It took a deep breath and blew hard at Sir Daljeet, causing a cyclonic whirlwind in the desert sand, but St Daljeet put up his magical bronze shield and leaned forward into the tempest.

As the phenomenal battle unfolded below her, Eyre tried to levitate down out of the blinding sandstorm. But strangely, her Viq didn't seem to work. After a few moments of frantically trying to generate the energy, she reverted to the old-fashioned way and climbed down, hanging on desperately in the wild wind. She sheltered behind the bulbous trunk of the baobab tree and kept her head down as the stinging sand whipped against her skin. And then there was silence. The tornado stopped and birds started singing.

When Eyre looked around the tree, St Daljeet was sliding his Mnae back into its scabbard. Although she hadn't seen it, from reading the books in the library, Eyre knew what had happened. St Daljeet had smashed the lamp with his Mnae, and the Djinn, unanchored, had been taken away in the whirling maelstrom, outwitted.

"Rather smart of me," the knight said, beaming, and struck a pose, the one that Eyre was familiar with.

Eyre's vision blurred and then she was standing in the pane that she knew was the first of the Alterworld series—Terra. She was by the cliffs and the azure grotto where the lux orbs were released by the Lux plant, with Tub-Bees buzzing around and Zhuzhu Flutters hovering over the water. The colours in the window were more vivid than in real life, giving the scene a surreal feeling. Eyre had to remember not to get too absorbed in the beauty of the sight, and she wandered around the pool looking for a clue that might help them. But before she had found anything, the scene shifted onto the Aqua window. She was under the water, swimming among the coloured coral and the strange fish, looking for any sign of the 'path' the Revelation had mentioned. But although enchanting, the scene changed again without her being any clearer. She traversed the Caelus and Incendium panels too, and began to feel desperate. What if the clue was there and she didn't see it? She could be searching for years.

The next series of designs were the 'artistry' set; six successive panels that celebrated the creative skills of the Lightworkers. Jolin the Second had designed a touching tribute to his father, Jolin the First, and Eyre watched the old man produce exquisite blown-glass designs from a red-hot furnace. In a nod to Lightworker skills, some of the glass spheres floated upwards like Bullio. But again, there was no obvious clue in this panel, or in the rest of the artistry series: the musicians, painters, and sculptors who had told the stories of Lightworker history.

Eyre was getting tired in this dreamlike world. The panels moved quickly and she didn't have much time to look around. She hoped she didn't have to go through the whole series again. Was this to be her fate—doomed to rotate endlessly through the panels in the diamond window? It was hard when she didn't know what she was looking for. An object? A magical spell? Even maybe a transit to somewhere else—she had no idea.

The window shifted again and Eyre found herself in the first of the scenic quintet. These were five panels that showed the beauty of Australia from the eye of one who had loved it dearly. The harsh, dry outback. The diverse wildlife. The blue seas and the incredible rainforests. One panel depicted the sunrise through to sunset over Lake Mackenzie on Fraser Island. They were the most detailed and intricate panels of the whole sequence, and Eyre suddenly realised she had stood through them all, mesmerised, without remembering to look for the sign to the Aura. She had a strange feeling of being unable to stop the treadmill she was on, and her head was spinning from the constantly changing surroundings.

Her vision blurred again and then she was in the enchanted forest of Montville. Hippogriffs wandered around and a pixie flew up to Eyre on shimmering wings.

"We've been waiting for you," it said crossly. "You took your time."

"Ah, sorry," Eyre said. "But I'm here now. Can you give me any information about the Aura? I need to find the path to reinstate it."

"Oh yes," the pixie said, and Eyre's heart leapt. "Kia Ora," the pixie continued importantly, "is the greeting of our Tasman neighbours. There's many flight paths over there, in state *and* out of state. As long as you wear a mask."

Eyre was so nonplussed she couldn't think of anything to say. Not *that* kind of Ora. Or path. Or state. She smiled weakly, and was about to try again when a horn blared from somewhere in the forest. A herd of multi-coloured unicorns came thundering out and dashed past her, followed by a hunting party of cheering fauns armed with bows and arrows.

With a small explosion of glitter, the pixie disappeared and Eyre stood uncomfortably as the fauns stopped across the dell and turned towards her.

"This one's easier," a hairy-legged member of the group sniggered. And before she could even think, he fired at her. A flaming arrow shot through the air and hit her at the top of her arm, burning her skin painfully.

"Hooray!" the fauns cried, and more arrows flew through the air towards her. Eyre tried to summon a shield, but nothing happened, and she realised that none of her Lightworking skills would work here. She ducked and dodged the blazing hail of arrows, and took off running into the forest. Holding her throbbing shoulder, she dashed amongst the trees as the fauns galloped behind her, shouting and cheering at the chase.

And then her vision shimmered and she was in the peaceful scene with the canoe and the two lovers drifting down the river. The woman in her old-fashioned hat looked over at Eyre and trailed her fingers in the water over the side of the canoe.

"You'll want to avoid *them*," she said to Eyre languidly, and she rested her chin on her hands as the canoe floated away around the bend.

Confused, Eyre turned around. 'Them' turned out to be the party of fauns, who were charging towards her across the rolling meadow, firing more flaming arrows into the air. The hunting horn was blaring and Eyre turned and ran...

...straight into the brink of a waterfall in the Snowy River. The winter scene, with pristine snow and a mostly-frozen lake. The freezing torrent of water hit her like a battering ram and blasted her over the edge and downwards, until she smashed through the lake's surface and plunged deep into the glacial water. The water was so cold she couldn't move for a minute, and then she desperately dragged herself up to the surface, gasping for air in her frozen lungs. The fauns were gathered at the top of the waterfall, firing down at her, and the burning arrows plunged into the frigid water with sharp fizzes. Eyre struck out with numbed limbs for the banks of the lake and crawled out into the deep snow. She was so cold she couldn't move, and she lay in the ice as the fauns stormed down the side of the cliffs towards her. On their two cloven hooves, they could handle the rocky slopes with ease, and they hooted as they drew near to their prey.

Who was suddenly lying before Sir Daljeet as the Djinn blew violently at him. The tornado of sand hit her hard and caught her up in a dizzying, brutal whirlwind.

And as Eyre lost consciousness, she realised that she had found the ending the Revelation had predicted.

CHAPTER FORTY-TWO

EYRE OPENED HER EYES groggily. She was so terribly cold that her jaw was locked in unmoveable rigor. She tried to draw a breath into her frozen lungs and rolled over onto her hands and knees to violently vomit up the contents of the Snowy River, mixed painfully with sand from the Thar desert. She took deep shuddering gulps of air down her raw throat as she tried to clear the black spots from her eyes. And then an astounding realisation dawned on her. She was still alive! But she also remembered, with a jolt of fear, that the fauns would be coming, and she had to keep moving. Faun. What a ridiculously sweet name for a horrible creature! A dark part of her nature wished she could bring a Saevus in here to entertain their hunting party.

She shook her head and looked around. She was back at the enchanted forest, and a sense of despair overcame her. She didn't know how many cycles the window had been through while she was lying there. She was utterly bone-weary already, and she didn't have a clue what to do. The scenes were moving too quickly for her to figure anything out, and it could take her countless cycles before she did—if ever.

She saw the pixie fluttering around a wattle tree and decided not to bother with it. And then she heard the thundering of approaching hooves. She hurtled into the forest and hid behind a tree, just as the fauns charged past, trumpets blaring.

"Took you long enough," an annoyed voice said. Eyre jumped and turned, and saw a small elf standing beside her, hands on his hips. He had a little peaked hat, and waistcoat and pants, all green.

"It's no wonder the cloven beasts keep finding you," he said, indicating the shimmer of her Lightworker uniform. "Dressed like that. You stand out like a neon light. Serves you right that you've had so much trouble. I doubt your mother would have."

Eyre's heart clenched. *What?* Her mother had been here?

The acerbic elf continued. "Now, you are looking for something, and I've been waiting for years to tell you where it is, and what to do with it."

Eyre's heart leapt and she knelt down, forgetting her mother and only focusing on the cranky little fellow. "Thank you," she whispered, with tears in her eyes.

The elf clicked his fingers and a golden chest, covered in rubies, emeralds, sapphires and other precious stones, appeared. Eyre realised that they were the stones of all the Sectors—amethyst, carnelian, citrine, golden quartz. What a glorious thing it was! The elf used a key on a chain to open the box and then gave an annoyed snort.

"We're out of time. See you on the next round."

The scene shimmered, and Eyre was back in the peaceful river scene.

"Hi again," the man in the canoe smiled at her. "Welcome back!" He poured a glass of champagne for his companion as Eyre ran to hide under a willow tree. She knew to avoid the fauns now, and she was determined they wouldn't catch her. With an irritated grimace she wished she had her Viq. *Then* she'd show them something! But she forced a smile and waved at the couple as they disappeared down the tranquil river.

Eventually, she travelled through all the panels again—fortunately, missing the waterfall dive this time, until she finally arrived back at the forest where the elf waited, tapping his foot impatiently.

"I will be so glad to get rid of this," he said in an annoyed tone. "Stuck in the forest waiting for someone to arrive. I'm going to the Aqua panel when we're done, for a bit of a holiday."

He reached into the chest and pulled out a crystal tile, a little like a flooring tile about 15 centimetres square. It was an interesting green colour, and Eyre couldn't identify it. It shone with a vibrant energy, and Eyre knew it was something very special.

The elf gave the square to Eyre, but then pulled a large pocket watch out of his trousers. "You've taken too long," he said. "Your time is nearly up. You put this—"

And then everything shimmered and Eyre felt an unpleasant tugging, and the world faded before her.

Eyre opened her eyes slowly. Every part of her body hurt, and she was lying on top of the crystal tile, which was cutting into her stomach. Slowly she sat up, breathing hard. And then joy flooded through her. She was back in the attic! How could that be? She wasn't meant to return! She looked at the precious object on the floor and picked it up carefully. It obviously had some great significance, but she'd been pulled back before the elf had been able to tell her what to do with it. Despite her exhaustion, she staggered to her feet, and when Sir Daljeet appeared again she tried to push back into the window. But only solid glass met her outstretched hand. There was no way in; apparently this was a one-time journey. Her shoulders slumped and she turned away and looked at the tile. She didn't know what to do with it, but she knew she needed to safeguard this incredible object.

She was still soaking wet from her swim in the Snowy River, so she tried to send a wave of Viq and dry herself off. But it didn't work. Confused, she tried again, and still nothing happened. Annoyed, and shaking with cold, she picked up the tile and walked slowly downstairs. She would have a shower, but first she wanted to find Beatrice, Abby and Nick.

She opened her cabin door, feeling like she'd just participated in the National Ferito Trials. Her whole body felt pummelled. Her friends weren't far away, sitting silently by the Mantle Basin when Eyre went outside, and they all turned in surprise at the sound of the door. Then an incredulous grin appeared on Abby's face and she charged over to wrap her arms around Eyre.

"You're back? But how?" She was crying with happiness and Beatrice and Nick came over too, their faces full of surprise and joy.

"Did you make any progress?" Beatrice asked as she too hugged Eyre.

"Agh," Eyre said through her blue lips, "partly." She held out the mysterious tile and sighed. "It's got something to do with the Aura, but I got chucked out of the window before I found out what to do with it."

Her teeth were chattering like miniature jackhammers and she felt she would never warm up, despite the hot spring sun. Abby sent a wave of Viq and dried her off.

"Thanks," Eyre said, "I don't seem to be able to use Viq at the moment."

"You're tired," Beatrice said. She waved her hand and a blanket appeared, which she draped around Eyre. "Let's go to your cabin—we've got to hear what happened!"

"And I have to put this in the basement," Eyre said. "It's not safe out here."

Nick gave her a hug, which was unlike his usually controlled manner. "We thought we'd never see you again. It's a miracle."

Inside the cabin they sat on the brightly-coloured couches as Beatrice bustled in the kitchen, making mochas in Eyre's emerald-green mugs. Leaning back into the soft cushions, Eyre told them all about her experience in the window. To her annoyance, they all laughed when she described running away from the fauns, and then after a moment she chuckled too. It really had been a bit of a shambles.

Beatrice brought the mugs over and sat down. The tile sat in the middle of the coffee table and they all studied it. It had taken such a long time to find, and the significance it had was not clear. But it was obviously incredibly important to have been hidden in the moving window. Eyre stroked the glossy surface of the green square. It wasn't completely even; there was a chip out of one of its edges—clearly it had been through some trauma. But they *had* it; it was another step forward in this mysterious journey.

"I wonder what stone it is?" Eyre pondered.

"It's Alexandrite," Beatrice said, as she examined the glowing square. "A type of chrysoberyl. One of the rarest of minerals."

A memory surfaced and Eyre's eyes widened.

"Jengles said, two years ago, that Alexandrite was the centre of everything! How did he know that? Does he know what to do with this?" Eyre was perplexed. If Jengles knew what they were looking for, why would he not just tell them what to look for? Or how to do it? She looked at the green tile, wishing for answers. But then she stood up, despite her weariness.

"Well, whatever it's for, we know it's important. I have to put it in the oak chest to keep it safe." Then she sighed. "It would have been better staying in the window if we don't know what to do with it."

"Can you go back?" Abby asked hesitantly. "Maybe you can find out?"

"I tried," Eyre replied miserably. "Obviously I only got one shot, and I blew it."

"No you didn't," Nick said. "You've been incredibly brave. You got the Alexandrite. We'll work it out, now we have it. You did so well to bring it back."

Eyre smiled at him gratefully, although she still felt that she'd failed. If only she'd been a bit quicker, she would have had the answer they were seeking. But she took the precious tile down to her oak chest and put it in, sending a prayer to her parents.

"You were so smart," she whispered. "I will try and work it out."

CHAPTER FORTY-THREE

THE NEXT MORNING EYRE woke and realised that if she *had* been in the National Ferito Competition, then she had most definitely lost. Every muscle and bone hurt and she moved like a very old person as she walked slowly to the kitchen to make a cup of tea. She tried to boil the water with Viq, but it didn't work. Frustrated, she tried harder, but the water sat in the green mug and did nothing. With growing dismay, Eyre rummaged in the cupboard for the kettle she'd used in the past to make tea and coffee. This was feeling awfully familiar—like second-year, when she'd lost all her Light powers. And then with a sick feeling, understanding dawned.

'*The traveller who enters will not return*'. It didn't mean that she would die, or be stuck in the window. It meant that she would come out of the window different than before—and obviously her Viq was now gone. She stood up with the kettle in her hand and tried to elevate. Nothing happened. Then she tried to communicate with Beatrice telepathically. It was just a blank void in her mind.

Tears streamed down her face as she put the kettle on the bench and realised that the price for the Alexandrite square had been the loss of her powers. It hurt more now than when she'd lost them previously. Back then, she'd had no expectations of regaining her Light powers, after her early poor performance at the Trials. When they did return, there was just gratitude and surprise that they had come back. But since then she'd become used to her growing powers; she was reliant on them and proud of them. She was used to seeing herself as both an Aether and a skilled Lightworker. It seemed bizarre that her Viq could be gone. But she now understood with certainty the meaning of the verses; entering the window had stripped Eyre of her Light energy. And her power as an Aether. The pain was like a Mnae going through her.

But then she slapped herself mentally. It was devastating to lose her powers but it was better than being dead. Or stuck in the window running away from fauns for the rest of her life. And she'd got the tile. *Move on, princess*, she admonished herself. Maybe her powers would come back anyway, like before. But deep down she knew that this change was permanent. It was a Revelation, and it couldn't be undone.

Just then, there was a knock on her door and she opened it to find her three friends grinning at her. Slightly nonplussed, she let them in.

"We're just so glad you're here," Abby said. "We thought you were gone forever."

Eyre smiled, and suddenly felt the sadness about her loss of Viq leave her. Abby's words resonated with her so strongly, and she realised it was *absolutely* how she felt as well. She hugged her friend.

"Me too, I'm so glad. But I have to tell you that I am again one of the proud Unlit."

At their enquiring glances, she explained. "I've lost my Light powers. I think I worked out what the Revelation meant. It's that *I'd* be changed when I came out of the window. Not dead, or disappeared—it just meant I'd lose my Viq. Come back different."

Her friends looked dismayed and then awkward, and Eyre jumped in. "I know, I'm not happy about it. But it's better than being dead, or stuck in that window. And if it means the Aura can be reinstated, it's worth it."

Beatrice looked relieved as she looked at Eyre's face and realised she meant it. "Well, that's why we're here. We've decided that we'll try and find out more in Russia—the Murzinka Mine in the Prigorodny District has a Golden Beryl mine. And it's located in the Middle-Urals Ring Structure, which is believed to be created by an impact event like the Proditio!" Then she frowned. "Except, we can't call it the Proditio anymore. There was no betrayal at all, was there. I'm calling it the Tunguska Event from now on."

"And I'd like to try and find out more about the Tomsk Prorok," Abby said.

Eyre smiled. "Well it's a great plan—but I'm going to have to hitch a ride with one of you. Where are we going first?"

"Let's go to the mine," Nick said, "perhaps the Mimir there can help us get started. And finding the Golden Beryl has to be the priority."

Everyone nodded; that made sense.

"I'll take you, Eyre," Beatrice said. "And everyone else too, to save time. I know where we're going. Grab hold!"

They all disappeared in a flash of light and when they reappeared, Beatrice generated a lux and Eyre could see that they were standing in an ancient tunnel propped up by ageing beams of timber. The marks of years of attack from pickaxes. and later on, impact-drilling implements, marked the granite walls with deep scars and pockmarks. Here and there, the discarded remnants of blasting apparatus lay scattered around, the indicators of years of back-breaking and dangerous work, and no doubt heartbreak. Boulders of volcanic and sedimentary rock lay where they had been blown from the metamorphic rock, crouching like strange animals in the gloom.

It was frigid in the passage, despite it being late-summer in Russia. Eyre shivered. Evidently, things didn't warm up too much here in the mountains, and especially below ground.

"Which way do you think?" she asked, as she rubbed the goosebumps on her arms. And then regretted it as her aching muscles complained loudly. Argh! She was sore.

Everyone looked around the tunnel. It was impossible to tell. It was even hard to know which way led down and which way up. Abby shrugged.

"Let's go this way," she said, and Eyre was happy to follow. Abby's psychic powers probably gave her a better idea than any of them about which way to go.

They hadn't gone very far when a gruff, strangely-accented voice stopped them.

"You'd better have a good reason to be here or my Crescent Blade is going to get a good workout today!"

A fierce red-haired creature stepped out of the dark, his gleaming curved blade raised and an unfriendly look on his face. His beard was plaited into two loops with garnets and copper wire, and Beatrice groaned out loud. The Mimir symbol of war. The short, sturdy creature was decked out in thick leather protective gear, and he uttered a loud cry in a language Eyre couldn't understand. Within seconds, the sound of running feet echoed off the cold rock walls. And then a whole battalion of Mimir stood behind the first, every blade raised.

"Great," Beatrice muttered as she regarded the irate form before her. "All we needed. Jengles' clone!"

But Nick stepped calmly forward and bowed. "General Gel Lithium Silica sends his regards, kind sir," he said calmly.

At that, the red-faced Mimir hesitated and he raised a cautionary hand to the troops behind him, who seemed intent on dealing forcefully with the intruders at any moment.

"From Australia?" he asked in his unusual brogue, as he studied them with narrowed eyes. Nick nodded, and the Mimir indicated that his troops should lower their blades.

"Why are you here?" the powerful Mimir demanded as he sheathed his blade. "War has broken out everywhere—the Gothak have overrun the Urals and there are pretenders everywhere." He glowered at Beatrice suspiciously and Eyre hid a smile. Perhaps he *was* Jengles' clone. Beatrice just sighed and rolled her eyes. Nothing new here!

"You speak English well," Abby said, knowing just the right thing to say. The muscular Mimir preened a little, which he tried to hide as a small smile appeared on his stern face.

"I studied in Ireland. I enjoyed it very much. There are many Mimir there and I enjoyed their purple ale. I am General Rhodonite, and I ensure the safety and protection of this section of the Prigorodny District. How can I be of assistance?"

Eyre stepped forward. "We are looking for 'The Golden Beryl'," she said. "Not *any* Golden Beryl, but something that is of note, or powerful somehow. We have been given secret information that it is the key to reinstating the Aura."

The General looked shocked. "There is a way to reinstate the Aura?" he breathed. "Lumen be praised!"

"Yes," Eyre said, "and it has something to do with a special Golden Beryl. We came here because the Proditio occurred here and we wondered if it might be linked."

"The *Tunguska Event*," Beatrice corrected her fiercely, and the General's eyes swung to her. She glowered back at him.

Eventually the General made a decision and waved his troops away, and then it was just the five of them as he sat on a boulder and indicated they should do the same.

"This is an old section of the mine," he said. "And no longer used. The newer section is where many different minerals are mined. But there are many people of Entis there, and we can't just walk in without causing an international incident."

Beatrice laughed and the General looked at her, his eyes warming a little.

"There have been many spectacular Golden Beryls mined here," he said, as his brow creased in thought. "But nothing of particular note. I wish I could help you." He shook his head. "The Overworld needs all the help it can get at the moment."

They all slumped in disappointment. This appeared to be a dead end, but Eyre rallied her dismal thoughts. There were many other Golden Beryl fields to visit.

"Thank you anyway," she said. "We appreciate your help."

The rugged General looked her, his eyes glinting. "We will fight to the end for the Overworld," he said grimly.

"Remember the spring," Eyre said, and the General smiled.

"And the summer that follows," he rejoined.

"Do you know anything about the Tomsk Prorok?" Abby asked. "We wanted to find a relative if possible, to see if they might be able to help us."

The General nodded. "Oh yes, she is very famous here, and has given many predictions. She has a sister who lives in Aqua I believe. And a second cousin in Entis, ah—Mrs... Shelf, I think?" He thought for a moment and then shook his head.

"No, that's not it—" but Beatrice interjected, her face astounded.

"*Madame Overmantle?*"

The General nodded. "Yes, that's it. Overmantle."

Abby looked astounded. "The Sea Crone is the Tomsk Prorok's sister?"

Eyre's thoughts spun, trying to catch up. "So is the Tomsk still alive?" she asked.

The General nodded. "Yes, but she's not very friendly." Beatrice gave a quiet snort. The General was probably good at assessing that.

"So how do we find her?" Nick asked. "Perhaps she can give us more information about The Golden Beryl?"

The General looked at him. "She lives on Mount Narodnaya, the highest mountain in the Urals. But she hasn't spoken for many years. She has given up on the Overworld and prefers to live alone." He sighed. "You may not— probably will not—have any success, but By the Light, I hope you do."

And then he stood. "I must return to my troops." He bowed. "I have enjoyed meeting you. Perhaps we might share a purple ale one day, if we all get through this."

He turned and disappeared into the gloom of the tunnel, which sort of echoed Eyre's feelings. Gloomy.

Beatrice sighed. "Pleasant fellow."

And they all roared with laughter.

"Oh Bea," Abby snorted, "I don't know what it is about you and the Mimir, but anyway, you've given me a good laugh! Maybe they don't like the fact that you're so much taller than them?"

"Well, let's get going to the mute Tomsk Prorok," Eyre laughed. "I'm sure that's going to be immensely helpful!" And they all chuckled again.

"Onwards!" Beatrice said, and they all held hands and disappeared into the ether in a flash of light.

CHAPTER FORTY-FOUR

THIS TIME, THEY WALKED out into a freezing blast of Arctic wind that howled like a wild animal down the vertical sides of the mountain. Narodnaya was certainly trying to show them who was boss, Eyre thought, as she wrapped her arms around herself. But she stopped for a moment to admire the incredible view. What a beautiful place this was! The mountain was covered, in parts, with permafrost and the white vertical curves of glaciers, but it just added to the beauty, along with green-grey firs that clambered up the rough rockface far below, in the alpine tree line. A sharp wind slapped her cheeks into red circles, and high above her, Steller's Sea Eagles circled and glided in the icy wind currents. She recognised them from her time with the Unlit, when they'd studied all the birds of prey across the Overworld. A sudden melancholy gripped her. She wished Florence was here. And Ischyros. She missed her creature companions desperately at that moment.

But they had no time to linger, and so they hid behind an outcrop to escape the freezing conditions.

Beatrice spoke to Abby, her teeth chattering. "Well, I think maybe you should ask 'Mrs Shelf'—" everyone laughed as they shivered, "—where her cousin might be. And quickly, before we turn into ice sculptures on this cliff!"

So Abby closed her eyes and concentrated, sending her powerful telepathic communication across the world.

After a moment she opened her eyes and sighed.

'The highest point, of course." She looked so mournful that everyone chuckled. Physical activity wasn't Abby's favourite pastime. But as Eyre's eyes traced the path to the top of the hill, she realised they were almost there.

For half an hour they trudged, heads down, up the rocky ridge of the mountain. Occasionally Nick, who led the way, would look up to check they were heading in the right direction, until finally they ended up at the peak. Wind buffeted them from all sides, and Eyre, despite the blasts of warm air her friends sent her way, felt that she didn't have much time left before hypothermia set in.

But then a rock rolled back from the ancient cliff face and a weather-beaten face peered out. And if Eyre had ever seen an expression of greater disdain, she couldn't remember when. Even Aowx seemed affable in comparison.

The old crone furiously waved them in, and without hesitation, they stumbled through the opening, desperate to escape the punishing conditions.

Inside was an incredible glow of violet and plum hues. Candles were lit all around the cave, and purple-coloured crystals gave off an incredible glow.

"Amethyst?" Abby asked softly, as she looked in awe at the beautiful structures.

"Alexandrite," Beatrice said, stroking a crystal with reverence. "So spectacular in candlelight."

The old crone took a hard look at Beatrice. After a long moment she indicated they should sit down, and they each took a seat on an outcrop of the purple crystal.

There was an awkward silence and then Eyre spoke.

"We are here because we need to know if you can help us to find the Golden Beryl," she said. "It is apparently critical in reinstating the Aura, and we are searching for information about it."

The old crone looked at her with an extremely annoyed expression on her face. Another long silence ensued, but none of the four could think of anything else to say. How to make someone who had decided not to speak, speak?

Eyre sighed, and tried. "If we don't find the Golden Beryl, it will be the end of the Overworld," she said. "I feel that might matter to you? You have a sister and a cousin in the Overworld."

A dry cackle emanated from the old woman, but there was no humour in it.

Abby, the ultimate diplomat, tried. "We met your sister in Aqua, and we know Madame Overmantle very well. They have helped us, and I'm sure each one of you would agree that it's crucial the Gothak don't take over the Overworld."

The wizened old crone turned fathomless black eyes towards them. After a very long time she spoke in a rusty voice that sounded as if it had not been used in many years. "I never asked for visitors. I don't want to talk to anyone, ever again. I chose my home to get as far away from people as I could, yet here you are, asking for favours. You gave my sister gifts of Angelite and Bloodstone for her help. Where are my gifts?"

Silence reigned, and Beatrice leapt in, always the logical one. "We are sorry to bring you nothing, but we are desperate, Wise One. All we can give you is our honesty. The reinstatement of the Aura is reliant on any information you might give us, and we are at a dead end. And Madame Overmantle has never required any gifts for her help."

Rage contorted the Tomsk Prorok's face. "That is because she is an altruist—stupid, *stupid*! I gave many things to many people for *nothing* in the past, and was berated for the truth I gave them. Never again! People don't want to hear the truth, only what they wish for."

Abby's face softened. "That's why you're up here."

The old woman didn't answer, and turned a tortured face away. But finally she spoke.

"I already gave the information you seek, years ago, and I *will not* repeat myself. But I will tell you that you will never succeed until you have the full force of the Lightworkers. One of your Sectors is missing. That is the idiocy of the Overworld, especially Entis. Forgetting that they must appreciate one another's gifts, that you need each other."

Reluctantly, she spat more words out. "The Penitent One needs to join you, or you will fail. But that is all I will tell you."

Then her face darkened and she turned towards them with an intent that Eyre knew would not end well.

"Go now!" the old crone hissed. "I tire of company and wish you gone."

Realising how serious the old woman was, Beatrice grabbed Eyre's hand, and the four of them disappeared before the Tomsk Prorok could act on her threat.

✕✕

The next day, Eyre wandered over to Beatrice's cabin for breakfast. She took a sip out of the golden quartz mug as Abby slumped, her hand under her chin and her elbow on the bench. Abby lifted her crystal blue mug and then put it down, as if it weighed too much.

"Well, that was a complete waste of time," she sighed. "Nobody liked us, and none of them could help at all."

Nick was pragmatic. He put his amethyst mug down on the bench. "We tried," he said. "There were no guarantees, and to be honest, to get the answers at the first attempt *would* be rather amazing."

Abby was petulant. "Yes, but that old woman *did* know something. Why wouldn't she tell us? I don't get it. The Penitent One—what help is that?"

Eyre nodded. "Obviously she's not like Mrs Shelf," she said solemnly, and they all laughed.

Beatrice put her citrine mug down too, and Eyre saw the familiar gleam in her eye that meant she was not giving up.

"Well," Beatrice said. "We'll solve it ourselves then. Let's head to the Transit today. We probably should have gone there first. It has every crystal there!"

Nick nodded slowly. "It would probably make sense that whatever we seek isn't too far away. It can't hurt to look anyway. I think we're struggling a bit at the moment."

Beatrice took another sip, and then sighed. "Well, I don't know if any of you have thought of this yet, and I didn't really want to mention it, but the old crone was right. Our team of eleven didn't have Rufa in it."

It hadn't even occurred to Eyre, to be honest. She'd just thought that the right people had been chosen for the task, and even now she didn't think they'd got that wrong.

"So... the Penitent One, then," Nick said slowly, as they all suddenly got it with a blast of dismay.

"*Ben Perrill?*" Abby was aghast. "Surely not! I don't want to go anywhere with that louse, reformed or not!"

It was obvious they all agreed, and Eyre shook her head. Penitent or not, how on Entis could they accept Ben into their trusted group, people who would each give their lives for each other? It was beyond comprehension.

"Could we find one of the good Rufa students, maybe?" she suggested. "What about Jensen Ross?" She was referring to the courageous student who had lost his leg to a Bunyip at the Lightworker Trials.

But Beatrice sighed. "The Penitent One seems pretty clear. Unless we want the Curtis brothers or Wyatt Rankins? They're penitent. About ever joining the Academy, I think. Or not asking Saskia out. Or tangling with Eyre!" Everyone howled with laughter. It was true enough to be hilarious. But then Beatrice shook her head in bewilderment at the thought of Ben Perrill joining their team. "Seriously," she said. "I really can't go there right now. Saving of the Overworld or not."

They all laughed, but there was an undertone. None of them wanted to work with Ben. None of them liked him. And although he had helped the

Overworld, the scars were too many and too deep to feel comfortable with the idea.

"Anyway, let's just go check out The Transit, *without* Perrill," Eyre suggested. "See if we can work anything out." They all looked at each other and it was obvious they all agreed. No one wanted to go anywhere with Ben Perrill, let alone into the depths of the mountain.

"We'll have to be careful though. Anything can happen down there, with or without Perrill," Beatrice said and everyone grimaced. *That* was for sure.

They finished their breakfast and returned to their cabins to get organised. Eyre took a moment to stick her head into Ischyros's stable as she walked past. She tossed some liquorice into his feed bin and gave him some fresh water. The old horse swung his head as he used his limited sight to see who it was.

"Ah, it's you. Back from wandering around? You do seem to be in a very confused state lately," he mumbled as he chewed on the liquorice. "Obviously not very intelligent. Make sure you come back. I'll need my feed this afternoon."

Eyre ran in and hugged the motley old creature. "I love you too, Ischyros," she whispered.

The four friends headed across the dusty earth towards the entrance in the cliffs that led to the Transit. Florence flew above them, and Eyre had Vulture Killer firmly in her baldrics. She may not have her Viq or staff any more, but she would make herself count.

The gloom as they went into the entrance caused Eyre's gut to tighten, as it probably always would. Ben Perrill had nearly killed her in this darkened tunnel, and her mind would never let her forget it. But Nick lit a lux and the passageway became dimly visible, and with Florence on her shoulder, she felt better. There were terrible things happening in the Overworld, but her little team was making progress. It wasn't clear yet, but they had a plan.

After an hour of walking, they arrived at the Transit. The beautiful cavern glowed with a rainbow of colours, and Eyre's heart suddenly sang. This location had been the source of so much heartbreak and pain that she had forgotten how glorious it was. Ben Perrill, George Wilson and Jemima Periwinkle had flavoured her memories so that all she remembered was fear and heartbreak here. But as she looked around, the awe she felt when she'd first visited this incredible cavern rose within her again. How could she have forgotten what a miraculous place it was? Great outcrops of glowing crystals of all sorts and sizes; shining examples of the most precious of minerals; a geologist's dream—if they knew it was here.

"Okay, the Golden Beryl! Let's go get it!" Beatrice announced pragmatically, breaking into Eyre's thoughts. Beatrice started marching around, her eagle eyes focused on the outcrops of stunning crystals. They all spread out, going in different directions as they tried to look for a golden-hued crystal.

They spent several hours looking, high and low, on the walls, under outcrops, being careful so they wouldn't miss the smallest crystal. After all, who knew how big the Golden Beryl was? They found citrines, yellow sapphires, yellow garnets, and chrysoberyls, tourmaline and topaz. *BTL*, Eyre thought, even yellow diamonds, which the Entis world would pay a fortune for... but eventually they gave up, sitting dismally in the centre of the magnificent cave.

"It's not here," Abby said.

"Can't be," Nick agreed.

"Well, at least we know the Transit's off the list," Eyre said, trying to be positive as Florence hopped restlessly on her shoulder. Florence was bored and wanted to be outside, flying. It was way too long for her to be underground, and actually, Eyre felt the same way.

But then, unexpectedly, Abby stood up. "I hear something," she said. Eyre's gut tightened. Anything unexpected down here usually led to trouble of a huge magnitude. She concentrated, but couldn't hear anything. Of course, she now had no Viq, so she probably wouldn't hear anything anyway. But Beatrice and Nick were listening hard, and it was obvious they couldn't hear anything either.

"This way," Abby said, starting towards one of the darkened corridors that led from the Transit to the Light knows where. Eyre felt her anxiety rise when she realised it was the same tunnel that George Wilson and 'Professor Vela' (in reality Jemima Periwinkle) had emerged from when she'd overheard them talking. But Eyre forced herself to stay calm. Abby was so gifted at clairvoyance and telepathy. If she said she heard something, it must be true. And hopefully, if it was anything nefarious, Abby would be aware of that too. Making a decision, she sent Florence back through the Transit.

"You go home, girl," she whispered as the golden eyes looked at her. "This is no place for you." Needing no further encouragement, the powerful Venator shot across the cavern and back into the tunnel that led back to camp.

The three of them followed Abby into the passage and they began walking into the shadows. It got dark pretty quickly, almost pitch black, and Eyre was about to ask one of them to generate a lux. But then suddenly, there was no need.

Rows of fairy lights strung along the sides of the passageway unexpectedly lit up and gave off enough light to navigate easily as they wandered into the centre of the mountain. The pinpricks of light were so pretty that Eyre looked closer, and realised that they were fireflies, lining up along the sandstone walls to help guide them the right way.

"What can you hear Ab?" Beatrice asked eventually.

"Someone calling my name," Abby said after a moment. "Or not really, or —maybe, I guess? But I can hear *'Nefelibata'* repeating over and over. I suppose that's me?"

"That's good enough for me," Eyre said. "You most definitely are Nefelibata—so, lead on, McNeff!"

The girls laughed They'd all studied 'A Midsummer Night's Dream' at their old school, St Jeffrey's—years ago, before all this. But Nick, who categorically and repeatedly had informed them over the years that he didn't like Shakespeare, didn't laugh. He just grimaced.

"Just imagine it's all a dream, Nick Bottom," Beatrice teased. "You'll turn into a donkey and wake up tomorrow!"

Nick rolled his eyes as the others roared with laughter.

"I'm already an ass, so no worries, Bea," he said, and Beatrice chortled loudly.

The echoing noise of their laughter startled the fireflies, who twinkled off in an instant, leaving the passage in complete blackness.

"Your fault, Eyre," Nick said in a whisper. "This is what Shakespeare does to a person."

But then a small light approached them, fluttering in the darkness. A tiny voice spoke.

"Hello! My name is Cobweb," the tiny being said as the fireflies erratically glimmered back on.

Abby groaned softly, and Eyre laughed internally as she understood Abby's pain. More spiders?

But Beatrice, of course, got the fairy's small joke, and laughed. She loved Shakespeare. "Is it really?"

Cobweb giggled. "Nope. But I do serve the Faerie Queen, Thi, second sister of Mab, Faerie Queen of the United Kingdom. So Cobweb is fine for now. We have been calling the Great One, and we are glad she is here."

Three people and one small one looked at Abby, and she jumped.

"*Me?*" she asked, completely astonished. Eyre laughed, softly this time, because she didn't want to startle the fireflies. Darkness definitely wasn't her thing. She touched Abby's shoulder, the most self-effacing one of them all.

"Nefelibata, Abby. You *are* the Great One, and rightly so. Let's go with Cobweb and see why they want you."

Cobweb grinned and flitted ahead of them as they walked down the firefly-lit corridor.

CHAPTER FORTY-FIVE

THEY HAD WALKED FOR about half an hour in the dimly-lit passageways, when there was a violent shudder from beside them, and Cobweb flittered in alarm. And then another alarming quake came from somewhere deep in the rock beside them.

"Capes," Nick said in a low voice, and in a second they were invisible, including Cobweb, who had dimmed her light, and the fireflies, who had turned off the moment the first shudder struck the tunnel. Eyre crowded under Beatrice's cape, unable to use her own.

As they stood silently against the walls, Gothak came swarming out of the passage, both in front of them and behind. There were so many that Eyre's heart clenched in fear, but she stood rigidly as the gross creatures charged past, oblivious to their presence. Her heart nearly stopped when Mudamir turned a furious face back to his troops.

"They are here! I *know* it! Bring the Strigis if you need to, but they must be caught!"

And he charged ahead into the darkness, with his foul troops behind him.

For a long moment no one spoke, or moved. And it was just as well, because a second wave of Gothak followed the first, storming into the tunnel of the Transit as if it was a familiar route. Eyre stayed stock still, but her mind was in turmoil. It *was* a familiar route for them. They'd been here many times, that was obvious, and there were so many of them, she was sure that despite the Lightworkers' drupe capes, it wouldn't take long for them to be discovered. Her mind was frantic. *What to do?*

But that decision was taken from her. Because just then something massive crashed through the wall into the tunnel.

Rocks started falling, and the ground disappeared from under her, and then Eyre was tumbling over and over.

She landed with a splash in cold water, as rocks rained like meteors around her. Something huge crashed into the water beside her, and she desperately tried to circular breathe as she plunged deeper into the water, but only choked on the icy water—circular breathing wasn't an option for her any more. Eyre struggled back up to the surface and scrambled out of the freezing water on her hands and knees onto the banks of the darkened limestone cave. As she gasped deeply, she looked around desperately for her friends in the faint blue-green light cast by the bioluminescent fungi that colonized the irregular walls. Her heart clamped in fear; she was terrified for her friends—were they alright?

Great chunks of stone continued to smash down around her as the destabilised foundations of the chamber disintegrated, and she ducked desperately to avoid them. Where was everyone? She finally managed to stand and turned to look behind her, and her blood ran cold. A Tuus Scorpion floundered in the water near the bank, its venomous stinger stabbing the water in panic. It must have been the cause of the rockfall—it had smashed through the wall and destabilised the tunnel so that the whole thing had collapsed into the underground cavern.

Eye slid carefully back to the wall, getting ready to run. But the freezing water of the cave was too much for the Underworld beast, used to far warmer temperatures. After a few minutes of struggling, the huge creature sank slowly beneath the surface. Eyre raced forward, looking up and down the banks.

"Guys?" she called, wracked with fear for her friends.

Abby suddenly popped up, gasping for air. She spat out a mouthful of water as she looked around desperately.

"Get out, Abby!" Eyre cried and Abby splashed across to the side of the huge grotto and crawled out, her drupe cape dragging behind her like a bedraggled creature. She sent a wave of Viq over herself, and then did the same for Eyre, who was soaking wet and shivering.

"Thanks Abby," Eyre sighed.

"By the Light, what happened?" Abby said, taking big gulps of air. She staggered to her feet and looked around. "And where are the others?"

"A Tuus," Eyre said. "It broke through the tunnel, but it's down the bottom of the pool somewhere." She looked into the dim waters, but it was too deep and dark to see where the creature was.

They sat at the side of the grotto, on rocks and crystals that were heaped up like sand on a sea shore.

"Bea? Nick?" she called over and over. Abby sent waves of telepathic communication, searching in the ether for their friends. There was no sign of Bea or Nick, but a sparkle of glitter from above announced the return of the little fairy. Cobweb fluttered down and sat beside them. Her purple eyes were serious.

"I am glad you are safe, Nefelibata and friend," Cobweb said. "The foul ones are stampeding through the tunnels above, going the wrong way."

Eyre save a sigh. "Well, that's good news, but we can't find our friends," she said, looking around the cave anxiously.

But then a voice came from the shadows.

"I'm here!" Someone was swimming across the surface of the water, and then Nick appeared in the light of the lux. Abby threw herself forward and helped him out of the shallows, showering his face with kisses.

Eyre was so relieved to see him that she hugged him too, and cleared a place for him to sit.

"Are you okay?" she asked, seeing the blood running down his arm.

"A rock got me," Nick said. "Nothing major. Where's Bea?"

Eyre shook her head and her face was pale with fear. But she just said, "Let's wait a while."

"Any idea where we are?" Nick asked, and Abby shook her head. They sat in silence.

"I will get help to search," Cobweb said, but at that moment Abby tilted her head. "I can hear Bea!"

She meant telepathically, and Eyre's heart leapt. "Is she okay?"

"And where's it coming from?" Nick asked. He obviously couldn't hear Beatrice either.

"Down that way," Abby answered, pointing into the darkness.

Eyre stood up. "Let's go find her," she said.

Nick brought the lux, which cast a soft light in the dark cave, and they began to walk in the direction Abby indicated, with Cobweb fluttering behind them.

The huge pool of water eventually came to an end, to be replaced by broken rock on the uneven ground of a massive cave. The walls were made of granite that arched above their heads, and as Eyre looked up her heart did a flip when she saw leathery wings and glowing eyes in the light of the lux. But then she realised they were just Eastern Bent-wing bats, the small cave-dwelling bats they'd seen last year at the Jenolan Caves, and were harmless.

After they'd walked for quite a while, Eyre began to hear Beatrice's voice faintly from the distance. Until finally, as they rounded a corner, Nick's lux lit up a pair of feet hanging down, ten metres above them.

"Get me off this!" Beatrice said crossly as she dangled from the roof. Her cape was jammed tight in a crack in the ceiling rock and she hung below it like a parachutist caught on a tree. If it wasn't so precious, she could have severed it with Viq, but of course she wouldn't do that.

"Bea!" Abby cried in delight. She and Nick levitated up to Beatrice, and worked carefully at the cape until finally they got it out of the crack without damaging it. Beatrice levitated to the ground and stood rubbing her shoulders, sighing theatrically. Although she was playing at being exasperated, Beatrice's face was pale and Eyre thought it must have been uncomfortable, and frightening, being strung up like that for so long with Gothak on the hunt. Like a lure in deep ocean waters.

They sat for a moment for Beatrice to catch her breath. "So, where to now?" she asked as she rested her forehead in her hand.

Cobweb gave a delighted smile. "Now I can take you to Queen Thi, we are not far. Come with me!"

The little posse followed the dancing wings as she led them into tunnels glowing with fireflies and bioluminescence, until they eventually emerged into a cavern, similar to the Transit, but even more spectacular. It was three times the size of the Transit and covered in crystal formations of all types. But interspersed among the crystals were little houses made of gemstones, and Eyre could see hundreds of tiny faces looking out at them curiously. Visitors in the Faerie kingdom were clearly an uncommon sight.

Cobweb looked at Abby importantly. "This way, Nefelibata," she said, just loudly enough for the watching Faeries to hear. Eyre grinned at the awkward look on Abby's face as they all followed the little being to the back of the magnificent cavern.

On a throne made of gold and encrusted with sparkling gems, Queen Thi awaited, holding a sparkling staff and wearing a diamond tiara on her head. Despite her tiny size, she had a regal bearing and an aura of serenity and authority. Several attendants flew around her, and a watchful blue-tongue lizard lay at her feet, its black eyes fixed on the new arrivals. Eye knew the lizard had a sharp bite, so she was careful to move slowly as they approached.

"Nefelibata," the Queen said softly. "We have waited a long while for you. Welcome to you and your friends."

"Thank you Queen Thi," Abby said, curtseying, and after a moment, Beatrice and Eyre did the same while Nick bowed. She was royalty, after all.

"Time is of the essence," the Queen said. "Already the Dark Ones choke our tunnels and pollute our world. An abomination beyond belief. I have information for you that will help, received from the energy of our powerful cave, older than time itself."

She closed her eyes and began to recite. Abby looked desperately at Beatrice as the melodic words fell from the lips of the Faerie Queen, and Beatrice nodded, understanding. *Remember!* Abby was saying.

The Faerie Queen's Verse

"Deglupta's strong duramen can aid
The fortunes of the Light Forces when it makes a stand
But only Nefelibata can help to see
The truth of the world that was betrayed
And lift the shrouds of the Druid's sphere to understand
What the way forward for the Overworld must be."

When she finished, Beatrice gave a thumbs up, confirming she had memorised the message from the mystical cave.

"But what does it mean?" Abby asked respectfully. Eyre knew that Abby shared her own dislike of puzzles and riddles, and just wanted clear directions. It was so frustrating.

Queen Thi just turned her calm eyes towards Abby. "That is why you are Nefelibata. We do not know the meaning of the verse; the cavern has communicated to you through me. It is up to you to figure out its importance."

The Faerie Queen's eyes clouded for a moment as a huge crash from somewhere in the tunnels above them made the rock walls shudder. A crystal tumbled down onto the floor.

"Let us hope you decipher its message soon," she added softly. "You must leave now."

"Thank you Queen Thi," Abby said. "I will do my best. Farewell Cobweb, thanks to you also."

They all held hands and left the glowing cave behind them, heading back to Highlight.

CHAPTER FORTY-SIX

THE FOUR OF THEM met again the next morning in Eyre's cabin. Bruised and battered, they sat drinking coffee as Beatrice transcribed The Faerie Queen's Verse into the Book of Bane using clairography.

Abby sighed. "Well, I don't understand this at all," she said, studying the verse with a perplexed and troubled expression. "But I do know that if we're relying on Ben Perrill to save the world, we are in dire straits indeed. So let's try and work this new clue out!"

She shook her head, and Eyre grimaced. "We don't seem to have made much progress in the past few days," she agreed, "other than to get ourselves even more confused."

Beatrice sat back in her chair, her eyes looking upwards as she thought hard.

But it was Nick who spoke. "Well, I know something about the verse," he said, and all eyes turned towards him.

"Deglupta is the Rainbow Eucalyptus. It's the scientific name."

"*What?*" Beatrice said. "By The Light! How do you know that?"

Nick shrugged. "It's fascinating, the beauty of wood. Jax and I often spent time in the woodworking shed when we could. He already knew so much because of his family business, but we both learnt more about the incredible trees that live in our world."

After a moment, Abby frowned. "Well then, do you know what a duramen is?" Abby asked him.

Nick nodded, but looked a bit puzzled. "The duramen is the heart of a tree," he said. "But how that might..."

Then Beatrice interrupted, an intense look on her face as she snapped her fingers. "Yes! That makes sense! I get it now - the heart, the *power* of the Rainbow Eucalyptus—if we can ask it to fight with us! Imagine the difference that ancient being could make! We have to find the Tree and ask!"

Eyre thought Beatrice had deciphered the verse, as usual. "Where would it be, I wonder?" she mused but Beatrice had already figured it out.

"Abby can find out telepathically," she said. "Surely the mighty Rainbow Eucalyptus will hear her?"

They all looked at each other, and then Eyre shrugged.

"Makes sense to me," she said to Abby. "Your telepathy is so strong."

After a moment, Abby sat completely still and shut her eyes, her face completely focused. Silence reigned as she sent the message out into the ether. Eyre knew that Beatrice and Nick could hear Abby, but of course she couldn't. She determinedly brushed away the wave of disappointment. There was no time to feel sorry for herself; they *had* to keep trying to solve the mystery of how to reinstate the Aura, and her own feelings were irrelevant when so much more was at stake.

After a while, Abby opened her eyes and gave a dejected smile. "Nope," she said softly and shrugged. "Nothing. I'm so sorry. I don't seem to be doing very well lately." Her mouth turned down, and her cornflower eyes looked at them apologetically.

Beatrice patted her on her back and they all smiled, understanding. This journey had been so confusing for so long, that no one had any expectations, and Eyre in particular was sympathetic. For years everything had been so baffling and unpredictable. So this latest failure didn't come as a shock. Another roadblock? Really? No surprise there.

They all turned back to the Book of Bane, studying the page for meaning or clues from the Faerie Queen's verse, but there was a very long silence that told each other they were all stumped. Even Beatrice sighed.

Their despondent looks were suddenly interrupted by a very annoyed voice that drifted in the window from the front of the cabin.

"Would someone please turn that dratted thing off? By the Light, the next thing I'll be blind in my other eye!"

Ischyros appeared very unhappy about something, so they crowded to the front door and opened it. The old horse was standing in front of the cabin steps with an extremely vexed look on his face.

"Who did this?" he complained, tossing his head towards something out of sight. "What a headache. It's like Kings Cross on a Friday night! Lights and flashing colours, trashy and showy. What a pain in the neck! Get rid of it immediately!"

Eyre was confused as she followed her friends out the door. But then they gasped. A blinding Iridis extended from a tetrahedron prism at the edge of the compound, over the eucalypts and high into the sky. It arced into the distance, way beyond sight, with only clouds intercepting its brilliant pathway. Eyre stood at the doorway and looked back at her friends.

"Ahhh..." said Abby.

'Err..." said Beatrice.

'Looks like the Rainbow Eucalyptus heard you after all," Nick said slowly. And then an ecstatic look came over his face. "I am so glad to have another go at this!"

Eyre grimaced. She wasn't so sure. Her last voyage on the Iridis had almost killed her, when a violent force had blasted her off the brilliant rainbow. If it wasn't for the Ranger, she would have died. The Iridis actually didn't hold great memories for her.

But she stepped forward, hope burgeoning within her.

"Bookends," she said. "So here we are. A rainbow at the beginning and ending of this journey—do we give it a go?"

Beatrice stepped by her side. "I am here, my friend," she said softly.

Abby moved to stand by Beatrice. "You can count on me too," she said.

Then Nick moved to stand by Abby. "We're all in it to the end."

They hugged each other tightly. Then they started towards the Iridis.

"Who's first?" Beatrice asked, but they all looked at Nick. His enthusiasm for another ride on the Iridis had definitely earned him first place. He grinned and walked up the steps cut into the side of the prism. A cluster of white crystals sat on the top—Anandalite, Eyre remembered, from their experience at the TEP trials—a crystal of extremely high energy.

"See you at the other end!" Nick laughed as he stepped on the green section of the rainbow, in the middle of the brilliant band of colours. They'd learnt last time that this was the most stable part of the Iridis. He started to slowly slide up the Iridis but quickly picked up speed up the steep incline until he had disappeared out of sight. The three girls could hear his whoops of glee as he vanished into the clouds.

"I hope there's a soft landing at the end," Beatrice said as she too mounted the steps. A short time later she had disappeared over the top of the arcing rainbow.

Abby looked mournful. "I am not looking forward to this," she said. Eyre rolled her eyes in agreement. Neither was she.

"You go," Eyre said. "I'll follow you." Eyre wanted to go last in case there was any trouble, so that her friends would be safely in front of her.

Abby jumped on and wobbled up the steep incline of the Iridis. As she picked up speed, Eyre could hear her petrified screeches as she hurtled along.

Eyre gave a grim smile as she ascended the prism. She felt just as terrified as Abby, the truth be told. She wasn't really looking forward to the wild ride either, and she was sure it was going to be an awful lot harder without Viq. She set her feet sideways on the green band in a snowboarding stance, and gritted her teeth as she began to slide upwards. Wind rushed through her hair and slapped her cheeks as the speed picked up. By the time she plunged through the clouds, everything was just a blur. Her feet were in agony from the pain of trying to stay on the narrow band of colour, and as she hurtled towards the top of the Iridis, Eyre knew one thing for sure. She was going to fall off.

And as she reached the curve at the top, that's exactly what happened. Instead of following the arc of the rainbow to begin the descent down the other side, Eyre's feet shot into the air, following the angle of the apex. With a sudden understanding, that definitely wasn't going to help her now, she realised why Viq was needed; to keep your feet bonded to the Iridis. Without it, she was launched into the air like a cannonball blasted from a cannon.

Screaming, she cartwheeled upwards until gravity caught her and tugged her towards the ground. Eyre closed her eyes and stopped her screeching, feeling suddenly peaceful. Death at least would put an end to this fear and confusion, and she would see her parents and her brother. She plunged through the clouds and accepted the inevitable, as she tumbled over and over through the frigid air, racing towards somewhere far over the Queensland border. Nice to visit Port Douglas, I guess, she thought. Would've been nicer in a bikini, rather than a hearse though, she mused, as her head began to freeze.

And then she thumped onto something soft and familiar.

"Thought I'd best make an entrance," the Ranger said cheerily, as Eyre desperately grasped the sides of the striped carpet. "You didn't seem to be doing so well."

"Good call," Eyre said weakly, choking. "The Iridis doesn't work very well without Viq."

The Ranger turned his purple eyes towards her. "So true," he said. "At the TEPs, staff kept you all on track for this test. Me mostly, but even," his eyes twinkled as Eyre hung on tightly, "Professor Vela was there in the background, in case anyone failed."

Eyre lost her grip in shock, and nearly blew off into the atmosphere as she considered this revelation. *BTL!* Professor Vela would always be an enigma to her. A good guy who didn't have a good heart? *There* was a puzzle for the Unlit, she thought.

"I've been keeping tabs on you," the Ranger said. "Never a dull moment, is there?"

Eyre nodded weakly. *True, that.* The Ranger sliced the carpet downwards at astonishing speed and she lay flat on the thick wool, grasping the edges as the wind whipped her hair into a wild tangle. But she knew she was safe and she grinned at the Ranger who sat at the back of the carpet, as calmly as if he was having a Sunday picnic in a park. Eyre suddenly felt so grateful to this incredible being who had always looked after Lightworkers, at any expense, even his own.

The Ranger plummeted through the icy atmosphere, heading downwards, following the arc of the rainbow. Eyre shut her streaming eyes until the Ranger pulled up suddenly and brought the striped carpet to a gentle landing in the middle of a rainforest.

"The Daintree," he said, sounding like he'd just re-encountered an old friend.

Eyre was so cold, she could hardly move, but she staggered off the orange and black carpet.

"Thank you," she said softly. "I know the whole Overworld thanks you, Ranger, ₅but I'm grateful for my life today. I hope I can make it count."

Ranger Chrysanthe's purple eyes twinkled. "Each one of you counts. No matter what you do. You *all* matter—every one of you has something to contribute. That's why I choose to be part of this world."

Eyre hugged him desperately. "Please don't ever leave us, Ranger," she whispered. "This world needs your help."

The Ranger lifted off the ground on his carpet. "I don't know about that," he said after a long moment. "It's been a frustrating journey for me. But I trust my ride..." he indicated the carpet, which was wriggling impatiently, "... and it's telling me that it's time to go. I'll be back at Highlight." His face was uncharacteristically serious. "See you there, Eyre, the Light willing."

As he spoke, Zyx appeared and began to circle above them, and then they shot downwards like missiles, talons extended. The bumble bee carpet lost its leisurely undulation and speared upwards through the black cloud. Black creatures were flung in all directions as the Ranger sliced through the swarm, heading upwards at Mach speed.

Eyre was safely hidden behind an Idiot Fruit Tree and felt a huge relief as she finally saw the Ranger break free from the horde. Dead Zyx thumped like hailstones into the rainforest's canopy as he soared above the rainbow.

"Onwards!" the Ranger shouted in glee as he took off further into the atmosphere, with more of the foul creatures streaming behind him. "Faith and Hope, Eyre!"

"Faith and hope," Eyre repeated softly, as the courageous Ranger headed above the Iridis, leading the swarm of Zyx away from her.

After a very long moment, she left the safety of the tree. Silence reigned. When a catbird called, Eyre relaxed. She knew she was safe if the cautious bird of the rainforest had emerged.

A shout from out of sight made her lift her head.

"Eyre?" Beatrice called desperately. "Where are you?" Then Eyre heard Nick and Abby calling for her as well.

Eyre charged into the rainforest. *"Here!"* she shouted. She leaped over the grotesque shapes of dead Zyx and ran through the trees until finally she saw Beatrice, Abby and Nick standing on the other side of the raging river she had visited three years ago.

"Where did you go? We've been so worried!" Beatrice called

"I got a bit sidetracked," Eyre shrugged. "Luckily the Ranger helped me out."

She headed downstream until she found some large rocks emerging from the swiftly-flowing stream, and she hopped across them to the other side. As she finally joined her friends, Nick looked at her curiously.

"The Ranger is here?" he asked, looking across to the other side of the river.

Eyre shook her head. "He was, but he's gone back to Highlight. I didn't navigate the Iridis very well and he caught me, luckily. If he hadn't been there I'd be smashed on the ground, back in Brisbane somewhere." She looked back over her shoulder uneasily. "There's Zyx around. We have to be careful."

"How on Entis will we find the Rainbow Eucalyptus in this?" Abby asked, as she took in the dense foliage that stretched along the sides of the river.

Beatrice sighed. "Well, it was somewhere on this side of the river. I guess we just keep looking. The Rainbow Eucalyptus organised the Iridis to bring us here, so it can't be too far away." She looked around and pointed to a narrow, damp track that led into the tangled vegetation. "Let's start there. I don't feel like hacking my way through the undergrowth."

They followed the path that led them deeper into the rainforest. Vines dangled from tall trees and mist drifted amongst the leafy canopy that arched over their heads. Occasionally a catbird or a whipbird broke the silence, but the rainforest was hushed, as if it was waiting for something.

Nick dragged a tangled creeper off his shoulder in exasperation. Then with an oath, he levitated upwards and disappeared through the leaves. Beatrice, Abby and Eyre grinned. They waited, happy to stop the bush-bashing and after a couple of minutes, Nick reappeared through the dark-green canopy.

"It's not far," he said as he landed back down on the track. "But we'll have to push on through for a bit. We have to get off the path to find it. Follow me."

He headed into the thick undergrowth, pushing his way through vines and a deep sea of ferns. The girls followed him, trying not to trip over the tangled roots and deep piles of old branches and fallen leaves. Golden-orb spiders decorated the rainforest with their shining golden webs, and Eyre was careful to walk around them. They weren't dangerous, she knew, but she really didn't want one crawling on her head!

Finally she caught a glimpse of bright colours through the thick trees. In this world of greens and shadows, the brilliant bark of the Rainbow Eucalyptus was like a shining beacon through the leaves.

"Hooray!" Beatrice shouted, as she too spotted it.

They pushed their way through the forest until they broke through into a clearing, with the Rainbow Eucalyptus standing at the centre of it. The mighty tree rose above them, its beautiful bark looking like a myriad of multi-coloured paints had been spilled down the trunk.

"Greetings," the ancient tree said in a deep bass voice.

All four of them bowed. "Thank you for seeing us," Eyre said. "We've come to ask for your assistance."

"Curious," the tree said, "and what for, pray tell?" The Moog rumbled, so low-pitched it was almost inaudible.

Abby stepped forward. "The Faerie Queen gave us a message and we believe it means that the only way to defeat the Gothak is if you join us in the fight."

The Moog sounded again, almost as if they could hear the ancient tree thinking.

"What did the message say?" the eucalyptus asked.

Beatrice looked upwards, concentrating, as her phenomenal memory retrieved the words. She began to recite.

"Deglupta's strong duramen can aid
The fortunes of the Light Forces when it makes a stand
But only Nefelibata can help to see
The truth of the world that was betrayed
And lift the shrouds of the Druid's sphere to understand
What the way forward for the Overworld must be"

"Ah," the tree said, the bass voice very soft. The way it said 'ah' made Eyre think that perhaps this wasn't good news.

"So we thought that with your heart and power, it might make a difference to the Overworld forces if you would stand with us," Abby explained.

After a very long pause the ancient eucalyptus spoke, so softly it was barely audible. "Well yes, you are correct," it said slowly. "It will make a difference. But I am afraid that it isn't my metaphorical heart you need. It's my literal one."

There was a lengthy silence and then understanding dawned.

"*What!* Your *real* heart?" Eyre said in horror. The tree rumbled in agreement.

"Well that's that, then," Beatrice said. "Impossible."

The four of them nodded in agreement. Another dead end, Eyre thought gloomily. But the Moog bass sounded again.

"The marked one of you has the skill and courage. He must cut my duramen out, and use it to make a stand for the beryl orbuculum. The Druid's sphere has guidance for you if you do this."

"But we can't cut your heart out!" Abby cried.

The leaves of the magnificent tree rustled. "Trees keep this world safe. We protect you, and our magnificent environment. And if this sacrifice is how I am to perform my duty for our wondrous Entis, I am ready. Every being has a cycle and a time, and a purpose. And now I know my time is upon me. Don't despair, little bird," the tree added as tears slipped down Abby's cheeks. "The Light has sent this message and if I can help the Overworld, I am content. I have had a long time on this earth and I am grateful."

Nick moved forward and ran his hand down the coloured bark. Instantly a range of notes filled the air like someone running their hands down a keyboard. "There must be another solution," he said, his voice barely a whisper.

Then the ancient tree sent four notes out, and Eyre knew them.

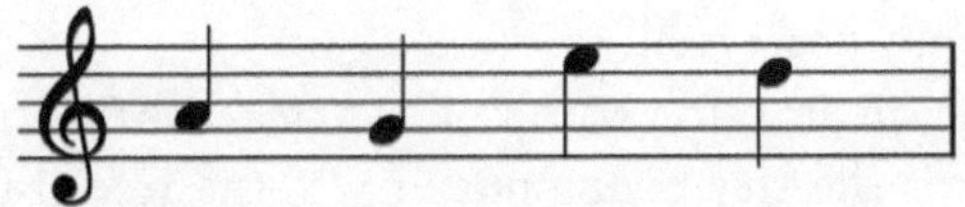

A-G-E-D. Aged, as in old. The tree was acknowledging its time on Entis was done. As she contemplated the bright sound of the quartet of notes, she felt a piercing pain at the irony of them, as she and her friends tried to comprehend the idea of cutting down this revered being.

And then, as they stood in the emerald canopy of the forest, a most astounding thing happened. Those four notes morphed into a song, a layer of sound, which became a heartbreaking, poignant reflection of life and its journey, as birds and trees and all the creatures joined in. It was a symphony of hope and understanding from the world they shared with these wondrous beings. When it finished, a cataclysmic silence reigned. Eyre, Beatrice, Abby and Nick looked at each other in anguish.

"I don't know that I can do this," Nick said softly, leaning his head against the tree. "Or how." Beatrice had her hand over her mouth, and Eyre wept too, tears coursing down her face.

The leaves rustled again. "Use your mighty Mimir blade," the tree whispered to Nick. "Its power will help to make it quick. Cut the very centre of my trunk out, and you will then need to carve it to make a smooth holder for the orbuculum. My power will release the secret the ancient crystal holds."

Nick closed his eyes for a second and then straightened.

"Is there no other way?" he asked, in a voice that was as tortured as Eyre had ever heard. His face was grief-stricken as he looked up at the ancient tree.

"You will be tested," the eucalyptus said slowly. "Your courage is how you will get through it."

Nick turned towards Beatrice, Abby and Eyre and saw his despair reflected in their faces. Eyre wiped the tears from her cheeks. How could this be the only way?

But the ancient tree shuffled and the deep voice sounded impatient. "You cannot delay. The Light has spoken. I am ready."

After a long silence, Nick shut his eyes and turned his face upwards. He raised his arm. A second later his Mnae spun from the ether and smacked into his open hand. He lowered his arm and turned slowly towards the tree.

"I'm sorry," he whispered as he put two hands on the hilt and braced one foot backwards. He drew the sword back.

"Farewell, young friends." The deep voice drifted over the top of them like a caress. "Use my heart well."

As Nick's Mnae bit into the trunk of the tree a shriek rang out over the forest. But it wasn't the tree crying out, it was the rest of the forest, as the rainforest community registered that their revered being was in mortal danger. Eyre covered her ears to try and block out the cacophony of cries and despairing wails that filled the air. But the sound pierced her to the very core, and she felt as if her own heart was being cut in two.

The first blow cut a third of the way through the magnificent tree, and it seemed to shudder in agony. Nick was weeping as he drew the blade back again and cut deeper into the trunk. The girls dropped to the forest floor in anguish, unable to bear the sight of this terrible deed. Finally, the powerful Mnae cut through the other side, and for a second the tree hung in the air, then slowly toppled over and crashed onto the ground. The sound was like the explosion of an atomic bomb, and the forest wailed in symbiotic pain. Thousands of birds rose into the air and screamed at the sight of the felled tree. They wheeled overhead, shrieking. The noise of the forest's grief was deafening as Nick cut the centre out of the stump that remained. His hand dropped to his side and the Mnae slipped to the earth as Nick fell to his knees and covered his eyes.

"What have I done?" he whispered.

Beatrice, Abby and Eyre ran over and they all embraced and wept, as the forest shook and wailed and railed with sorrow.

"We're sorry," Eyre said in an agonised voice, and then Beatrice took her away from the unbearable sight in a flash of light.

CHAPTER FORTY-SEVEN

EYRE TOOK A BREATH, steadying herself against the vertigo as she emerged from the flash of light. Abby and Nick arrived soon after, Nick straining to hold the heavy wood in his arms. He placed it gently on the ground by the Mantle Basin, struggling not to drop it. They all sat on sandstone blocks and stared at the dark wood, sap dripping from it like blood. Indeed, Eyre felt as if they had committed murder, and an overwhelming despair threatened to drive her into the ground. *So much sacrifice!* It seemed this terrible agony would never end.

After a moment Nick stirred. His eyes were dull as he summoned his Antaraks and his Kulbeda.

"I guess we need to keep moving forward," he said softly. "Make it count."

He knelt by the uneven chunk of wood and leaned his forehead on the centre for a moment. "I'm so sorry," he whispered.

Then he picked up an Antarak and sliced a chip off the outer layer. But the chip flew back at him and cut a deep slice in his arm. Nick grimaced but said nothing and took another swing. Once again, the hardwood ricocheted back at him and gouged his skin. Blood was dripping down his arm as he turned and looked at his friends.

"The ordeal the Tree mentioned," he said softly. "This is such a tragedy, I welcome the pain." Then he gritted his teeth, and began with efficient strokes to chop the outer layers from the wood. Each piece of wood hurtled back at him like a sharp knife and each one slashed into his body. But Nick didn't make a sound. He worked his way inwards as the lethal chips cut him deeply until only the inner core of the log remained.

Eyre held her hand over her mouth as Nick paused and took a deep breath. He looked like a demon, covered in blood and surrounded by pieces of wood like shattered bones.

"I need the orbuculum," he said, agony tightening his words.

Eyre ran to the basement and pulled the heavy crystal ball from her oak chest. She cradled it carefully as she hurried back to the clearing. Abby was weeping and trying to dress Nick's wounds, but he pushed her away gently when he saw Eyre returning.

"By the time I'm finished," he said to Abby softly. "I'll have a few more."

Eyre placed the orbuculum in the dust by Nick. His face was pale and sweating and his hand shook as he picked up the Kulbeda. He studied the curve of the crystal sphere and then began carefully to whittle away at the magical duramen, taking his time, despite the shavings piercing his body like shotgun pellets. As he gradually carved a bowl-shape into the piece of wood, he picked up the orbuculum occasionally and tested to see if it would fit. But his movements were getting slower and he was swaying so much, and Eyre could tell he was about to pass out. She was terrified; there was so much blood. And she couldn't imagine the pain he was in—such courage, forged from his past hardships. She, Abby and Beatrice stood close behind him, wanting to help. But Nick waved their hovering forms away and clenched his jaw as he cut the final strokes into the wood. He'd shaped the duramen into a perfect bowl that cradled the orbuculum like a hand.

Nick looked at the beautiful stand he'd carved and then his eyes glazed over and he fell backwards into the dirt.

When Eyre came back up from the basement, Beatrice and Abby were tending to Nick on the couch. Abby washed his wounds with a bowl of water and Beatrice wrapped gauze around them, which quickly became stained with blood. Nick was unconscious and very pale, the healed scars from wounds sustained in his previous life standing out like a roadmap of misery. *A few more for his collection*, Nick had once said, and now he had so many more it was like his body was more scar tissue than skin.

It was hard to comprehend the pain Nick had endured to carve the stand for the orbuculum. But one thing was for sure, Eyre thought grimly as she looked at Nick's ashen face, they would make this *count*. So many sacrifices over the past few years, by so many good souls.

After a few minutes, Nick began to stir and he eventually sat up. "Where's the stand?" he asked weakly.

"In the basement," Eyre said, and held up her hand, which was covered in deep cuts. "We put the shavings and chips in the Mantle Basin, and they weren't kind to us."

Beatrice and Abby held out their own hands, which were also cut and bleeding. The shavings had zapped around like violent butterflies, slicing whoever was unlucky enough to encounter them.

"The Ranger suggested we put the shavings and the gumnuts in the basin—they should give the Mantle extra power," Eyre added. "The Ranger went back to the forest and brought the huge trunk and most of the Rainbow Eucalyptus branches back. Some of them had gumnuts on them. He said the wood was too magical and too beautiful to be wasted, and the Mimir sorted it all out. When the Domain is clear—" She hesitated and there was an awkward pause. Eyre knew everyone was wondering whether the Domain would *ever* be clear.

She gave a wry smile and forged on, "—they will store the branches in the Domain and use them to craft only the most precious items in the years ahead." There was a silence as they gathered the small comfort this information gave them.

Then Beatrice continued. "The Ranger isn't going back to the Front for now; he's staying to help us." Eyre felt a great relief as Beatrice said it, although Eyre already knew. It would be wonderful if she and her friends didn't have to make all the decisions all the time. And to have someone as smart as the Ranger by their side for once.

As if he had heard her thoughts, the door opened and the Ranger walked in. His bright green hair was crazier than usual, no doubt a result of his wild ride back to Highlight from the Daintree, Eyre thought. The iridescent beetles circled madly around his head, and his purple eyes were serious as he looked at Nick's wan face.

"How are you doing?" the Ranger asked as he leaned up against the breakfast bar. "That was incredibly brave of you Nick."

Beatrice was solemn. "A wood chip could have cut an artery. It was so awful but we couldn't do anything."

Nick laughed weakly. "Nothing I haven't encountered before." Abby's eyes brimmed, but she just patted his shoulder.

Just then a shadow passed over the campsite and their eyes turned towards the open door. The light darkened outside as something flew above them. An inhuman shrieking came from the forest, somewhere beyond the perimeter of the Mantle and Eyre's stomach dropped. She knew that sound.

From the stand of eucalypts at the side of the clearing, a monstrous beast crashed through, heading for the Mantle at enormous speed. All three heads screeched deafeningly as an Elapidus Viper smashed down entire stands of trees. Dark shapes plummeted from above, following the foul creature as it charged towards the perimeter. The air was filled with the shrieks and cries of Strigis. Eyre jumped up and stared out the doorway in horror. Flying in behind the Zyx was a swarm of Gothak on Interfector Hornets. They hooted with glee as they spotted the Lightworkers staring up at them from the veranda of Eyre's cabin.

And then more Strigis appeared. A horde of Characs, their wide-spaced eyes glinting. Tuus Scorpions scuttled round the edge of the Mantle, deflected by its power, but increasing in numbers. No doubt they had come from the sandstone cliffs that surrounded Highlight, from the Transit, Eyre thought dismally. Slavering Saevus skulked behind the cabins and Gryllus Wetas chittered at the edge of the clearing. So many of the terrible creatures, and Eyre felt an overwhelming despair. How could they hope to overcome this powerful force?

Flames shot from the Mantle as the Gothak on Interfector Hornets neared the protective barrier, incinerating the ones that were closest. The swarm veered away from the shining light, but the Elapidus Viper kept charging. It slammed into the energy field at the perimeter and the whole ground shook from the impact. Electricity fired into the beast and it shrieked, but reeled back and smashed into the Mantle again and again, trying to break through. The swarm of Hornets wheeled back around, and Eyre realised with horror that it was Mudamir at the forefront of the pack, holding something horrible in his hands.

"Get down!" the Ranger shouted, suddenly realising what it was, and they all dropped to the ground instantly. Being a Lightworker meant never asking questions.

Mudamir held the object high above his head and then hurled it at the Mantle. Eyre gasped and covered her ears as she also recognised it; *the Egeo Blackstone!* The Gothak had brought their most foul and powerful talisman, which had *somehow* survived the explosion in the Underworld, to Highlight. Eyre's heart filled with dread as the pulsating object tumbled over and over towards the silvery barrier.

As the Blackstone hit the Mantle, the protective barrier exploded violently, sending Strigis and Gothak flying in all directions. Several carcasses thumped down into the campsite and smouldered, emitting foul fumes, and chunks of burnt flesh and bits of skin littered the ground. The Egeo Blackstone lay in a grotesque, pulsating lump as the Strigis charged into Highlight. Interfector Hornets landed on the ground and the Gothak jumped off their mounts, streaming into the clearing. Two of them picked up the Egeo Blackstone and disappeared into the woods. The other Gothak taunted the Lightworkers as they trampled over the silvery bits of the shattered Mantle, until there was nothing left of it but sparkling dust.

"Eredicco! *Eredicco!* EREDICCO!" they chanted over and over. Eyre recognised the words after her visit to the Underworld. Kill. Kill. *Kill!*

The horde of Characs raced forward, their mouths opening and shutting in anticipation.

Beatrice stepped forward and her staff flew into her hand. In one smooth movement she sent a violent flame of Viq towards a Saevus that had reached the upturned Mantle Basin. Abby had her staff in hand too and she stood beside Beatrice and sent a flamethrower blast through the ranks of Characs. Even Nick had managed to get to his feet and he leant against the rail at the end of the veranda and sent meteors of Viq at the Gothak who were creaking in towards them. There were screams as the grotesque creatures fell to the ground from the combined assault of searing Light energy, and an awful stench filled the air. But more were coming and it seemed impossible, unstoppable. The Ranger swore as the Elapidus Viper slid into the campsite, all three heads screaming, its six red eyes fixed on the figures standing on the veranda.

"Inside," the Ranger hissed, and they retreated to the cabin and slammed the front door. Eyre opened the windows and Beatrice, Nick and Abby looked out the opening, their staffs raised. Never had Eyre felt so impotent in her life as at this moment. She could do nothing, just cower inside without the ability to help her friends in this dire peril.

The jeering horde of Gothak suddenly fell still, then parted to allow Mudamir to walk through. Mudamir shouted something in a guttural language and there was movement from the perimeter of the clearing.

The Elapidus Viper slithered closer to Eyre's cabin, the monstrous body coiling and uncoiling as it drew near the steps.

"Slaughter them," Mudamir shouted as he reached the Mantle Basin. His black eyes looked at Eyre through her window, and a sneer of triumph crossed his face. At that moment, Eyre would have given anything to have Viq; she would have sent a Kulbeda spinning straight into his heart. Her blood boiled but she could do nothing but tilt her chin.

"It's not over yet," she shouted through the window. "I'm going to kill you one day like I slaughtered your useless brother."

The sneer fell from Mudamir's face and his control left him. "MAKE THEM SUFFER!" he screamed, and the Gothak roared and pumped their Luxoccisors, the evil, curved blades flashing high in the air.

A howl filled the air as the horde shouted in unison, *"EREDICCO!"* The foul creatures charged towards the cabin as the Elapidus Viper reared back to strike.

But then, a soft rumbling from the ground began as the earth started to move. Cracks zigzagged across the clearing and deep fissures were rent in the earth. The whole clearing shuddered and the ground moved like the crest of a rolling wave, toppling the Elapidus Viper. Several Gothak fell screaming into the deep chasms and the Strigis staggered, trying hopelessly to keep their balance. The Zepp at the edge of the clearing did a full somersault and smashed down violently, upside down in the dirt.

There was a massive explosion that sent chunks of earth and rock shooting upwards, and a creature blasted out of the earth with a primordial scream, blowing smoke and flames from its nostrils. It gave a deafening roar as it took to the sky on powerful bronze-coloured wings. Then it tilted sideways, folded the wings close to its body and speared like a missile through the swarm of Zyx, incinerating them in blasts of flame.

Eyre's mouth dropped open as realisation dawned, and her eyes filled with tears. *Aowx! But how?* And on his back—something... *someone...?*

Private Ammonite shouted with glee as he held on tightly to the attacking dragon. "*Yeeha!*" he shouted, as they wheeled around and came back through the horde, scorching the ground like napalm. "Payback's an itch, and I'm scratching it, you disgusting vermin!"

He raised a fist in the air as Aowx roared furiously in agreement, and they streaked in low for another strafe.

The cries of wounded Gothak filled the air, and for the first time, panic hit the Underworld creatures. They ran in all directions, sometimes directly into the path of the Strigis, which were snapping and biting at the unknown danger. Eyre watched the head of a Gothak roll across the ground, bitten off by a confused Tuus Scorpion. It was complete chaos as Aowx scorched the earth with a fury that was breathtaking. Smoke and flames filled the air and the piles of corpses grew.

But then the Elapidus Viper lifted its massive heads and turned towards the cabins, as Mudamir urged the monstrous creature on.

"Eredicco!" he screamed. "*EREDICCO!*"

One of the Elapidus Viper's heads reared back and it struck at Eyre's cabin. But with amazing speed, Aowx shot sideways and intercepted the Viper before its teeth could connect with the door. The powerful downdraft of the dragon's wings discharged a cyclone of wind and dust and leaves that swept through the windows. Eyre covered her eyes and watched in wonder from beneath her palm as the mighty dragon swooped past the veranda, bit the Viper's head off without even changing trajectory, then spat it out like it was nothing more than an olive pit. The grotesque diamond-shaped head skidded across the earth and slapped into the base of the Mantle Basin, as black blood poured from the Viper's headless neck.

"One down, two to go," Private Ammonite taunted, as they shot upwards in the sky. Mudamir's face turned black with fury, and he turned towards his troops.

"Reform! *REFORM!*" he shrieked, out of his mind with rage.

Aowx swooped in from behind the hideous snake and opened his formidable jaws. With a snap that echoed across the clearing, he bit the Viper's body in two and flew sideways past the cabin, sending another blast of dirt into the cabin. The top half of the Elapidus, the remaining two heads still striking blindly in the air, wriggled impotently across the ground until it teetered on the edge of a chasm and finally slipped over into the void.

The spectacular bronze dragon had decimated the battalion of Gothak, but more were coming. Another Elapidus Viper towered from behind the eucalypts, and the air was dark with Zyx. Eyre was overcome with fear for the courageous dragon and his fearless pilot. Even they could not survive this onslaught.

But before it could attack again, from behind Mudamir rose a monstrous creature and Eyre's heart clenched. This Strigis was gigantic—a chimera of Sublabor, Menax Lizard and Interfector Hornet. It stood thirty metres tall, a horned, leathery skinned creature with hundreds of legs and massive pincers, and a pair of powerful wings. Aowx banked around and was heading at speed towards it when suddenly the colossal beast reared high on its legs and reached down. With a single scythe it sliced a Saevus in two. As Private Ammonite and Aowx pulled up in astonishment, it screamed a victorious shriek and stampeded through the Strigis. It speared a Tuus scorpion with its sharp horns and crushed a Gryllus Weta to dust, then swung around and knocked a swathe through the Strigis that gathered at the edge of the clearing. The horrible creatures screeched and attacked, but they were no match for the powerful chimera, which blasted them flat and annihilated them. Then, honing in on Mudamir, the chimera plummeted towards the leader of the Dark Forces, forcing Mudamir to retreat and disappear in a swirl of smoke. He reappeared in the midst of the Gothak troops, halfway back towards the perimeter.

"Clever boy," the Ranger said softly. And as understanding dawned, Eyre realised who he was talking about. It was *Warrigal* who had joined the fight! Somehow, he had transformed himself into that lethal, powerful mutant, a strange combination of terrible Strigis. But her awe was tinged with fear. Not only for his physical safety as he fought the Dark Forces, but from worry—could he ever recover from this? Changing from a Sublabor back to himself had taken weeks—so what would *this* take? Was it even possible? As she watched Aowx and Warrigal battle from the sky, Beatrice, Abby and Nick stepped back onto the veranda and the three of them sent violent blasts of Light energy into the oncoming Gothak. Defending the treasures that lay in the basement. Eyre joined them on the veranda, but she could only watch helplessly, feeling ashamed at her impotence as their desperate battle for survival raged. The Ranger appeared beside her and patted her shoulder. As always, he understood.

Aowx gave an ear-splitting roar and joined the chimera as they both flew upwards, hurling Zyx in all directions. Then they dived back towards the ground to once again churn a lethal path through the Strigis. The Ranger followed their flight with his purple eyes. Then he snapped his fingers and his bumble bee carpet materialised.

"No aerial fight without me," he said cheerily and leapt aboard. In less than a second, he had taken to the skies and was cutting Zyx in half. He did loop the loops and flew the carpet vertically, on its side and even upside down, to navigate through the foul swarms of Zyx and Interfector Hornets. It was prodigious flying and if events weren't so desperate, Eyre might have enjoyed the show.

She gripped the handrail as she looked upwards, watching as the Ranger flew right through a Sublabor Pede, sending its head tumbling to the ground. He, Aowx, and Warrigal were cutting down the Gothak and the Strigis in swathes. But still more kept coming. Somehow, Mudamir had found out that something of significance was occurring here, and he wasn't giving up. Eyre knew they could not win this battle, and she glanced over at Abby, who apparently thought the same.

"I've been sending messages to Madame Overmantle," she shouted, as she fired beams of light at the Gothak. "By the Light, they had better send reinforcements soon!"

Eyre could only agree in silence as she watched the Ranger duck and dive around Interfector Hornets, as the Gothak swung their sharp long-handled scythes at him. Aowx and Warrigal were fighting valiantly, but there were too many of the evil creatures massed against them.

And then a loud trumpet blared from above and Eyre turned towards the sound. Clearly, *someone* had picked up on Abby's psychic cries, because blasting out of the clouds came a shining golden chariot. Gegenees blew the horn with one hand and steered the chariot with another. The other three hands held weapons: a massive longsword, a Flail and a long, nail-studded whip. He bellowed a ferocious war cry, dropped the trumpet and flew into the plague of Zyx. Black bodies flew everywhere as he cut them to pieces with his sword and mashed them with the Flail. Whenever an Interfector Hornet drew near, he used the whip to flick the Gothak off its back, sending the evil warriors tumbling to their deaths.

The squadron of four was causing immense damage to the Dark Forces. But the evil reinforcements kept coming—an endless procession of Strigis, Gothak and weapons. Eyre's heart clenched—she knew it was only time before one of the courageous fighters fell.

But then the biggest lightning strike Eyre had ever seen smashed into the ground, sending Gothak and Strigis flying in all directions and scorching a massive black circle into the earth. There was a clap of thunder and a sonic boom as Eyre blinked desperately, trying to clear the spots that danced in front of her eyes. *What was that? Good news or bad?* she thought anxiously, scanning the campsite. Her ears were ringing and she peered into the thick smoke that coiled up from the ground. The Dark Forces had fallen silent at the blast and Mudamir had turned to stare behind him. The Gothak turned too, and the Zyx circled aimlessly. After a sharp command from Mudamir, even the Strigis stopped their attack. The Ranger, Aowx, Gegenees and Warrigal drifted in the air above the camp, waiting to see what was happening. A strange cease-fire had fallen over the battleground, and after a moment, Eyre realised why.

Emerging from the smoke and burning embers at the perimeter of the clearing was a figure, holding something in one hand before him. In the other hand, a Mnae was raised, the magical blade gleaming with reflected fire. *A Lightworker!* The figure strode slowly but confidently forward and Eyre wondered why none of the Gothak attacked. And then she gasped as she recognised who it was. *Jax!* She wanted to weep in fear for him, and shout at him to RUN! He walked steadily up to Mudamir, who stood just beyond the Mantle Basin. Eyre was confused at the expression on Mudamir's face. The evil Gothak had a look of absolute terror on his face.

Finally, Jax stopped, and Eyre realised that he had the Egeo Blackstone in his hand. His blade had streaks of black blood on it, and she knew how he had acquired the grotesque talisman of the Dark Forces; two Gothak must now lie somewhere in the bush, slaughtered by the Mimir's lethal blade. Jax held his Mnae just above the Blackstone and Eyre understood why he hadn't been attacked. If he dropped his Mnae, it would slice the pulsating object in half. Several Gothak had fallen to their knees in horror, and a heavy silence hung over the clearing.

"Give me the Blackstone," Mudamir said in a tight voice, "and I will let you live."

"Wait a minute," Jax said brightly. "I'll be right back."

And before anyone could move, he had disappeared in a flare of light. Mudamir gave a shriek of fury, but when he spoke, his voice was flat and lethal, his movements tightly controlled.

"Find him, and bring him to me," he ordered the Gothak. The soldiers jumped to their feet and were reforming into ranks, when there was another flash and Jax reappeared in exactly the same position, but without the Blackstone this time.

If it weren't such a terrible scene, Eyre might almost have laughed at the startled expression on Mudamir's face. Evidently, he hadn't been expecting *this.*

When Jax spoke, his voice was calm and authoritative. Eyre's heart swelled with both love and dread as she looked at his fearless stance. You would never know he was facing such a frightening creature. He looked like he was addressing a Country Women's Association luncheon.

"Your precious, *revolting* Blackstone is somewhere in the Overworld," Jax began. "In the last five minutes I have visited each one of the Alterworlds, as well as Entis, so you will not be able to follow my tracks. The Blackstone is hidden in a place only I know, and you are very unlikely to find it in decades."

The Gothak wailed and ranted, and Mudamir appeared ready to explode with rage. But Jax continued before the foul creature could speak.

"You will take your forces away from this place. Right now. And none of us are to be harmed. If you do this, I will leave the gross filth where it is. If you don't withdraw, I will destroy it. But if you kill me, you will never find it. And if you kill anyone else here, I will destroy it before you have a *chance* of finding it. Get out of here. And then we will meet you at Mt Augustus to decide this thing once and for all."

A long silence followed Jax's speech. Mudamir's face was suffused at being outsmarted, and when he finally replied his voice was tight with suppressed fury.

"When the Protector gave his life to help you escape, I realised there must be more to your group than I had thought. That is why we are here." He turned towards the cabin and his black eyes speared into Eyre's as he said archly. "I have been here before you know, many years ago, when I believe I might have killed your brother?"

Eyre understood and a tear rolled down her cheek. Mudamir had been the Gothak that had killed Eric, Nick's mother and Ben's brother. But he had been targeting *her* mother. Mudamir's vile brother Kaar had finally been successful at accomplishing that foul deed. She already hated the evil creature, but now her blood burned with a violent lust for revenge. One day she would make good on her promise to Mudamir, and she would kill him like she'd killed his brother.

"We will withdraw. But this is not the end of it," Mudamir said softly. "We will meet you at Mt Augustus, where you will all most certainly pay for this. In a very, very painful way. The outcome is inevitable. Pity." His voice lowered to a bare whisper as he finished the sentence and his lips drew back in a ferocious snarl. Despite herself, Eyre shuddered. The evil of this creature was so potent.

Then, Mudamir turned and uttered some guttural words to the Strigis. A tall smoking Seam appeared in the centre of the campsite, and the Strigis flooded into it. The Gothak flew their Interfector Hornets into the undulating blackness, followed by a coiling stream of Zyx. Finally, the foot troops followed. Mudamir was last, and he turned before he stepped into the oily smoking Seam.

"We will meet again," he promised, his eyes black. "And I will look forward to it."

He stepped through and disappeared. A second later, the Seam vanished.

CHAPTER FORTY-EIGHT

EYRE RACED DOWN THE front steps and flung herself into Jax's arms. He held her gently as tears streamed down her cheeks, and his hand stroked her hair.

"It's okay, my love," he said. "We're safe for now."

"Why are you here?" Eyre said as her chest heaved. "And what were you *doing?* You could have been killed!"

"I heard you," Jax said softly, and as Eyre turned her face up with questioning eyes, he added, "you were in danger, and I heard your fear." He held her out and looked deeply into her eyes before brushing her forehead with a kiss. "Somehow we are attuned. I can't explain it, but I *knew* you were in trouble. I'm glad I came."

They held each other for a long moment. "Well, it was a pretty impressive display of fulminology," Eyre said finally, and gave a weak laugh.

"I've been practising," Jax replied grimly, as they walked back to the veranda, avoiding the gaping crevasses in the ground.

Nick was sitting on the veranda floor, exhausted after the battle. He had been weakened by the ordeal of carving the stand, and using so much Viq shortly after that had brought him to the brink of unconsciousness. Abby sat beside him, stunned and silent, and Beatrice leaned on the rail, looking outwards as if not convinced it was all over.

With a swoop, the Ranger brought the bumble bee carpet down to settle gently in front of the stairs, and stepped off. He snapped his fingers and the carpet disappeared. The colossal chimera whumped down beside the Mantle Basin. Gegenees glided down in his shining chariot to the perimeter of the clearing. And Aowx flapped his huge wings once and spiralled down to land on the ground beside the chimera. Private Ammonite, his face blackened with soot, slid down from Aowx's back and he strode towards them, completely unconcerned that he had been so close to death only moments before. He grinned and his white teeth showed starkly against the smut on his face.

"We sure showed 'em!" he beamed. Shortly after, he was overwhelmed with hugs as Beatrice, Abby and Eyre hurtled over and wrapped their arms around him. Nick staggered up and shook his hand, and Jax did too.

"How on Entis...?" Beatrice asked, unable to even complete the question. She wiped a sweaty lock of hair from her face as she looked in disbelief at the grinning Mimir. They all waited for the explanation. How on Entis, indeed! The last anyone had seen of Private Ammonite and Aowx, they had been disappearing under the ocean of treasures in Aowx's lair after the Elapidus Viper had severed Aowx's tail.

"Lizard tails grow back," the Private said with great satisfaction. "A bit of TLC down in the caves, a bit of rest, and the mighty Aowx was back!" His voice was light-hearted, but Eyre could see from the way that he looked at the crusty old dragon, that he actually really did care for him. When the dragon's orange eyes softened, Eyre realised that the feeling was probably mutual. Perhaps Aowx had finally discovered something more valuable than treasure down in the depths of the earth.

A strange sound from behind Private Ammonite made them all turn. The chimera was groaning and writhing, and its skin moved as if something was crawling beneath it. As they watched, the creature slowly reduced in size and its shape changed until human-like limbs began to emerge. Finally, the creature had morphed and shrunk until it was Warrigal, bent over on one knee, with his head down and his palms flat on the ground. He shuddered and inhaled deeply, and then finally lifted his head. With an enormous effort, he forced himself to stand up, where he swayed for a second as if he might faint.

The Ranger swiftly moved forwards and steadied him. "You are a prodigy," he said softly. "There has never been anyone with your skills, ever. And you are so incredibly brave." He patted the boy on the shoulder and helped him to walk over to the group. They all hugged him tightly. He had risked his life in order to save theirs.

Gegenees had finally finished examining his chariot for damage and he strode over to join them and shook the Ranger's hand. "Nice flying Leo!" he said. Then he spotted Abby. "Ah, warrior girl," he said. "You truly are worthy of the Argonaut's medallion. Courage under fire indeed!" All five arms saluted her, and everyone laughed.

The Ranger scanned the skies and then the perimeter. "That was very smart, Jax," he said as the beetles whirled wildly around his head. Despite the curious sight, Jax looked well-pleased by the compliment. The Ranger had such vast vision and abilities, his comment was true praise indeed. The Ranger finished, "Very impressive tactics—you are to be commended. And well done to the rest of you too! We should be safe here for a short while."

"Maybe longer," Jax said smugly, and they all chuckled. Obviously Jax thought the Blackstone was well hidden.

"Go and clean up, have something to eat and a rest," the Ranger said. "And then we can meet back and make a plan to save the world."

"The entire Overworld, actually," Abby said solemnly, "not to add any pressure," and they all laughed softly.

Eyre woke from a very deep sleep, and sighed happily when she realised that someone was stroking her hair. *Jax.* Earlier, she'd had a hot shower and then a ham and cheese sandwich, which was close to being the most delicious thing she had ever tasted. She ate it in about two minutes flat, and was then completely overcome by exhaustion. So exactly thirty minutes after she'd walked into her cabin, she was sound asleep on her bed.

She smiled up at Jax as he brushed her hair from her face and leaned over to kiss her deeply.

"It's getting late," he whispered.

Eyre blinked her eyes and then sat up gingerly. Every muscle hurt. The wild ride on the Iridis and the trip on the Ranger's carpet, followed by the hike through the bush, had evidently not been much appreciated by her muscles.

"What time is it?" she asked.

"It's eight o'clock."

"I slept 'til almost bedtime?" Eyre gasped and Jax chortled.

"'Til get-out-of-bed time, actually," he laughed, pointing at the window, where morning light was streaming through.

Eyre stood up, and her eyes were round as she realised that she had slept all afternoon and all through the night. It was eight o'clock in the morning!

"Why didn't anyone wake me?" she said in disbelief. "I can't believe I slept that long! We have to get onto things!"

Jax shrugged. "We all slept that long, Eyre. And the Ranger decided the risk was worth it. He wants us to rest up before we head to Mt Augustus."

Eyre felt frantic, but yawned despite herself. "Are Beatrice, Nick and Abby up? Because, what you don't know is that we may have found a way to move forward with the whole Aura thing!"

Jax's eyebrows raised. "What—the solution?"

Eyre nodded, her face hopeful. "Maybe."

Jax stood up too. "Well the others have only just woken up. I guess it's time for a pow wow at the Mantle Basin. I'll go let them know."

He embraced Eyre gently and then headed out the door. Eyre made herself a coffee and grabbed a piece of vegemite toast, and then walked slowly down the front stairs. Every step hurt; evidently there was a price to pay for riding the Iridis.

The first thing she saw as she walked out the door was a large sleeping dragon in the middle of the campsite. Private Ammonite was lying on the ground between Aowx's massive arms, and he was snoring loudly. They must have also needed time to recover. She smiled and headed to the Mantle Basin.

Warrigal was already standing by the battered metal dish.

"Jengles is not going to like that," Eyre said solemnly as she took a sip of coffee and studied the upturned basin.

Warrigal smiled. "I'm waiting for Nick. He and I are going to turn it over."

"Thank you for helping yesterday," Eyre said. "You were unbelievable."

Warrigal shrugged. "Anything to fight the Darkness. Especially for friends."

"How is the Front then?" Eyre asked hesitantly, and a cloud passed over Warrigal's face. His eyes closed and he said nothing for a long moment.

"Bad," he said eventually. "We're being massacred. So many dead. Todd is gone. And Saskia. Lindi too."

Eyre gasped in shock. Todd, the amiable boy who the echidna had put to sleep at the TEP trials. Saskia, the vain girl who expected to be first in everything. And now among the first to die. First for the ultimate sacrifice. She'd died protecting the Overworld, and Eyre suddenly understood that not everything is black and white with people. And Lindi, the girl with such strong Viq, but still not strong enough to survive. They'd all sacrificed their lives for good, and Eyre felt her heart clench in pain. She would avenge them, and all the others who had died fighting the Darkness.

Jax arrived next, so he and Warrigal righted the Mantle Basin, using a combination of Viq and strength.

"Warrigal was with me when I had the vision that I needed to come and check on you," Jax said. "And he said he'd come too." He slapped Warrigal softly on the back. "Thanks so much, mate. Others would probably have questioned why."

Eyre smiled gratefully at Warrigal, and then her smile widened as she caught a glimpse of Beatrice trying to make her way over to the Mantle

Basin. She was staggering along with a very cross look on her face, obviously feeling as sore as Eyre was.

"By the Light," Beatrice complained. "If we ever get this Aura reinstated, I want my name on a plaque right outside Professor Vela's office!"

She sat down gingerly on a sandstone block and Eyre joined her, laughing at Beatrice's annoyance. Eventually the Ranger joined them, and finally Nick and Abby, also moving rather slowly.

They all sat down on blocks and Eyre studied the empty Mantle Basin. That alone was reason enough to hurry today. No protective Mantle and a horde of furious Gothak, who might return, if by some luck they stumbled across the Egeo Blackstone quickly.

"Yesterday we found another clue in the quest for the Aura," Eyre began.

"A stand," Abby said.

"Made from the Rainbow Eucalyptus," Beatrice added.

"So that Abby can see something in the beryl orbuculum that will help us," Nick finished.

"We need to hustle," Eyre said. "Before they come back." She felt a terrible anxiety that they had wasted precious time by sleeping so long. As usual, the Ranger understood.

"You need strong Viq to read the Orbuculum," the Ranger said softly. "It was important you slept and recovered. There is still a long journey ahead, and I was banking on Jax's ability to find a good hiding spot for the Gothak's foul Blackstone."

Eyre agreed. The Ranger was right of course. By the end of the battle yesterday, Abby had barely been able to stand up, let alone focus on something as mentally draining as scrying. She'd needed to rest and sleep and recharge. But now, they had to try and find the secrets in the orbuculum.

"The Gothak have lost the advantage of surprise. Now they will anticipate that we will call for reinforcements, so it is not in their interest to return. Mudamir, undoubtedly, will take the battle to Mt Augustus. So we have a little time. You should bring the orbuculum and stand out here," the Ranger said. "Abby will need strong light to see properly." His voice had softened, but it was as hard as steel when he added, "The rest of us will stand guard."

So Eyre stood up carefully and made her way to the basement to retrieve the crystal sphere and the carved stand. Time was of the essence, but she still took an unusually long time to walk back to the sandstone seats with the precious objects. Her muscles were definitely staging a mutiny. By the time she got back, Private Ammonite had woken and was rubbing his eyes and yawning by the Mantle Basin. Aowx had drawn nearer, studying them all with his unfathomable orange eyes. And Gegenees was seated on a sandstone block with a piece of toast in one hand, a bowl of cereal in another, a spoon in the third, a banana in the fourth and a cup of coffee in the fifth. It was a choreographer's triumph getting it all in his mouth in a coordinated fashion.

Beatrice had fetched a table and Abby had found a supple throw made from Va Flax she had bought in Terra, that had been spun, woven and dyed by the Nemoris. It was a deep purple, shot with gold; a mystical cloth that gleamed when she slipped it over the table. The Ranger clicked his fingers and suddenly a sparkling chair, made completely out of quartz, stood before the table.

"Quartz, the bringer of Light," he said. "A chair worthy of the great Nefelibata."

Abby smiled gratefully and took a seat as Eyre put the stand in the centre of the table and carefully set the orbuculum on top. And then an irritated voice came from behind her.

"Well, obviously you're trying to kill me," Ischyros grumbled. "Atomic bombs going off, stampeding creatures, earthquakes. And then you try to starve me to death! No dinner. No breakfast. By the Light, what is going on?" He came and stood at the side of the sandstone blocks, turning to look at them with his one good eye, and harrumphed loudly. And then to Eyre's delight, Florence flew out and landed on his back.

"Babysitting a chicken," Ischyros muttered. "Clearly my only value."

But when Florence scratched him behind his ear with her beak a dreamy look came over his face and Eyre grinned. Apparently, Florence wasn't a complete nuisance.

"We have something to do, Ischyros," Eyre said, "and then I'll get you the best breakfast you've ever seen!"

Ischyros snorted again, but stayed with them.

Abby took a seat at the table and for a moment her eyes turned upwards. Then she wrapped her hands around the rainbow-coloured stand and looked deeply into the orbuculum. She didn't make a noise as she searched the now gold-tinged swirling mists in the crystal ball. For fully five minutes she stared intently at the ethereal clouds in the orb, and she didn't utter a word. Eyre had to stop herself from moving in agitation as the silence continued.

Finally, Abby looked up. Tears were brimming in her eyes and she shook her head.

"It's no good," she whispered, staring unseeingly into the glowing sphere. "I seem to have lost my skills. Madame Overmantle should have kept the orbuculum after all."

Eyre felt so sorry for her friend. Abby had tried so hard, and Eyre knew the bitter taste of failure.

"It's okay Abby," Eyre said, and patted her gently on the shoulder. Then she gasped loudly and jumped back. Everyone was already so much on edge, four staffs made a sudden appearance as Beatrice, Nick, Jax and Warrigal leapt to their feet. Aowx's eyes narrowed and Private Ammonite drew his Crescent Blade as he looked around wildly. Even Ischyros got a fright, and Florence took off screeching into the sky.

"What is it?" Beatrice cried, searching the skies.

Eyre felt silly. "I—ah—I'm sorry, I thought I saw something." She peered over at the orbuculum but now all she could see was swirling clouds. Her shoulder touched Abby's as she leant closer and then she jumped again. *What?* She leaned forward and put both hands beside the crystal ball and stared frantically into the golden mist.

Abby wiped her eyes and looked at Eyre curiously. "What is it, Eyre?"

Eyre's eyes raked the interior of the ball, and then she slumped.

"I guess it was my imagination," she said, and laughed shakily. "For a moment—well, for a moment I thought I saw Mum in there."

Abby looked sympathetic and patted Eyre's shoulder. Eyre jerked again.

"She's there!" Eyre cried, pointing a finger into the ball. Abby frowned and turned back to the orbuculum, squinting at the mists. She gave an annoyed huff.

"I can't see anything, I have to be honest," she said.

Eyre looked at Abby, perplexed. "She was there, I'm sure—as clear as a photograph. Are you sure you didn't see it?" Abby just gave a dejected shrug. But she wrapped her hands more tightly around the magical base and tried.

Eyre leaned in to study the orb again, and grimaced. "I guess not. I'm sorry I gave you all a fright." Ischyros tossed his head and grumbled as Florence settled on his back again.

"Chicken heart," he accused Florence, as if he himself hadn't leapt in the air at the commotion. Then he wandered off grumpily to eat some grass by Eyre's steps, suddenly losing interest in the proceedings.

Eyre took a shuddering breath. Her imagination had tricked her, seeing visions like images in clouds on a windy day. She put one hand on her head and groaned.

She must be going mad.

CHAPTER FORTY-NINE

EYRE LOOKED SO MISERABLE and Abby reached over and squeezed her hand. Once again Eyre exclaimed, but quieter this time. She blinked.

"I *can* see something!" she said in wonderment. "But... I think maybe it's only when you touch me, and the base, Abby. You have a look—can you see it?"

Abby looked baffled, but kept holding Eyre's hand as she looked back into the whirling clouds in the crystal ball. "Nope," she said after a moment, sighing. "I can't see anything. Is it still there?"

Eyre shuffled closer and tilted her head in wonderment. "Yes, I can see so much happening in there. How can that be?"

Abby nodded her head despondently and let Eyre's hand go. "Yes indeed, how can that be? I must be a complete fake if you can see it and I can't." She stood up and her mouth turned down. She sighed. "You take my seat Eyre, I'll stand behind."

There was an awkward silence, and then the Ranger stepped forward and his eyes were kind. "No, Abby, it is you that has the gift. You must be a very powerful conduit indeed for Eyre to be able to see what is within the beryl orbuculum." He snapped his fingers and a second quartz chair sat beside the first. "It takes a talented medium to bridge the gap between the living and the deceased, but only an *extraordinary* one can reveal the events of the past to those that are still here. Be proud, my girl. You are Nefelibata, the Cloud Walker indeed."

Abby smiled uncertainly, but her look was grateful as both she and Eyre sat down on the crystal chairs. "Thank you Ranger Chrysanthe."

Eyre was mesmerised by the swirling clouds she could see in the orbuculum, and she didn't take her eyes off the magical sphere. She called over her shoulder in a distracted tone.

"Bea, could you transcribe what I see, and we'll transfer it to the Book of Bane later?" Beatrice nodded and a second later her Felsic appeared in her hand.

"Good idea," Beatrice said slowly as she placed it in her lap. But Eyre could tell by her preoccupied voice that she was thinking about something else. Then Beatrice snapped her fingers.

"*Yes!* That's it. I was trying to figure out the Faerie Queen's verse—*only Nefelibata can help to see!*" Her musings drifted over Eyre's shoulder like holographic formulae.

"The Druid's sphere is the beryl orbuculum—so Abby, *you* are helping Eyre to see how we can help the Overworld. It sort of all makes sense."

The Ranger smiled, and immediately another crystal chair appeared and Beatrice sat down on the other side of Eyre. Then Abby held Eyre's hand again as Eyre stared into the orbuculum. Once Abby touched her, Eyre could see pictures moving in the golden mists of the orb. Her awareness of anything outside the crystal ball dimmed, and she began to describe the visions she could see. Silvery writing appeared on the screen as Beatrice used clairography to transcribe her words on to the Felsic.

Eyre's mother and father, walking around the Mantle Basin at Highlight, with two energetic toddlers running around madly beside them. Neither of the toddlers had much hair, but the wisps Eyre could see were definitely flaming red. A moment later Eyre could see Whittaker Ray coming over to join her parents, and she saw her mother quickly covering the children's heads with hats. *Hiding the fact they were Aethers*, Eyre thought.

Eyre was scarcely breathing as she studied this window into the past. Seeing her parents again created a terrible yearning in her, and a sadness so great she felt she might lie on the ground and weep for a thousand years. But she was unable to take her eyes off the crystal ball, and unable to move, as the mesmerising scene changed.

This time she saw the Gothak streaming through Highlight, Mudamir at the forefront, and then there was complete chaos as Eyre's mother, obviously in the middle of a happy playgroup picnic, lunged forward desperately to fight the vile creatures, Mudamir at the front of them. George Wilson and the Edmunsuns charged in after the Gothak arrived and a violent battle ensued, with Light and weapons and fury. But at the end of the conflict, Nick's mother lay dead, and Ben Perrill's tiny brother too, pale and lifeless on the ground beside little Eric. Tears ran continuously down Eyre's face as she saw her brother's still form, and her mother and father running over desperately to try and save him. She saw Ben Perrill's mother skulking away with Nick's father, and rage flooded through her at the sight.

The damage those people had caused. They were worse than the Gothak, because they had betrayed their own kind in the foulest way possible.

Eyre stared at the crystal ball, as if in a trance, and related the events she saw. All awareness of the outside world had gone and she sat like a statue as the events of long ago were revealed by the golden mists. A Gothak could have appeared right beside her and she wouldn't have reacted, she was so completely and utterly ensnared by the unfolding story.

The mists swirled and the scene changed again. Eyre's heart clenched when she saw her parents sitting in their old house in Canberra. Seeing the beloved home, with its bright, familiar colours and its warm, cosy furniture, caused a solitary tear to run down her cheek. It hurt so badly to see this so clearly, but to realise that she could never experience it again. However, she knew she had to concentrate, and she wiped her face as she leaned in closer. Her Wisdom was on the table before her parents, and several piles of notes lay beside it. Her parents appeared to be mid-conversation with an old man with a long white beard, who Eyre recognised as Professor Aperito, the Chairman of the Echelon before Chairman Essendon. Professor Aperito had died and Rigmar's father had been elected to replace him. Eyre knew the Professor from the portraits of past Board members that lined the walls in the Central Administration building at the Academy.

"Somewhere out there is the missing piece of the Aura, disguised as a square of Alexandrite," Professor Aperito was saying, and Alia and Rufus looked at each other and laughed, and the puzzled Professor paused for a moment before continuing. "When we find it, after all these years of investigation, we will be able to reinstate the Aura. My trip to the archives of the National Library of Russia has finally yielded the information we needed in order to proceed."

"Oh well done, Julius," Rufus Lightward exclaimed, and clapped the Professor on the back. "Where did you find the answer?"

"It was in an old manuscript written about the Tunguska Event by Adolf Hamlen's wife, Bertha, who was horrified by his perfidy. But the manuscript was filed in the fantasy fiction section of the Library by Entis librarians, and subsequently lost for years. The Entis librarians didn't see it as a serious document, because it outlined in great detail the Proditio and the truth of that day—which we now know was misreported at the time by others—when the Aura was destroyed. It described and debunked the widely-held belief that the Protector had attempted to pass over the Aura's power to the Gothak, and that he had been prevented by the Ranger's actions.

"Bertha contacted the greatest mystic in Lightworker history, the Tomsk Prorok, to find out how to reinstate the Aura, and then wrote the remedy down in great detail in the manuscript—I guess it was her attempt to atone for her husband's terrible actions. Bertha was killed shortly after completing the document, before she could give it to the Lightworkers, and it was passed on to the National Library of Russia. But back then, it was treated as fantasy by the Entis librarians and relegated to an old box in the basement. It has taken me all year to go through the archives to find it. I had a hunch the answer might lie somewhere in the area that the Proditio occurred."

"So tell us, Julius, what is the solution? How *do* we reinstate the Aura?" Eyre could hear the excitement in her mother's voice, and she felt her own anticipation rising. Could she really be about to find out?

Professor Aperito paced the floor and waved his hands animatedly. "The inert Aura must be taken back up to the original height of the Proditio—which was 28,000 feet—to catalyse the rebirth of Entis's protective energy. And only the Protector can take the seeder; he is a crucial link to the energy of the original events that happened in 1908."

The scene changed and Eyre saw the Ranger, flying—on his own ability—up to the rainbow-coloured Aura. The Ranger's skin was blue and he had no hair, but his features showed unmistakeably that it was him. He hovered over the Aura as the Protector flew in on a shining silver Lighthorse and then the Ranger plucked out a section of the Aura. The piece of the Aura, about 15 centimetres square, glowed brightly with a life of its own for a second, and then faded to a purplish-green colour. *The Alexandrite tile!* Eyre thought. A wild storm was picking up, and Eyre could see that below the Ranger and the Protector hundreds of Gothak on Interfector Hornets were circling like a school of sharks. The swarm of Dark Forces was led by a Lightworker, who looked remarkably like Carrison Hamlen, riding a massive black Lighthorse. The black swarm didn't seem able to rise any higher, but it made an impenetrable barrier to anyone wanting to descend.

"If they get you now, they will take the Aura. It is contracting and slowly descending. I am going to break it up so they can't seize its power," the Ranger shouted to the Protector. "I am sorry my friend, but you need to go down there and allow yourself to be captured, to distract them. It's the only way. But then you *must* escape so you can bring the Aura's fragment back up here to regenerate the energy field. Only you have the power." He held his hand up in a gesture of valediction as the wind picked up and howled around them. "I may not survive this, but we have no other option. Farewell, my good friend."

The Protector looked devastated, but he did as the Ranger had instructed. He waved his hand slightly, like a salute. "Farewell Heliodor. I hope I see you again." Then the Protector's silver Lighthorse dived into the black mass of Zyx and Hornets below. Within minutes the Protector was wrenched from his Lighthorse's back and hauled into a smoking Seam. The horse screamed and fought ferociously to follow him, but the Seam disappeared and the valiant Lighthorse was soon covered in Zyx. Eyre saw the Ranger take a deep breath, close his eyes and then a blast of nuclear proportions exploded the Aura into four spinning Isars. The silver bars whirled wildly, then they spun away from each other in four different directions. As Eyre watched, transfixed, each bar was enveloped by a vertical Seam, and vanished.

The horde of Gothak was blown apart violently and bodies plummeted downwards like massive black hailstones. The Ranger was falling too, hurtling towards Entis and turning over and over like a ragdoll. Eyre saw a silver shape plummeting after him; the Protector's Lighthorse, knocked unconscious by the explosion, alive only because he had been shielded by the bodies of the Zyx. Shortly after, Eyre saw the Ranger and the horse plunge into a tumbling river and disappear.

The vision cut back to Eyre's father as he shook his head, astonished at what the Professor had just revealed. He looked at Professor Aperito.

"So, the solution was sitting in Russia, all these years? This is truly a day for celebration!"

"We made progress too," Alia said modestly. Professor Aperito raised an eyebrow and Alia continued. "We have also been to Russia—and we've found the missing piece of the Aura!" The Professor gasped and sat down, and both Rufus and Alia laughed. "Rufus and I went to Aqua to visit the Sea Crone this week and she told us we would find the Alexandrite square in the river below the Proditio. We realised it must be in the Podkamennaya Tunguska River, and we found it! Although after *quite* a lot of circular breathing, and *digging!*" They all laughed.

"The Sea Crone told us that the Alexandrite square was crucial to reinstating the Aura, but not why, or what to do with it. But I told Jengles that the Alexandrite was at the centre of it all," Eyre's mother said, and then her eyes turned down. "Just in case. He must know it is critical to the Overworld."

Professor Aperito looked stunned. "Incredible," he whispered. "Where is the tile?"

"It's in Jolin the Second's window, well hidden," Alia said, then her face fell slightly and she added softly, "although, there is a price to pay for any Aether that enters the window."

Rufus touched her arm gently. "But we don't know what to do with the square yet," he said.

Professor Aperito's eyes gleamed. "Ah, but *I* do! My research at the Russian National Library, and the work of Bertha Hamlen, has revealed the secret!" As Alia and Rufus looked up in surprise, the old Professor beamed.

"The Protector must find the Isars," he continued, "and then take them to the avaricious dragon (Eyre vaguely heard Aowx mutter his annoyance at this comment) to be forged into Kenaz. Once the Kenaz are formed, the Protector must arrange them to form the shape of an Inguz and the Alexandrite is placed in the centre. Then, the resulting Inguz is used by the Protector to reinstate the Aura."

His face was alight with hope. "We are so close!"

Rufus nodded. "We must record the final instalment in the Wisdom without delay, and then all the information will be secure." He opened the Wisdom and flipped the pages over. "Next week we will meet with the Determinant Dozen to inform them of our findings. In November we begin the search for the Isars. But our first task must be to free the Protector, that courageous soul, so he can take the Alexandrite upwards! Ahhh, my friends," he finished, with a faraway look in his eyes. "It is hard to believe that our long, clandestine journey is almost over!"

As Eyre watched, totally absorbed in the gripping visions, her father opened a bottle of champagne and handed Eyre's mother and the Professor a glass. And then, magically, as they all sipped the champagne, Rufus and Professor Aperito sat over the open Wisdom and carefully crafted spinning holograms in the air that disappeared into the pages of the book. Finally, they were done and they shut the book with a content look on their faces. There was a flash of light and the book disappeared.

"It's safely in the warded basement of our cabin," Rufus said, linking arms with Alia as the Professor took off his spectacles and returned them to his pocket. "Just to be safe." They clinked glasses and beamed at one another.

"Will you still love me without my powers?" Alia whispered to Rufus, and his eyes crinkled. "Forever, my love." They kissed softly and then Alia brushed her red hair back and headed for the kitchen. "I'll just go get—"

But what she had been going to get would never be known, because just then the front door was blown open by a flaming ball of atra, and the door cartwheeled past the startled Lightworkers and slammed into the wall. Alia jumped to one side of the room to avoid it and Rufus and Professor Aperito to the other as Kaar stalked in the door, a satisfied expression on his face.

"I do believe you might be able to instruct me on how to acquire the Aura's energy," the pallid creature breathed. Rufus sent a ball of Light energy flying at Kaar, but he ducked and it hurtled out the front door. More

Gothak flooded in through the doorway, forcing the Lightworkers further to each side of the room. When their backs hit the walls, Professor Aperito and Rufus summoned their staffs and aimed them at the foul creatures. From her seat four years in the future, Eyre's heart clenched, even though she already knew what was coming.

There was a second of silence, and then Rufus blasted away half the Gothak in the room. But Kaar was lightning quick and he hurled a meteor of atra at them. As Professor Aperito deflected the burning missile, a spear hurtled in the front door and caught him full in the chest. His face had a look of profound shock as he dropped to his knees and fell forward, lifeless. Eyre was willing her parents to teleport out of there, but then she saw the problem. They were standing too far away from each other to touch, and they couldn't get closer with the Gothak between them. Her mother had no Light energy to teleport, and her father wouldn't leave her. Alia gave Eyre's father such a look of love and resignation that tears started to run down Eyre's face. In a flash of light, Rufus teleported to Alia's side but Kaar was expecting it, and as Rufus appeared, Kaar incinerated him with a violent blast of flame and soot.

Alia, her face contorted with grief, turned towards Kaar as he stalked over to her. Fearlessly, she raised her chin and faced the grotesque creature.

"Tell me what you know," Kaar said softly, "and perhaps I'll let your daughter live."

An anguished groan fell from Alia's lips. "*You obscene piece of filth!*" She moved so quickly that Kaar was taken by surprise as a dagger flew towards him. But he batted it away like an inconsequential fly. A knife without Viq was no threat to him.

"I see you are not going to cooperate," he said. "Pity."

"You will not win," Alia hissed. "You will die screaming!"

Kaar's eyes darkened and he flung the dagger back at Alia. It spun through the air with such speed she couldn't react, and buried to the hilt in her heart. Her mouth opened as if to say something, but she dropped soundlessly to the floor. Kaar looked down at the three dead Lightworkers and nudged Professor Aperito with his foot. A mocking sneer appeared on his face. Then he looked back at the remaining Gothak.

"Burn it," he said disdainfully. "Burn it to the ground." And he turned and walked out the front door.

The mists began to swirl and twist and the visions in the golden clouds dimmed until there was nothing left for Eyre to see.

CHAPTER FIFTY

EYRE STARED FRANTICALLY INTO the orbuculum, her heart breaking and desperate for *just one more!* glimpse of her parents. And then Abby slid off the quartz chair, unconscious, and the beryl orbuculum cleared. Eyre gave an agonised cry. She wrapped her arms around the crystal ball and sobbed desperately when she saw that it was now completely clear. Tears, and years of weariness, pain and loss racked her body until a soft nose nudged her shoulder.

"Seems a shame to cover such a priceless object in snot," Ischyros commented. But he dipped his head down to her chest, and Eyre turned and buried her face in his neck.

"It's not fair," she wailed, and Ischyros blew softly on her arm.

"No, it's not," he agreed. "But you are strong. And I am here."

That caused Eyre to sob again, great wrenching spasms of grief. Finally she knew what had happened to her parents, their reasons for secrecy, and their determination to protect her. Their courage and their enormous sacrifice for the Overworld, which until now, no one had known about. As Ischyros nuzzled at her back, and Florence played with her hair, everyone else waited, knowing there was nothing they could do. Eventually, Eyre calmed a little and lifted her head off the table. Her eyes were red from howling and she rubbed the tears away as she stood up on shaking legs.

"All that for nothing," she whispered in a voice devoid of hope. "The Protector is dead."

Beatrice put the Felsic on the table and hugged Eyre. "I'll make us a coffee," she said, and headed slowly into Eyre's cabin. Eyre walked over and sat down beside Jax on a sandstone block and he put his arms around her. His lips brushed the top of her head.

"I'm sorry," he said softly.

They all sat in silence, a black gloom swirling. To have come so far! Only to discover that all hope was gone. There was nowhere to go.

Eyre picked up the orbuculum. It had to go back to the basement. The five students stood up and headed for Eyre's cabin. But then Abby turned back, her psychic sense picking up on something.

"Are you okay, Ranger?" she said hesitantly.

Ranger Chrysanthe's head was tilted and he looked into the distance, his purple eyes focusing on something unseen. His face was as serious as Eyre had ever seen it. Then he sighed heavily. "Whittaker Ray has just contacted me; we must all head to Mt Augustus today, in case the Gothak return to Highlight. Apparently, they are desperately searching for the Egeo Blackstone. They do not have it yet, but there have been catastrophic losses in the Overworld. Incendium and Caelus have now fallen, along with Terra and Aqua. The final front is being fought at Mt Augustus, and they need our help." He took in the serious faces that looked at him. "I'm sorry. Have your coffee, but then we must get organised to leave. We need to take the Zepp to carry medical supplies and weapons, so you can sleep on the way over. Hopefully your batteries will be fully recharged by the morning."

Private Ammonite twirled his Crescent Blade around in circles and the light glinted brilliantly on the polished metal as it spun. "I'm ready for war," he said in a fierce tone. "Let me at 'em! I'll go get my stuff—see you at the Mantle Basin." He strode down the steps and past the cabins, before disappearing into one of the circular trapdoors that led underground.

Gegenees nodded and flexed his five arms. "It's time for a final showdown." He grinned, showing his white teeth in his black beard, but it was not a friendly smile. "I am going to service my chariot." And he left too.

Aowx stood up, tilted his head and blew a torrent of fire into the air. A deafening roar filled the valley and echoed off the sandstone cliffs. His eyes narrowed. "And I am going to remind them of the consequences of entering my lair," he whispered, in a voice that sent shivers down Eyre's spine.

The students walked up the steps of Eyre's cabin in silence. There was nothing more to say. Time had run out for searching and conjecture, for running around after elusive answers that were never quite resolved. The Overworld troops needed them, and they were going.

They piled into Eyre's living room. Eyre headed down the hall to put the orbuculum away as the others sprawled on the couches, and Beatrice clattered around in the kitchen organising the coffee.

Eyre shut the lid of her oak chest with a huge sadness. The journey was over. But in a way it was a relief. No more running around after confusing puzzles; the time had come to fight. The final showdown. She contemplated the courage of her parents and Professor Aperito and tears ran down her face as she thought of their sacrifice. All for nothing. But the least she could do was honour them by fighting; to try and overcome the foul Gothak. She wiped the tears away and stood up.

When she joined the others in her living room, they were talking about the Blackstone.

"Well, I'm glad to hear they are having a bit of trouble finding it," Jax said. "I like the image of them swimming around Aqua with a Nodolagem after them."

Everyone laughed at the thought of the frightening monster that they'd encountered in Aqua. It was indeed a satisfying thought.

"Or conversing with a Garman in Terra," Abby sniggered.

"I hope you left the Blackstone at the crater of Mt Incendius," Nick laughed.

"Or inside a Lux flower," Warrigal added, and they all snorted. The carnivorous Terra flower would be a great hiding place. Jax grinned, but didn't say where he'd left the Blackstone. That was something he had obviously decided to keep to himself.

"*By the Light!*" Beatrice exclaimed, and instantly they were all on their feet, staffs in hand. Recent experiences had left them ready for trouble at any moment.

"What is it, Bea?" Abby cried as she raced to the kitchen. Beatrice was standing with a coffee cup in each hand, a stunned expression on her face. She was speechless, and shaking her head.

"Are you alright, Bea?" Nick asked as he lowered his staff.

Beatrice suddenly looked apologetic. "Oh, I'm so sorry," she said. "I just had an idea, and it hit me like an extra-terrestrial cyclone. *St Illuminado be praised,* come and look."

Staffs disappeared as everyone crowded to the breakfast bar and the entrance to the kitchen.

Beatrice plunked the coffee cups on the bench and beckoned. "No," she said, her eyes agleam. "Come in *here!*"

They all jammed into the small kitchen, mystified. What on Entis could be in here to create such excitement? Maybe the dust on my shelves, Eyre thought ruefully.

But she could see the cogs turning in Beatrice's brilliant mind. And then the lanky girl pointed at the cupboards, her eyes shining with excitement.

"I'm so slow! Look at the carving around the edges! I've always thought it was just decoration around the initials of your family, Eyre. But what if *that,*" she pointed to the double horizontal lines between the three letters, "is an *equals* sign? Then it reads—AER *equals* AER!" she exclaimed. "Or, to take it further—E-Y-R-E equals H-E-I-R. *Eyre equals heir.* Why have I not seen this before? It's a code, a puzzle! The Protector said he had been waiting a long time to meet 'The Eyre', but what if he really meant 'The Heir'?"

Eyre looked confused. "The Heir to what?"

Everyone stood still as Beatrice paced around, thinking out loud.

"The Protector was a good guy, we know that. We also know that the Protector is the only one who can reinstate the Aura. So why would he kill himself, knowing it would effectively render the Isars powerless? Unless," she wagged an 'aha' finger at Eyre, "he knew there was someone to step up. *The Heir.* He was sending a message. And giving the world a new Protector, one that the Gothak didn't know about. That's *you*, Eyre!"

Abby thought about it. "You *have* had some very powerful energy over the years, Eyre. Inexplicable things have happened to you, right from the TEPs. Healing quickly, cyclonic tempests, Viq before you elevated, not to mention butterflies flocking around your energy—you've always been different somehow. Even your Inguz is different." She snapped her fingers and looked at Eyre. "And your drupe cape! Plumipes put an 'H' on it. Perhaps she didn't mean—*Hese*—maybe the H stood for 'Heir'? Could it be that she knew about all this too?—After all, she has actually been around for aeons!" She looked upwards, thinking. "I think Beatrice might be right!"

Beatrice raised her eyebrows. "Of course I am!"

Eyre looked dubious. She mulled the outrageous idea over in her mind. "Any unusual powers I've had have always been totally out of control. Not much use to anyone, really, if I'm blowing things up left, right and centre. I just thought it was because I was a rather inept Aether. And, remember that Aowx said the Kenaz had to be pushed together by the Protector. I did that—and nothing happened."

Beatrice frowned and stopped pacing. She looked deflated for a moment, and then stuck her chin out, thinking furiously. "No, it's *got* to be right. That border was added later, after Eric had died. You told me that Whittaker Ray said you used to be called Er 1 and Er 2—for Erin and Eric. But, what if it meant 'Heir 1' and 'Heir 2'? Back before Eric died? Your parents knew you were Aethers, and it's got to be a code, I'm *sure* I'm on the right track." She snapped her fingers. "And when you did it last time, the Alexandrite tile wasn't in the middle."

Eyre looked unsure, and then shook her head. "I have absolutely *no* powers at the moment. How could *I* be the next Protector?"

Nick pragmatically said, "Well, there's only one way to find out. Why don't you try again, Eyre?"

After a moment, Eyre shrugged. "Can't hurt, I guess. I'll go get them—Jax, will you give me a hand?"

She and Jax headed to the basement and Eyre carefully pulled the Kenaz and the Alexandrite square out of the oak chest. Could these objects be the key to reinstating the Aura, as Professor Aperito had said? But, as for Eyre being the new Protector, that seemed way too far-fetched to be possible. She hadn't really shown Protector-ish skills over the years. Half the time she was struggling to catch up, slower than other students to pick up skills, and trying to manage embarrassing, out-of-control powers that were no use to anyone. And after her visit to the window, she had no powers at all.

She sighed as she closed the lid. Puzzles and mysteries, and nothing was straightforward. But at least there was still hope. Although it seemed ludicrous to her that *she* might be the next step forward.

Jax carried the Kenaz up the metal stairs and Eyre followed with the precious Alexandrite square. She walked carefully; all I need is to trip and crack it, she thought. That *would* put a spanner in the works.

Ischyros had ambled around the side of Eyre's cabin with Florence on his back, tearing up grass around the edges with his old teeth. He looked up as the six students came out, and he scowled at them, his face most displeased.

"You said I'd have a wonderful breakfast," he accused, through cheeks stuffed with grass. "Liar." Then he turned his old rump towards them to demonstrate his chagrin.

Jax walked over near the Mantle Basin and put the angled gold bars on the table, where they gleamed dully in the morning sunlight. Eyre carefully lay the Alexandrite tile beside them as she studied the five treasures dubiously. Could the Kenaz and the Alexandrite really hold the secret to reinstating the Aura? All the years of sadness and pain, of death and despair, ultimately centred around these strange objects? It seemed hard to believe.

The Ranger emerged from the Perrills' cabin and saw the group surrounding the table. He walked over to them, looking at the gleaming objects curiously. Eyre was sure she saw a spark of recognition in his eyes when he looked at the Alexandrite, but then it was gone again. The titanic blast when the Aura disintegrated had blown his memory away with it and he looked so frustrated that Eyre felt sorry for him.

After a few minutes, Gegenees dropped the grease and rags, tools and brushes he held in his hands, and left his chariot at the side of the clearing to join them. Private Ammonite emerged from his trapdoor with a backpack and his Crescent Blade and when he saw the group he headed over too. For a moment everyone studied the objects on the table as Beatrice explained her theory.

"Well, have a go," Warrigal coaxed Eyre, who couldn't seem to move. Finally, she gave a small smile, and leaned over. First, she put the Kenaz in the shape of an Inguz, like Aowx had shown them.

And then she placed the Alexandrite square in the middle.

There was an expectant silence, but nothing happened. Eyre felt embarrassed, and pushed the bars more tightly together. There was not a sound as everyone collectively willed something magical to happen. But nothing did. After a very long and awkward five minutes, Eyre pulled the objects apart and laughed uncomfortably.

"Well, it was a good theory, Bea, but I'm obviously not 'it'." She looked around at the sympathetic faces that watched her, and shrugged. "I didn't really believe it."

Abby patted Eyre on the shoulder. "We're all struggling to figure it out, Eyre. I thought Bea's theory made complete sense."

Beatrice was gloomy, not only because the Aura hadn't been reinstated, but because for once, she'd got a puzzle wrong. It was aggravating to her, as well as disappointing. She heaved a sigh as her eyes scanned the air one last time, looking for a change in the atmosphere. "But, hang on, I feel like there's something else. I'm just thinking," she said, frowning and rubbing her forehead.

Nick, ever pragmatic, raised his eyebrows. "Well, what do we do now? Off to Mt Augustus I guess."

And then Abby recited the prophesy of the Sea Crone softly.

"When all seems forsaken
And the Darkness awakens
To dispel chaos and peril
Find the Golden Beryl
And at 7.17
When the colour is green
Free the last treasure of Pandora
From the diapaused Aura"

Everyone who was there listened again to the prophesy that they already knew well. It had been debated and mulled over ever since Eyre had come back from Aqua, and they had all heard the words many times. Abby shook her head.

"Well," she said after a moment. "We know that the last treasure in Pandora's box was *hope*, and I think we've officially reached the 'forsaken' status that the Sea Crone mentioned," she said. "We definitely need Pandora's 'hope'. The Alexandrite is the tear from the Aura, the diapaused —what Whittaker Ray said meant 'the inert'—Aura, so what do we do? We couldn't be more qualified for the category of 'chaos and peril' if we tried!"

As if to support her statement, a huge explosion came from the south. Flames lit the night sky and the whistle of atra shrieked in the air. Abby continued softly, with her eyes on the orange horizon. "We need to find the Golden Beryl the Sea Crone told us about. Maybe it's time to go back to the Library."

"Heliodor," Jax said as he stared into the Mantle Basin. "A stone of the sun, to regain what has been lost." Eyre raised her eyebrows. He'd obviously done well in Minerals and Crystals 301.

Then suddenly, Beatrice snapped her fingers and grabbed the Felsic. She had the look of someone who'd just solved the Goldbach Conjecture. "Yes! That's it!" She scrolled wildly down and pointed at the transcript of what Eyre had seen in the crystal orbuculum. "Heliodor!"

"Ah... yeah," Jax said, trying to follow her. "It's related to emeralds and aquamarines, they are beryls too."

"BY THE LIGHT!" Beatrice exclaimed, turning to the Ranger and looking back at Eyre. "That was what the Protector called Ranger Chrysanthe!"

"Yes," Eyre said slowly. "Heliodor, when the Aura blew up. But he also called him Doron Helios, in the Underworld."

"Yes, but remember, Whittaker Ray said it might be L-i-o—for short?" Beatrice said excitedly.

The Ranger looked nonplussed and ran his hand through his green hair. "I wish I could remember that day. I've always been Leo—apparently that was the name I gave when the Russian peasants dragged me out of the Podkamennaya Tunguska River. I don't recall it."

Eyre pointed at the Alexandrite square and the Kenaz on the table. "You have a go, Ranger! Maybe *you* are the Golden Beryl we were supposed to find! And maybe it's *you* that is the new Protector!"

The Ranger looked doubtful. "I do not think this is my destiny, Eyre," he said gently, and then his eyes crinkled. "But I'm happy to try." He moved closer to the table, and like Eyre, pushed the Kenaz together and then slipped the Alexandrite in the centre as everyone watched anxiously. But the Kenaz remained the same, and the green Alexandrite square was unchanged. Eyre felt as low as she ever had in her life. The tears she'd cried earlier were still salty on her cheeks, and she felt so tired. They really had reached the end of the track. If Ranger Chrysanthe wasn't the Golden Beryl —then how would they ever figure out what was?

But then Nick cried out, and pointed at the Ranger's neck. "What's that?"

Everyone looked, and they saw something green, glowing on and off like a neon light, under the Ranger's shirt.

The Ranger pulled it out and stood up with a bemused expression on his face. "It's my pendant," he said, holding it out to the watching group. It was an irregular shaped piece of green stone that Eyre had noticed many times before around his neck. Set into a silver holder and hung on a thong, Eyre had always assumed the gleaming crystal was an emerald. But now it was flashing on and off like a green torchlight.

"It was in my pocket, along with other stones from the bottom of the river when they hauled me out," the Ranger said. "I've always liked it, and I've worn it ever since."

Jax picked the Alexandrite square up and turned it over to examine it. Then he pointed at the chip in the crystal tile. "The imperfection in this tile—it looks like perhaps *you* are wearing the bit that's missing."

Everyone crowded around to see. And Eyre realised that Jax was right. The chip that they already knew was in the flat surface of the tile matched the shape of the Ranger's crystal perfectly. The Ranger took his leather thong off and carefully pulled the crystal out of the silver setting. Then he lay it on the hollow in the Alexandrite tile. Immediately there was a green flash and the chip was absorbed into the crystal square, so that it formed a perfectly smooth surface. Eyre's mouth hung open. She really hadn't expected anything to happen—for so long they had struggled to take a step forward in this perplexing journey.

Beatrice turned towards Eyre, her eyes gleaming. "*Now* have a go, Eyre," she whispered.

A hush fell again, but this time there was a difference. This time, Eyre realised, the atmosphere was tinged with hope, and she almost couldn't bear to try again, in case she didn't succeed.

But she bent over the Kenaz, and carefully placed the Alexandrite in the centre.

For a moment nothing happened. Then the four Kenaz started to glow brightly. White rays of light shot outwards from the silver bars, and a low-pitched humming arose from them. As Eyre watched, a brilliant hologram of the Inguz rose above it, and moved across to the side of the cabin where Ischyros and Florence were standing. Then, without warning, the Inguz hologram sent off a violent shockwave of energy that knocked everyone in Highlight over and Ischyros screamed. A sonic boom exploded above them and Eyre was deafened; all she could hear was a high-pitched ringing in her ears as she stumbled to her feet and raced over to the Kenaz arrangement. The four bars were now gleaming gold and had been blown off the table and burnt into the ground where they landed. The Kenaz had merged and melted permanently together, forged into an Inguz, with a centre of gleaming green Alexandrite solidly joined to the golden frame.

Florence flapped and squawked above, alarmed by the massive explosion, and Eyre shook her head groggily. She had a sudden, petrified thought. *Where was Ischyros?*

She limped over to where Ischyros had been standing only a moment before, as Florence wheeled above in panic, desperately looking for her friend.

But the old horse was gone.

CHAPTER FIFTY-ONE

BEATRICE WAS ON HER hands and knees, gasping for breath, and Abby had been blown six metres away, between the cabins. Warrigal and Jax, who had been standing slightly further away, had somehow ended up on the veranda of Eyre's cabin and Nick was on the roof. He groaned as he rolled over and slid off the edge, landing on his back with a loud *oof*, next to Warrigal and Jax. "By the Light," he muttered. "I guess it worked."

As they all picked themselves up, Eyre ran around frantically, calling for Ischyros. But the old horse was nowhere to be seen and Eyre sobbed when she finally realised that he had disappeared. He was gone, blown up by the Light. Tears ran down her face as her heart broke.

Abby was crying too. "I'm so sorry, Eyre," she said, and put an arm around Eyre's shoulders.

And then someone pointed upwards. Eyre rubbed her eyes and looked where they were indicating. Was the Aura back? Had they managed to regenerate the powerful force? She shaded her eyes against the sun as she scrutinized the sky for some sign that they might have succeeded. All she could see was a bird high up in the sky. And then she looked again. No, not a bird. Her jaw dropped as a shining silver-white Pegasus plummeted down from the sky at incredible speed, landing gently in the clearing. A magnificent creature, larger than a normal Lighthorse, it pranced in place on golden hoofs as its brilliant golden mane and tail flowed in the breeze.

Eyre's wasn't the only jaw that had dropped. Everyone there stood up slowly, mesmerised by the beautiful creature. Where had it come from?

And then Florence shot across and landed on its back. The horse jumped and looked over its shoulder.

"Dimmog," the shining creature said. "Dratted chicken!"

Eyre's heart stopped. She walked forward slowly. "I-Ischyros?" she said tentatively.

The magnificent creature harrumphed in a definitely familiar voice. "I know, I know," he said. "You're definitely punching above your weight."

Eyre rushed forward and threw her arms around her glorious Lighthorse. She buried her face in his mane as tears coursed down her cheeks. "How can this be?" she whispered.

Ischyros tossed his head. "*You* did it," he said. "Four years of running around after the silly old Isars. Personally, I'd rather have stayed as I was."

Eyre looked at the shining horse and felt the same. Where was her grumpy old warhorse? This glorious animal did not seem like her beloved old companion.

"Where have you gone, my old friend?" she asked softly. Ischyros turned his head and after a moment, *nipped* her.

"Ow!" Eyre said crossly, rubbing her shoulder. "That hurt!" And to her chagrin, everyone in the clearing laughed. Chuckles became chortles, then outright guffaws, as everyone looked at the badly-behaved, magical animal.

And Eyre's heart melted. It didn't matter what he looked like—decrepit, burnt and scarred, or rippling with breathtaking beauty—he was her Lighthorse and she loved him dearly. She flung her arms around him again and sobbed.

"I thought I'd lost you!"

Eventually, she stepped back and rubbed her eyes, feeling slightly self-conscious, as her audience of friends stood silently watching. And then there was a bright flash in the clearing and the Kikkuli Master walked out.

"Hello, old friend," he said, recognising Ischyros immediately. "You've been to the salon?"

No nipping for the Kikkuli Master. Ischyros trotted up to him and rested his head on the Master's shoulder.

"He summoned me," the Kikkuli Master said. "Because he is upset. He doesn't want another Protector."

Another Protector? Eyre was shocked. Did that mean that—

"Yes," the Kikkuli Master nodded, reading her thoughts. "Ischyros was the Protector's Lighthorse. When the Aura was destroyed, he was transformed and hid for decades in the Equestrian Centre. The previous Kikkuli Master was the only one who knew his identity, and only then because he found out where the old horse had come from. The Podkamennaya Tunguska River could only mean the Protector's Lighthorse. Ischyros was told who he was, but his memory of that day was gone. So all he knew was what people were saying about the Proditio, and the Protector's betrayal. It's no wonder he didn't let on who he was. But I knew, because the previous Kikkuli Master told me." The Kikkuli Master scratched the mighty horse gently on his forehead. "Ischyros hated all Lightworkers and all Lighthorses, didn't you, old friend."

Ischyros harrumphed again and tossed his head, then reared up on his hind legs and pawed the air.

"Stupid, brainless horses who put their faith in untrustworthy, evil Lightworkers," he snapped. But of course, only Eyre and the Kikkuli Master could hear him.

"What you don't know yet, Ischyros," the Kikkuli Master said gently, "is that the Protector, *your* previous Lightworker, did not betray the Overworld. He did not cause the Proditio, the Betrayal."

Ischyros stamped back down to the ground, and for the first time since Eyre had met the recalcitrant old horse, seemed lost for words.

The Kikkuli Master continued slowly, so Ischyros could understand. "We only recently discovered that the Protector was trapped in the Underworld. He did not cause the Proditio, he tried to prevent it, along with another courageous being." He shot Ranger Chrysanthe a look and Gegenees patted the Ranger on the back with all five hands.

"Your Protector sacrificed himself so the Isars could come back to the Overworld," the Kikkuli Master finished. "He has released you, Ischyros."

And as Eyre watched, a golden tear ran down the beautiful horse's face. It fell through the air and landed on the ground by his golden hoofs, and an incredible silence reigned. Ischyros bent his head until all the tears had finished falling, then he looked over at Eyre. He trotted up to her and she fully expected another nip, or a swift kick with those massive feet. But instead, he put his nose in her hand and nuzzled her. Tears ran down her own face as the incredible Lighthorse blew gently into her hand. He had *chosen* her! After all these years! Her heart singing, Eyre stroked his muscular, silver neck and whispered lovingly in his ear. They had already been bonded for life, but now it felt like they had merged, much as the Kenaz had to become the Inguz; she and Ischyros were now a single entity.

Zyx had begun flying across Highlight above them. In the distance, the sound of fighting and explosions seemed nearer, and black smoke spiralled up from somewhere out of sight; another town plundered, more lives lost. An ominous feeling hung over Highlight.

And then Abby exclaimed. "Eyre, your *arm!*" She pointed at the top of Eyre's shoulder, and when Eyre looked down, her eyes grew round. Because her Inguz was now a gleaming gold on the outside, with a sparkling silver centre. Completely baffled, Eyre rubbed it to see if it would disappear, but she realised that the symbol was permanent. The combination of the Kenaz and Alexandrite had somehow caused the indistinct black outline and dull grey centre of her old Inguz to morph into this glorious thing.

And then like a light going on, Beatrice's eyes blazed. "Nostradamus! '*The late return will make the grieved ones contended*'—she recited. "Nostradamus predicted in his quatrain X that the return of the Protector will avenge the souls of those who have been wronged. *You* are the 'girl so high, high' that Nostradamus spoke of. And this is your late return!"

Eyre's thoughts were whirling. "But the Aura is not here," she said. "The Zyx are still above us, and although Ischyros and I certainly look sparkly, that's no use to the Overworld, unless Highlight is holding a disco?" She shook her head as she studied her new Inguz.

"On the contrary," Beatrice said. "You are *so* crucial! *You* are the new Protector, so only *you* can take the Inguz up to the height of the Proditio! That's how the Sea Crone told us the Aura will be reinstated."

"Well I don't feel any different," Eyre said apologetically, looking around at the expectant faces.

"Ride with me," Jax whispered. And a sudden jubilation rose within Eyre. *Were* her powers back? Could she do it? She looked at the Ranger uncertainly and his purple eyes twinkled, taking in the smoke and fires, the swarm of Zyx above and the distant sound of explosions.

"Lovely day for a jaunt," he said.

Taking that as a yes, Eyre swung herself up on her beautiful Lighthorse and he *pranced* in place with her on his back, to her utter amazement. He was taller than he was before, and much more muscular, and it felt strange for a moment. But then she lay fully down on his neck and hugged him.

"Look after me, Ischyros," she whispered, and for once, there was no harrumph.

There was a flash of light and Firestorm emerged, and he stood quietly as Jax leapt onto his back. Then he and Eyre exchanged a look and charged along the ground in front of the cabins. A few strides later and the powerful wings of the Lighthorses pulled downwards and lifted them off the ground.

Eyre held on tightly as Ischyros soared upwards, towards the clouds. About fifty metres off the ground they encountered the swirling Zyx, but they blasted through the leathery creatures as if they were confetti and sent them hurtling in all directions. Jax flew beside Eyre and the mighty horses headed higher, into the cumulonimbus formations. The air was frigid, but Eyre felt strangely warm as they plunged in and out of the towering clouds, whooping and hollering. The stress of the past days made the experience even more fun, and they charged at each other, swooping horizontally and then plummeting vertically as fast as they could go, then zooming along the top of the sandstone cliffs, before climbing back up again to the clouds. Eyre shouted in glee. She'd thought she'd never have a Lighthorse that could fly, and to be able to do *this*, was beyond wonderful.

"Here, copy me!" Jax called, and summoned his staff. He fired a beam of light through the nearest cloud and it formed a perfect circle before closing over again. Eyre felt a wave of doubt. Did she have Viq again? She focused hard and held out her hand. To her joy, her staff thwacked solidly into her palm and she grabbed it. Then she fired a brilliant stream of light into the cloud, forming the outline of a heart shape. Quick as a flash, Jax seared J&E into the middle of it.

The Lighthorses circled slowly in the air as Jax and Eyre drew nearer and nearer to each other until they held hands, still circling. Jax leant in and kissed Eyre deeply.

"You are quite something, Eyre with the red hair," he said softly. "Let's hope that soon we might end all this."

Eyre put her hand on his cheek. "Thank you for always being there for me, Jax," she whispered. "My Light and your Light will be together forever, no matter what happens."

They spiralled gently downwards until Firestorm landed on one side of the Mantle Basin and Ischyros on the other.

"I think we can safely say that Eyre's powers are back," Jax said as he dismounted, and everyone chuckled.

"You *are* the Protector," Beatrice breathed, and then fell to her knees with her hands outstretched on the ground. "Oh, mighty one!"

Abby giggled and did the same. "Protect us, we beseech thee!"

Eyre snorted. "Oh, get up!" she said in exasperation. Everyone started to laugh. Eyre saw the shining Inguz had been placed on the table, where it gave off a hypnotic, magical aura. There was no doubt that this glistening object was something extraordinary; it seemed almost alive. The power it contained was a palpable thing.

Beatrice studied it and shook her head. "We did it," she breathed. "Only one step to go. It seems unbelievable."

Then she walked around, thinking aloud in a tone like a PA giving her CEO his daily directives. "Well, at 7.00 we should launch you up there, to give you time to get to the right height by 7.17," she said. "It's a few hours yet, so let's rest and then go."

But Jax interrupted. "Nope, that won't work," he said, and Beatrice looked peeved.

"Why not?" she asked. "We need to get onto this as soon as possible!"

Jax stroked the smooth centre of the Inguz reverently. "If the Alexandrite has to be green—as the Sea Crone said in her prophesy— *'And at 7.17 when the colour is green'*— then it can only be at 7.17 in the morning. Alexandrite is red at night, green in daylight. The Tunguska Event occurred at 7.17am, so that would make sense."

Beatrice nodded, but her face was slightly vexed. She'd obviously remembered from crystallography that Jax was right, and she wasn't happy that she hadn't worked it out herself. But then her eyes turned upwards to where the swarm of circling Zyx was growing thicker. "We may not *have* any time in the morning, if this continues," Beatrice said in a subdued tone.

The Ranger understood. "We have to go," he said softly, "Gegenees spotted Strigis in the next valley, and they'll be heading this way. We must leave this afternoon and go to Western Australia. Whittaker Ray is on his way and I have filled him in on all you have discovered. So, tomorrow morning you can take the Inguz and depart from the top of Mt Augustus, with the protection of the Overworld forces below. If Mudamir comes back here he will find only an empty campsite, which will buy us some time. So, go and rest for a couple of hours, as you may not get another opportunity for quite some time. Then pack your gear and we'll all meet back here at 5pm."

Eyre stroked Ischyros's golden mane. He was a stunning creature and she still couldn't believe it was him. But part of her was mourning her cranky, shabby old horse, and a tear ran down her face as she realised that she wouldn't see that version of him again. But then, as if Ischyros could read her thoughts, he seemed to shudder and jerk, much like Warrigal undergoing therianthropy. A minute later, the old Ischyros stood in front of her, complete with his burned coat and blind eye. Eyre cried out and wrapped her arms around him, weeping.

"Camouflage," Ischyros said craftily. "Keep 'em guessing."

Eyre led him to his stall and gave him the promised spectacular breakfast, with every possible treat she could find. Ischyros chewed blissfully on some liquorice with his old teeth as Florence landed on his back.

"Don't think I'm sharing," he said tetchily. Florence ignored him and tucked her head under her wing, and went to sleep.

CHAPTER FIFTY-TWO

AFTER PACKING HER BAG, Eyre headed down to the basement to look at her Wisdom. She didn't know if she would ever be back here, and she wanted one last look at the holograms, in case it was a farewell forever.

She sat on the floor and turned the precious pages and felt the familiar pain, and joy, at seeing the images of her parents. And then she turned the last page. She wasn't really surprised to see a new hologram twirling around; part of her had hoped for it, after her past experiences. But the message she got was so much more than she had ever expected.

As soon as the page lay flat, Alia began to speak.

"My courageous girl, you have had a long journey, and the fact you are seeing this means that somehow you have worked your way through the morass of intrigue to solve the mystery of the Aura.

"When you and Eric were born, you both had a silver Inguz on your head, which is a sign that you are an Heir to the Protector, a very rare event. The silver Inguz remains for two years and then disappears. We had to keep this information completely secret, as we had realised that not all Lightworkers around us were working for the Light. An Heir is born only once every fifty years, and the Dark Forces would kill any Heir that they knew of."

Alia stopped talking and Rufus took over. "The Heir to the Protector will metamorphose into the Protector only when there is no living Protector, and only when they are in the presence of the Aura, in this case the diapaused, or resting, Aura. *The Inguz with the Alexandrite heart.* By now you will have gone through this process, and can we tell you how proud we are of you? What you must have endured to reach this point. We only wish we were there with you now."

A tear rolled down Eyre's cheek. She wished that too. If only they were here. Life would have been so different. But she wiped it away as Alia continued to speak.

"Future Heirs will need to go up to the Aura, when it is restored, and bathe in the spectrum in order to ascend to the position of Protector, if a new Protector is needed. We have embedded in the Wisdom the secret information that we have discovered, from the efforts and writings of Bertha Hamlen, which is intended in actuality only for Protectors of the Aura. We have bonded it with Light energy, so that the information will activate only in the presence of a Protector. You will see it. But no one else will see anything on this page. It is up to you to pass this on, from now on, only to the one who is worthy."

Rufus finished their dialogue, and his eyes were sad. "Go with the Light, my girl. Be strong. And one day, we will see you again in the Ether." He raised a hand, and Alia did too, and then the spinning hologram gradually faded away.

At the same time, silvery writing was appearing on the page in front of Eyre, and she was grateful, as tears coursed down her cheeks. Her heart felt like it might crack in two as the dim light of the hologram vanished, and the words that were materialising on the page took her mind off seeing the images of her parents for the last time.

She took a deep breath and wiped her eyes, and after a moment began reading.

The Protector's Mandate

The Protector is the guardian of the Aura until he or she dies, Eyre read. *And also, the Custodian of the following critical, and inviolable information. Only the Protector should be aware of these facts; it is imperative that the information is not passed on to anyone. No one but the Protector should know this information, and the book by Bertha Hamlen, which violated that ancient edict, has now been destroyed.*

As Protector, your mandate is to sacrifice anything to protect the Overworld.

The Aura is vulnerable during the 'contraction' from 90,000 ft (the highest altitude before space) to 10,000 ft and back again, between June 5 and 18 during the Beta Taurids, and the Protector must be vigilant while this is happening. Like a tide, the Aura comes in and out from the surface of Entis. The Protector is also at risk during this time.

The Gothak can reach 30,000 ft on their Interfector Hornets, so there is a window when they can attack the Protector, but they do not know this. In 1908, Vigil Argenti (Eyre hiccupped in sorrow as she realized that this was the name of the old man who had suffered for decades in the depths of the foul Underworld) *was set upon by the Dark Forces during this vulnerable time—they had been given the information by Adolf Hamlen, who discovered it by chance. The Revelation came from a translation made of an ancient Egyptian manuscript by a hieroglyph expert in 1907. From this, Adolf learned that the contraction was predictable, and infinite, but shifting, like the rhythms of a tide.*

Fortunately, the destruction of the Aura exterminated any of the Dark beings who knew this information. So once again, the knowledge is safe.

Be strong, Protector. And defend the Overworld, at any cost. It is worth it.

That is your mandate.

Eyre shut her Wisdom with a finality that recognised she had seen the last of the messages from her parents. She was filled with grief, but at the same time energised with purpose. She would not let their deaths be in vain. Her parents and Professor Aperito had sacrificed so much for the Overworld, ultimately their lives, in the quest to reinstate the Aura. They had been so very, very close to achieving that goal before they had paid the ultimate price.

A cold rage had overtaken Eyre. She was fuelled by a determination to avenge their deaths, but also to complete their mission. She returned her Wisdom to her oak chest and then stood up with a resolve that filled her to her very core; a violent, undeniable conviction. *She would avenge them.* And the Aura was coming back, or she would die trying.

She spent the afternoon practising her newly-returned Light skills. She would never again take them for granted, and she was elated as she ran through her Ferito, her Staff skills, levitation, fulminology and psychic skills. It was a joy and a privilege, she realised, and her energy was boundless. She didn't know if it was because she was now the new Protector and had an extra level of power, or if it was simply because of her joy at having her Viq back, she just knew that she was filled with an overwhelming euphoria at being able to perform the difficult skills again. And not only perform them, she had a force within her that bubbled close to the surface, like a volcano about to erupt, and it gave her an intense energy that she'd never experienced before.

After she had been practising for almost two hours, a disturbance from above made her look up.

Circling above was the blue Zepp of the Echelon. It swooped in large, circles until finally it landed and trundled in an ungainly manner towards the campsite. When it finally came to a stop, the side door opened and

Madame Overmantle stepped out. Whittaker Ray descended from the pilot seat and they both walked over to the Mantle Basin.

Whittaker Ray smiled at Eyre, although his eyes were serious. "Well done," he said. "You and your friends have solved the mystery, when others have been trying for over a century and failed. Your courage and tenacity are a credit to you all."

Madame Overmantle's brown eyes were warm as she patted Eyre on the shoulder. "So *you* are the new Protector? Perhaps I should have known. Your cards at the TEPs indicated a time of trial, but a life ahead that was large. But the Light kept your true destiny well hidden."

Whittaker Ray shrugged. "No one could know, Cheska," he said. "It does seem that the Light intended this to be a well-buried secret. And Alia kept her children's heads covered with hats at all times, something I always attributed to their fair skin and her respect for the Australian sun. So no one could have known. But now I understand." He turned towards Eyre. "Aethers have a blue Inguz on their scalps when they are young, but you and Eric were even more unique. Alia knew that her children—*you*—would be in danger should anyone find out that you were Heirs." He looked sorrowful as he added, "She didn't even tell me."

The conversation was interrupted as Beatrice, Nick and Abby came out of their cabins, each with a backpack over their shoulder. They tossed them by the Basin and beamed at Whittaker Ray and Madame Overmantle. Shortly after, Warrigal and Jax arrived, with the Ranger behind them. Gegenees wandered over and finally Private Ammonite jumped out of a trapdoor and charged over to join them. There was an expectant silence as they waited for the Dean to speak.

"I am not going to sugar-coat this," he eventually said. "The situation is dire, and the battle at the Front, at the base of Mt Augustus, is not going well. We are taking crucial supplies with us today, which we hope will help our forces. We have lost many of our troops, and at this point, the Dark Forces are crushing us. What you have done—" he looked at all of them, "— may make the difference between the annihilation and the survival of the Overworld." He sighed heavily. "*If* successful. Tomorrow will be arduous, and we will support you with the full might of the Overworld. But the Gothak have gained a powerful trajectory, and it will be a terrible fight; one we are not guaranteed to win. We can only have faith that the Light will endure."

The late afternoon air was cooling as the sun began to lower, still in the grasp of late winter. Private Ammonite leapt on Aowx's back and the shining dragon stood up and yawned, revealing massive, white teeth.

"We will escort you!" Private Ammonite called.

Gegenees marched towards his gleaming chariot. "And I too!" He climbed aboard and waited at the edge of the clearing, organising weapons and getting his reins straight.

The students filed into the Zepp with their bags and took a seat, buckling up tight. None of them had any illusions about the trip; at any moment they might be shot out of the sky if the Gothak located them. Eyre sat between Jax and Abby, and pulled her strap over her shoulder snugly. There were huge piles of medical supplies stacked in the available spaces, and so many weapons were crammed in every nook and cranny, it was difficult to find a place to sit comfortably. Eyre placed her feet on top of a crate of arrows and leaned back into her chair.

The Ranger took the pilot's seat and Whittaker Ray, Madame Overmantle and the Kikkuli Master sat in the back with the students. Whittaker Ray carried the miraculous Inguz into the Zepp, but after a moment, he passed it to Eyre.

"If things go awry, then it will be up to you," he said in a soft voice.

Eyre held the precious object in her lap with reverence. The dimming light had caused a change in the colour of the Alexandrite and it was now a deep purple colour. The golden frame of the Inguz hummed as an ethereal wave of rainbow colours hovered above it, like a miniature Aurora Australis. Despite her trepidation, a profound joy filled Eyre's soul; she was determined that tomorrow it would be back in its rightful place. After all these decades of sacrifice and confusion and loss.

Keeping this image firmly in her mind, she stared out the window as the Zepp took off, banking west over the Blue Mountains.

CHAPTER FIFTY-THREE

EYRE WATCHED, MESMERISED, AS the brilliant colours of the sunset deepened, and she was so lost in thought, she jumped when Abby nudged her with a grin and pointed to the window opposite.

Flapping lazily along by their side was a large copper-coloured dragon with a grinning Mimir on his back.

"First one there gets a pet rock!" Private Ammonite hollered at them.

Despite her apprehension, Eyre had to laugh. He was irrepressible.

As they flew towards the centre of Australia, Eyre sighed and ran her fingers over the golden Inguz with its Alexandrite centre. So much death and destruction to get to this point. Would it work? *By the Light,* she thought grimly. *It had better work!* As if the Inguz could read her thoughts, a melodic singing drifted from it to her ears.

It was comforting, and she stared out the window as darkness fell and the Zepp flew steadily over the vast interior of Australia, heading for the largest rock formation in the world.

The pitching movement and hum of the Zepp, and the approaching darkness, was hypnotising after the stress of the past few days, and before long Eyre fell into a deep sleep.

Many hours later, a change in the rhythm of the motor woke Eyre, and alerted her to the fact that they were descending. Eyre leaned her head against the cold window and waited for the Ranger to land the vehicle. She didn't want to even think about what this day might hold.

It was still pitch-black outside, but the stars twinkled brightly in the vast sky, and she found it strangely reassuring—it was a reminder that time was endless, and that hope could survive any ordeal.

Below her she could see fires and smoke drifting up in the darkness, and she desperately hoped that this might be the final day of this foul war. Perhaps today they might finally bring this horrible saga to a close.

The Zepp landed on the bumpy terrain and Eyre could see the looming shadow of Mt Augustus beside them as they came to a stop. They had come around to land at the back of the mountain, behind the battlefront where the fighting was most brutal. The choice of location was a move designed to keep their mission a secret—if the Gothak realised how close the small group of Lightworkers were to reinstating the Aura, the whole strength of the Underworld would fall on their heads.

The occasional explosion sounded in the distance, but the troops on both sides had fallen silent, waiting until morning to begin the fight again.

Aowx landed with a soft whump in the darkness beside the Zepp, and Gegenees pulled up silently in his chariot, which glinted in the moonlight.

Whittaker Ray stood up.

"It is five hours 'til dawn," he said to Eyre and her friends. "And that is when you must make your move. I am in contact with Lord Clarembout and Professor Vela, and the leaders of the Alterworlds—Field Marshall Xenolith of the Armatura, Brigadier Lunar Zephyr of the Caelites, Admiral Murchadh of the Pinnae and General Magna O Fyre of the Nemoris, and they are all ready to create a diversion upon my signal. Gegenees and Aowx have also agreed to help with this operation. The fewer there are of you heading up from this side of the mountain, the less attention you will create—the aim is to act before the Dark Forces realise what is going on.

"As soon as the first light dawns, you must be ready to go. You *must* sleep now, to regenerate your energy after the trials of the past few days. I will wake you when it is time, and then this momentous day will unfold."

Eyre fell into an uneasy sleep, with Jax's hand in hers. As she drifted off, she was comforted by the hope that there might come a day when they could be with each other in peacetime, when each moment wasn't filled with apprehension for the future. Her long red locks entwined with Jax's black hair as they leaned against each other and slept.

A few hours later, a thin orange glow lined the horizon, and then expanded as the sun lifted itself into the cool air. Eyre had already been awake for an hour, her eyes scanning the darkness, and she watched the day unfold with the glorious sunrise. She held the Inguz tightly with both hands, unable to rest knowing the Gothak were so close. As the sun rose, the red plains that Eyre knew was the Gascoyne region in the north-west of Western Australia was revealed, the sun turning the vast desert into an undulating ocean of orange, red and terracotta hues. Beside them they could now clearly see the massive rock called Mt Augustus, lying like a colossal sleeping creature on the uneven desert terrain.

Whittaker Ray stood up, looking as if he had not slept at all, and probably he hadn't, Eyre thought. As he slid the door open on the Zepp, a troupe of foraging wallabies jumped away in fright. Eyre hoped they hopped far away from here today.

Cool air flooded in the doorway, the deceptive start to what Eyre knew would soon be a scorching day, despite the fact it was still officially winter. She breathed the fresh air in and shut her eyes, savouring the momentary peace.

And then there was a flash and the massive form of Sergeant Tottingham strode out of the light by a Balga Grass plant, marched over and stuck her head in the door of the Zepp next to Eyre.

"Anyone awake yet?" she boomed. The sleeping students in the Zepp opened bleary eyes and sat up slowly. None of them looked well-rested, and Eyre was sure they'd had as restless a sleep as she had. They looked at each other with wan faces, and Beatrice raised an eyebrow.

"Well, here we go then," she said in an intense voice as she headed for the door to join the Sergeant.

The six students descended stiffly from the doorway of the Zepp in the early dawn, and Eyre felt a fire of fear and anticipation fill her body. If she concentrated, she could hear the faint roar of warfare, even at this distance. First light had brought the continuation of the violence from the day before; Light versus Dark. The ultimate battle had begun again on the other side of the mountain.

"The conflict is coming this way," Whittaker Ray said heavily. "And it won't be long before they are over this side. We had hoped we might have a bit longer, but that is now not the case. We must act quickly."

He handed out sandwiches and fruit as the students milled around the side of the Zepp, stretching aching muscles, which had seized up from sitting in one position for so long on the six-hour journey. They all ate quickly and then headed for the rocky boulders at the base of the mountain. It looked like a good place for cover, and they crowded between the rocks as they saw the first dotted lines of Zyx cross the sky.

Eyre summoned her staff, and felt her mental strength surge back as she heard the noise of the fighting increase. The feel of her staff as it hit her hand gave her courage; the branch of the martyred Rainbow Eucalyptus filling her with a ferocious determination. They were here at the point of no return, and there was no doubt that today would decide the future of the Overworld. But no matter what happened, she would fight as hard as she could and take down as many Gothak as possible. The thought gave her great satisfaction.

A fleeing mob of kangaroos bounded past and Eyre looked where they had come from. Red dust hovered in the air and then a horde of Characs came shrieking out of the whirling sand. They appeared so unexpectedly that Eyre's heart jumped. But her hands were so practised she didn't even need to think. In a second, she had strafed the Characs with a stream of burning energy, and those that survived veered away, screeching in agony. The power from Eyre's staff was so great she could hardly control it, and she stepped back in shock.

"Take cover!" the Sergeant's booming voice called.

She had barely called out the warning when a deafening noise like a freight train approaching arose from behind the massive rock. And in a few minutes, the first of the Lightworking troops appeared around the side, battling the Gothak. The clang of Mnaes rang through the air, and the boom of atra made the ground shake. From across the plains the smell of burnt flesh made Eyre cough and gag.

And then the full mass of the warriors emerged. Eyre's jaw dropped. Because there were tens of thousands of Lightworkers battling the Gothak. The troops streamed across the flat plains, fighting furiously, and the smell of blood filled the air. Alterworld warriors were interspersed with hordes of Gothak, and it was a scene from Dante's Inferno, with flames and blood and maniacal creatures attacking the struggling Lightworkers. All over the battlefield bodies lay where they fell. There was no code of ethics in this war, and anyone attempting to rescue the wounded was cut down. All the troops were merely trying to survive, battling for their lives. There was no chance for Eyre, or any of the other students, to surreptitiously crawl up the sides of Mt Augustus. All they could do was fight and try to breathe, like a swimmer in the surf churned up by a monstrous dumper.

"For the Light!" the Sergeant roared, and charged into the fray, her huge Mnae gleaming as she smashed it into the Dark Forces. A Charac's head rolled as she swung her mighty blade around. And then the Sergeant disappeared into the seething mass of violence.

Aowx gave a savage roar and unfolded his massive wings. He took to the air with powerful downward beats, Private Ammonite astride his back. The huge dragon soared high in the air, then plummeted downwards, screaming in rage as he torched the Gothak's ever-increasing ranks.

Jax seized Eyre and pulled her close in to him, kissing her fervently. His green eyes locked onto hers and his voice was rough as he whispered, "Stay alive."

Then both he and Eyre charged into the fracas, their staffs already blazing lethal energy at the Gothak.

Eyre was dimly aware of Abby and Beatrice fighting desperately not far from her, but she couldn't turn to look. It was too important to concentrate—one lapse and it could all be over for her. She burned countless Gothak, and plunged her Mnae to the hilt in the necks of the Characs. As if possessed by a demon, she cut and stabbed and slashed and burned the vile creatures, but always there were more to take their place. The Strigis ran amok through the struggling figures and the spine-chilling sound of their cries reverberated off the steep flanks of Mt Augustus. Eyre was sweating, and starting to tire, but she had to keep going. The Gothak could *not* win!

Battalions of Armatura, shoulder-to-shoulder with Caelites and Nemoris, marched into the whirling maelstrom of pain and death. The brave Alterworld soldiers fought courageously, but they were overwhelmed by the sheer numbers of the Underworld troops. Strigis, Characs and Gothak on Interfector Hornets surged forwards endlessly, inundating the Light Forces with their incredible numbers. Even the Pinnae, sending tidal waves of water over the parched earth, could not make a difference. For every one of the Dark Forces they swamped or drowned or smashed into the earth under a powerful breaker, ten more emerged.

Suddenly, there was a deafening screech and the earth-shaking thud of immense feet, and Eyre saw Warrigal go thundering by—transformed into the Strigis chimera. In a short while he had dispatched scores of Gothak, tossing them in the air like a cat with the carcass of a dead mouse. But the flood of Gothak was inexorable; they seemed endless, and they were unafraid to die. Eyre felt despair wash over her. This was an impossible fight. When a mighty Armatura disappeared into the jaws of a Gryllus Weta, she knew they were going to lose.

And then the familiar rage started to boil within her and the violent energy took over her body. Her hair stood on end and her skin felt like it was on fire. As if by some other force than herself, her staff raised slowly.

As the tumultuous battle neared, she aimed at the towering heads of the Strigis with the pink crystal on the end of her staff. Her eyes glowed golden, and with a humourless glee she turned towards the flood of Strigis emerging from the Underworld. Her heart sang as the dormant energy that had been within her for years finally found its full force and she focused her fury on the foul beings who approached.

Look out, she thought.

CHAPTER FIFTY-FOUR

A FIRM HAND GRABBED Eyre's shoulder, and she was dragged backwards behind a sandstone rock. Eyre was so far gone in her mindless rage, it took Whittaker Ray some time to calm her down, speaking to her quietly as the battle surged past the crevice where they were concealed. Gradually, the golden fury left Eyre's eyes and she looked around vacantly, breathing deeply as her mind finally took control again. But her face contorted as she saw the Overworld forces being decimated on the plains before her.

Whittaker Ray's eyes were sombre.

"You are not here to fight right now," he said softly. "We can't let them know who you are, or it will all be over before you have a chance to take the Inguz up. You must remain hidden."

Eyre looked at him contritely. The battle had overwhelmed them all so quickly, she felt that she'd had no choice but to fight. Tactics and strategies had not even crossed her mind. She hadn't thought about the Inguz, or where it was, or her ultimate mission.

"I'm so sorry," she whispered. "I just wanted to kill them all."

Whittaker Ray looked sympathetic. "I understand. We all do. But *focus*, Eyre! Call for Ischyros. And here is the thing that will change the world forever."

He brought the Inguz out from behind a rock. It shone brilliantly, despite the shadows of Mt Augustus, and Whittaker Ray slid it into a long-handled burlap bag which he gave to Eyre. She slung it across her body so the precious object could not be seen.

Then Whittaker Ray handed her a strange geometric crystal, shaped like a pyramid, that had a rainbow metallic sheen.

"Bismuth," he said. "An element of transformation. This will help you keep time, and find the right altitude to release the Inguz.

"The time is coded within the metal, and the tiers of the structure will light up as you ascend. Each tier is 1000 ft. When the final tier is lit, the single cube at the top, you are at the correct altitude of 28,000 ft." Then he laughed shortly. "Don't drop it."

Eyre laughed too and put the bismuth carefully in the bag with the Inguz.

Then Whittaker Ray, the proper, ever-disciplined, courteous mentor of the Academy of Light, grasped Eyre's shoulder and a grim expression crossed his face.

"Thank you, Eyre," he said. "Make it happen."

Eyre lifted her chin. "Yes sir. My honour and privilege." She held tightly on to her staff and called for Ischyros, the first time in her life she thought he might actually come.

And he did.

And when he arrived, she was startled at his appearance—she had been expecting the old, decrepit Ischyros and had forgotten that he had transformed. His silver coat shone in the sunlight and he tossed his head. The golden mane streamed behind him and he looked like an ancient, mythical deity as he arrived from the Ether.

"I was in the middle of lunch," he complained. "I hope it's important."

Eyre smothered a laugh, despite the circumstances. "To the top of the mountain, post-haste my steed!"

She swung herself up on his back and held on tightly to his golden mane as he reared up on his hind legs. What a difference it was to sit on his back now, Eyre thought. He was broad and strong, and his muscles bunched with power as he leapt into the air and kept going upwards with huge strokes of his mighty wings. It would have been exhilarating if she wasn't so churned up with anxiety

Ischyros flew steeply up the sides of the 715-metre-high mountain. As they climbed higher, she could see further around the plateau and her heart fell as she saw the extent of the massacre. Bodies lay strewn for kilometres, and there were burning Zepps dotted all over the vast expanse of red earth. Squadrons of Lighthorses were battling in the air as Zyx and Interfector Hornets attacked, and Eyre's heart clenched when she saw Lord Clarembout roaring in rage and charging into a horde of Characs on the dusty red earth far below. His troops fearlessly followed him, and she could hear the distant clash of their blades. She sent a silent prayer to the Light for Sir Philius's safety.

But she had to keep going. Whatever was happening below couldn't impact on her resolve.

At the top of Mt Augustus, Ischyros curved around and landed lightly on the scrubby rock. Any other time and Eyre would have marvelled at the precision and lightness of his landing. But today she needed to focus on the next phase of her mission.

She stroked Ischyros gently. "Thank you, my friend, for this incredible journey," she whispered. "I'm grateful for the path we have shared. Whatever happens, I will always be thankful you were in my life."

Ischyros rested his head on her shoulder. "And I will always be grateful for the chicken," he said solemnly, causing Eyre to crack up and throw her arms around his neck.

"I love you, Ischyros," she said softly. "Thank you."

"And I love you," Ischyros replied after a long moment, causing floods of tears to course down Eyre's cheeks.

"Well then," she said. "By the Light, let's do some *damage!*"

A sudden movement from above caused Eyre to raise her staff swiftly. But fortunately she recognised Firestorm before she blew the beautiful gelding out of the sky. Jax plummeted down and landed on the rock beside them.

Another flare of light flashed beside Jax, and Nick appeared. Then two more flashes as Beatrice and Abby emerged from the light. Despite her worry for her friends, being so high on this exposed rock, Eyre was grateful they had come to say farewell.

And then a further surprise as Rigmar, Pheria, Tina, Colton and Carly materialised beside the others.

"You didn't think you were leaving us out of this stampede?" Carly asked as the amethyst crystal on top of her staff glowed a vivid purple.

"Oplo is keen for some action," Pheria said, indicating her sturdy staff, and as if to demonstrate, she lifted it up and sent a torrent of fire into the swarm of Zyx that was beginning to circle above them. Charred bodies dropped from the sky and hurtled down the cliff face.

"We'll cover you," Nick said as he peered over the edge of the cliff. "We've got company."

The students crowded to look down the rocky slope and Eyre could see hundreds of Gothak climbing the steep sides, with their strange, double-jointed limbs. It was an eerie sight, and she felt a frisson of dread travel across her skin. A Gryllus Weta had started to scuttle from the base of Mt Augustus and she knew it wouldn't be long until it reached the top. She saw hundreds of lamprey-mouthed Characs clambering up the rockface and she knew Nick was right; she had to go.

Eyre kissed Jax lightly on the lips, but her eyes were intense. "They're coming," she whispered. "There's not much time. Half an hour until 7.17

and I had better be up there."

Eyre swung up onto Ischyros's back. "I suppose I've got to do some work then?" he grumbled. But she could see the gleam in his eye. He was a true Lighthorse, invigorated by the adrenaline rush of battle, and always keen to take to the skies.

"You and me both, my friend," she said softly, and wound her hands in his golden mane. She looked at the group who now stood guard, staffs aimed high at the Zyx and Gothak, and pointed downwards at the horde that ascended the mountain, and she gave a crooked smile.

"The Light be with you, my wonderful friends."

And then Ischyros galloped along the top of the mountain and launched into the air as everyone left behind on the mountain cheered.

Ischyros flapped his huge silver wings and caught an updraft that took them rapidly above the mountain. From her vantage point, Eyre could see the struggling Lightworker and Overworld troops below, and the blackened plains where the Gothak had been. She gritted her teeth. As Whittaker Ray had instructed, she would make this happen, if it was the last thing she did.

A movement behind her made her swivel, but it was Firestorm again in the air. Jax sat on his powerful steed's back and circled up to them.

"What are you doing?" Eyre cried. "You won't be able to make it!"

"Maybe not," Jax said grimly, "but you're not going on your own."

Eyre felt torn. She was so worried for him. But at the same time, she felt a huge relief at not having to do this alone. In any case, there was no time to argue, so she started to turn around again. But then she noticed more flying shapes in the air, and with a start, she realised that Beatrice, Abby, Nick, Pheria, Rigmar and Colton had left the mountain-top to join them. Tina was sitting behind Colton on Nox, facing backwards, with an arrow already nocked in her bow. And then Eyre realised that Carly, and Warrigal, now transformed back to himself and rocketing upwards on Bunu, had arrived and were also risking their lives to be part of the mission. Her heart swelled at the courage and determination of her friends. The Eleven were with her. So be it—they had journeyed so far together, and they would continue that way, until this thing was done.

She turned back with renewed energy to continue the journey, as her friends caught up with her and formed a squadron. And then she nearly fell off Ischyros as a late arrival joined them. Ben Perrill, on his big bay Lighthorse swooped in at the rear. He looked at Eyre and after a moment she nodded. So be it—the Eleven were now Twelve, the angel number of light and love that the ancient old crone in Russia, the Tomsk Prorok, had said would make a difference. And all the Sectors were included.

Ischyros flapped his wings and they shot up almost vertically. Each second that they delayed regenerating the Aura meant more lives lost, and Eyre urged him upwards. They had to *hurry!* The eleven other students hung valiantly on her heels, but after a while the gap started to widen as her phenomenal Lighthorse found his stride and stretched out.

But then something dark and black shot by Ischyros's nose. A Zyx! And then, like a school of piranhas, hundreds of the horrible creatures flew into the squadron and attacked. They were too close for Eyre to use her staff, so with a blood curdling cry, she drew her Antaraks and sliced and chopped madly at the foul horde. Leathery wings scraped her face and sharp fangs snapped viciously, and the lethal clawed feet tried to drag her off her steed. But she was driven by a wild and manic fury, and all the skills of Clasis with Multiple Weapons suddenly seemed to fuel her veins—she swapped between weapons without even thinking, and the corpses of the Zyx fell downwards like a toxic black rain.

Eyre's friends were battling the awful flock too, and Eyre saw the Interfectors whirring in, their lethal barbs curved and ready to strike. Gothak sat on the backs of the huge Hornets, and their dead eyes looked triumphant. There was only one way this was going to go, their faces seemed to say. Well, my story goes differently, Eyre thought furiously, and she incinerated the nearest sneering face with a dead-centre blast from her staff.

But the Interfector Hornets were agile, and they flew around the Lighthorses looking for a vulnerable spot as the Gothak drove them on. And then, a terrible cry from Carly. Eyre turned and saw with horrified eyes that Carly's Lighthorse had been stung by an Interfector. As Eyre watched the massive Clydesdale battle for his life, the Gothak that rode the Interfector sliced Carly across her neck with his Luxoccisor. Carly didn't even make a sound; she slipped off her massive horse and they both tumbled downwards through the black swarm of Zyx.

"Nooo!" Eyre cried. But the huge-hearted girl who had been her friend from the beginning was gone. Tears ran down Eyre's face as she cried for the brave warrior, and she felt as if she too had been pierced through her heart. But all she could do was fight the onslaught of vermin that were trying to bring the squadron down—she had to keep going.

Just when Eyre felt that they would all share Carly's fate, reinforcements arrived to give them respite. Sergeant Tottingham appeared on her huge grey Percheron, Audo, leading a contingent of Lightworkers of all ages. Many of them were wounded, but they came in with a ferocity that was breathtaking. Jensen Ross, the boy that had lost his leg to the Bunyip at the

TEP trials, was there on his white mare, and he took out three Zyx and an Interfector within seconds. Pheria's brothers, Will and Stratt, soared up beside him. Will had his Mnae drawn and was slaughtering any Gothak that came close, and Stratt was showing his athletic prowess with his sparkling Antaraks. The brothers fought back to back in the skies as the Gothak swirled around them. And Eyre saw Iris Goff and Amanda Lorraine, unlikely comrades in normal life, flying side by side, their staffs firing flames of wrath as they swooped amongst the Gothak.

Aowx came charging through as Private Ammonite whooped with manic glee. "A pleasure doing battle with you!" he shouted as he sliced the head off a Gothak with his Crescent Blade.

And then Eyre ducked as something came flying towards her like a bullet. She raised an Antarak, but stopped as she recognised Florence, hurtling through the air like a missile with her strong claws extended. Her three yellow eyes glowed and she let out a piercing cry as she grabbed a Zyx and tore its head off without even slowing down.

A moment later, a huge flock of Venators appeared out of the Ether. Florence shrieked proudly and headed upwards at the head of the lethal predators. No longer Florence, Ischyros's amiable companion, Eyre's apex bird was now in her element as Ne-Ne, the most powerful of the Venator flock, and she led the Caelorian birds as she was born to do. Their leader. Head of an unstoppable force. With a shrill cry, the V-formation cut through the swarm of Zyx and black bodies dropped like stones towards the earth.

Gegenees arrived in his magical chariot, and he swung a Flail around his head as a colossal, spiked Nahtaivel swooped in from the side. The Flail struck the armoured creature in the centre of its forehead, and it screamed as it swung around to attack again. Its large jaws opened, revealing three rows of razor-sharp teeth, and it lunged towards Gegenees with incredible speed.

But a black and orange streak zipped between the beast and the chariot and something was lobbed into the Nahtaivel's open maw before the streak rocketed out of reach again. A second later, the leathery creature blew apart, sending blood and guts all over Gegenees and his chariot.

"World War II hand grenade," the Ranger called. "Very effective."

Gegenees wiped his face, rolling his eyes. "Thanks, I guess." But his voice was dark. He knew the Overworld was losing.

Eyre and Jax flew higher as the Defence Forces below battled to keep the Dark creatures from following.

"What is the time?" Jax called as they soared high above Mt Augustus.

"7.02, 15,000 feet," Eyre answered, checking the bismuth pyramid as the Lighthorses powered upwards. By 18,000 feet, Eyre could see that Jax was beginning to slow down. It was ten minutes to the deadline, and Firestorm was struggling in the thin air. He was lagging behind slightly when a meteor of atra blasted by them.

Ischyros reared and Eyre turned in shock. What could have made it up here with them?

Her heart clenched when she saw Mudamir on an Interfector hornet, larger than normal, a black, lethal-looking creature covered in metal, flying up towards Jax. Jax wheeled around on Firestorm, but he was tired, and Eyre knew he couldn't breathe properly. Only the Protector could operate at this altitude, and she berated herself for allowing Jax to come with her; he was completely vulnerable.

Hauling Ischyros around, she charged towards Mudamir, but she was too late. He fired a black beam of fire into Jax's chest, and Jax tumbled off and dropped down towards the earth. Firestorm shrieked in grief and plunged after him, disappearing through the cloud cover.

Mudamir grinned as the black Interfector hovered. "My dear, I am very glad to see you again. We found the Egeo Blackstone. Very clever of your compatriot to hide it in a Terra sailing rock. We might never have found it. But what you don't know is that Saevus are trained to scent specific objects for us, and one of them found it, gliding along in the middle of the Pyre of Va."

He sighed mock-happily. "I'm sure you'll be glad to know that Rhabdor is now carrying the Blackstone in his chariot. It has definitely given us the edge since it re-joined us. Unfortunately, to the detriment of your troops. So anyway, what are you doing up here on your silver horse, all on your own?"

Eyre was weeping inside as Mudamir gloated. Jax was gone, and her heart felt like it would break in two. Time was counting down to 7.17 and she still had thousands of feet to go. Mudamir was certain of his power, and taking his time. But he didn't know who she was.

A sudden calm descended upon her. It was as if the four years of heartache, searching and sadness had culminated in this one moment. It didn't matter about her life, or her grief, or the difficulty of the journey. All that mattered was the Overworld. And it was her job to protect it.

Her eyes blazed and she smiled at Mudamir. The evil creature looked slightly disconcerted as she bared her teeth, but he raised his Luxoccisor.

"I'm going to enjoy this," he smirked.

"Me first," Eyre whispered. And as Mudamir raised the scythed weapon, she summoned her Kulbeda and hurled it at him, slashing his arm. Then, controlling the golden dagger, she spun it past his other arm, and cut him deeply before the weapon flew back to her.

Mudamir hurled a spear of flaming atra at her but she sent up a shield and it bounced back at the sneering Gothak. He hurtled upwards and attacked from above, raising his Luxoccisor above his head.

"A valiant attempt, my dear," he snarled. "But inconsequential, I'm afraid."

"I promised that you would die screaming," Eyre replied in a soft voice, and hurled an Antarak at Mudamir. The spinning sword, crafted from the Zha'kara diamonds from Incendium, moved too fast for him to react. He raised his hand and the Antarak sliced cleanly through it, leaving him screaming as black blood gushed from the stump of his wrist. His hand, still holding the Luxoccisor, tumbled down into the clouds.

Eyre grinned, her eyes dead. She summoned her Mnae with barely a thought.

"Clasis for Multiple Weapons," she said. "I have many of them, and you are going to experience their pleasure at close quarters today."

Mudamir spun away on the Hornet, but Ischyros hurtled after him. Eyre drew nearer, until she could look directly into the Gothak's black eyes.

"*I am the Protector,*" she breathed. "The Guardian of the Overworld. And you will soon be lying on the plains of the Gascoyne. A piece of filth that everyone will trample over, unnoticed, reviled by your people as a failure. You will be forgotten before this day is finished."

She swung her Mnae and severed Mudamir's other arm at the shoulder. He screamed in agony, his black eyes unable to believe that this small girl was besting him.

"*How can this be?*" he howled. "*Where did you come from?*"

"I come from the Light," Eyre said in a voice that was as large as eternity, as she summoned Vulture Killer. Ischyros swept away from the Interfector's lethal barb and Eyre nocked an arrow. In one smooth movement, and as Mudamir roared in anguish, she shot an arrow straight through his heart. She was so fast, he was dead before he had even blinked.

Mudamir slid slowly off the Interfector Hornet and Eyre dispatched the black creature with another arrow, so that they fell out of the sky together, plummeting towards the base of Mt Augustus.

Tears were flooding down her face as she looked at the bismuth crystal. 7.12, and still 7,000 feet to go. She leaned over and patted Ischyros on the neck.

"Come on, my valiant friend, we need to be swift," she whispered, and kissed his ear.

Ischyros flapped his wings mightily and he surged upwards. Eyre was suddenly filled with a surge of breathtaking power, beyond anything she had ever experienced before. And she knew with certainty that she was going to do this, no matter what it took. She looked up into the indigo stratosphere and dug her heels in to Ischyros's flanks. From deep within her an explosion of energy burst outwards, a spiral of light that lifted them higher like a formidable updraft. As they reached 28,000 ft, the final cube on the bismuth pyramid glowed brilliantly. She looked at the time. 7.16.

Carefully, Eyre pulled the Inguz from the hessian bag. The Alexandrite square in the centre of the Inguz was glowing green, and she waited until the time ticked over to 7.17. Then she hurled the Inguz horizontally, like a shining frisbee, into the frigid air.

For a second, nothing happened, and Eyre was terrified she would see the heavy object plunge ineffectually back down towards Mt Augustus. But then some other power caught the shining talisman and bathed it in a glowing golden light, and it hovered for a moment. Then, with an explosion of rainbow colours, a band of brilliant light emanated from the Inguz and radiated outwards. The Inguz disappeared, and the spectrum of colour shot away from Eyre, too fast for her to follow. There was an ear-splitting *boom* as the energy circumnavigated the globe and returned to complete the circle above Entis. Eyre could almost hear Entis sigh as the protective barrier was re-established after so many long and difficult years.

The Aura was back!

Eyre waited a moment as the rainbow spectrum faded and disappeared, and then she turned Ischyros downwards.

"We did it, my friend," she said softly, but nothing about this moment felt jubilant. The vision of Jax and Carly plummeting down to Entis was like a Kulbeda in her own heart. Her shoulders bowed in grief as tears streamed down her face. Feeling as if her soul had been destroyed, Eyre wheeled Ischyros around and began the descent from the Aura.

CHAPTER FIFTY-FIVE

AS ISCHYROS PLUNGED DOWNWARDS, Eyre began to see the larger picture. She could see the violent battle below and was filled with a cyclonic rage at the sight of the bodies strewn across the plains. Good souls from all the Alterworlds and Entis, sacrificing their lives to keep the Overworld safe. Eyre sped downwards, determined to join the fight. She would make the Dark Forces *hurt*.

Something came charging up beside her and she flinched and raised her hands. *What was that?* Ischyros was startled and he swerved away as Eyre summoned her Mnae.

But then her mouth gaped open.

"How on Entis did you reinstate the Aura without me?" Jax asked weakly, as he hung over Firestorm's neck.

Eyre burst into waterfalls of tears and charged towards him. She hugged him desperately as she wept in relief. "I thought you were dead," she hiccupped. "How can you be here?"

Jax pulled the pendant out of his shirt, the plume agate that Eyre had cut and polished for him in second-year, the rare stone she had found in the Transit. "*It wards off evil, for protection*, you told me," he said, breathing hard. "The atra hit me right in the middle of it. I'm still here—so I guess you were right."

Eyre held Jax tight as the Lighthorses danced around each other, thousands of feet above the ground. She was struggling to believe that she hadn't lost him.

Just then, a soaring black and orange carpet swept by them.

"So," the Ranger said. "There's a fight going on down below. And I think it's time we remind them of the power of the Light."

Eyre pulled back from Jax and wiped her eyes.

"We will do our best, Ranger Chrysanthe," she said.

The Ranger's purple eyes focused and his jaw tightened.

"I am Doron Helios. Or Heliodor to my friends; aka The Hope Stone. And I *finally* remember."

He flew around Eyre, and Ischyros neighed softly as the Ranger continued.

"We will avenge Vigil Argenti, our brave, selfless friend. And history will rewrite the facts of this story."

The Ranger's eyes softened. "I know you remember now, too, my friend," he said to Ischyros. "Let's go make them remember who *we* are."

Ischyros's coat shimmered for a moment, sending off a blinding silver light in agreement.

The day was clear, the crisp winter air giving way to the sun's warmth, but the glorious weather contrasted starkly with the desolation that spread out before them. The flat plains made it easy to see the extent of the battle; a bloody scene of pain and despair. The bodies of Lightworkers and Lighthorses lay amongst the Mimir, the Armatura, the Pinnae, the Caelites and the Nemoris. Amongst the carcasses of the Strigis and Gothak. A horrible stench filled the air, and already blowflies were buzzing around the dead. There was no attempt to retrieve the fallen; the Overworld troops were decimated and all they could do was try to keep the unending Dark Forces from completely slaughtering them all.

Ranger Chrysanthe spotted Aowx in the distance, strafing the ground with fire, and he smiled.

"Time for me to join the battle," he said in a very unfriendly voice.

Eyre held out her hand and the Ranger took it. "I will see you on the battlefield Doron Helios," she whispered. "But I have to check in with the leaders first."

The Ranger's purple eyes crinkled. "All will be well, little one," he said softly, and then zoomed off towards the explosions in the distance, performing a loop-the-loop on the way.

Eyre and Jax landed behind a makeshift tent that was set up in the shadow of Mt Augustus. Eyre could see runners charging in and out of the tent, carrying small white squares that she assumed were Peragros with secret information. Not that there was much to be secretive about. '*Losing*' could only be written in so many ways. She slid off Ischyros and headed for the entrance as Jax limped behind her.

The first person she saw as she ducked under the flap was Lord Clarembout, who looked exhausted. The huge man was in discussion with

Sergeant Tottingham and another man, obviously of high rank. They were studying a map and pointing at the diagram, but their faces were sombre. It was clear that things were not going well.

"Lord Clarembout? Sir?" Eyre said, as she approached the trio. Sir Philius turned, and his weary face lightened as he saw Eyre. The Sergeant exclaimed and enveloped her in a bear hug.

"You're alive?" she exclaimed in astonishment.

"The Aura is restored," Eyre said simply.

The unknown man gave a short, disbelieving laugh, as if Eyre might be some sort of lying Dark infiltrator.

"How can that be?" he said in a stunned voice. "If so, this is *magie*, indeed!" His meaning was clear. *Magic* or *Lies!*

Lord Clarembout shook his head. "No Gerrit, these are students of the finest calibre. Eyre, Jax, this is General Gerrit Meijer, the head of the Dutch forces."

Jax stepped forward. "The Aura *is* back, sir," he said. "Thanks to Eyre."

After an incredulous moment where they all simply stared at each other, the three leaders finally walked quickly to the entrance of the tent and looked upwards. A faint, undulating haze was just visible, high above them. General Meijer's eyes were round and the Sergeant patted Eyre on the back as she studied the sky.

"You are truly remarkable, Eyre," she said in a voice that hitched, and Eyre could see that the Sergeant was emotional. After the Sergeant's own tireless fight for the Light, with a traitorous sister who had sullied the family name, Eyre realised how much this meant to her steadfast and courageous mentor.

A gleam came into Lord Clarembout's eyes. "This might make all the difference," he said, and stood straighter. "I must call Cheska!"

General Meijer bowed to Eyre. "Apologies for my uncertainty. My nation thanks you," he said as he headed off back to the fray.

"We have perilous wars going on in all the Alterworlds, and every country in Entis is suffering," Lord Clarembout said heavily to Eyre. "The Forces have been through terrible hardship, and—I have to be honest—the Overworld is losing. Sit down for a moment," he said to Eyre and Jax. "You will need to rest; you have both been through a terrible experience. But no matter the outcome, the whole Overworld will thank you for what you have done, and for your courage.

"The Dark Forces have been planning this for decades; they came in with unexpected strength, and they have exploded upon us. But with the Aura, we may have a chance. We have a grave battle ahead of us, and you have brought us hope."

Eyre wasn't sure what hope she could offer. Supposedly she was the Protector of the Overworld. But what did that mean? She'd reinstated the Aura, and to be honest, she'd expected that her job would be over. She had assumed that Lightworkers higher up in the hierarchy would now take over and tell her what to do next. And that somehow, magically, the horror and danger would be over.

But it seemed that nobody knew. It had been too long since the Aura protected the Overworld and those that lived now had no knowledge of what should follow.

Black despair clamped down upon her. She sat in a flimsy tent, with vicious creatures shrieking overhead, charging around outside and tearing her friends to pieces. And she didn't know what to do. She'd thought she'd fixed everything. But nothing was happening.

And then an ancient voice spoke to her suddenly, the deep tones chastising her. "Move on," it said. "You have a part of me, and I am still here. Stand up. Walk forward. The rest will come to you."

So Eyre did stand up, although tentatively at first. The Rainbow Eucalyptus was not going to let its sacrifice be in vain. Speaking from the Ether, it was still keeping Eyre in line. And so she got to her feet to honour that selfless being; she owed the ancient tree this much respect. She didn't really know how she would move forward. She was just pretending.

But then, as the Moog tones reverberated in Eyre's mind like a wave washing over the sand, the advice from the wise entity who had sacrificed itself for the benefit of the Overworld suddenly registered, and she understood the message.

None of them knew where this was going, or what to do next. All they could do was the right thing, as they saw it. Every one of the Overworld troops had faced that dilemma and found the courage to move forward, with faith, and sometimes sacrificing their lives. And she suddenly knew what the right thing for her was at this moment. Move forward, with faith. *Faith.* The lesson she had learnt so many years ago.

And even if she sacrificed her life, she was going to *fight.*

Uncertainty left her, and she twirled the rainbow staff in her hand. "Thank you," she whispered to the aeons-old tree, wherever it was. And then she turned to Jax.

"Let's go," she said with a reverberating conviction. "A war awaits."

CHAPTER FIFTY-SIX

EYRE AND JAX WERE heading towards the front of the tent, their staffs in hand, when Madame Overmantle arrived in a flash of light, her wispy hair in a mess and her purple-rimmed spectacles askew, the strong glass of the lenses magnifying her brown eyes like an owl. She smiled at them as she straightened her bright floral dress. Evidently, fighting to the end of the world had not affected her wardrobe choice.

"My faith in you has been confirmed," she whispered as she hugged them both. "You students are the way forward for this world." Her face fell as she added, "Now you are Eleven, again. Make Carly proud."

Tears sprang from Eyre's eyes again. "I will make them *suffer*," she said softly, and Jax put his arm around her.

"I am communicating with the leaders of the Overworld," Madame Overmantle said. "The Determinant Dozen. The Echelon of every nation on Entis. The Alterworld Commanders. The Mimir and the Lightworking leaders of Australia. I am letting them know that the Aura has been reinstated. It will give them hope, and faith, and hopefully the strength to carry on and *finish* this war." Her eyes were solemn and she suddenly looked very tired and very old as she added, "My cousins could have helped us to end this war so long ago, but I am here to end it *now*. The Light be with you, my very special students. It seems the path forward for the Overworld may lie with you."

Tears dripped from Eyre's eyes as she hugged the elderly woman. She didn't know if any of them would see each other again.

She and Jax headed outside into the maelstrom.

As if in sympathy with the foul Underworld, the wind was rising across the plains, and the skies had darkened. The Aura may have been reinstated, but the world seemed a darker place, as charcoal clouds scudded across the sky and obscured the sun, warning of a violent, impending storm. Venators battled against the powerful gusts, and although it was only early-morning, it seemed like suddenly the day was over. Eyre hoped it wasn't symbolic.

The plains were in complete chaos. Lightworkers and Mimir were fighting Characs and Gothak, who wielded sharpened Luxoccisors and metal-studded clubs. The Unlit were there, with the indomitable UD1 at the forefront, and Rachis at his side, making inroads with their archery and their incredible physical skills. It was so difficult for the Underworld forces to battle a foe who did not fear them. There was a fire in the Unlit as they fought with a ferocity that Eyre understood. Again, but *better*! Kill the foe, at whatever cost. Eyre saw Julia sending lethal arrows into the Underworld ranks with a focus that was fearsome. Her training had paid off; she was definitely avenging her father's death, with a furious joy, and the Gothak fell in swathes before her.

All the Alterworld forces were in full battle mode; the underdogs fighting to the death against tens of thousands of huge Strigis: Sublabors, Saevus, Menax and Tuus, Gryllus, and the horrific Elapidus Vipers. And the ultimate flying fighting weapon, the Nahtaivel. Swarms of Zyx filled the sky, overwhelming the Overworld squadrons with their sheer numbers, and hordes of Characs stormed across the plains; nerveless, evil creatures, who felt nothing, their sharp teeth bared and ready to slice and bite. For a moment Eyre felt complete hopelessness. And then she raised her rainbow staff as the pink diamond glowed vividly, and she kissed Jax gently.

"Whatever happens, we have tried," she said. "If I don't see you again in this world, I will see you in the next."

And they charged into the fray.

Their reality disappeared into a vortex of madness. Eyre was barely aware of anything other than trying to stay alive as she slashed stabbed and burned; switching weapons in Multiple Clasis as she did anything but Tego —only *Aditus* today. *Attack, attack, attack!* Kulbeda flying, Antaraks slicing, her powerful Mnae thrusting, but most of all, her beloved staff— incinerating countless horrible creatures as she fired flaming Viq into their midst. Every thrust and parry was for Carly, and she fought with a force that her long-time friend would have approved of.

Aowx careered overhead, with Private Ammonite shouting in joy every time they dispatched more of the Dark Forces in a flame of pyrotechnic expertise. And Gegenees charged in his chariot beside them, his five arms hacking the heads off Strigis as soon as they were unwise enough to approach him.

And then Eyre saw that a new defender of the Light had joined them.

Plumipes, her massive wings in full power, was swooping down to attack the Gothak, her fangs gleaming. The Gothak looked up in shock as the terrible creature plunged from above and sunk her fangs into their necks. They died instantly from the potent venom and the Gothak scrambled to get away from the ferocious creature. A squadron of smaller winged spiders dressed in soft knitted jackets followed her like satellites, and Eyre gave a small laugh.

"Dinner!" one of them squealed as they smothered the troops. The Underworld ranks were terrified, and ran away screaming from the aerial attack. Eyre couldn't help herself; she smiled as she watched the joy of the spiderlings from below. *Eat 'em up*, she thought grimly.

Armatura, with Devil Wolves by their sides, battled ferociously, cutting the Gothak down in swathes. Their swordsmanship was unparalleled in the Overworld, and they churned through the Dark Forces with grim faces, making each blow count as the Devil Wolves mauled any Dark creature they encountered. And Jotnar and Tumba fought side by side, attacking the Characs with their razor-sharp weapons. But then, as Eyre battled a Gothak with her Mnae, her heart clenched. Because as her blade smashed against the Gothak's Luxoccisor, she saw Goong Goong, the kind-hearted Tumba from Incendium, completely surrounded by Saevus. The massive Strigis stalked towards the small, leathery creature, their dripping fangs bared. Eyre sliced the head off the Gothak she was fighting and craned her neck desperately to look for Goong. But the body of the Gothak fell on top of her, and she fought furiously to get out. *BTL!* Eyre thought. *Don't let this happen!*

Charging in from *somewhere* came an uncoordinated, lanky form, long legs pumping with her staff ahead of her. Beatrice stormed towards the little Tumba, her staff blazing with a righteous light. The emerald glowed with an unearthly force, and in a few seconds, Beatrice had burnt the circling Saevus around Goong Goong into a pile of soot.

"So be *Lit*," she said, as she furiously stamped the remnants into the ground.

Beatrice stood for a moment with tears flooding down her face as she put her arms around Goong Goong.

"This terrible war. So many good souls, but I'm thankful you're not one of them right now, my good friend."

Beatrice raised her staff, and Goong Goong raised her sharp fork, and together they charged forward into the morass.

Eyre watched them wearily and managed to shove the heavy body of the Gothak off her, its foul black blood spouting over the ground. Slowly, she raised her staff and looked for her next foe. More Strigis were swarming from Seams all over the battlefield, too many for the Forces to match. Eyre brushed her grimy hair from her forehead, despairing. For a moment, she faltered. But as she watched Rachis standing atop a pile of dead Strigis far across the battlefield, nocking arrow after arrow as he bellowed in triumph, she set her jaw. *Again, but better.* So be it! And she charged forwards again.

The skies were black, with huge clouds towering and tumbling over themselves. Eyre fought off her despair as she swung her Mnae with two hands, and with a mighty blow, decapitated a Sublabor. And then some unusual allies charged from the rear—a huge pack of hundreds of dingoes, that snarled and yelped as they swarmed over a Menax, taking it down like lions attacking a buffalo. The creature screeched, kicking on the ground as the pack overcame it, until it finally fell still. Eyre dropped her Mnae for a moment and saw that elapid snakes, spiders, scorpions, ants and wasps had joined the fray, swarming over the Gothak with lethal intent. Entis creatures were making their allegiance clear, Eyre thought. And she realised that Alterworld creatures were there in force too: Garmin, Zeguardagens and other vicious-looking creatures she'd never seen before; they all knew their worlds were at stake and were fighting alongside the Overworld battalions. But she knew that even this was not enough. All of the Overworld beings were just waiting for death.

Suddenly, there was a break in the melee and an eerie silence descended on the battlefield. The Strigis stopped their onslaught and the Gothak stood to attention. Eyre stepped back in surprise, wiping smut and blood from her face. What was happening?

Her heart dropped as she realised. A dull black chariot, pulled by Saevus, charged into the throng of fighters, smashing both Underworld and Overworld troops into the ground as the heavy iron wheels ran over the top of them. Commandeering the ugly vehicle was the hideous Rhabdor. Pale and flaccid, and covered in pustulating, weeping sores, he was a gross being with not an ounce of Light within him.

He charged in like a victorious god, waving his hand in the air for approval from his troops, who prostrated themselves on the ground in front of him. The Overworld troops were caught unawares, and milled around aimlessly as they waited to see what would happen. There was a terrible silence, and an ominous feeling in the air as Rhabdor ascended gloatingly to the front of the chariot.

An icy fear passed over Eyre, as she saw he held the Egeo Blackstone in his hands. *So Mudamir had been telling the truth.* They had found it. Pulsating, huge, evil. The heart of the *true* Betrayer, who Eyre now knew was Carrison Hamlen's great-grandfather. A foul, sickening talisman of power. But completely terrifying. Its potency far exceeded the Overworld troops on the ground.

She lowered her staff and waited. And then, there was a startling movement from behind her. And another. And another. As she turned in alarm, her fear turned to relief. First, Rigmar landed beside her on his Lighthorse. Then Pheria. Warrigal, Beatrice, Abby and Nick followed. And finally, Ben Perrill, and Colton and Tina on Nox. They dismounted and summoned their staffs, forming a barrier beside Eyre and Jax.

Rhabdor seemed greatly entertained. He was well aware that the Overworld troops had been suffering, and that the Dark Forces were winning this war. He took his time as he hefted the bloated Blackstone in the air.

"I hear the Aura may or may not have been reinstated," he shouted in an amused tone, and on cue, his troops laughed uncomfortably.

"*NO THANKS TO YOU!*" he suddenly shouted, and blasted a spear of Atra at Ben Perrill. But Ben stood tall and deflected the beam without difficulty. Rufa. The most physical of the Lightworker Sectors.

"You decimated my family," Ben said softly. "And made me a pawn. I will die trying to make this right."

And then, as the Lightworkers jumped in surprise, Ben sent a beam of Viq towards Rhabdor's heart. If a Charac hadn't jumped in front of the foul being—instantly incinerated—Rhabdor would most certainly have been blown out of his chariot, the smug smile still on his face.

Eyre looked at Ben, gobsmacked. Until this moment, she had never been convinced of his loyalty. But she suddenly understood. He was *with* them. And he'd lost so much, as they all had.

Rhabdor was incensed, and his taunting good humour vanished. Standing up high, he lifted the Egeo Blackstone into the air with both arms.

"If the Aura does indeed exist, it must be destroyed! Perhaps you damned creatures of the Light did not count on *this!*"

And with supernatural strength, the grotesque creature hurled the Blackstone upwards. It hurtled higher and higher, with a power beyond the normal physics of Entis, ascending at huge speed towards the Aura.

Eyre's blood cooled. In less than a second she had mounted Ischyros, and her ten friends were also seated on their Lighthorses, holding Rhabdor at bay with their focused staffs.

Eyre was beyond rational thought as Ischyros flapped his mighty wings and they hurtled up into the stratosphere, chasing the gross, misshapen object. She careered after it like a dog after a ball, with no other thought than she absolutely *had* to *stop it!*

The Egeo Blackstone spun over and over, soaring powerfully upwards, until suddenly, a red-gold bullet of energy shot past Eyre. Jax, contender for the Australian Lightworking polo team titles, overtook her, and swatted the horrible object with his sapphire-topped staff—smacking the ball for the goal. Jax's time in the Academy Hawks had evidently paid off; the trajectory of the Blackstone stopped as it shot sideways and started to tumble downwards.

Ischyros dived after it and Eyre drew her Mnae. Ischyros plummeted downwards until they caught up to the falling black heart, and lifting her magical blade from the Mimir, Eyre cut the Blackstone into sixteen pieces with eight swift blows. Before the parts of the ancient Adolf Hamlen's black heart could hit the ground, she blasted it with the full force of the Rainbow Eucalyptus's staff, burning the darkness away. By the time the Egeo Blackstone hit the earth, it was a softly fluttering waft of soot and smut. Gone forever.

Rhabdor was incandescent with rage, and he screamed at the Underworld troops to kill the perpetrators. "GET THEM NOW!" he screeched, as the foul creatures rose from the ground.

And then Rhabdor reared back in his chariot and called for the leader of his defence force.

"MUDAMIR!" he shrieked. "You shrinking coward—where are you?"

Eyre landed on the ground and slid off Ischyros's back, her staff in her hand. She stalked towards Rhabdor, grinning blackly. "Dead," she said. "I did it. By now he is ground under the feet of the Overworld troops, into the stinking mud."

She stood in front of the disgusting creature with her Mnae in her hand. Many good souls have died because of you," she said softly. "I'm here to stop anyone else going."

Rhabdor was unsettled, but still utterly convinced that the Overworld had no hope. "We have taken all the Alterworlds," he sneered. "And perhaps, I applaud your confidence. But I'm afraid your pathetic conglomeration of cobbled-together troops have no chance. It is only a matter of time."

"Look out Eyre!" Beatrice called, and Eyre turned to look behind her. Rhabdor had been distracting her—evidently, he wasn't completely convinced she wasn't a threat. As she tried to rally, a violent comet of atra shot straight at her, but she couldn't react. She was trying to keep an eye on

Rhabdor, and it was impossible to look both ways as she aimed her pink diamond at his heart.

A black missile flew in from above to intercept the stream of dark energy, as Colton and Tina on Nox hurtled between Eyre and Rhabdor. Just before the lethal mortar hit Eyre, Colton sent a blinding shield of Light to protect her. Only Colton had the horsemanship to achieve such a feat; he had moved with Light speed to intercept the lethal blast—no one else on Entis could have flown so fast. Tina shot an arrow into the heart of the Gothak that had sent the burning atra as Colton tried to lift off out of the conflagration. But even his magnificent flying skills couldn't achieve this, and a second flaming blast of black soot hurled by another Gothak hit Nox and his riders square on.

Colton and Tina's faces were shocked but accepting as they looked at Eyre with a sad farewell. This was their journey, and they'd chosen. Then the three of them—Colton, Tina and Nox—disappeared in an explosion of flames, and the rest of the Twelve wailed in pain and desolation.

CHAPTER FIFTY-SEVEN

"NOOO..." EYRE SHRIEKED, AND incinerated the Gothak with one violent blast from her staff. As she stared in disbelief at the place where her beloved friends had been only seconds ago, Eyre's heart exploded with anguish at their loss. Colton, so pure of soul, had sacrificed himself for the Overworld—and *her*, and so had Tina, Eyre's clever, courageous comrade from the Unlit. She could have jumped off Nox, but she had stayed with Colton, at her post. Tears streaked down her face as Eyre realised she would never see them again.

Almost completely derailed by grief, she looked at Rhabdor's triumphant smirk, and the sneer on the bloated creature's face made her blood begin to boil.

"You total maggot," she whispered. She summoned Vulture Killer and shot an arrow at the monstrous Gothak. But he moved fast and it whistled over his shoulder. And then he sniggered.

It was that sound that suddenly caused a deeply-embedded energy force to ignite within her. Ever since her early teens, Eyre had had moments of uncontrollable rage, something her parents had attempted to help her deal with. They'd tried to hide it from the world, to tamp it down.

But now, there was no need for that. Wrath, violent, uncontrolled, erupted from within her, and it was most welcome. *She wanted it!* Finally she knew what she was here to do—and she looked at the smug Rhabdor like she was a Great White shark lining up a fat seal. She let go of all thought and let the fury come.

As her mindless rage increased, she felt a ferocious, uncontrollable surge of energy travel up her body, and then a vertical beam of light exploded upwards from the pink diamond in her staff, shooting to the stratosphere at incredible speed. The beam of energy hit the Aura with a blinding rose-coloured light. Eyre let go of the staff and it stood upright on the ground, with the light still tethered to the Aura.

Nothing happened for a few seconds and then a deafening boom shook the entire world. The Aura shimmered and sent an undulating wave of energy blasting downwards to the earth like a shining curtain of rainbow-coloured light. The shimmering curtain followed the curve of the Aura and disappeared out of sight before reappearing from the opposite direction and joining up—a beacon of hope and power that encircled the world. Four Seams appeared and the spectrum of light shot into them, through to the Alterworlds, illuminating the openings with a blast of rainbow hues.

The ferocity of Eyre's energy lifted her off the ground, as the full force of her power finally exploded. Her hair stood on end and her eyes were golden as she screamed at Rhabdor, who was looking up at her with his mouth hanging open.

"Darkness will never usurp the Light. You, who have crawled out of your foul, septic chambers, have made a grave error in underestimating the strength of the Overworld. You will regret that decision!" she screamed.

The power of the Aura swept down from above, bathing the Lightworking Forces in a saintly glow, and they were energised tenfold by the magical energy. At the same time, the Underworld Forces were weakened; the Aura sapped their strength and left them staggering around in dazed confusion. A mighty roar echoed from around the world as the Overworld felt the power and turned with new energy towards their hated foe.

"You forsook your comrades, your family and the Light," Eyre shouted at Rhabdor as she hovered above him. "You are a creature from the darkest, most stinking dungeon, and the world will be well-rid of you, you grotesque mutant!" And as Strigis and Gothak stumbled around in confusion, she held the mighty Vulture Killer steady and sent a flaming arrow straight through Rhabdor's heart. He screamed and exploded in a flash of light.

Eyre descended to the ground and called for Ischyros. In a second she was on his back and leading the charge into the Dark Forces, her Mnae raised. Without their leaders, and weakened by the Aura, the Dark Forces milled around in disarray. They were easy pickings for the Lightworking Forces, who dispatched them one after another until the corpses piled high across the vast plains of the Gascoyne.

Eyre, and the remainder of the Twelve, fought shoulder to shoulder, and took their revenge on the creatures who had killed so many from the Overworld. The Gothak retreated from the might of the advancing troops until eventually they knew they were beaten.

Smoking Seams appeared around the battlefield and those that were left scrambled through them, retreating to the Underworld.

A thunderous cheer arose from the exhausted Overworld army and weapons were thrust in the air and clanged together in jubilation.

Lord Clarembout raised his Mnae and Gegenees hollered from above in his golden chariot, and then blew a resounding blast on his trumpet. The Ranger hugged Madame Overmantle and the Sergeant saluted Aowx as he roared past, blasting celebratory bursts of fire. The fearless Unlit, with UDı and Rachis at the forefront shook their bows high in the air. And the Squadrons of Lightworkers on Lighthorses high-fived each other, as the Mimir raised their Crescent Blades and bellowed in victory.

Plumipes and her offspring winged off into the distance, each one with a Gothak in its mouth. The soldiers of the Alterworlds mingled to congratulate each other: the valiant battalions of Armatura, the Caelites, the Pinnae and the Nemoris. The air was filled with triumphant cheers that reverberated off Mt Augustus and filled the plains with joy.

One by one, across the plains, the Overworld troops dropped to their knee and crossed their arms before their chests, bowing their heads to the new Protector.

The Overworld had won! The Light would Endure!

Jax stuck his head through Eyre's door. "Are you ready?" he asked, and Eyre gave a crooked smile. She nodded. "I guess so," and picked up her guitar before following him down the front steps. She saw Jengles in the distance, busying himself with some chore. He'd lost some fingers in the terrible warfare, and had been cut and burnt and bludgeoned, but he'd survived.

Ischyros—the old version of himself—was chewing on some grass with his 'chicken' on his back. Florence had also survived the Overworld War, as it was now called, and she was happy being back with her old friend. Eyre gave Ischyros a piece of liquorice as she walked past, before heading to the Mantle Basin where the group waited, the remnants of the Twelve. Including Ben Perrill, who Eyre now regarded as a friend. He had shown great courage and had fought with them to end the terrible war. And now that she understood his past, she had forgiven him.

Like Eyre, the student's faces were sombre, but resolute.

"Nick's got the plaque he made," Abby said, and after a moment, he held it out. It was a bronze rectangle, fired by Aowx to a high sheen. On it, Nick had engraved: "*To the courageous fallen, who gave their lives for others and for the Light. They will not be forgotten.*"

Carly, Colton and Tina's names were listed underneath, as well as the names of other Academy students who had died fighting the Gothak. Including Pheria's brother Stratt. It was a long list and the students by the Basin were silent as they mourned the courageous souls. Whittaker Ray and Peter and Robyn Edmunsun, and Dr Perrill watched from their verandahs, and gave a small wave, but they didn't come to join them. They knew this was something the friends had to do themselves.

The nine remaining students began the long walk to the Buyabarra Billabong. It was hot, despite being early spring, but no one complained, and no one spoke. It seemed disrespectful somehow. This time, there was no fear of being stalked by a Saevus, or being out late and vulnerable to the Zyx. The Underworld denizens had not been seen since the war finished a month ago, and Eyre doubted they would make an appearance anytime soon. Even the Mantle wasn't lit anymore. It was no longer needed. Spring, she mused. Sort of appropriate for the Overworld's new beginning. And she realised the great Mimir poet Esor had been right: *Remember the spring.*

The environment was supporting their venture today, and had turned on glorious weather. The sky arced above in a brilliant blue swathe, without a cloud in sight. The trees whispered in a gentle breeze, and a soft light danced before them as they walked along the sandy track.

Finally, they arrived at the magical billabong, after climbing down the rocky sides of the steep cliff that surrounded it. The dark water was still and unfathomable, almost as if it was watching and waiting to be a participant in the proceedings. It was soon to be the guardian of something very precious.

Abby produced a paper bag she had been nursing for a couple of weeks. Nick dug a hole in the rich soil that edged the sandstone rocks surrounding the billabong, and Abby tipped the contents in; seeds from the Rainbow Eucalyptus. They had gathered them from the burnt gumnuts of the fallen tree that had been in the Mantle Basin. Nick covered the seeds gently with the fertile soil. The scars from his recent cuts from the Rainbow Eucalyptus's wood stood out starkly on his skin, and he bent his head as his hand rested on the soil above the newly-buried seeds. Eyre understood the pain he felt; he would never get over the trauma of cutting down the magnificent tree, even though that act had ultimately helped to save the Overworld.

"Grow and be strong, like your valiant predecessor, young plant," Nick whispered.

And then he attached the brass plaque to the sandstone rock in front of the hole with a blast of Viq.

Tears fell as Beatrice, Abby, Nick, Jax, Warrigal, Rigmar, Pheria, Eyre and Ben studied the plaque, swamped by the pain of losing the magical tree, and their friends. The ones who had helped to save the world. And as if those souls were somehow watching, the top of the normally-still billabong rippled, as if someone had just danced over it.

Eyre sat down with her guitar and her friends joined her, surrounding the brass plaque. And then Eyre sang a song that she'd written to honour the courageous souls.

"Rest in the shade of the Rainbow Tree
Your names won't be forgotten, you live in our hearts
Without you our future might have ceased to be
You've gifted the world a new start
So sleep lightly by the Buyabarra
In the wind and the peace and the trees
We weep quietly, because we're here without you
But your names are revered in the breeze
Go to the Light, we know one day that we
Will all be together though we're now apart
Rest as the branches grow strong and free
We'll thank you forever 'til we too depart."

As the haunting strains finished, all the trees in the area moved and rustled and bent.

"Thanks Eyre," Beatrice hiccupped as she wiped tears from her face.

They all stood and started up the steep sides of the cliff. But their steps were lighter; somehow, by honouring their friends and comrades, those they knew and those they didn't, they were able to cope with their sadness. The world was rid of the Dark Forces, and peace would now reign in the Overworld because of the efforts of the fallen, but also of those who had lived. They would rebuild after the decimation of war, and life would again be good.

Eyre followed at the rear, scanning the skies for any sign of trouble, as she would forever now.

She was the Protector, the Defender of the Overworld, and as long as she lived, the Dark Forces would never again pollute this earth.

Jax took her hand and kissed her lightly as they made their way back to Highlight.

DEAR READER, THANK YOU so much for reading the Quest for the Aura series! As a special gift from me to acknowledge your loyalty to Eyre and her friends in this grand Australian adventure, I'm delighted to offer you a special, free bonus...

She had to piece together a complex series of clues to save the planet. Download the keys to all the secrets in the confidential Book of Bane!

Eyre Lightward faced some tricky challenges when it came to fulfilling her destiny. And with messages and ancient mysteries buried in complicated riddles, Eyre needed every ounce of her legendary sharp wit to restore Earth's failing protective shield. Now you can join with Eyre and connect the dots between all of the formidable, prophetic puzzles.

Warning: spoilers!

If you're about to download the free Book of Bane codes, make sure you've read all five books in the Quest for the Aura YA contemporary fantasy series!

Download your free copy of The Book of Bane here: https://thequestfortheaura.com/book-of-bane

Psst! Don't share this secret link until you're sure the recipient has read all five books!

About the Quest for the Aura

Discover more exciting facts about the Quest for the Aura and download a free glossary from R.S. O'Neal's website here:

https://thequestfortheaura.com/